NEXT MOVE: TERROR

The police ignored Hakluyt. One of them went straight to the two-way radio in his car and called headquarters for reinforcements. That's when Hakluyt said something about a man being innocent until proven guilty.

Angers turned his eyes on him. "No," he said. "You're wrong. Our laws are like the *Code Napoléon.* The onus is on the accused."

Faces full of hate came to the entrance of the slum, stared down at them. Distantly there was the howl of police sirens. But Hakluyt wasn't thinking about any of that. He had stuck, as though walking up a down escalator, in front of a billboardlike vision of Señora Posador, informing him that whether he liked it or not he had importance in the scheme of affairs.

Enough importance to kill a man.

And that's when Hakluyt knew that all the decisions he thought he had made up to that point, had not been his at all . . .

Also by John Brunner
Published by Ballantine Books:

THE SHEEP LOOK UP

THE WHOLE MAN

THE SHOCKWAVE RIDER

STAND ON ZANZIBAR

The Squares of the City

John Brunner

A Del Rey Book

BALLANTINE BOOKS • NEW YORK

A Del Rey Book
Published by Ballantine Books

Copyright © 1965 by John Brunner

All rights reserved under International and Pan-American
Copyright Conventions. Published in the United States by
Ballantine Books, a division of Random House, Inc., New
York, and simultaneously in Canada by Ballantine Books of
Canada, Ltd., Toronto, Canada.

ISBN 0-345-27739-2

Manufactured in the United States of America

First Edition: December 1965
Fourth Printing: December 1978

First Canadian Printing: February 1966

Cover art by Murray Tinkelman

INTRODUCTION

The story told by John Brunner in *The Squares of the City* held me spellbound from beginning to end. It had a special attraction for me because all the people in the book are chess-mad, and chess is my favorite pastime. But even the reader who knows nothing about the game will be thoroughly fascinated by this story in which the two chief political antagonists in a South American country attempt to direct the actions of their followers by using the unconscious but powerful influence of "subliminal perception," a technique which may well threaten all our futures.

Under its baleful persuasion, members of the two hostile parties commit all sorts of crimes as they unknowingly carry out the actions suggested to them by a confidant of their leaders who is an expert in subliminal perception and who is the Director of the television network that controls The City. Only gradually does one realize that The City is a chessboard—its chief inhabitants taking actions that are the counterparts of moves in a vicious game of chess being played out by their leaders.

The author has added an ingenious twist to his story which will be particularly intriguing to chess fans. The game in which his characters move as living pieces has not been artificially designed by him to suit the progress of his plot. It had actually been played, move for move, some seventy years ago in a match for the world championship between the title holder, the American master William Steinitz, and the Russian master Mikhail Ivanovich Tchigorin.

—Edward Lasker, M.E., E.E.

The
Squares
of the
City

I

On the flight down from Florida I talked with my seat companion—or, to be more exact, he talked at me. He was a European-born Jew in his middle fifties whose family had been thrown out by a Nazi invasion early in World War Two, but although he was very proud of the fact that he spoke with a European accent and said so at least a dozen times—"You have noticed my accent, of course!"—I didn't manage to establish his actual place of origin.

He had not been "home" for four years, and in fact appeared to have spent much more time in the States than he had in Aguazul, but there was no questioning his fervor for his adopted country. He insisted on addressing the stewardess in ludicrously bad Spanish—worse even than mine—although on this route, of course, all the stewardesses spoke English, Spanish, and Portuguese with equal fluency. And when the plane was circling in toward landing, he almost climbed into my lap in an effort to point past me through the porthole and indicate locations of interest in Vados.

Eventually the stewardess commanded him sternly—in English—to fasten his seat belt. I think it was more the fact that she addressed him in a "foreign" language than the actual order that made him calm himself and sit down. After that I was able to close my mind, if not my ears, to his glowing descriptions.

I forebore to tell him (it would have been very unkind) that although I had never set foot in Vados, I almost certainly knew more about the city than he did—more indeed than any of its citizens who hadn't deliberately tramped the streets for a week on end, exploring and observing. I knew that ten years or so before they had gone to a barren, rocky stretch of land and decreed that there should be a new capital city; they had built roads and put wild mountain torrents into concrete

conduits and hoisted solar electricity generators into the surrounding hills, first on muleback and then by helicopter into
places where even a mule could not scramble. Now it was a
flourishing city of half a million people.

I had studied the essential structure of the city, too: developed organically from four gigantic plazas or squares,
modulated by the three great traffic arteries—six-lane superhighways with ten-foot shoulders clear from Astoria Negra
and Puerto Joaquin on the coast, and Cuatrovientos, the oil
center on which the wealth of Aguazul—and therefore the
city—was ultimately based.

But, looking down on the reality as the plane nosed toward
the airport cut in the mountainside, I felt a stir of my seat
companion's excitement.

For I suppose I had never before seen anything so completely of the twentieth century.

"Ten years ago," I said to myself, "this was wasteland.
Scrub. Rock. And now *look* at it." A shiver of awe clambered
down my spine. My feelings must have shown in my expression, for my companion chuckled.

"*Magnifico,* no?" he said with a smirk of satisfaction, as
though he himself had been responsible for the graceful tow-
ers, the splendid avenues, the richly flowering parks.

It did indeed look magnificent. But—if it was as good as it
looked, I wouldn't have been here. I hesitated over whether or
not I should try to explain, and in the end said nothing.

When we parted in the customs hall of the air terminal, my
temporary acquaintance insisted on shaking my hand and
giving me his card. The name on it was Flores, with an
address on Madison Avenue and another right here in Vados.

Flores. *Blum*? I wondered. *Rosenblum*? Possibly; the intervening years had smoothed out his vaunted European accent
till it was cosmopolitan, featureless.

He was torn between a desire to continue bragging of his
adopted homeland to a stranger and the wish to take his place
in the citizens' line at the customs desk, asserting his national
rights. In the end the latter pull triumphed. But before we

separated, his hand shot out and indicated a picture placed—
not conspicuously, but visibly—behind the customs officers.

"That's a great man!" he said impressively. "The man they
named Vados for, of course. *El Presidente!*"

I was apparently the only alien aboard the plane this flight,
and, as happens most places these days, the natives received
precedence. I went to a bench across the narrow hall and lit a
cigarette, composing myself to wait.

The hall was quiet, lined with sound-absorptive material;
although the sun beat down pitilessly on the gray concrete of
the runways outside, in here it was cool. The light came
through high green louvers, and not a single fly buzzed
through the still air. That in these latitudes was an achievement.

I occupied myself by looking at the picture. It was not only
that I was interested in the appearance of a man who could
have a city called after him in his own lifetime, and a capital
city, moreover. He was also indirectly my new employer.
Officially I would be responsible to the Ciudad de Vados city
council, but Vados was mayor of the city as well as president
of the republic, and from everything I had heard it seemed
that what he said was what counted.

The portrait—which, of course, had no caption—showed *el
Presidente* in a plain white suit. A thin black tie seemed to
cut his chest into equal halves. His heavy-set body was carried
erectly, in a military posture; he gave the impression of tall-
ness, and I knew he was in fact over six feet. He had been
taken gazing directly into the camera and so directly at me
where I sat studying him. The picture was very well done and
suggested a certain immediacy of presence. His face was very
pale in contrast to his thin black moustache and smooth dark
hair. He grasped a gold-knobbed swagger cane in both hands
as if intending to twist the ends in opposite directions and
make it as spiral as a piece of sugar-candy.

Juan Sebastian Vados. A lucky man, an astute man. And,
Flores had claimed, a great man. Certainly a brilliant one: for
more than twenty years now he had ruled Aguazul, and he
had prosperity and contentment to show for it—not to mention Ciudad de Vados, the greatest showpiece of all.

I grew aware that I was being beckoned. I dropped my

cigarette in a sand bowl and crossed the resilient floor to the customs desk. A porter trundled my bags down a roller conveyor to within reach of the official who had waved to me. This was a swarthy man in a severe black uniform with silver rank badges; his fingers were discolored with the blue chalk used for okaying passengers' bags.

He glanced down at the passenger manifest and said in a bored tone, "*Quiere Vd. decirme su nombre?*"

"*Me llamo* Boyd Hakluyt," I told him, reaching into my pocket for my passport. "*Habla Vd. inglés?*"

He put his elbow on the desk top, hand outstretched. "*Si*," he agreed. "The señor is *Norteamericano?*"

"No, Australian. I've been in the States some time."

His eyebrows arched a little as he studied my Australian passport. Quite probably he hadn't seen one before. "And what is it brings the señor to Aguazul?" he asked, as though genuinely interested. "Tourism, yes?"

He took up the stub of blue chalk lying nearest his hand and began to move it toward my bags. I told him no, in fact I was working in Vados as of the following day.

His eyes narrowed a very little. The hand with the chalk stopped an inch from the first bag. "So?" he said. "And what is the señor's profession?"

"I'm a traffic analyst," I answered. "I specialize in such problems as how to get cars moving faster in busy streets, how to prevent people blocking the exits at subway stations—"

He nodded impatiently. "*Yo comprendo*," he snapped, as if I had implied he was of inferior intelligence. "And what do you do here in Vados?"

"I'm supposed to suggest a solution to a traffic problem."

This was factually accurate, and as I said it, I felt again a tingle of excitement—the same excitement that I had felt on first being assigned the job. Perhaps it wasn't so much simple excitement as a sense of being awarded an accolade—Ciudad de Vados was more than a brand-new city in the circles where I worked; it was a byword for ultimate achievement in city planning and traffic analysis. And to be chosen to improve on near perfection was a kind of climax to a career.

Of course, it was to be expected that improvement had now become possible; it was twelve years since the plans had been approved, and there had been progress in that time. More to the point, the finest analogue computers in the world couldn't get all the bugs out of a traffic plan—experiment was the only way of establishing where faults might lie.

And yet . . .

The customs officer seemed to be affected by the same kind of puzzlement as I. But he had a way of resolving it. He tossed the chalk in the air and as it fell closed his hand around it with a gesture of finality. "I shall require to examine your baggage, Señor Hakluyt," he said.

I sighed, wondering what had made him change his mind. But experience had taught me it was always quicker not to raise objections. So I said only, "Everything I have with me is my personal property, and I checked with your consulate in Miami to make sure I wasn't bringing any proscribed items."

"*Puede ser,*" he answered noncommittally, and took my keys.

He asked questions about almost everything he found, but it was the quantity of clothing I had with me that he harped on most. He kept trying to insist that I could not possibly need everything I had brought; again and again I had to explain that my work often took me out on highway and other construction projects where there were no laundry facilities, and if I was to dress reasonably well, I had to bring as much as this.

"Señor Hakluyt, then, is a very wealthy man?" he pressed, altering his line of attack.

I resisted the growing temptation to make a smart crack in reply and shook my head.

"The señor is not wealthy and yet has so much baggage," he said, as though propounding a major philosophical paradox to himself. "Will the señor tell me at what rate he is to be paid for the work he does in Vados?"

That was a little too much. "Is it any of your business?" I countered.

He showed his teeth, with the air of a card-player producing a fourteenth trump. I disliked him intensely from that moment on. "Señor Hakluyt is perhaps not aware that I am a police officer," he purred. "But I am—and it is therefore illegal to refuse an answer to any question I may put."

I gave ground. "I'm being paid twenty thousand dolaros and expenses," I said.

He pushed down the lid on the last of my bags and slashed crosses on each item with the blue chalk. Then he dusted his hands off against each other in a way that suggested he was getting rid of something more than just smears of chalk. "It is to be hoped, then, that the señor is generous with his money," he said. "Perhaps it is there, the reason why he is not already a wealthy man."

He turned on his heel and stalked away.

The examination had taken so long that the airline buses had all left for the center of town. I dug into my inadequate knowledge of Spanish and managed to persuade a porter to call me a cab and load my bags into it while I went to a change booth and turned a few dollars into a supply of dolaros—crisp new red-and-yellow paper bearing portraits of *el Presidente*, nominally at par to the United States dollar but worth in actual purchasing power about eighty-five cents. They were a monument to one of Vados's first great achievements—the major currency reform he had carried through a year after coming to power. It was said that he had called his new monetary unit the *dolaro* in hope that it would become as hard a currency as its North American original; by Latin American standards he had worked miracles in even approaching this goal.

When I came to tip the porter who'd called my cab, I remembered what the customs officer had said about being generous with my money. By way of experiment I gave him two dolaros and looked for a reaction. There wasn't one. He probably thought I was a tourist who couldn't be bothered keeping track of foreign currency because he subconsciously felt it wasn't real money anyway. I tried to shrug the whole thing off.

However, it wasn't until the cab was on its way down from

the mountainside airport that the matter was driven to the back of my mind. The road swung around in a wide quarter circle to ease the sharp descent into Vados, and since the air was clear and the sun was shining brilliantly, I had a perfect bird's-eye view out over the area. I could even make out Puerto Joaquin, forty-odd miles distant, as a dark blur where the land merged into the ocean.

But after a superficial glance around, I didn't again trouble to look so far away. I was too fascinated by Ciudad de Vados in the immediate foreground.

There was an impressive quality about the city that no amount of maps and plans had been able to convey to me. Without the distraction of Flores importuning me to look at things, I was able to soak up the true magnificence of it all.

Somehow—it was hard to define how—those who had planned this city had managed to give it an organic vitality akin to that of a giant machine. There was a slumbering controlled power that could be felt, implying business to be done; yet it was matched by a functional perfection that meant economy, simplicity, unity without uniformity. Just about everything, in fact, that idealistic city-planners had ever hoped for.

I told the cabdriver to pull off the road for a moment and got out to stare down through the limpid air from the edge of a bushy bluff. I recognized almost everything I could see: residential there, business there, government offices there, the parks, the museums, the opera house, the four great plazas, the viaducts carrying the superhighways.

Fantastic. On the surface not a single flaw.

I stayed long enough on the bluff to smoke half a cigarette; then I went back to the cab and told the driver to take me into town. I went on staring out of the window as we hurried down the mountainside.

Then something came between the window and the view, and I turned my head barely in time to see a sort of shack parked—it didn't look substantial enough for one to say it was *built*—alongside the road. I had no chance to take in details, but that didn't matter; fifty yards farther on there was another, and then a whole cluster of them—matchboard shanties roofed with flattened oildrums, their walls made gaudy here and there by advertising placards, ragged washing hung out to dry between them on poles and lines. Naked or nearly naked children played around the huts in company with straggly roosters, goats, and the odd emaciated piglet.

I was so taken aback I had no chance to order the driver to stop again before the road straightened for its final nose dive into Vados proper. But as we passed the gate of the first real house on the outskirts—it was a handsome colonial-style villa set among palms—I saw a peasant family trudging up the hill: father carrying a bundle on the traditional strap around his forehead, mother with one child in her arms and another wearily plodding at her heels. They paid the cab no attention as it hummed past, except to screw up their eyes against dust.

A memory filled my mind suddenly: the memory of a man I had met while working on the clearance of an industrial slum area. He had been born there; he had been lucky enough to climb out of it and all that it implied. And he had said, as we talked about what was being abolished, "You know, I always knew it wasn't permanent. That was what enabled me to get the hell out, when other people gave up. Because it was a shock to me, every time I saw a paving stone taken up, to find that there was earth underneath—the aboriginal dirt. Most of the time the town seemed so implacable, so solid and squat and loathsome—but whenever I was reminded that the earth was underneath, I managed to see through that façade and go on fighting."

It was as though cold water had been thrown in my face. I suddenly saw a possible explanation of why I was here. And—in the most peculiar way—the explanation frightened me.

II

The layout of Ciudad de Vados was so straightforward and logical it would probably have been impossible for a cabby to try taking even a complete stranger by a roundabout route. Nonetheless, force of habit and professional interest made me follow the track of my cab on a mental map, at the same time as I studied the buildings and the people on the streets.

With the twentieth-century homogenization of culture, most of the route we took could have been approximated in any large city in the Americas or Western Europe, aside from obvious differences, such as the language on the street signs and the frequent appearance of priests and nuns in their religious habits. Here a trio of pretty girls in new summer frocks stood waiting for a crosstown monorail; the high platform was windy, and their skirts whirled as they laughed and chattered. Below, a thoughtful youth in an open convertible eyed them with careful consideration; a few yards away two respectable women debated whether to be more disapproving of the girls for being attractive or the boy for being attracted.

Huge stores, designed according to modern sales-promotion techniques, proffered their goods; money flowed like a river over their counters. The cars and cabs whirled forward; despite the fact that the traffic flow was nowhere near its theoretical optimum, there were still fifty per cent fewer traffic holdups than I had ever before seen in a city this size. Bright clothes and bright faces on the sidewalks; bright sunlight on the bright light walls of the tall buildings and on the clean—incredibly clean—streets.

I looked around, and the buildings said proudly, "Progress!" The laughter on the faces of youths and girls said, "Success!" The satisfied look of businessmen said, "Prosperity!"

But even in that moment, in my first hour in Vados, I found myself wondering what the peasant family would have answered, trudging up the hill toward their shantytown.

My hotel—the Hotel del Principe—was on the Plaza del Sur, one of the four main squares of Ciudad de Vados. The squares had been named unimaginatively enough after the four points of the compass. We were nearing the end of the trip when that part of my mind that had been following our route on an imaginary map warned me that we had taken a wrong turn at a traffic signal. I was leaning forward to remonstrate with the driver when I saw that the whole stream of cars and other vehicles was being diverted from the entrance to the Plaza del Sur. I caught one glimpse of the palms and flowers in the parklike center of the square, and then the cab pulled in at the side of the road and the driver reached for a cigarette.

I asked him what was happening; he shrugged an enormous and expressive Latin American shrug.

"No tengo la culpa," he said defensively, but giving one brief glance at the meter clocking up my fare. "It isn't my fault."

I opened the window and craned my head around. An excited crowd (but where in Latin America is a crowd not excited?) had gathered at the entrance to the square. It had a holiday atmosphere about it, for peddlers were going to and fro with tamale wagons and trays of knickknacks, but it was plain from the many parked trucks and cars bearing the neatly lettered word POLICIA that there was nothing festive about whatever had happened.

After a few minutes a line of police appeared from inside the square and began to disperse the crowd with extravagant waves of their long white batons. My driver snuffed his cigarette out, carefully returning the unfinished butt to his pocket, and pulled the wheel down hard. We crossed the road to an accompaniment of other cars' brakes shrieking and entered the square.

Though there were still many people on the gravel walks between the trees, there was no sign of anything police might have been needed to break up. The single indicative point was that a man in a shabby cotton uniform—a municipal street cleaner, perhaps—was going carefully about picking up bits of paper that looked like leaflets and stuffing them in a long gray bag.

The cab rolled around the square to the Hotel del Principe, a white-and-bronze building with a kind of loggia along its line of frontage, and three shallow steps underlining the effective façade. There were three doors of plain glass in the glass face of the loggia; the cab halted before the first of them.

Instantly a trio of ragged youths and one ragged girl, who had been squatting on the sidewalk with their backs against the hardboard side of a portable news kiosk, eyes screwed up against the sun, bounced to their feet. They attempted to open the door, get my bags out, shine my shoes, and show me the way up the hotel steps, all the time keeping one palm free and poised to catch money if it flew in their direction. The cab-driver didn't move from his seat; he merely spat into the gutter, making the act convey a whole bookful of disgusted annoyance.

At the head of the steps a majestic commissionaire turned toward the commotion. He summed it up in a glance and sent the ragged children running with some awful and probably obscene threat in a raucous voice and coarse accent. Then he walked down and opened my door.

"Buenas dias, señor," he said affably, but this time in so polite and polished a voice I gave him a sharp stare, almost not believing this could be the same man. *"Es Vd. el señor Hakluyt?"*

I agreed that I was, and paid the driver, giving him a tip that proved large enough to startle him out of his seat to help the hotel bellhop with my bags. I looked around the plaza again.

"What was going on here just now?" I demanded. "Why had they closed the square to traffic?"

The commissionaire interrupted himself in the middle of instructing the bellhop. He turned a cool and sardonic eye on me. "I do not know, señor," he said. "It cannot have been of much importance."

From which, naturally, I deduced that it was of very great importance—sufficiently so to make a bad impression on a new arrival. I reminded myself to find out at the earliest opportunity what it was.

I checked into my room, which was high up in the building and had a good view on the side away from the square. The first thing I had to do was phone the city council offices and make an appointment to see the head of the traffic department the following morning; the second was to clean up after the trip and change clothes; and the third was to do nothing at all for the rest of the day. In my sort of work, at the beginning of a new job it's usually essential to spend up to fourteen hours a day on absorbing facts and impressions; I might as well make the most of my last chance to relax and be idle.

The bellhop unpacked my bags quickly and efficiently while I was making my appointment; a couple of times when he came to items he did not recognize, like my theodolites and my portable analogue computer, he crossed the room and held them mutely before me, asking with his eyes where he should put them. I indicated that he should dump them on the bed. After he had gone, I gave them a quick inspection to make sure they had suffered no damage on the way.

When I was through, I went down to the lounge in search of a drink and a comfortable chair.

The lounge was large and pleasant. The architect's fancy had led him to ornament it with palms and colorful-leaved creepers growing inside glass pillars; aside from that, the decor was mainly black-and-white, repeating a motif which appeared explicitly in the low tables whose tops were inlaid with a checkered pattern. I'd been staring for some time at the table beside my own chair, but it was not until I noticed that a man and a woman sitting a few feet from me were brooding over a set of pieces in play that I realized the pattern was actually a chessboard, eight by eight and intended to be used.

Once my attention was caught, the imperious presence of the woman held it. She could have been any age 'rom thirty to fifty; her face was an almost perfect oval, disturbed—but not marred—by a sharp and determined chin, and framed by sleek, shining black hair. I could not see what the color of her eyes was; they were shaded, as she looked down at the game, by sweeping long lashes. She wore a straight dress of a rich dark red; the slimness of her bare arms and the fine carving of her face suggested that the slenderness of her figure would be natural, not dieted down. She was tanned to a gold almost as rich as the gold of the watch on her wrist, and those two together suggested great wealth and much leisure. In the slim hand with which she moved her pieces she held a black Russian cigarette, unlit.

She played well, with a straightforward directness in attack that had already got her opponent into serious difficulties. I shifted a little in my chair to follow the play.

I had been watching for several minutes when a waiter came to call the opponent to the phone. He stood up and excused himself, not—so I thought—without some relief, and the woman nodded to him and sat back in her chair. At last the thin cigarette went to her lips, and she picked up a black handbag to open it and find a lighter.

The fact that I was holding mine before her, open and lit, did not surprise her in the least. I guessed that in her cosmos automatic attention of this kind was predictable. She put her cigarette to the flame, let smoke curl from her nostrils, and looked up at me. Her eyes were violet.

"*Gracias*," she said pleasantly.

A hovering waiter came up with a tray and was on the point of removing the chessmen; she stopped him with a gesture and waved her hand over the board. "Would you care to complete the game?" she suggested to me.

I smiled and shook my head. White was too near defeat for any attempt at salvage.

She indicated to the waiter that he should take the pieces away, after all, and continued the gesture as an invitation to me to take the chair opposite her.

"The señor is a stranger in Vados," she said factually. "And it is probably his first visit."

"Quite right. But is it so obvious?"

"Oh, indeed. From your expression. You seemed surprised a little to find that these chessboards were for use."

I wondered how she had contrived to study me closely enough to notice that, and shrugged. "I was, a little," I acknowledged.

"But this is a thing you find everywhere in Vados, indeed throughout the country. It is perhaps our national game so much as it is of the Russians, let us say." As though mention of the name had reminded her, she took another draw on her Russian cigarette and tapped the first ash into a tray on the table. "It is, of course, a dream of our president that one day such another as the Cuban Capablanca should be found here in Ciudad de Vados. For that reason we play from childhood."

"Is Vados himself a chess player, then?" I inquired, more for conversation's sake than out of any real interest.

"Oh, indeed!" She seemed surprised that I asked the question. "He is, they say, very good at the game. You play yourself, perhaps?"

"Badly. But I do play."

"Then if the señor is staying here, he must do me the honor of a match sometime. May I be acquainted with the señor's name?"

I gave it, and she repeated it thoughtfully. "Hakluyt. A famous name. I am Maria Posador," she added, as though by afterthought.

A few more trivialities disposed of, I managed to ask what had been going on in the square when I arrived this afternoon, and she smiled.

"That is a feature of our life in Vados, Señor Hakluyt. It is a daily occurrence."

"Really? I had the idea you were comparatively free from—uh—such things."

She smiled, revealing superbly regular teeth. "You mistake my meaning. The arrival of great numbers of police is a rarity. But—well, the señor has perhaps been to London?"

"No, never."

"But you do perhaps know of a place they call the Corner of Speakers, in one of the great plazas there?"

I caught on. "Ah, Speakers' Corner in Hyde Park. Yes, I know what you mean. Is that the sort of thing you have in the Plaza del Sur?"

"Exactly. Only—our national temperament being what it is—our discussions sometimes grow more heated than among the phlegmatic English." She laughed; it was a mellow sound that made me think of ripe apples. "Each day about noon there assemble a few persons with ideas to preach or grievances to complain about. Occasionally tempers rise. That is all."

"And what was all the trouble about today, then?"

She spread one hand gracefully, and I had the impression that she had suddenly drawn a veil over her eyes. "Oh, it may have been one of many things—more than likely a difference about a religious matter. I did not go to inquire."

She plainly preferred not to pursue the subject. I fell in with the wish and turned back to generalities. "It's very interesting to hear you have a Speakers' Corner here. Is that another original notion of your president's?"

"Possibly. Or perhaps—like many of *el President*'s more striking innovations—it was the idea of Diaz." The name meant nothing to me, but she went on without noticing my failure to respond. "Certainly it has proved of benefit to us all; what could be more useful than a theater where the discontents of the people can be brought to light?"

"Who's Diaz?" I asked. "And what makes you think this idea might have come from him? I thought Vados *was* the government here."

"Not at all," she said crisply. I had the impression that I had touched a sore spot. "Vados would not be the man he is without his cabinet, and most of all without Diaz. Diaz is the Minister of the Interior. Thus, of course, his name comes less before the public than does Vados's; outside Aguazul Vados's name is known because the name of his city is known. But surely it is obvious that the strongest ruler depends on the strength of his supporters."

I agreed that it was obvious, and Señora Posador—though she had not mentioned it, she wore a marriage ring—glanced at her little gold watch.

"Well, Señor Hakluyt, it has been pleasant to speak with you. You are staying in this hotel?"

I said I was.

"Then we shall meet here again and perhaps have that

game of chess I suggested. But at this moment I fear I must go. *Hasta mañana, señor!"*

I rose hastily and managed an awkward bow over her hand, which, since she accepted automatically, I took to be still customary. And with a final dazzling smile she was gone.

I sat down again and ordered another drink. There were only two things seriously wrong with all this. The first was that wedding ring, the second the irritating fact that although I was perfectly sure Señora Posador knew very well what had been going on in the plaza when I arrived, I still had not found out what it was about.

I looked for reports in the papers the following morning, because for some reason this question went on irritating me. My Spanish was just about up to newspaper standard, if I took it slowly and guessed every fifth word.

There were two important dailies in Vados: one was the government organ, *Liberdad,* and the other an independent called *Tiempo. Liberdad* gave only about twenty lines to the whole affair, saying that arrests had been made and that a certain Juan Tezol was due to appear in court today on a charge of inciting to riot. *Tiempo,* on the other hand, made this item the main front-page news and gave it a large spread.

Struggling, I managed to make out that the villain of this paper's version was not Tezol at all; it was someone called Mario Guerrero, who was alleged to have urged his followers to tear down Tezol's speaker's platform and burn the owner in the wreckage. The argument that had given rise to this—literally—inflammatory language didn't seem to be religious, as Señora Posador had tried to make out; it must be political. But the reporters in both papers assumed their readers would be familiar with the background, and the details were tantalizingly inadequate for a stranger like me. There was mention of a Citizens' Party and a National Party, associated with Guerrero and Tezol respectively, and so far as *Tiempo* was concerned, the former were inhuman monsters. That was the best I could gather from the reports.

I had been under the impression that—for a Latin American country—Aguazul was comparatively free from internal strife. Seemingly I was wrong. But local politics were outside my province. I brushed the matter to the back of my mind and finished my breakfast. This morning I was due to start work.

~ III

The city administration was housed in buildings near the government quarter, north and east of the Plaza del Norte and about a mile from my hotel on the Plaza del Sur. Since it was fine and warm and I had time to spare before my appointment, I decided to walk there and get a preliminary feel of the city.

I came quickly to the central traffic intersection that lay at the focal point of the flow generated and governed by the four great squares. I stopped there for some time on the sidewalk, watching the vehicles move—and they did move, with no breaks. Ingenious use of precedence lanes and total avoidance of same-level crossing had eliminated the need for stoppages altogether, and there wasn't a traffic signal in sight—nothing but one bored-looking policeman filing his nails in a small booth high above the middle of the maze. A bright red telephone handset was his only visible equipment, connected presumably to the public address system whose speakers formed bulbs like coconuts on nearby lamp posts.

With the feeder roads for the three superhighways debouching here, and seven access roads for local traffic, pedestrians had to be kept well out of the way. Accordingly, there was a complex network of subways forming an underpass. After the bright morning sun outside, I found the mercury vapor lighting hard to adjust to at first when I'd finally dragged myself away from admiring the smooth flow of traffic. Somehow I overlooked one of the direction signs and found myself going the wrong way; while trying to retrace my steps, I had the first and less pleasant of two major surprises.

Dodging a fat woman with a large basket on one arm and a little girl on the other, I almost tripped over a boy sitting on the floor.

Between his legs rested a beautiful hand-painted Indian clay pot; around his shoulders was a handsome but threadbare *serape,* with the fringe of which his right hand played endlessly. He had no left hand, and his battered sombrero was tilted back to show that he had no left eye, either—the whole of that quarter of his face was one great weeping sore.

Startled, I halted in mid-stride. He fixed me with his one eye and whined something in a harsh voice. I felt embarrassed and appalled at the sight of him, as though I had found obscene words scribbled on the Parthenon. I kept my eyes averted as I fumbled in my pocket and found about a dolaro and a half in odd coins which I dropped in his clay pot.

Badly shaken, I went on my way. I had seen sights like that in India fifteen years ago, when I was first working away from home, although even then beggars were rapidly disappearing; I'd seen them in the UAR before it quit bickering and settled down to clean house. But I had thought they belonged to past history.

I had gone only a short distance farther when I felt a tap on my shoulder and turned to find a fresh-faced young policeman trying to regard me sternly. He banged some quick-fire Spanish at me, the thread of which I lost after two words.

"*No habla español,*" I told him.

"*Ah, Norteamericano,*" he said with an air of having had everything explained to him. "The señor please not again geev—geev *dinero* to so kind of people."

"You mean people like that beggar-boy?" I said, and waved in the boy's direction to clarify the meaning.

He nodded vigorously. "*Si, si!* Not to geev to heem. We try ver', ver' mooch feenish so kind of people—we not want any more. Not good have in Ciudad de Vados," he added triumphantly.

"You mean he's allowed to sit there and ask for money, but it's illegal to give him any?" I felt slightly confused.

"Ah, no, no, no, no, no! He seet zere, a'right. He ask for *dinero,* not good. Señor geev *dinero,* mooch bad."

"I see," I said. I wasn't sure that I did, completely. But they were trying to discourage beggars; that was plain. The boy seemed like a deserving case—still, I wasn't prepared to take up the question of social welfare services in pidgin Spanish.

The policeman gave me a beaming smile and went back along the subway.

When I came to the next intersection, I found I'd taken a wrong turning *again* and would have to go back. That was how I happened to find the policeman, baton thrust against the beggar-boy's chest, fumbling in the clay pot for the money I had put there. The boy was weeping and protesting.

The policeman made certain he had all the coins and stood up. He made his baton swish through the air an inch from the boy's face, yelling at him to be quiet, as though he were a disobedient animal, and turned away.

In the same instant he saw me standing looking at him.

He seemed to turn green—or perhaps that was an illusion caused by the mercury vapor lights. His mouth worked as if he were trying to find words to explain his action. He failed. When I silently put out my hand, he sheepishly dropped his plunder into it.

I just stood there. After a while he gave a foolish, apologetic smile and marched rapidly off down the passage, trying to look as though nothing had happened.

I put the money back in the boy's pot and got across to him the idea that he would be better off somewhere else. Smiling and nodding his grotesque head, he gathered his *serape* around him, hid the pot under it, and shambled away.

I had no further difficulty in finding my way to the correct exit from the subway, which brought me out on the edge of the Plaza del Norte. I stood there for a moment, getting my bearings by reference to the two statues in the square. One was of *el Liberador,* Fernando Armendariz, first president of the Republic of Aguazul; the other—inevitably—was of Vados. Armendariz faced right, toward the palatial old-gold frontage of the Congress building, Vados left, toward the vast, plain City Hall.

It was only to be expected that there was a tremendous

bustle of people coming and going before the City Hall—and nearly complete stillness in front of Congress.

I had just identified the third great building that fronted on the plaza as the Courts of Justice when there was a tug at my sleeve. I turned to find a small man with glasses, a notebook, and a fistful of ball-point pens. Behind him, two identically tall men in dark suits watched me closely. I disliked the look of them at once—"bodyguard" was the word they brought to my mind.

The small man addressed me rapidly in Spanish; it was too much for me to follow, and I said so. He laughed forcedly at his mistake.

"It is an error of mine, señor," he said importantly. "I am asking the questions for the government, and I regret that I took you for a citizen."

"What questions for the government?"

"Ah, the señor is perhaps not acquainted with some of our enlightened and progressive ideas!" He beamed at me. "Why, it is simple. When there is a matter of public importance to be decided, we take what is called a random sampling of the people's opinion."

"I see," I nodded. This seemed much of a piece with what Señora Posador had told me yesterday about the Speakers' Corner in the Plaza del Sur; it might even be another of Diaz's ideas. Governmental public-opinion polls seemed like pretty good insurance for an absolute ruler, to find out which of his proposed decrees he would be unable to shove down his people's throats.

"And what's the current survey about?"

"It is on the citizenship rights in Ciudad de Vados," said the small man. "But since the señor is not a citizen, he will excuse me for returning to my business."

He bustled back importantly to the subway exit, and I saw him stop and question a pretty girl as she emerged. I wondered, watching her, whether, had I been a citizen, I could have spoken my mind honestly with those two tall and menacing characters staring at me.

I checked my watch and found I had spent five minutes too

long on my way to the traffic department. I hurried across the plaza toward City Hall.

The head of the traffic department had signed the contract that brought me to Vados; I knew therefore that his name was Donald Angers, and I had naturally assumed him to be North American.

He wasn't. He was type-English almost to the point of affectation, and my first reaction to the discovery was to feel that he was almost as much out of place in Vados as the one-eyed beggar-boy.

He studied me hard as he shook my hand and then waved me to a chair. "I see you've caught a dose of the local mañana temperament already, Mr. Hakluyt," he said, with a glance at the clock on his office wall that was just discreet enough not to be offensive.

"I ran into one of your organs of government," I said, and told him about the public-opinion pollster.

Angers gave a thin, wintry smile. "Ye-es . . . I suppose President Vados is one of the very few people ever to have put into practice the old saw about a government standing or falling by its public relations."

He offered me a cigarette, and I accepted. "Is this another of Diaz's ideas?" I suggested as I held out my lighter.

Angers hesitated momentarily before setting his cigarette to the flame. "What makes you think that?" he countered.

"It seems on a par with this sort of Speakers' Corner they run in the Plaza del Sur, and a woman I met at my hotel last night told me that was one of Diaz's notions."

Again the wintry smile, this time a little broader. "Yes, that's one of the best pieces of gallery play we have." He made a note on a memorandum pad before him; he used a fine-nib fountain pen with light blue ink.

"Purely out of curiosity," I said, "what the hell was going on in the Plaza del Sur when I arrived yesterday afternoon? I see the papers are full of it today, but I don't speak very good Spanish."

Angers drew in smoke thoughtfully, looking past me. "That isn't strictly true," he said. "*Tiempo* played it up, as was to be expected, but they naturally magnified it out of all proportion. As it happens, though, it was one minor aspect of a problem with which your work here is directly involved."

"Oh?"

"Yes. I'll brief you as well as I can. The situation's very complex, but I can at least give you an outline at once." He stretched out a thin arm and tugged down the cord of a roller-mounted wall map on his right.

"You've probably made yourself acquainted with the history of Ciudad de Vados?" he added with a passing glance at me.

I nodded.

"Good. Then you'll know it was planned about as thoroughly as a city could well be. But the human element is always the most difficult to legislate for, particularly when the human element concerned is *not* the population of the city itself, but the extremely balky and obstinate native group."

There was a pause. I became aware that a comment was expected from me. I said, "This doesn't sound much like an orthodox traffic problem."

"Not much in Vados *is* orthodox," said Angers pointedly. "As you have no doubt gathered. However, the essence of the problem is simple enough.

"Vados, of course, is an exceptionally farsighted and astute man. I believe that he had for a long time envisaged the possibility of building his new capital city before there was a chance of really doing it, but he was forced to admit that if he simply used up the funds and resources he had available in employing—uh—native talent, he would get not the handsome new town he hoped for, but something petty and rather squalid, like Cuatrovientos or Puerto Joaquin. You should visit those towns while you're here, if you want to see a traffic man's nightmare.

"Well, there was one possible solution, and he rather courageously went ahead and adopted it, in face—so I'm told—of extremely strong opposition from Diaz and a good few of his other supporters. That was to invite anyone and everyone who could make a positive contribution to his new city to invest their efforts in its building. Naturally enough, he wanted the very best of everything, and the very best simply wasn't to be found in Aguazul.

"I myself was supervisory engineer on the road-building project between here and Puerto Joaquin, and like everyone who had played a major part in the creation of the city I was granted citizens' rights and the offer of a permanent post when the job was over. The great majority of us took the posts we were offered, naturally; in fact, about thirty per cent of the city's present population, the most influential and important section, acquired their citizens' rights the same way. After all, a city isn't something you can put down in the middle of nowhere, fill with people, and expect to run itself, is it?"

I murmured that I supposed not.

"Exactly. Some such scheme was essential to the success of the project. The natives could never have produced the Ciudad de Vados you see today without this help from outside—you take that from me.

"A few years ago, however, unforeseen trouble arose. Here's what I mean about the human element. The people of the villages and half-pint towns up-country from here saw this prosperous new city on their doorstep, so to speak, and decided they wanted to move in. Why, they argued, shouldn't they cut a slice of this cake? Of course, to people like you and me it's obvious why not, but imagine trying to explain the facts to an illiterate Indian peasant. Why, until we managed to put a stop to it recently, we were getting whole families moving in not only from the West Indies but even, so help me, from Hawaii—people with no more right to the streets of Vados than—than Laplanders!

"One of the less savory effects of this you may have noticed already—the fringe of shantytowns just outside the city boundary, populated by a shiftless crowd of spongers and beggars: illiterate, forming a positive cesspool of disease, contributing nothing to the life of Vados and expecting everything in return."

He was growing quite heated with the force of his expostulations. I took advantage of the fact that he seemed to have worked himself up to a climax, and interrupted.

"How exactly does this become my problem, Mr. Angers?"

He relaxed a little, remembered his cigarette, and knocked off its accumulated ash. "Well, as you can understand, we citizens don't like the situation. We played an indispensable part in creating Vados, and we expect the terms of our citizens' rights to be honored. We don't want our town smeared with patches of slum development. Matters came to a head some months ago, and it was obvious that something was going to have to be done—something really drastic. Diaz, who is, strictly speaking, the minister to whom the various administrative departments of the city are responsible, wanted to try to integrate this new floating population into the town. I told him it was ridiculous, because the natives just aren't city-dwellers—they're backward peasants. But Diaz is a hard-to-persuade sort of man, son of the soil and all that—I sometimes wonder, actually, whether he's really superior to these people in the shantytowns or whether he's just more cunning. It would be hard to imagine two people less alike than Diaz and the president, who's a very intelligent and cultured man. Still, I suppose it's for precisely that reason that Diaz managed to make himself indispensable—the common touch, you know, and all that sort of thing.

"Anyway, as it turned out, the president fortunately saw the citizens' point of view. But it wasn't just a matter of passing a few bylaws, because it's Vados's policy to give with one hand if he's forced to take away with the other, and there's no denying that a vocal minority exists on Diaz's side. So the solution that was finally adopted was to remodel the 'black spots' of Vados in such a way that the sponging existence of these people became insupportable—and at the same time to confer positive benefits on the whole population. There are four million dolaros at your disposal, Mr. Hakluyt. I'm certain that someone of your qualifications can be relied on to produce a satisfactory solution."

He gave me his wintry smile again. In thoughtful silence, I digested the statement he had just made.

I had often quoted to people who asked me about my work the standard platitude to the effect that traffic is the lifeblood of the city society. I had never expected to find myself in the position of a leukocyte charged with eliminating an undesirable social germ from that bloodstream. Nevertheless, the idea was logical.

And could probably be made to work.

I told Angers as much, and he put out his cigarette with a nod. "I was fairly certain you would say so right away, Mr. Hakluyt. Well, the next step, of course, is to make you acquainted with the various officials with whom you'll be cooperating, in addition to myself—the chief of police, for example, and Señor Seixas in the treasury department, and our various planning and administrative personnel. But before we really get stuck in, there's one point I've been asked to bring to your attention, which I'm sure you'll see the necessity for. I'd like to impress on you the need for you to remain absolutely detached in this matter.

"You'll probably find that I sometimes get a bit—a bit worked up, as they say. But that's because the whole thing is pretty personal to me, or to any other citizen. The reason we selected you for the task—in addition to your outstanding record, of course—was that you'd never been to Aguazul in your life. It will be much more satisfactory for everyone concerned, and will cut the ground from under the feet of the people who've tried to oppose the plan, if we can go on pointing to your verdict as that of a wholly independent and disinterested expert."

"I presume," I said, "that that was why you called in an outside traffic analyst anyway, instead of having the job done by your own traffic department."

He looked slightly embarrassed, as though I had put my finger on a sensitive point, and I had a vision—so sharp it almost brought a smile to my lips—of the opposition he had probably put up to my being engaged.

"Yes, of course," he answered with a hint of severity. "Well, now that I've made that point clear, perhaps you'll give me an idea whether there's any special equipment or assistance you'll be needing."

I took a sheaf of paper from an inside pocket; I had typed it out before leaving Florida. "That, broadly speaking," I said, and lit another cigarette while he was running down the list.

I'd put down only the obvious items—scraped off the top of my head—but nonetheless they added up to a respectable length. A car to be permanently at my disposal; an official *laissez-passer* in case the police got inquisitive—I'd more than once been picked up for loitering while standing at an intersection counting the traffic flow; the use of an office in the traffic department with a computer at least up to MAXIAC standard, and a secretary speaking English and Spanish with equal fluency; addresses of every important organization and company in the city, a supply of maps, a team of qualified statisticians, borrowed if need be from a business research firm; comprehensive cost figures for the last half-dozen major construction jobs in Aguazul, down to hard core per cubic meter and standard-rate fees for demolition squads—I was always careful about this now and had been ever since the time when, as a green novice, I produced a beautiful scheme for a budget of sixteen thousand pounds Australian, which costed out at four hundred per cent over; and, not least important, English translations of all relevant bylaws and regulations governing construction work in Aguazul.

Angers seemed to be favorably impressed with the comprehensive list—at any rate, his manner thawed perceptibly as the morning leaked away, and when we had finished going into the details of my requirements, he gave me the warmest smile I had yet seen from him.

"I can tell it's going to be a pleasure working with you, Mr. Hakluyt," he said confidentially. "You're obviously a methodical man, and we appreciate that sort of thing. I don't imagine I need refer again to the question of being detached about all this, do I? After all, I suppose you people down under look at things pretty much the same way as we do, really."

I couldn't have thought of an adequate reply to that if I had tried for a week; fortunately he turned to his clock and stood up.

"It's about time for lunch," he said briskly. "Suppose you join me, eh? We can eat in the plaza—it's a beautiful day."

I had a wild vision of sitting on the grass and having a picnic when Angers suggested lunching in the plaza; I should have guessed that his dignity implied something different.

In actual fact, a restaurant was what we found—twenty tables for four and a complete portable kitchen that appeared with near miraculous suddenness under the trees every noon and evening except when the weather forecast was bad. I learned afterwards that it was the most expensive place to eat in the whole of Vados, but it was extremely pleasant if you had no objection to being watched by groups of workers who had come to eat their tortilla-and-frijole lunch and take their siesta on the benches all around the square.

We were halfway through the main course—Angers holding forth on the history of the city again—when a stir caught my eye on the steps outside the Courts of Justice, which, as I had previously noted, also fronted on the Plaza del Norte. A tall, good-looking man in his forties was coming out, surrounded by a group of admirers and hangers-on. A big black car pulled up to the sidewalk as he descended the long half-spiral of steps that crossed the frontage of the courts; he called something to the driver of the car and continued across the plaza to take a table not far from where Angers and I were sitting. Here he sat down with three of his friends, and the waiters rushed to serve him. I noticed that whereas they were merely polite to Angers and myself, they were positively deferential to the new arrival.

"Who's that over there?" I asked Angers, and he turned his head.

"Oh, one of our most distinguished citizens! Excuse me—I must ask the result of the case. Though I'm pretty sure it was a foregone conclusion." He beckoned to a waiter and gave him instructions in Spanish; the waiter crossed to the newcomer's table, spoke briefly with him, and returned to us.

"Excellent," exclaimed Angers when the waiter had conveyed his news. "We must have another bottle of wine on that, Hakluyt—it's worth celebrating."

I reminded him delicately that I still didn't know what he was talking about.

"Oh, I'm terribly sorry! That's Mario Guerrero, chairman of the Citizens of Vados. You'll recall that our professional troublemaker Tezol made himself a nuisance in the Plaza del

Sur yesterday—you said you arrived in the middle of the row. Guerrero has just been giving evidence, because he happened to be present when it all happened, and he says Tezol was heavily fined. I wish they could get rid of him altogether, though."

"Who is he? Tezol, I mean."

"Oh, some Indian rabble-rouser from the villages, I believe. Not a citizen."

Angers raised his glass toward Guerrero, who caught the movement and inclined his head in acknowledgment, smiling.

After that, Angers went on recounting the history of the city and mainly his part in building its highways; I let the flow of words wash over my head and reflected on the function of a white corpuscle.

Somehow, the sense of elation I'd had at being invited to work in Vados was beginning to evaporate.

IV

Angers, so he told me, had arranged appointments for me with the police chief, whose name was O'Rourke, and with the treasury department official he had previously mentioned, Seixas, who was handling the estimates for the replanning. But these were not until late in the afternoon, and I saw no point in hanging around the traffic department while they got things ready for me; besides, I'd probably have been in Angers' way.

Accordingly, having finished lunch, I left him and made my way back to the Plaza del Sur to have a look at the day's parade of grievances.

The speakers were in full swing when I arrived, and some thousand-odd people were idly listening to them or dozing on the ground or the benches under the palms. I dawdled through the crowd to see what the speakers' hobbyhorses might be.

The two most heavily patronized were on opposite sides of the square: one under a Citizens of Vados banner, one a swarthy mulatto with a demagogue's manner who emphasized his remarks by pounding fist into palm and who stood beneath a banner saying NACIONAL.

Beside him on his small dais, legs dangling, sat a man with a long, morose Indian face, wrapped in a gorgeous *serape;* he seemed to be paying no attention.

After a while the mulatto stopped talking, there was a spatter of applause mixed with booing from the hundred or so people clustered in front of the dais, and a troupe of Indian musicians in traditional costume came forward and played the pipe and drums in an insistent, repetitive style. Obviously this was not to everyone's taste; as I pushed forward to hear better and to get a sight of the players, I noticed a strange coincidence—even with my Florida tan, I was the palest among the people who had stayed to hear the music, whereas on the other side of the square, where I had been at first, it was a swarthy skin that was a rarity. A division of sophistication, perhaps.

A collection box jangled under my nose; I presumed this was for the musicians, so I thrust a folded one-dolaro bill into it. The man carrying the box had a face as wooden as a cigar-store Indian's; his only reaction was to incline his head a few degrees forward before passing on.

A familiar, husky voice addressed me as the collector went away.

"Are you aware what you have just paid for, Señor Hakluyt?"

I turned to see Maria Posador standing beside me. She wore narrow biscuit-colored linen slacks today, a white tailored shirt, and sandals on her bare feet; she looked dressed more for an expensive holiday resort than for this crowd. Enormous dark glasses made her face inscrutable, and her tone of voice had been absolutely neutral.

"For the musicians, I suppose," I said, belatedly answering her question.

"That, and other things. Indirectly, you have helped to get Juan Tezol out of an impossible situation. You have heard perhaps that they fined him one thousand dolaros this morning?" She gestured at the group of people around us. "If you went through the pockets of all these people—those who have pockets—you would find perhaps one hundred dolaros."

I shrugged. "I have no great interest in the matter."

"No?" The great dark lenses searched my face. "You would perhaps not even recognize Tezol?"

"I'm sure I wouldn't."

"There he is, sitting like one of his ancestors' idols on the steps of the speaker's platform. He is wondering how the world can be so unjust to him. If you showed him a thousand dolaros, he would be able to count them in a week—perhaps. The man of mixed blood who was addressing the crowd on his behalf is a certain Sam Francis. He had just assured the crowd—and I, for one, believe him—that he will not spend a cento on himself until the fine is paid. And yet there are holes in his shoes."

She swung around and pointed at the speaker under the Citizens of Vados banner. "There you see Andres Lucas, secretary of the Citizens Party. The shoes *he* is wearing probably cost him fifty dolaros, and he probably has more than twenty pairs. I do not know where Guerrero is, their chairman."

"I do," I said after a pause. "Lunching in the Plaza del Norte."

She nodded without surprise. "The check there will be as much as a pair of Lucas's shoes. You may consider you are lucky, señor, not to have a great interest in the matter." She uttered the last sentence bitingly.

"I begin to see what the customs officer meant," I murmured, and she snapped a quick "Who?" at me.

I explained, and she laughed without humor. "You may expect to find that often in Vados, Señor Hakluyt. The reason, of course, is that much money has already been swallowed up in this city—and while we are all proud of it, there are those here, and many more in Cuatrovientos and Astoria Negra and Puerto Joaquin, who think that it is about time money was spent elsewhere. Perhaps they are right; perhaps they are."

The crowd was breaking up; two men of middle age carefully carrying a chessboard with an unfinished game went past us, dispersing like the rest back to their work. The speakers had come down from their platforms, and energetic youths were dismantling these and carrying them and the banners away.

We watched in silence for a few minutes. Then Señora Posador came to herself briskly. "Well, señor, I will delay you no longer—indeed, I cannot, for I have an appointment. But we shall meet again, and we must have this match at chess sometime. *Hasta la vista!*"

"*Hasta la vista!*" I echoed automatically; then she was gone, striding like a man with an air of purpose and determination across the square.

I stayed looking thoughtfully after her until she disappeared from sight. There had been a quality of bitterness in what she had said about Tezol that made me revise my original assessment of her as a woman of wealth with much leisure and no more.

Not just a person, plainly—a personality. I would have to find out more about her—and since she was not the sort of woman to be overlooked, almost certainly Angers would be able to tell me about her.

There was only one thing I regretted. I had almost failed when I started out as a free-lance, through inability to discipline myself; after two false starts I'd imposed rules on myself that included one about not chasing women while on a job, and now after ten or twelve years it had become second nature to me. Accordingly, I was making no effort at all to interest her in me.

But it seemed a pity, all the same.

I came back to the traffic department a few minutes ahead of time and was shown into Angers' office. The Englishman was smoking at his desk, reading through a typed report; he gestured that I should take the same chair I had had this morning.

"Won't keep you a moment," he said. "Just got to finish this memo. Then we'll go over to Seixas' and get him to brief you on the financial side of it."

I nodded and sat down. A few minutes passed in silence.

At length Angers folded the report, rattled its sheets together, and scribbled a minute on the flyleaf before ringing for a secretary to collect it and pass it on its way.

"Fine," he said with a glance at the clock. "We only have to go next door, and I'm afraid Seixas is like too many other people in Vados—doesn't know what time is, I sometimes think. Still, that's no reason why we should be late. Let's go."

We strolled through clean, bright passages out of the building and across the intervening lawns to the treasury offices. We were almost at the entrance when Angers said, as though struck by a sudden thought, "Oh, by the way, I meant to ask you—there's a woman called Maria Posador who spends a lot of time around your hotel. Have you run into her?"

Surprised, I nodded.

Angers gave me his habitual wintry smile. "A word to the wise, and all that, then," he said. "She's not good company."

"What do you mean?"

He shrugged. "Well . . . just that maybe you oughtn't to cultivate her acquaintance. Bear in mind what I said about remaining detached, won't you?"

I don't think I showed it, but I found the flat, dogmatic, English way in which Angers put his warning very unpleasant. I said shortly, "Why?"

"Uh—" He ushered me forward through the revolving door of the treasury building. "Well, she's a well-known local personality and something of an opponent of the president— it's a long story, and I won't go into it. Take it from me, though: if you're seen about with her, it would make people assume you weren't a disinterested outside expert."

"Well, here's something for you to bear in mind," I said. "The best way to ensure that I stay disinterested is to treat me as though I were and not to jump to the conclusion that because Señora Posador is prettier than you I'm going to take orders from her."

"My dear chap!" said Angers, distressed. "I assure you—"

"Forget it," I said.

A tense silence took us into Seixas' office, which, although basically identical with Angers', bore the stamp of an altogether different personality. Seixas, who rose from behind his desk to greet us with both hands outstretched, was a stout, sweating man with a round red face and black hair. A large black cigar like an exclamation mark jutted up from his wide-lipped mouth; it bore the widest band I had ever seen—gaudy with gold and red. He wore a sky-blue suit and a white shirt, down the front of which a tie with a design of pineapples poured like an illuminated cascade. As well as the office equipment on his desk, there was a large jug of something sickly-looking with ice cubes floating in it, and an enormous pinup calendar with a steatopygic nude hung from the tag of the rolled-up wall map.

"So you're Hakluyt, hey?" he said. "Siddown, siddown! Have a drink! Have a cigar!"

We both refused the drink—it seemed to be Bols *Parfait Amour,* which is a sickly liqueur the color of methylated spirit, cut with gin and water—but I took a cigar and found it surprisingly mild for all its coal-black appearance.

"Brazilian, hey!" said Seixas with satisfaction, sucking hard on his own. "Well, whaddya think of Vados, Hakluyt? The burg, not the man!"

"Impressive," I said, watching Angers out of the corner of my eye. It was plain that he found Seixas unbearable; it was equally plain that Seixas was thick-skinned enough not to realize the fact. I found this amusing.

"Yeah!" said Seixas with deep satisfaction. "This is one *hell* of a town! And you're gonna bring it one step nearer heaven, hey?" He shook with laughter, squeezing up his eyes, and the ash from his cigar fell down the geometrical center of his brilliant tie.

"Well, with Angers there looking sour like a fresh lime, guess we'd better get on with the business." He shoved his large body forward in his chair so that he could put his elbows on the desk, and swiveled his cigar up to an angle that he had probably copied from a bad Hollywood movie when he was in his teens: the tycoon angle.

"Well, 's pretty straightforward. Back a few years—oh, eight years ago—there was a hell of a big dock fire at Puerto Joaquin. Tanker blew up. The docks didn't do so bad, in the end, but the city fire department wasn't worth a spit on the sidewalk. 'Bout four hundred people roasted to death; houses burnt like paper, y'know? Well, year or two an' they got the town put back together, built lotsa new apartment blocks an' like that—nowhere so good as Vados, though, all scrappy and bitty.

"Anyways, after that Vados gets the cabinet together an' says we gotta be ready for it happening again, so he puts a levy on oil shipments—the big companies kick up a squawk, but hell, Vados is a good man in their books, straightened out their labor problems, done lotsa good work, so they give in. An' offa this levy he gets a 'mergency fund, sorta like insurance. Y'see, they was building this burg then, already got started—hadn't anything left over for Puerto Joaquin or any place else. There's about eight million dolaros in the fund right now, an' *el Presidente* himself says how it gets spent. If. You got four million of 'em if you need."

He hauled a drawer of his desk open and rummaged inside for something. After taking out a gaudy-covered novel, a flat gin bottle—empty; he dropped it in the wastebasket—and a soiled shirt, he extracted a large file of papers and set it on the desktop with a grunt of satisfaction.

"Now le's get this straight," he muttered. "Ah—yeah!"

He selected a sheet of paper with a magnificent embossed letterhead and several wet rings adorning it, and held it up between beringed fingers. "This here's the official authorization, y'see," he said. "You get paid twenty thousand plus expenses; you can spend up to ten thousand on research, computing, and like that, but you have to get out a scheme for it. You cost your own scheme, that right?"

"That's the arrangement."

"Great—*hate* costing construction projects. Damn muddle of figures, all those loose ends like sickness losses an' God knows what. . . . Want I should put y' on to the firms who'll be doing the job?"

"That can wait. I'm not interested in who does it—it's what has to be done that concerns me."

"Uh-huh," he said, regarding me thoughtfully. And then a second time, "Uh-huh."

We spent about twenty minutes after that going into a few

of the most significant figures—he sent for some recent records of work done under government contract so that I could get a rough picture of costs, and Angers sat impatiently at the side of the room while we got technical. I was rather surprised to find that under his casual exterior Seixas had a mind like a razor. Of course, I shouldn't have been—Vados wasn't the kind of man to tolerate easy riders in his beloved city's administration.

Our interview over, Seixas got to his feet, beaming. "A helluva lot of luck, Hakluyt!" he said. "Me, I think it's too damn much money to spend anyway—we could dig those sonsabitches out in half a day with bayonets. Then they'd come back, though, so maybe it ain't a waste. See you!"

Evidently relieved, Angers got up eagerly, shook Seixas' hand with a distant expression on his face, and hurried me out of the room.

"Quite a character, isn't he?" I said when the door was closed behind me.

"By no means unique, I'm afraid," said Angers glumly. "I mean—well, you saw for yourself. The empty bottles and the dirty clothes in his office desk—I *ask* you!" He sighed. "Still, one has to admit he's clever enough. He's a native, of course," he added as an afterthought.

"He spoke very good English."

"Says he taught himself at the cinema." Angers looked about him as we emerged once more into daylight. "Well, we have to go about a quarter of a mile—do you feel like walking, or shall I call a cab?"

I mentally pictured the layout of this locality; the police headquarters were in a block a short distance north of the Plaza del Norte, behind the Courts of Justice. "I'd like to walk, if you don't mind," I said. "The more I can see of the city on foot, the better, at the moment."

"As you like."

We walked silently for a while. "By the way," I said eventually, "why is the chief of police one of the first people I have to see?"

"Oh, a variety of reasons," said Angers offhandedly. "I don't mind saying you may find him a little awkward—

he seems to be in two minds about the whole affair."

I digested the remark blankly. After a pause Angers explained further.

"Well—uh—the people squatting in these shantytowns, of course, are a thorn in his side; there's a tremendous amount of petty thievery that goes on, and often enough a wanted man can just vanish into the hills with the help of relatives of people here. So he wants to get rid of the mess, like the rest of us. On the other hand, he's rather the same kind of man as Diaz—country-born, not an educated man at all, or rather, not a *cultured* man. I'm told that this is one of the reasons why Vados preferred him as police chief—he's far better able to enter the minds of native criminals than anyone from outside Aguazul. But he has a gruff sort of dislike for—well, for people like myself, for example. For the foreign-born citizens."

"And what's his force like?"

Angers shrugged. "Venal and corrupt by our standards, but pretty good, so I'm assured, for Latin America. Vados cleared out the worst offenders when he took office, and they come down very heavily on policemen who take bribes or falsify evidence out of personal grudges. That's to say, they come down heavily on the ones they catch; I'm sure there's a lot more going on than ever comes to light."

"That was my impression," I said, and told him about the policeman who had tried to steal from the beggar-boy's pot.

"What can you expect?" said Angers in a tone of unexpected toleration. "After all, it's probably only the fact that he has both eyes and both hands that divides the policeman from the beggar. It's going to take a lot of determination to ensure that the substance of Vados matches the appearance of it. Some of these people are a few generations at most away from the Stone Age; it's really asking too much of them to turn them into civilized city-dwellers. In another twenty years perhaps— not yet."

El Jefe—Captain O'Rourke—looked as Irish as his name, aside from an Indian cast to his cheekbones. His short brown hair topped a stage-Irish face, knobby like a potato, with wide lips. He had a wart on his nose and another on the back of his left hand. His fingers were thick, stubby, and ill-kept; there was a mat of coarse hair on the back of each wrist. He wore black uniform pants and boots, a black shirt, and a red tie with the knot pulled down two inches so that he could open his collar. On a peg on the wall behind him hung a shiny-peaked cap and an automatic in a leather holster.

His office smelled a little of frying-oil, as though the air-conditioning had been turned off at noon and had failed to carry away the smell of his subordinates' packed meals. A huge array of photographs of himself framed him as he sat behind his desk—from a faded street-photographer's shot of him as a small boy en route to first communion, to a glossy eight-by-ten of him resplendent in dress uniform shaking hands with *el Presidente*.

On other walls there were also photographs—mainly gory ones. Three bodies being dragged out of a wrecked car. A man bleeding from the corner of his mouth, both eyes closed by bruises. A woman drawing down the top of her blouse to expose an ugly burn scar across one shoulder. Probably mementos of past cases.

He gestured us gruffly to a chair; it was almost a shock to hear his gutteral accented Spanish, in view of his name and his appearance.

"*No habla inglés*," he said shortly, as though confessing to a serious fault—perhaps in his eyes, it was one. He added something else rapid, which I failed to follow. I glanced at Angers.

"Uh—in spite of his name," Angers translated with a bad grace. "I'll have to interpret for you, I suppose." He turned to O'Rourke and spoke haltingly.

The interview, such as it was, took a long time and covered very little ground. Since it was practically all platitudes and dull questions to which the answers were obvious, I let Angers do the talking after a while, meantime looking at the pictures on the walls.

A sudden barking exclamation from O'Rourke brought me back to the here and now with a start. I glanced around to find his brown eyes fixed on me, and Angers looking uncomfortable.

"What's the trouble?" I said.

"I—uh—well, I was telling him about this disgraceful affair of the policeman stealing from a beggar this morning, and—"

"You *what*?" I said.

"Well, it oughtn't to be allowed to pass without action," said Angers defensively.

"All right, if you've done it, you've done it. What's the comment?"

Angers licked his lips, with a sidelong look at O'Rourke, whose face was like thunder. "I—I can't quite make out. He either wants to sack the offender, because he was stealing from his own people—as though it would have been better for him to steal from you instead—or prove that there's no truth in the accusation at all."

"It wasn't that important," I said wearily. "It probably goes on all the time—don't translate that! Tell him—oh, hell! Tell him the boy got his money back; tell him there oughtn't to be any need for beggars in Ciudad de Vados."

Angers translated hesitantly; astonished, I saw O'Rourke suddenly break into a smile, and he rose from behind his desk to extend his thick-fingered hand.

"He says you are perfectly right," Angers interpreted. "He hopes you will do a lot of good for the people of the city."

"So do I," I said, and rose to shake hands. Then I got up to go, and Angers caught at my arm.

"Not so fast," he said. "There's—uh—there's one other thing."

I sat down again while he exchanged a few more sentences with *el Jefe*. Then the interview was in fact over, and we went out again into the warm afternoon air.

"What was the bit at the end all about?" I asked.

Angers shrugged. "Nothing of importance," he said. "I was just telling him what you'd probably be doing for the next day or two. Officially, or course, aliens have to register with the police and report once a week if they're staying over a month and all kinds of rigmarole like that—but we can avoid your going to so much trouble, O'Rourke says. You'll only have to notify the police if you move away from your hotel."

"Fine."

"Well, that's about it for tonight, then. Tomorrow I'll take you out and show you the extent of the problem we have to solve."

V

The first "black spot" due for our inspection was a cheap market that had grown up in what was intended to be a quiet lower-income-group residential backwater in the angle between two of the access roads coming from the main highway nexus. Itinerant merchants had found it a convenient spot to set up shop when the city was being built; they traded there with the construction workers. And somehow, through some loophole in the regulations, it had continued as a permanent feature of the area.

But if it hadn't been for the arrival of the squatters in the shantytowns, so Angers told me, it would naturally have withered away, and the area would have continued the way it was designed. Here the squatters garnered practically the whole of their exiguous income, and their tenacious persistence was rapidly making the section degenerate toward a slum.

Complicating the issue, the high cost of living made many people prefer to buy their vegetables here—too many for a simple city ordinance to decree it out of existence without strong and vocal opposition. It was part of the technique that had made Vados's regime so durable that he always preferred to replace the substance of a nuisance to himself or his supporters with the *fait accompli* of a universal benefit.

And in this case it was going to take a lot of doing.

The market was colorful—but it stank like a pigsty; picturesque—but so noisy it was hardly to be wondered that the dwellings in the vicinity were going downhill toward tenement standards.

"Does this go on all day?" I asked Angers. "Every day?"

"Except for Sunday," he confirmed. "These people have no

conception of time, of course—and nothing better to do
anyway. It's all one to them whether they sit here twelve
hours or two hours—look at the flies on that baby's face!
Isn't it disgusting? —so long as they sell what they've
brought."

I swatted a fly as it buzzed past, but missed. "All right," I
grunted. "Let's take a look at the next on the list."

The next eyesore was—of all places—right underneath the
main monorail nexus. Ciudad de Vados had a first-class cross-
and around-town network of tracks, in the so-called "spider's
web" pattern that is rather efficient but suffers from one
serious drawback—the need for a large central interchange
station.

In Vados, of course, this hadn't been such a disadvantage
as it usually was; they were building from scratch and could
afford to be lavish with space for the central. The result was
that a good acre or more of surface was barred from the sun
by the overhead concrete platforms.

"What happened here was largely due to sheer greed,"
Angers told me flatly. "It's also a sample of what would
probably have been Ciudad de Vados if Diaz had had his
way instead of the president. The owner of this land was the
original director of the monorail system. He asked for a !ease
on the area under the station as part of his citizens' rights
endowment when the city was first incorporated. It seemed
like an innocuous enough request—everyone assumed he
would rent it out as warehouse space, or something harmless
like that. So no one took the precaution of placing limitations
on his use of it.

"What happened? He fitted up the spaces between the
foundations with flimsy partitions and rickety flooring, let the
resulting chicken coops to his friends and relatives, and found
it so profitable to be a landlord that he resigned his job. Now
he devotes his full time to *this*."

He pointed; I looked at "this," and it wasn't pretty.

The lie of the ground here was a series of sloping ridges
over which the platforms of the station jutted out. Standing
where we were on the crest of one of the banks that ran
between the two main entrances for passengers, we could see

directly down into the space between the steel girders and thick concrete pillars that carried the platforms. There was a smell down there of rotting food and close-packed human beings and their waste products. Smoke from fires drifted up to us; the squalling of children merged into one hideous row together with the braying of donkeys, mooing of cows, grunting of pigs, and the wail of an elderly phonograph playing a record long worn past comprehensibility.

"Tezol lives here, by the way," Angers informed me.

"It hardly seems possible that human beings *could* live down there," I muttered.

Angers laughed sourly. "Either the natives desire nothing better, or this is actually an improvement on what they're used to. I say, we're honored! Look who's coming to see us—the proprietor himself."

A fat Negro was hauling himself up from the depths beneath the station. The path was very steep and very slippery, for dogs, domestic cattle, and, it appeared, children had used it indiscriminately to relieve themselves, so the landlord was forced to use his arms more than his legs in the ascent.

He pulled himself over the lip of the bank, grunting, and wiped his face with a large red bandanna. Thrusting it back in the pocket of his bulging jeans, he called out to us.

"You back again, Señor Angers, hey?"

"Yes, Sigueiras, I'm back," said Angers, not trying to hide the distaste on his face. "We'll be clearing out that muck heap of yours soon."

Sigueiras chuckled. "You tried that before, señor! Always it is not possible. If you try to take away *my* citizens' rights, what happen to *your* citizens' rights? That a big joke, hey?"

"He's talking about a legal decision that went in his favor a few months ago," explained Angers to me in an undertone. Raising his voice, he went on, "But citizens' rights are subordinate to city development plans, aren't they, Sigueiras?"

"Yes, señor. And I would very willingly give up this little patch of darkness—but where else are my people to go? They wish homes, you will give them no homes, I am *forced* to give them homes!"

"They must have had homes where they came from," said Angers sharply.

"Had, Señor Angers! Had! When they were starving because their water was taken for the city, when their land was dry, where else should they go but to the city? Each night and morning I pray to Our Lady and to Saint Joseph that new homes may be built for these people and work be found for them—"

"The old hypocrite!" said Angers under his breath.

Sigueiras interrupted himself. "You say—you say city development plans, Señor Angers? I hear you say that! Is it that my prayers are answered?"

"Your prayers are more likely to be for some of your tenants to die so you can move in more at higher rents," said Angers coldly. "This is Señor Hakluyt, who is going to redesign this area so that it's all turned into a new road. Or something," he added, glancing at me.

Sigueiras clubbed his fist and raised it toward me, suppressed fury choking him for a moment. I took a step back for fear he would strike me, almost losing my footing on the bank.

"So you come to Vados from over sea and take away all the home my people have?" he screamed. "You make your living by taking away home from people? I spit on you! I tread you in the dirt! Señor Angers, this I swear on the name of my dead father, rest his soul." He uttered the last statement with a peculiar passionless intensity, looking again at my companion. "I swear that if you do this thing, if you take away my people only home, I bring them all—all—their cows, their burros, everything—and I move them into your big, beautiful apartment. *Then* you see!"

"Let's not waste any more time on this hysterical old fool," said Angers sourly, and turned to go. I, hesitating, was about to follow him, but Sigueiras caught my sleeve.

"You make your living taking away home from people," he said, gritting the words. "I give up my living to make home for people. Which of us do better thing, hey?"

And he was gone, slipping-sliding down the path back into his personal inferno.

Angers was already back at the car before I caught up with him again. He was wiping his forehead with a large handkerchief.

"I'm sorry about that outburst," he said wryly. "I'd have warned you if I'd known we were likely to run into him. You don't have to take any notice, of course—he always acts abusive like that."

I shrugged and got into the car. But as we rolled back toward the main road, I saw a long-faced man with a bowed head, wearing a bright *serape* I was sure I had seen the previous afternoon in the Plaza del Sur. Juan Tezol, going home. I wondered if he had found his thousand dolaros yet.

"It's a strange comedown for Sigueiras," said Angers as the car fled along smooth concrete roadway. "I suppose it's the type—but I remember him as an apparently intelligent and sensible man."

"And now?" I said, keeping my face absolutely straight.

He gave me a sharp glance. "You saw for yourself," he said. Then he realized there was more to my remark than a foolish question and nodded reluctantly.

"You're probably right," he admitted. "He could still be a formidable person."

He lapsed into a thoughtful silence. I wondered if he was picturing scores of peasants, cattle and all, actually forcing their way into his rooms.

We went next on a tour of the three shantytowns, and all of them were very much like Sigueiras's slum spread out over a wider area, except that since they weren't closed in, the smell hanging over them was less repulsive. But although they were superficially alike, I found that each of them had its own kind of organic structure and function, perhaps due to the fact that they were on different sides of Vados and the inhabitants came from districts differing slightly in cultural pattern. There was also, naturally, a marked difference between them because of the local traffic pattern, but this operated at third or fourth remove, and was not especially significant.

"I don't quite understand how you fellows do it," Angers said as he watched me doodling flow-curves on a scratch pad, standing on the shoulder of the highway overlooking one of the shantytowns.

"Coming from a highway engineer, that's a handsome admission," I said, more sardonically than I'd intended. "Most of the time your boys make me feel I want their permission to breathe in their vicinity."

Angers colored a little. "No offense," he said.

"I mean it. Oh, it's largely a matter of instinct and a particular sort of mind. Hard to explain. I suppose the closest analogy is with the way a river deposits silt at a bend—the direction and strength of the current and the nature of the silt determine the way the course of the river develops. In roughly the same way you can establish principles of traffic flow that sometimes—almost invariably in the case of unplanned towns or villages—determine the primary nature and layout of the result."

I stripped off the sheet of the pad I'd been working on and screwed it up. "No luck?" Angers suggested.

"Oh, it could be done. But . . . well, I suppose you wouldn't be interested in the obvious solution."

Angers raised a sandy eyebrow at me. "I thought we'd considered all the obvious solutions," he said rather stiffly. "That was why we called in an expert."

"It's still obvious. Use the money to build these people a nice clean new housing development and educate them into living there."

"It may be obvious, but it's superficial," he said with the relieved air of one who has met and defeated the same argument many times before. "These aren't the only peasants we have to cope with, remember. What do you think their relations back in the hills would say when they saw Cousin Pedro and his family of fourteen installed—and I mean in a stall, because they'd take their animals with them!—by the government for nothing?" He shook his head. "No, that would merely aggravate the problem."

"All right," I shrugged. "But I can tell you now that if that would aggravate the problem, the best I could do would be to alleviate it. I can make life difficult for these people; I can eliminate their market, so they have to tramp from door to door to sell their vegetables and chickens; I can make their shantytowns into nice clean new—something. But these people are fatalists, damn it! To them it will merely be something new to be endured, like a drought or a famine. The most that can be hoped for is to make things *so* difficult they can be persuaded back to their villages—but unless something is done there, too, they'll come back, and you'll get precisely the same thing happening all over again under new circumstances."

"Yes, but—well, frankly, Hakluyt, we aren't looking for much more than a palliative, you know," said Angers, blinking. "We're tackling the other aspects of the problem, but that's long-term stuff, you know. I mean, there are United Nations teams up in the villages, teaching elementary things like hygiene and baby-care, and there are Vados's own educational shock troops trying to bring the literacy level up a few per cent. Oh, in another generation these people will probably be pretty well civilized! What we object to, we who are citizens and sweated blood over Vados, is seeing uncivilized people mucking up everything we've worked for so hard."

I judged it better not to pursue the matter. "Well, I'm a stranger," I said. "All I can do is warn you."

I turned back toward the car and began to stroll down the shoulder of the highway.

"I think you've given me everything I need to be going on with—most other points I can clear up with maps and reference books. For the next week or so I want mainly to be left alone; I can't say for sure what I'll be doing, but I'll most likely be standing around on street corners, taking the mono, getting into crowds wherever they form. Things like that."

Angers hesitated. "Well, you're in charge," he allowed finally, and I had to hide a smile. Like most traffic men who've come up by way of highway engineering, he was used to dealing in—literally—more concrete things. Accordingly, I went into a bit more detail as we returned to the city center.

"For instance," I said, "consider the problem of that market you want to get rid of. As you pointed out, one reason why it continued to exist after the city was built was that the shanty-town squatters took over the tradition established by the peddlers who traded with the construction gangs in the first place. But a contributory factor to its survival must have been the absence of heavy traffic flow through the roads it occupies. So we have to create such a flow—and it has to be a functional flow in the sense that people have got to be better off when it operates. Okay, achieve that, and you create a sense that the market is a nuisance because it's a brake on the smooth passage of people who want to get past it. Six months of that kind of irritation, and a contagious urge to get rid of it will enable the city council to legislate it away with the support of a large majority of the public."

Angers nodded his head in reluctant admiration. "It amazes me that the abstract factors you traffic analysts handle can produce such positive results," he said.

"It's the way people work. We're subject to a lot of pressures we're not conscious of; some of them influence us out of proportion to their importance. But the problem lies here: a new traffic flow through the market quarter will have to pour into the main traffic nexus—there's no room for it to do anything else. And that complex of intersections was designed—and very well designed—to cope with *exactly* its present amount and direction of traffic flow. You can't just open a new road into it; you might very well slow the traffic down instead of speeding it up."

I looked thoughtfully out of the car. We were traversing the Plaza del Este, just in front of the magnificent cathedral. Like ants against the blazing whites, blues, and reds of the frontage, a family of peasants was standing. Their heads were tilted back, staring at the three-hundred-foot aluminum cross rearing into the clear sky overhead, wondering whether the deity inhabiting this august edifice might not be different from the one occupying their little adobe-built village shrine at home.

"At home"; yes, that was the trouble in Vados. Or a good part of it, anyway. Twenty thousand people who couldn't regard the city as their home, although they lived in it—simply because it *wasn't* their home. They were in a foreign country in their own homeland.

"Where would you like me to drop you off?" Angers asked as we rolled on toward his office.

"Anywhere around here will do."

"And shall we not be seeing anything of you at all for the next week, then?"

"I'll drop in every morning, of course—find out if there is anything important I should know, ask any questions I've dreamed up. Don't worry about me—I'll make out fine."

Angers nodded, looking past me at the street. "Any special time?"

"After the morning rush is over, probably. I want to get a complete picture of the type and density of the traffic flow in the city center all around the clock, but I'll probably be out in all the rush hours, for the first week at least."

He sighed. "All right. Keep us posted, won't you? Cheerio."

I shook his hand and left him when the car pulled up to the curb, and strolled slowly along the sidewalk back toward the pedestrian underpass at the main traffic nexus.

Well, one thing that was going to be essential if I was to work completely on my own, as I always preferred in the first stages of a job like this, was for me to do something about my rudimentary Spanish. Another was to post myself in better detail on the attitudes and reactions of the average citizen. I'm a firm believer in the platitude that people get the popular press they deserve; accordingly, I bought a copy of the afternoon edition of the government paper, *Liberdad*, and took it to a bar to look through it. I had a vest-pocket dictionary I'd bought in Florida, and though it didn't give some of the words I needed, I got ahead quite well with the paper.

One headline caught my eye because it mentioned the name of Mario Guerrero, the chairman of the Citizens of Vados. I struggled through the story under the heading and found that a man called Miguel Dominguez had brought a charge of dangerous driving against Guerrero's chauffeur, and another of aiding and abetting against Guerrero himself. There was a picture of Guerrero standing beside a big black sedan, the same I had seen roll toward him as he left the Courts of Justice in the Plaza del Norte.

Once again the reporter failed to include a lot of things I wanted to know; he did, however, make it plain that in his view the whole affair was a plot by the National Party, of which Miguel Dominguez was a prominent supporter, to discredit the chairman of their opponents. Of course, it was ridiculous to suppose that Guerrero would do anything to injure the citizens of his beloved Vados—or anyone in Aguazul, for that matter, Fortunately for Guerrero's honor, the charge against him would be defeated by the legal skill of his close friend and colleague Andres Lucas, and the stigma on his good name would unfailingly be removed.

It was that kind of report.

I inquired for a *Tiempo*, because I felt pretty sure the independent paper would regard the affair rather differently. But I was told that it wasn't well enough off to afford more than one edition a day—*Liberdad* was government subsidized, of course—and in any case it was getting on toward the end-of-work rush hour, so I left it till the following morning.

I was out early the next day, assessing the incoming traffic as the stores and offices opened up for the day—the regular hours of work seemed to be eight-thirty to noon and two to five-thirty for offices. Around nine-thirty I went back to the hotel for a leisurely late breakfast and found the follow-up I was looking for in *Tiempo*.

As I'd guessed, the independent organ had a totally different slant on the matter. Their report explained to the world how Guerrero had ordered his chauffeur to drive through a group of children playing with a ball in a side street; the public-spirited Miguel Dominguez had seen the event and had been so shocked at the risk to the children that he had done his duty as a citizen, fearless of the powerful entrenched interests which were bound to smear his act as a political trick.

I cursed local politics and turned over to the inside pages.

Here I found an article that concerned me much more directly—indeed, I was mentioned in it by name, and not at all politely. It was on the shantytown problem; the writer's name, Felipe Mendoza, rang a bell with me, and I wondered where I had heard it before. I found the clue in the caption to a badly reproduced portrait of Mendoza in a little box at the foot of the page; he was a distinguished local novelist whose work had been published in translation in the States. I'd seen his books but never read any. According to the reviews I'd read, he seemed to be a sort of Latin American William Faulkner, with a dash of Erskine Caldwell.

According to his view of the matter, I was a hireling brought in by the despots of the government to take away the people's homes—but this was comparatively mild. He reserved his real scorn for Seixas and the other treasury department officials. Seixas, he alleged, had persuaded the president to choose this way of tackling the shantytown problem, instead of rehousing the squatters, because he held shares in a highway construction company which was likely to benefit.

I wondered what the laws of libel were like in Aguazul. Fairly elastic, to judge from this.

As I'd promised, when I was through with breakfast, I went down to the traffic department to look in on Angers and see if there was any news. I found him talking to a pale, fair-haired young man with a slight speech impediment and horn-rimmed glasses.

Angers, serious-faced, interrupted the conversation to introduce his companion as Mr. Caldwell of the city health department, and waved me to a chair.

"I've just been hearing some rather interesting news, Hakluyt," he said. "Caldwell, maybe you'd tell Hakluyt what you just told me. I think he ought to hear it right away."

I sat down and looked attentive. Caldwell cleared his throat nervously and gave me one quick glance before settling his eyes on the wall behind me and speaking in a low, monotonous voice.

"It was yesterday afternoon," he said. "I was making my regular visit to S-s-sigueiras's—his s-slum. We've been trying literally for years to get him to improve the c-conditions down there. I th-think I must have been there about the s-same time you were.

"Because when he came back he was s-saying he was going to file s-suit against Mr. Angers for this attempt to get rid of his s-slum."

"Citizens' rights again, I suppose?" interjected Angers, and Caldwell nodded, swallowing. His Adam's apple bobbed.

Angers turned to me. "Of course, immediately I heard this, Hakluyt," he said, "I felt I must ask you to concentrate on this aspect of the problem first, if you can. We don't want to exert pressure on you in any way—after all, you're the expert—but you do see what we're up against, don't you?"

"I hope you see what I'm up against, too," I answered dryly. "You asked me to keep personal considerations out of this, and I think that had better go on applying. You've given me a budget and a problem to solve; suppose you let me be the judge of the best way to tackle it, and you'll get the best results. Besides—damn it, if the legal mills grind as slowly here as they do most other places, it'll take months for Sigueiras to show results in his suit."

Angers looked unhappy. "Well, that's the unfortunate part of it," he said. "The legal mills, as you put it, in Vados grind pretty quickly. It's a different matter anywhere else in the country, but one of the things that Diaz has always insisted on ever since the city was built was quick handling of law cases—both civil and criminal. He was suspicious of us foreign-born citizens, you see, and he seems to have been afraid that we'd litigate the simple-minded native-born citizens out of their rights. Well, that's beside the point—in the abstract, it's a damned good thing that cases don't hang around for months on end, of course, but Diaz has his own man in as Secretary of Justice—fellow called Gonzales—and he sees to it that if there's a dispute involving a foreign-born citizen and a native-born citizen, it moves like lightning."

He looked down at the top of his desk; he had picked up a paper clip and was nervously toying with it.

"I've got a nasty feeling that I haven't been told the whole truth about this problem I've been asked to solve," I said. "What is this legal question involving Sigueiras, anyway?"

"Well, it's damnably complicated, actually. But I'll try to boil it down for you." Angers sat back, avoiding my eyes as Caldwell had done, but for a different reason. "When the city was incorporated, all of us foreign-born citizens, and those native-born citizens who'd qualified in particular ways by contributing to the creation of the city, were given what we call a citizens' rights endowment. That's to say, guarantees of options on particular official positions, at fixed levels of salary, or leases on undeveloped land, or something of the kind, and their duration was to be fifty years or the lifetime of the recipient, whichever was shorter. They can't be inherited, you see—although citizenship as such descends to the progeny and all that.

"The problem with Sigueiras, of course, is that he managed to fiddle the undisputed use of that land under the monorail central as part of his citizens' rights endowment, and it's legally unassailable. The only loophole lies in the proviso that the city council retains powers of development, and it can dispossess any leaseholder on payment of compensation. Well, what we've got to try to do is dispossess Sigueiras—using this city development clause."

Caldwell had been listening in mounting excitement to Angers; now he burst out as though unable to control himself any longer.

"We've *got* to get him out. Everybody s-says we must! The health problems are gh-ghastly; the education department is t-terribly worried; it's affecting the tourists—it's sh-shocking, Mr. Hakluyt!"

I got up. "Look," I said, "for the last time. You hired me to do a job, and I'm going to do it if it can be done. I don't have to be *told* that this slum development is a blot on the face of Ciudad de Vados—I can *see*. Suppose you try to be patient—and better still, let me get on with the work."

I was leaving the traffic department building when I had my first sight of *el Presidente* in person—from a distance, but unmistakable. Well, how could one mistake him when he drove down the street and into the Plaza del Norte behind a flying wedge of black-uniformed motorcyclists with police sirens howling?

He sat in the back of an open convertible, one arm resting along the side. Next to him was a dark and very beautiful girl—his second wife, presumably. His first, so I had vaguely heard, was a girl he had married in his twenties and who had died soon after the foundation of Ciudad de Vados. He looked older than he had in the photograph at the airport, even behind the dark glasses that hid his eyes.

There was no doubt that he was still popular. People on the sidewalks and in the middle of the square stopped talking to turn and wave at the passing cavalcade, and a bunch of children ran yelling behind his car. *El Presidente* acknowledged the acclaim with no more than a languid lift of his hand, but his wife smiled and blew kisses at the children.

The car pulled up outside the City Hall, and Vados went inside—to attend to his mayoral duties, presumably. As soon as he had disappeared from sight, his wife leaned forward and said something to the driver; still attended by the motorcycles, the car purred off in the direction of the main shopping streets.

I strolled away, deep in thought, when the interruption was over. Angers, plainly, hadn't much liked my parting remarks; it was certain that if he got to hear about my actions for the next few days, he wasn't going to approve of that, either. I intended to spend the immediate future on foot, looking at the places I was supposed to clear up, with a camera slung around my neck, a white Panama hat on my head, and the biggest dark glasses I could find on my nose.

And, in direct contradiction to Angers' request, I proposed to concentrate first on what I considered the major problem: the street market and the attendant slum area. Sigueiras's set of pigsties were not in fact essentially a traffic problem; if there were as many people who wanted to get rid of them as Caldwell had claimed, they could be cleared away on the basis of something little stronger than a pretext. But to get rid of the market was going to call for some rather subtle and organic planning.

I'd arrived on Tuesday; today was Friday. The market area deserved at least three days' close study, and the fact that I would have the end and beginning of the working week in the period meant that I would see it in both its busiest and slackest moments, which was ideal.

The slackest period of all, of course, was Sunday—there was no market at all, and I concentrated on the outward and return flow of cars bearing people out of town for the day.

But with that interruption, I stayed in and around the market area until Monday evening; three or four times a day I worked my way through the market and its surrounding streets, noting the volume of traffic on foot and on wheels at different times of day, estimating how many people had to pass this way, anyway, how many came here only because the market was here, and how many might come this way if it weren't for the market and the resulting low character of the neighborhood.

There were valuable pointers to public opinion, too, to be followed up—sources of irritation and resentment against the market that could be gently magnified until it became possible to decree it out of existence without opposition.

It was fascinating. But then I'm one of those lucky people to whom it is given to enjoy his regular job. There are so many aspects of human existence reflected in the way people move through their streets. I'd had to allow for the snarls in traffic flow caused by the muezzins in Moslem cities calling the devout to prayer, and the consequent five-times-daily interruption of everything, much to the annoyance of the nonreligious citizens. I'd had to work out a design for an embankment along the Ganges where it was certain that at least a million people would suddenly turn up once a year, but which had to cope with them and with its ordinary traffic without wasting unduly much space on the million-strong crowd which would remain idle the rest of the year. I'd helped develop the signal system in Galveston, Texas, designed to get every fire appliance within twenty miles nonstop to any outbreak without interfering with traffic on any route not used by the engines. Those were large-scale tasks, and they had their own interest. But this—by comparison—half-pint puzzle was equally intriguing.

By Monday afternoon I was coming to a tentative conclusion.

I was wandering along the sidewalk, pausing to turn over things displayed for sale and rechecking my guess about how many people came this way just to do their shopping when the offices and businesses nearby closed for the night, when a hoarse voice called out to me.

"Ay, señor!"

I glanced around. The only people in the direction from which the yell had come were two shabby old men deep in thought over a chessboard resting on an empty packing case—I saw that the white king was lost or broken and had been replaced by the neck of a bottle, broken off short and stood on its jagged end—and a fat man in a white suit that was soaked with sweat under the arms. He sat on a rickety chair tilted back against the wall. A hat shaded his plump face; one pudgy hand clutched a bottle of some sickly-colored soft drink with a straw in it; the other held a ropy cigar.

I looked inquiring; he beckoned; I went over to him. As I came up, he said something in rapid Spanish, and I had to ask for a repeat.

"Ah, that's all right," he said with a sudden surprising switch into strong New York. "Figured you weren't one of these stuck-up spicks. Tourist?"

I nodded; that was my role at the moment.

"Drink?" he suggested, and before I could accept or refuse, he had thrown back his head and yelled, "Pepe!"

I looked at the nearest doorway and found that I was in fact standing outside a shabby bar, converted in makeshift fashion from the entrance hall of a house. A misspelled name scrawled on the wall in black paint announced the fact.

"What'll it be?" said the fat man.

"Something long and cool," I said in my best tourist manner, wiping my face.

The fat man snorted. "In a hole like this? Pal, if they had a frigidaire here, they'd have to use it for cooking tamales. The power company cut the supply a month ago. Makes it a choice between beer and this muck I'm drinking. Better have beer—at least it doesn't get dirty inside the cans. *Cerveza!*" he added sharply as a worried little man appeared in the doorway, wiping his hands on an apron or maybe the flapping tail of his shirt.

"Siddown," he went on, indicating a folding chair propped against the wall near him. "Reason I called you over was 'cause I figure I've seen you around here a few times before. Didn't I?"

"You might have," I acknowledged, finding that the chair, seemingly on the point of collapse, was still strong enough to take my weight. I hadn't seen him; that I was sure of. But I didn't comment on the fact.

"You seem to be spending a hell of a lot of time down here." His eyes fixed on me. "Mind my askin' why? Sort of—uh—unusual for a tourist."

"A girl I know back home told me to get her one of those fancy Indian shawls—*rebozos*," I answered, thinking in high gear. "You know how it is," I added, trying to make the words imply I thought he was irresistible to every girl for miles. "I wanted to make it something—something classy, if you get me. Can't find anything I like."

The fat man spat with great deliberation into the gutter, three inches from the bare feet of a woman carrying a basket of clay pots. "Should think not. Stuff you get here's not worth a damn. You'd do better to stop off for a couple hours in Mexico City on your way home an' spend a few bucks in a big store there. These people can't afford to spin their own thread any more, y'see. Have to make do with lousy commercial stuff—won't dye properly, won't weave the same way. No good."

"Looks like I've been wasting my time, then," I said. Beer arrived, brought by the worried man; I took it as it was—in the can—and sipped it.

"Maybe not altogether. Get better stuff here than anywhere else in Vados, that's for sure. And cheaper. Trying to clear this market away—hear about that?"

"No!" I said, feigning astonishment. "Why? Don't people like having a genuine Indian-style village market right in the heart of Vados? I'd have thought tourists would go for it in a big way."

"Nuts. Vados is '*the*—most—modern—city—inaworld.'" He managed to make the slogan sound faintly obscene. "That's what tourists come looking for. Old-world crap they can find back in New Mexico or somewhere. What they want here is the day afer tomorrow, not the day before yesterday. 'Sides, the place stinks. Don't it?"

The smell was pretty thick, and likewise indescribable. Cooking oil and frijoles and rotting fruit and human bodies all had a place in it. So did sun on dust, which smells like nothing else in the world.

"What are these poor bastards gonna do for a living when they clear this market up? Hafta live in that dump of Sigueiras's—they don't show *that* to tourists. Heard about it?"

"Under the main monorail station?"

"Tha's right." He looked at me with a speculative expression. "For a tourist, you got eyes, pal—say that for you. Guess you didn't go down inside, though." I shook my head. "Guessed right. There's a guy called Angers in a city traffic department been shooting off his mouth about cleaning out market, shacks, whole damn lot. Him an' that money-grabbing bum Seixas."

He gestured with his now empty bottle; he had been sucking enormous gulps between sentences. The movement took in the big-eyed children and the back-bowed women and the shabby men playing chess, the barrows and the baskets and the fruit and corn and clay pots and trinkets. "Riles me! I'm a citizen, same as Angers. I got my stake here, same as him. But it's these poor bastards' own damn country, and they don't get much of a share."

On the last word he hurled the empty bottle at a rotten melon lying in the gutter; it sank in without breaking and stuck up at an angle, the straw still in the neck. "Have another on me?" I suggested.

"Next time you're by," he said, and hauled himself ponderously to his feet. "Got to go make room for it before I have another. Think about Angers while I'm doing it. Maybe we'll fix him one of these days. Still a law in this country—of sorts. Wouldn't think I was a lawyer, would you?"

"No," I said, genuinely astonished.

"Pretty good one, too. Not the sort that gets the classy clients, like that bastard Andres Lucas, but I am a lawyer, and I'm out here drinking in the atmosphere so I can plead a case good tomorrow. Sigueiras filed suit on the traffic people—

Angers' lot—an' I'm handling it. Name's Brown. Everyone calls me Fats, even the spicks. Don't give a damn—I *am* fat."

He glared at me as though challenging me to deny it.

"Well, thanks for the beer," I said, getting up and wondering whether I could safely admit that I *was* going to be by here again.

"Oh, hell, that's okay, Hakluyt. Nothin' against you. Mucky stinkin' business, but not your fault. Wouldn't buy Angers a beer, so help me. But don't blame me if you're out of a job before you're started."

For a moment I was completely stunned. "How did you know who I was?" I asked at length.

"One of Sigueiras's boys saw you around here Friday and Saturday. I didn't. Wasn't here. Won't be tomorrow. If you want to buy me that drink, you'll have to come to the courts. So long."

He disappeared into the dark entry of the bar; he must have turned back immediately, because I hadn't taken more than one step away before he was calling me back.

"Oughta warn you," he said. "These lousy double-crossing sonsabitches at the top won't pay a cent 'less your plan is just what they wanted anyway. Watch yourself."

He vanished again—so quickly this time that I suspected his succession of soft drinks must finally have made the matter urgent—and left me to walk very thoughtfully off down the street.

VI

I had been up late the three previous nights, watching the weekend flow of late-night traffic in the main traffic nexus. It appeared that at no time was it dense enough for me to worry about; it consisted mainly of heavy trucks on through journeys and a few cruising taxis. Except for a comparatively small area on the far side of the Plaza del Oeste where nightclubs were concentrated, Vados seemed to close down fairly completely by about one in the morning. There were, of course, parties and theaters and movies and so on which contributed irregular bulges in the flow, but nothing very significant, even on a weekend, on the generous scale of the streets here.

That, combined with the shock Fats Brown had given me, decided me in favor of knocking off work early.

It was about half past six when I got back to the hotel. The evening was warm, and the glass panels separating the loggia bar that ran along most of the ground-floor frontage from the sidewalk had been slid back. Several tables had been set outside under a wide green awning. Inside, the bar was crowded with men and women in evening clothes: the women's jewels glittered brilliantly. I realized that since the opera house was only two blocks south, the Hotel del Principe was conveniently situated for a drink before the show, and there must be some kind of gala performance tonight.

Few people were sitting outside, except for a small group at the far end table; a bored, dark-haired, dark-complexioned girl with a guitar was idly plucking chords on a seat just outside the loggia, stopping every few moments to pick up a cigarette. I was intending to go inside, into the lounge, but a quiet voice called to me.

"Señor Hakluyt!"

I glanced around. Maria Posador was looking at me over her shoulder; she was sitting in one of the chairs at the far end of the awning, with her back to me. I had not noticed her as I came up. Beside her was a dark, scowling man whom I thought I ought to recognize but could not identify.

I walked over and said hello, and she signaled a waiter. "You will drink with us?" she suggested, eyes twinkling. "You have had a thirsty day, no doubt. Please be seated."

I couldn't think of a reason for objecting, except for Angers' ill-phrased advice to stay clear of this woman, and I had reacted against that. I took the place next to the dark man, who continued to scowl. He looked extraordinarily out of place next to Señora Posador's elegance, for his hands were like a workman's, blunt-fingered and with broken nails, and he wore a floral shirt and grimy off-white trousers. His feet were thrust without socks into rope-soled espadrilles.

"Señor Hakluyt, I should like you to meet Sam Francis," said Señora Posador equably, but with a hint of mischief in her tone. "You remember you were listening to him speak in the Plaza del Sur last week. Sam, this is our visiting traffic expert."

The swarthy man's scowl didn't lighten. I managed to smile, though his brooding presence made me uneasy. I wondered what Juan Tezol's right-hand man was doing here, among the kind of people he seemed to have made his deadly opponents.

The waiter took my order and was back almost immediately. I raised the cool glass to my companions, and was taking the first sip when Francis stubbed out the cigarette he had been smoking and spoke angrily to Señora Posador.

"Maria, what the hell you do around here, anyway? Ain't things bad enough without you waste time 'mong these sonsabitches?" He jerked a large thumb at my glass. "Why not you put that cash to help Juan pay his fine, hey? What's the reason?"

He had a sweet, thick Caribbean accent that was hard for me to follow at once; Señora Posador was used to it. "The idea is that Señor Hakluyt had a thirst," she answered. "Didn't you?" she added, glancing at me.

I realized I'd come in halfway through an argument. "I— was thirsty," I agreed. "And this was very welcome."

Señora Posador half-smiled. She took from her handbag a thin gold case containing half a dozen of her black Russian cigarettes, offered me one, which I took, offered another to Francis, which was refused with a gesture of disgust, and took one herself.

"I should explain to you," she said urbanely. "Sam and I have had a difference of opinion regarding yourself. I've been maintaining that as an independent expert called in to solve a problem here in Vados you can be relied on to give a satisfactory answer to it, regardless of personal interests. I remember you saying to me in so many words that you had no interest in affairs here. Whereas Sam—"

Sam Francis made his opinion plain enough without uttering a word.

"So you see it was very gratifying that you arrived when

you did," Señora Posador finished with gravity. "We now have a chance to decide our argument."

Then they both looked at me, very hard and very closely, in a way that made me feel like a specimen under a microscope.

"I have to admit," I said slowly, "that when I took the job I didn't realize there was so much local feeling involved. I was told I just had to straighten out some kinks in a traffic pattern. That's my job; that's what I came here to do. If I find myself instructed to solve a social problem, and it's been made pretty clear to me that's what I'm really supposed to do, then I tell them: any halfway proposition designed to fit what they want and not what's really needed will land them in a whole mess more of trouble."

Francis turned to me, laying one enormous fist on the table before him. "You better mean that, man," he rumbled. " 'Cause trouble is something we got too much of right now."

He sat back glowering; Señora Posador put a calming hand on his arm. "That seems a fair answer to me, Sam," she said. "Have another drink, Señor Hakluyt—we'll toast a solution satisfactory to all parties."

I was about to insist on buying this one when a big car halted at the curb and a man and a woman got out. The woman was plumply attractive, wearing an evening gown and a diamond tiara, with a stole around her bare shoulders; the man was thin and good-looking, and I recognized him at once. It was Mario Guerrero, chairman of the Citizens of Vados.

Sam's eyes followed them closely as they crossed the sidewalk toward the bar. Guerrero, looking around rather languidly, caught sight of him and halted in his tracks. When he spoke, he did so, of course, in Spanish, but my ear had been improving rapidly over the weekend, and I followed the gist of what was said.

"Well, good evening, Señor Francis!" Guerrero exclaimed. "Who would have thought to see you here? Surely it's not good for your relations with your peasant supporters to be seen indulging your taste for gracious living like this!"

Sam snapped back his answer crisply. "Possibly they will

think I deserve it more than you, for I spend my time working on their behalf, and you—you work only for yourself." His Spanish was better than his English and had as polished a ring to it as Guerrero's own.

As though by magic, a small group had gathered around us; they included a man with a news camera and flashgun. Guerrero's eye fell on this man, and he smiled to himself. The woman he was with plucked at his sleeve; he ignored her and continued: "Is there perhaps a photographer here from that rag of your party's—*Tiempo?*"

"Of course not! *Tiempo* has better things to fill its pages than pictures of a bunch of idlers."

"Really?" said Guerrero smoothly. "Yet I seem to remember seeing pictures of you in it almost every time I ever glanced at it."

I noticed that the man with the news camera was grinning, and realized suddenly what was being worked out.

"Well, I don't doubt that those of your supporters who are literate enough to read *Liberdad* occasionally will be very interested to see a picture of you lounging here," Guerrero said, and as the photographer whipped his camera into position adopted a friendly smile.

A picture of that could have been a very damaging weapon indeed, obviously. For the followers of the National Party to see their leader's right-hand man apparently chatting in a friendly way with the head of their opponents—and in such surroundings—might be damaging to Sam's prestige. Guerrero was plainly a very clever man.

But, for this moment, Maria Posador was cleverer. She had obviously reached the same conclusion that I had; she had decided what to do about it. She stood up. That was all. But the glare of the flashbulb shone on her back, and I saw that her shadow would have masked Sam Francis completely. Guerrero's hastily adopted smile vanished like frost in sunlight.

"I think perhaps we should not keep Señor Guerrero any longer, Sam," she said quietly, but loudly enough for it to be emphatic. "He doubtless has—pressing business."

Her eyes brushed over Guerrero's companion just long enough for her meaning to be unmistakable, and then the two of them pushed away through the bystanders. Guerrero watched them go, eyes narrowed; then he gave me a long, hard stare and finally yielded to the insistence of his companion and entered the bar.

The girl with the guitar shook back her hair and began to sing an old lullaby, very softly; I finished my drink and went into the hotel.

Who the hell was this Posador woman, anyway?

I bypassed the crowded bar, which was slowly beginning to lose its customers as curtaintime at the opera house drew near, and was going through the foyer to collect my key at the registration desk when one of the bellhops trotted toward me.

"Señor Hakluyt!" he said. *"Una señora preguntó por Vd."*

I reflected that I seemed to be pretty much in demand. *"Donde está?"* I inquired, hoping to hear she had gone home.

She hadn't; she was waiting for me in the lounge—a slim middle-aged woman with iron-gray hair and green-framed spectacles, idly stirring a long, cool-looking drink with a gold pencil. A young man with a shaven head and a broken nose lounged in the chair next to her, drawing shapeless patterns on a notepad.

"Señor Hakluyt," the bellhop told the woman, and left me to it.

She hastily took the pencil out of her glass and gave me a beaming smile, extending her hand. "Señor Hakluyt!" she purred. "I'm so glad we caught you. Do sit down. This is my assistant, Señor Rioco. My name is Isabela Cortés, and I'm from the state broadcasting commission."

I sat down; Rioco shut his notebook with a snap and put away his pencil. "I hope you haven't been waiting too long for me," I said.

She waved a carefully manicured hand on which an emerald ring glistened gigantically. "We have been here no more than ten minutes, truly," she declared. "In any case, that is of no importance whatever, since we have found you. It is a special request we have to make of you."

I looked expectant and cooperative.

"I am the director of—of what you might in English call current affairs broadcasts on both our radio and television

networks," Señora Cortés expounded. "Each day on the television we produce a program about life in Vados and the
interesting people who come here, and we have also the news,
of course. Señor Rioco has been preparing for tonight a program about the new developments that are planned for the
city. We are desolated that we approach you on such short
notice, but—"

She glanced expectantly at her companion, who jerked his
jacket higher up around his body and leaned forward. When
he spoke, he sounded as though he'd learned his English
somewhere around Louisiana and then crossed it with Hollywood.

"Ought to have thought of it earlier," he said in this half-
lazy, half-tough accent. "It was Angers in the traffic department who put us on to you—we canned an interview with
him this morning, and he said you were the only guy who
knew what was in your mind, so we been trying to track you
down. We reckoned we'd best try to catch you when you got
in here an' run you straight out to the studio." He checked his
watch. "Program goes out in—uh—hour an' a quarter, at
twenty-oh-five. Mind comin' along to say a few words?"

"We do hope you'll agree," said Señora Cortés sweetly.

"I don't see why not," I said. "Just give me time to clean
up and change clothes, and I'll be right with you."

"That's great!" said Rioco, and sat back in his chair,
composing himself visibly for the short wait.

As I ran my razor over my chin in the hotel bedroom, I
reflected there were certain other things I didn't see, as well
as why not. Such as why I was considered important enough
for the director of current affairs broadcasting and the producer of the program both to come calling; why, if Angers
had suggested enlisting my cooperation for the program, he'd
left it as late as today to bring the matter up—presumably it
hadn't just been sprung on him this morning without notice.

And more important than either of these: how Señora
Cortés had known I was going to be here, now, when the
previous evenings I'd stayed out till the small hours.

Was it a lucky guess? Or information received?

If it hadn't been for the few minutes' conversation I'd had with Señora Posador and Sam Francis before coming into the hotel, I'd have arrived coincidentally at almost the same moment as Señora Cortés and this shaven-headed assistant of hers. It looked altogether too much as though someone had worked out my estimated time of arrival; logically, this implied that someone was keeping an eye on me, probably had been since I started work—and further implied that someone didn't trust me.

Or—another alternative occurred to me as I was going down to the lounge again—or else someone was protecting me. The idea stopped me in my tracks, and a cold shiver threaded beneath my jacket. With the high-running feeling against the project I was supposed to be undertaking, it struck me now for the first time that I *could* become a target.

VII

The slab-sided bulk of the television and radio center was set high up on the hillside across the city from the airport, so as to keep the towering antennae well clear of incoming planes. We whirled up toward it in a luxuriously comfortable car driven by a girl in a dark green uniform.

The evening lights of Ciudad de Vados spread out below us like a carpet of jewels. It was the finest view I had yet had of the city; I said so to Señora Cortés.

"Yes, we have a beautiful city," she answered, smiling faintly. "It is good to know that you, señor, will help us to keep it so."

Rioco, sitting in the front beside the driver, gave a short laugh, perhaps not at Señora Cortés's remark.

Like everything else in Vados, the studio building was spacious and impressive. We pulled up in front of the brilliantly lit main foyer whose high glass doors stood open to the warm night. An attendant—a man, but uniformed in the same shade of green as the girl driving our car—whisked the door open for us to get out.

In the foyer people were coming and going with an air of quiet busyness; several of them greeted Señora Cortés as we entered. There were bored-looking actors, actresses, and commentators whose makeup gave them a slightly inhuman appearance; executives and technicians dashing from office to office; a man leading a trio of carefully clipped French poodles by blue ribbons around their necks; an unshaven man with narrow eyes, carrying a trumpet without a case, who looked lost; several tall, slim girls who from their movements could only be precision dancers—it was the sort of mixture one might see anywhere in the vicinity of a TV studio.

Altogether unexpected, though, was what happened when our elevator arrived.

We crossed the floor of the foyer directly to the elevator doors; Señora Cortés pressed the button and stood tapping her foot impatiently while the signal light over the door moved from 3 to 2 to 1. The moment the door started to slide open, she moved forward, only to fall back in astonishment and confusion.

There was a bishop in the car, in full episcopal regalia.

He nodded to us, eyes twinkling, and moved forward with the stateliness of a one-man procession, surrounded by lesser clerics, and a hush fell on the foyer as he approached the exit. I glanced back as we got into the elevator, and saw one of the dancers stop him and drop on one knee to kiss his ring.

Noting my amazement, Rioco chuckled. "That is our good Bishop Cruz," he said. "He comes each week to record a— a—how do you say it? A lecture?"

"A sermon," I said, and he nodded.

"A sermon, that would be it. But that's the first time I ever saw him go out in all his fine clothes like that." He chuckled again. "Me, I thought for a moment it was someone dressed up for a show!"

The elevator disgorged us on the top floor, and as we emerged into the corridor, a stout man going thin on top caught sight of my companions and addressed them sternly in Spanish.

"Where in the name of the good God have you been, Isabela? You know this evening's program has to be good!

What was the reason for running off *and* taking Enrique with you?" He flung out an arm in a grandiose gesture. "The chaos in the place is beyond conceiving!"

Señora Cortés blanched slightly, but replied peaceably, explaining who I was and where she had been. "Go into the studio, Enrique," she added to Rioco. "Things can't be in too bad a muddle, but something probably needs setting right."

Rioco nodded and disappeared through the nearest door. The balding man seemed to have been pacified by what Señora Cortés had to say and shook my hand absentmindedly. "I'm beginning to think I should have handled the details of this program myself," he said in a depressed voice, not paying me any more attention. "Please make sure it is good, won't you, Isabela?"

He turned away and strode down the corridor. Showing signs of relief at his departure, Señora Cortés turned to me again.

"Please come with me," she said. "I will show you the studio from which we make this broadcast. Much of it is on tape already, of course, but the interview with you and some other parts will transmit live. This way."

We went through the same door as that which Rioco had taken, picked our way through a tangle of cables snaking across the floor, dodged technicians and avoided cameramen lining up angles. Finally we took refuge in an alcove next to the director's goldfish bowl.

Rioco had changed his personality as soon as he entered the studio, obviously. Now, standing between a girl in glasses who held a pile of duplicated scripts and a man with cigarette-yellowed fingers who seemed to be the lighting technician, he was crackling out authoritative directions to his staff.

"Francisco!" called Señora Cortés to a pleasant-faced young man crossing the floor. He turned and came up to us, and she introduced him as Francisco Córdoban. "Our regular interviewer on this program," she explained.

"Glad to meet you, Mr. Hakluyt," said Córdoban, gripping my hand squarely. "Bit short notice, I'm afraid, asking you to appear for us, but it's extremely good of you to come. The interview won't run too long, I'm afraid—I'm figuring on between seven and nine minutes near the end of the program. How's your Spanish? I can run it in either English or Spanish, but we lose a lot of time if I have to interpret, of course."

I shrugged. "Well, my Spanish is pretty poor, but I'm willing to try it if you like."

"Excellent. Look, let's step into the control room for a few minutes—Enrique won't be ready to come in for a while, I imagine. I can give you an idea of the questions I want to ask and find out if answering them in Spanish gives you any trouble."

He pushed open the door and stood aside to let me pass. The goldfish bowl was fairly cramped, but of course as soon as the door was closed again it was dead silent. None of the monitor screens was working yet, and only a whisper indicating that current was flowing came from the speakers.

Córdoban gave me a chair and himself leaned back against a panel of lights. "Well, I'll start off with a bit about your background and the kind of work you do—you're a traffic analyst, isn't that correct? And you've worked almost all over the world. Anywhere in particular you'd like me to mention?"

"Oh—India, the UAR, the States. And my native Australia, of course."

"Ah-hah. Good. Well, that bit doesn't involve you; I'll just do the spiel with you out of shot. Then I'll start putting questions to you directly. The first ones will be quite simple, about what you think of Vados. Let's try it through. *Ha estado Vd. otra vez en Ciudad de Vados?*"

"*Nunca,*" I answered.

"*Le gusta a Vd. nuestra ciudad?*"

And so it went smoothly enough: it was much as I had expected—mostly platitudes about how impressive Vados was. The nearest Córdoban came to treading on the edge of the controversy regarding the proposed redesigning was to ask me if I had yet made up my mind about what I would recommend.

I told him that I had been here only a few days and it was too early to say.

"*Bueno!*" he exclaimed, pushing himself away from the

panel where he had been leaning. "That'll do nicely, Mr. Hakluyt. Well, we still have twenty minutes before we go on the air—we could step around to the bar for a drink if you like—"

He looked out onto the floor of the studio and corrected himself. "Sorry—Enrique's doing a run-through, so we'll have to stick around a moment. Cigarette?"

I accepted the offer.

"Have you been on television before?" Córdoban inquired. "I didn't think to ask. Maybe you'd be more interested to stay here and watch what's happening."

"I get put on TV quite often," I said. "I've been in charge of two or three quite big projects in the States, and reporters sometimes come swarming around when work's in progress."

"Ah-hah," Córdoban nodded. "I can well understand that. We'll be making a very big feature of the reconstruction when it starts, I imagine."

"No matter what form it takes?" I couldn't resist the jab; it missed, and he gave me a puzzled look.

"Does it matter what the details are? It's news, anyway."

I passed it off as inconsequential. "Tell me," I said. "You have quite a setup here—far bigger than I'd expected. Is your broadcasting very extensive?"

"It's the highest coverage in Latin America, as a matter of fact," he said with a hint of pride. "We've used television a lot over the past twenty-odd years. I'm not sure what the current percentage is, but according to the last survey a year ago, we were getting to two-thirds of the total population, except, of course, at the big festivals like Easter. Even then there's television playing in bars and places, of course, and the smallest villages have at least one set apiece now. Then we go over the border to some extent, of course, but the number of sets there is so much smaller it's negligible."

I was impressed. "How about radio?" I said. "I suppose you don't pay that much attention if your TV audience is so large."

"Oh, on the contrary! Except for the hour-a-day educational programs, we only telecast from six in the evening, you know. There isn't much of an audience during the day, except on Sunday afternoons when we come on at two. But we do radio programs from six in the morning until midnight. Workers in factories listen, peasants take portable radios into the fields with them, drivers on the road and housewives at home listen in—why should we waste a potential audience like that?"

The way he put it puzzled me slightly; I didn't press the matter, though, and simply nodded. He looked past me through the glass wall. "Enrique's still having trouble" he noted. "I don't think we'd better disturb him for another few moments."

I glanced around the room; as he spoke, my eye fell on a small row of books alongside the control panel, and I thought there was something familiar about the nearest of them. They were mainly cheap novels, presumably what the technicians or producer read during lulls or transmission of intercut tape. The one that caught my eye, however, was obviously out of place; it was stout and well-thumbed, and its red binding bore several cigarette burns. It looked like a textbook; I presumed it was a manual of television engineering, but— perhaps the author's name rang a bell with me—I picked it up.

A book whose title, even in Spanish, meant something to me because the name of the author was very well-known to me indeed: Alejandro Mayor.

Several years rolled back in my mind; I was back at the university, arguing heatedly over the most controversial of many controversial books in our social science curriculum. In its English edition the book was called *The Administration of the Twentieth-Century State,* and the author was this same Alejandro Mayor.

I opened the book with interest; its title was *El Hombre de la Ciudad de Hoy—The Modern City Man.* I wondered if it was as pungent and original as the earlier work, for I saw it had only been published a matter of five years ago. Probably not, I decided with regret; in those days Mayor had been a firebrand type of youthful iconoclast causing a scandal in academic circles with every lecture course he gave at the Mexico City School of Social Science. Now he was probably a

sedate conformist. That fate usually overtakes innovators—
their ideas cease to be revolutionary.

Córdoban had been grinning at the inaudible difficulties
Rioco was having with his run-through. Now he turned back
and saw what I was doing.

"You've read that, perhaps?" he suggested.

I shook my head. "Not this one. But I read his first book
in college. It's rather an odd sort of book to find in a TV
studio, isn't it?" I stuck it back in the rack. "I wonder what
became of that man—I don't seem to have heard of him for
years."

Córdoban regarded me with mild astonishment. "No?" he
said quizzically. "Why—"

He glanced around through the glass wall and stiffened as
the door of the studio swung open. "Why, there he is now."

I followed his gaze and saw the balding, stout man whom I
had met with Señora Cortés on my arrival.

"Him?" I said blankly.

"But of course. Dr. Mayor has been Minister of Information and Communications in Aguazul for nearly eighteen
years."

"Why—that's from long before the founding of Ciudad de
Vados."

Córdoban nodded. "That's right. I'm surprised, though, at
your saying his books were strange things to find in a television studio. Why, we regard them as indispensable hand-
books."

I frowned my way back into my memory. "I'm beginning
to remember more clearly," I said. "Didn't he maintain from
the start that communications were the essential tool of modern government? Yes, of course he did." A further thought
struck me. "Eighteen years, did you say? I was still in college
then. But I thought Mayor had a chair of social science in
Mexico City at that time."

"I believe he did," said Córdoban indifferently. "He lectures
at the university here, too, of course."

Out on the studio floor Enrique Rioco had finished his
run-through; he seemed satisfied and had gone to have a
word with Mayor.

"We just have time for that drink," Córdoban said. "If you'd like one."

I nodded, and we hurried out of the studio to a small but comfortable bar at the far end of the corridor. Over our drinks I came back to the previous subject.

"Does Dr. Mayor speak English?" I asked.

"I think so—I don't know how well. Why? Do you want to meet him?"

"I'd be very interested," I confirmed. "Maybe he'd be interested, too—he was a great influence on me when I was developing my own style."

"Traffic analysts have styles?" Córdoban inquired sardonically. "How?"

"Why not? Architects have; they develop designs for living or designs for working; we develop designs for moving. There are half a dozen traffic analysts today with individual styles."

Córdoban looked down at his glass. "I'm not quite sure I see how that's possible," he said. "But it's interesting to know. Are you one of the half-dozen? I'm sorry—that's a stupid question. You must be, or they wouldn't have asked you to Ciudad de Vados." He laughed. "We always say it, and we always flatter ourselves by saying it—only the best for Ciudad de Vados."

He glanced at the wall clock and tossed down the rest of his drink.

"Time to get to our places," he said. "Come on."

Two minutes before the start of the program we were back in the studio. Córdoban ensconced me in a chair out of camera shot, explaining that he would signal to me to come up and take my place alongside him when he was ready to start the interview. Then he himself took a chair facing the number one camera, glanced at Rioco in the control room, and ringed his finger and thumb to signify okay. The first lines of his commentary went up on the teleprompter beside the camera. The red light came on.

The program was extremely well handled, if rather naïve. It ran for thirty-five minutes, much of it on tape, and I watched it all on a master screen set high above Rioco's head in the goldfish bowl. It started with a few shots of the planning and building of Vados, the opening ceremony with *el Presidente* himself officiating, and of traffic in the wide streets. I had little trouble following Córdoban's smooth clear-spoken commentáry, and I felt my interest more and more engaged as the program developed. This magnificent city really was, I thought, one of the greatest achievements of the twentieth century.

After opening on a grandiose note, Córdoban tinged his voice with sadness as he referred to the recent problems that had developed in and around Vados. Shots of the most squalid dwellings imaginable, of diseased children sharing huts with pigs and burros, of overcrowding and overbreeding. The contrast with the clean, attractive city itself was appalling. Apparently one of the cameramen had actually gone down into Sigueiras's slum under the monorail station; effective shots stressed the difference between the bright sunlit platforms of the station above and the dark, unsanitary warren below.

There was a brief taped interview with Caldwell, the young man from the city health department whom I had met in Angers' office, who gave some alarming figures about disease and malnutrition in the shantytowns; then another, slightly longer, with Angers, taped in his office with the wall map of Vados unrolled behind him. He deplored the existing situation in tones of grave concern, and then cheered up slightly as he explained that the enlightened president had taken steps to remedy the evils now current.

He mentioned my name, and Córdoban signaled to me. I went over to the chair alongside his and sat down just out of shot.

Cheerfully Córdoban announced to the audience that he was privileged to have the person responsible for setting things to rights in the studio this evening.

"Aquí está el señor Hakluyt—" and the camera turned on me.

After what I had seen from the taped shots, I got rather more heated in my replies to Córdoban's questions than I had in the rehearsal, but my command of Spanish held out okay, and I received nods of approval and encouragement from

Córdoban whenever he was off-camera. I really was feeling that it was a hell of a shame to mar the sleek beauty of Ciudad de Vados with these slums, and I did my best to reassure the viewers that a way would be found to cure the trouble. Then the program was suddenly over; Córdoban was getting up, smiling, to congratulate me on getting through it in Spanish; Señora Cortés came from the control room with Rioco to thank me for appearing, and as I was trying to find words to express my appreciation, the door of the studio opened and Mayor came in, beaming plumply and apologizing to Señora Cortés for doubting her ability to make a success of the program.

Gradually the turmoil subsided; some of the technicians departed for the bar, talking volubly, and others set about rearranging the cameras and lighting for another transmission later on. Córdoban gestured to me to hang on for a moment; he himself hovered at Mayor's side, and when the balding man had finished reviewing the program with Señora Cortés, caught his attention.

Sharp brown eyes, the whites a little bloodshot, skewered me as Mayor swiveled his head toward me; he listened to Córdoban intently, paused—not hesitated; there was something about his manner that suggested he never needed to hesitate over a decision—and then nodded and smiled.

His smile was quick, unforced, and unlasting: a tool, an expression that communicated a particular implication, to be ended when the significance had been put across. I went up to him with a feeling that this meeting was not quite real; for so long Alejandro Mayor's name had not been associated in my mind with a man, but with a set of precepts, and to find them embodied in an individual was disconcerting.

He shook my hand briefly. "I have heard all about you," he said in good English. "All, that is, except what I only now hear from Francisco here—that in one sense I can claim you as a pupil of mine."

He cocked his head a little to one side, as though he had thrown out a challenging statement in a debate and wanted me to worry about it. I said, "In one sense, yes, doctor. I was much influenced by your book *The Administration of the Twentieth-Century State.*"

He frowned—briefly again; it seemed that he did everything by precisely measured small doses. "Ah, that," he said distastefully. "My first book, señor—full of inaccurate theorizing and pure guesswork. I disclaim it; it was a firework, nothing better."

"How so?"

Mayor spread his hands. "Why, when I wrote it, I was innocent of experience in practical government. There were a thousand, a hundred thousand errors in points of detail, which only practical government could expose for what they were. I can excuse it on only one good ground—that it caused our president to interest himself in my work."

A technician signaled for his attention; he excused himself for a moment and listened to what the man had to say. I used the interlude to run over in my mind what I could remember of that first book which had so impressed me and which he now declared to have been full of mistakes.

A firework, he called it—well, that was accurate enough. It was a virtuoso display of paradoxes: opposing arguments brilliantly set forth so that one could hardly question the logic on either side. He presented, among other things, a picture of the free democratic state as the high point of the social evolution of man; then, with shattering precision, he proceeded to demonstrate that the free democratic state was far too unstable to endure and therefore guaranteed its citizens misery and destruction. He presented totalitarian systems as stable, enduring, reliable—and then mercilessly exposed one by one the factors which rendered their eventual downfall inevitable. By the time the reader was dizzy, Mayor was tossing out provocative suggestions for remedying these defects, and the total impression left on students like myself—who went through college faced with what seemed like equally appalling alternative futures: nuclear war or a population explosion that would pass the six billion mark by the end of the century— was that for the first time the West had produced a man capable of forging social techniques to match the situation.

For myself, convinced as I had been that the ant heap state

of People's China was the only place where adequate social techniques to cope with the population explosion were being evolved, his book had been a revelation. Even now, eighteen years after I had first read it, I could hardly imagine where lay these flaws of which Mayor had just spoken. Of course, if I were actually to reread it or read some of his newer work in which presumably these faults had been rectified, I'd see what he meant.

I watched him as he disposed crisply of the problem raised by the inquiring technician. So he had been a minister here since the time I read that first book of his. . . . The fact struck me as amazing at first—my automatic reaction was that if he had in fact been applying his theory of government and administration of the state, practically every move he made ought to have had sensation value.

Then I recalled a passage from his first book which had stuck in my mind: "People do not object to government; to be governed, whether by custom or by decree, is part of the human condition. People object to what might be called the scaffolding of government. With the spread of literacy and the drawing together by communications of our small planet, more and more individuals became aware of that scaffolding; more and more individuals oppose it because they can see it. How do we create government without scaffolding? There is a central problem for modern society."

Well, of course, if he hadn't dismissed that, too, as an error, it would explain a lot.

He was turning back toward us now—toward me in particular. "You have dined this evening, Señor Hakluyt?" he was asking.

I shook my head.

"Then please join us here. Consider it a fee for your appearance; I may say it has been most valuable to us."

I pondered the significance of that all through the meal, which we had in the bar where Córdoban had bought me a drink before the program. Señora Cortés, Rioco, and Córdoban came with us; they discussed future current affairs broadcasts in Spanish with Mayor, which rather irritated me, because I had hoped to probe further into the evolution of his theory which Mayor had hinted at. It was only toward the end of the meal that I managed to gain his undivided attention and put some of the questions that were irking me.

"Dr. Mayor," I said, "you mentioned errors in your first book. What were they? Or what were the important ones? I've been thinking back, and I can't decide."

"I underestimated progress," said Mayor shortly. "Señor Hakluyt, you are a stranger in Aguazul. You will therefore be inclined to dispute the dogmatic assertion that this is the most governed country in the world."

Again that air of throwing down a gauntlet in debate, again that cocking of the head to imply a challenge. I said, "All right—I dispute it. Demonstrate."

"The demonstration is all about you. We make it our business, first, to know what people think; we make it our business, next, to direct that thinking. We are not ashamed of that, señor, incidentally. Shall we say that—just as specific factors influence the flow of traffic, and you understand the factors and can gauge their relative importance—we now understand many of the factors that shape and direct public opinion? What is a man, considered socially? He is a complex of reactions; he takes the line of least resistance. We govern not by barring socially unhealthy paths, but by opening most wide those paths which are desirable. That is why you are here."

"Go on," I invited after a pause.

He blinked at me. "Say rather what is your view. Why is it we have adopted this round-and-round policy of inviting an expensive expert to solve our problems subtly, instead of saying, 'Do this!' and seeing it done?"

I hesitated, then counter-questioned. "Is this, then, the extension of an existing policy rather than a compromise between opposed personal interests?"

He threw up his hands. "But naturally!" he exclaimed, as though surprised to find me so obtuse. "Oh, it is ostensibly that there is conflict between one faction and another—but we *create* factions in this country! Conformism is a slow death; anarchy is a rapid one. Between the two lies a control which"—he chuckled—"like a lady's corset in an advertisement, constricts and yet bestows a sense of freedom. We govern our country with a precision that would amaze you, I believe."

His eyes shone suddenly, like a crusader's faced with the first glimpse of Jerusalem. Like the crusader, too, his fire was somewhat quenched by the fact that his imagined ideal city was far from divine in appearance. But I had no chance to press the questions further; Córdoban, who had been following our talk with an air of repressed boredom, crumbling a roll on his dessert plate, seized his opportunity to interrupt.

"Chess, doctor?" he proposed, and Mayor turned to him with a sardonic expression.

"You wish to try again, Francisco?"

He did not wait for an answer, but snapped his fingers at a passing waiter, who cleared the table and deposited a board and pieces on it. Señora Cortés and Rioco shifted their chairs and bent forward with an air of expectancy which I found it hard to emulate—though a mediocre player myself, I had never found watching chess so fascinating. Obviously, though, these two were old opponents; their first half-dozen moves chased across the board. Then Córdoban, with a smug expression, made a pawn move that departed from the established pattern, and Mayor blinked and rubbed his chin.

"You learn, Francisco—piece by piece you learn," he rumbled approvingly, and took the pawn. A series of exchanges as devastating as machine-gun fire cleared the board down to essentials, and then the pair of them settled to a long, thoughtful end game with three pawns apiece.

That part of chess had never seemed to me much more enthralling than checkers; obviously, though, Señora Cortés and Rioco did not share my opinion. They were as tense with excitement as fans at a Shield match waiting to see if the third wicket of a hat-trick would fall or not.

It fell. After fifteen or so more moves, Mayor rubbed his chin, shook his head, and indicated the square next to his opponent's king. The significance of the gesture was lost on me, but the other two watching sighed in unison and Córdoban sat back with a crestfallen expression.

"What you should have done—" said Mayor, rapidly setting an enemy pawn back one square and bringing its neighbor forward. "So!"

We all stared at the board in silence for a few moments. Then Mayor grunted and got to his feet.

"Mañana está otra día," he said comfortingly to Córdoban. "That is enough for today, I think. But there will be another time. *Hasta la vista,* Señor Hakluyt," he added, turning to me and putting out his hand. If you have time to spare before you leave Aguazul, perhaps it would interest you to pay another visit here and see how our transmitting system operates."

I shook hands. "Certainly," I said. "Thanks for the invitation."

And that was an invitation I would take up, I told myself. Moreover, from now on I was going to look out rather carefully for proof of these assertions Mayor had made—about Aguazul being the most governed country in the world. It sounded to me like wishful thinking; the system, if indeed it operated at all, could hardly be faultless, if only because it was still necessary to call out the police to break up a riot brewing in the Plaza del Sur on the day of my arrival. Possibly it was true compared with the country's neighbors or with its own past; I didn't see that this precision to which Mayor made claim was borne out in practice. Unless—and this possibility I found peculiarly disturbing—unless the government did things like turning out the police simply because the people expected it of them. In that case the underlying assumption was that, if it chose, the government could abolish the meeting in the Plaza del Sur without anyone feeling the need for them afterwards.

Could it be like that? Could it? Angers had said something about Vados's regime taking seriously the saw that a government stands or falls by its public relations. . . .

I checked myself. I was building a dizzy tower of speculation on secondhand evidence. The only solid facts I had to go on were the fact of my being here, the nature of the job I'd been given, and what I had been able to find out with my own observation. And those combined to indicate that—

Mayor's assertions to the contrary—the government of Aguazul was a reasonably beneficent authoritarian regime, competently administering a rather prosperous country without treading so hard on anyone's feet that people felt it worth the trouble of changing it. Twenty years' duration testified to the success of the formula they used—Mayor's, or whoever else's it might be.

But "the most governed country in the world"? That was to be taken with a grain of salt.

VIII

"So you starred in a television program yesterday, Señor Hakluyt," said a quiet, husky voice near me. I looked up from the paper I was reading with my breakfast coffee in the lounge of the Hotel del Principe and saw Maria Posador.

"Buenas días, señora," I said, indicating the empty chair beside me. "Yes, as a matter of fact I did. You saw the program?"

She sat down, unsmiling, not taking her eyes from my face. "No, I only heard about it," she said. "It is too dangerous to watch television in Aguazul."

"Too dangerous?"

She nodded. "You are a stranger in Vados, señor. I cannot blame you for that. But there is information I think it is my duty to give you."

I searched her exquisite face for a hint of the real meaning behind her obscure words and failed. "Go ahead," I shrugged. "I'm always willing to listen. Cigarette?"

"If you don't mind, I prefer these of my own." She slipped her gold case from her handbag; I held my lighter for her. Then she sat back in her chair and regarded me fixedly.

"You doubtless know," she began, "that our Minister of Information and Communications is one Alejandro Mayor—a man of certain notoriety."

"If being the author of a theory of government is a claim to notoriety, I suppose he qualifies," I agreed.

"No longer a theory only," corrected Señora Posador, and looked for a brief instant extremely unhappy. "A practical form."

"It always seemed to me that he had something, when I read his stuff in college."

"The señor will forgive a personal remark, but I judge that he is about in his late thirties, and his university studies would have been fifteen to twenty years ago, no? Much has changed since then. It would be best if you could read Mayor's recent books, but they are substantial and very technical, and I do not believe any have been translated into English for many years. He has been too taken up with his duties in Vados— and in any case in most countries speaking English his precepts would be without value."

"How come? It struck me that he spoke in pretty universal terms."

"Oh, to some extent one may say so. . . ." She delicately deposited ash in a tray at her side. "But—let us take this program on which you appeared yesterday. Did you find that it impressed you? Did it appeal to you, excite you?"

"I thought it was very well done and presented the facts in a balanced manner."

She studied me again with those rich violet eyes. At last she shrugged. "There are indeed things you ought to know. Do you have one hour to spare, Señor Hakluyt? Unless I have badly misjudged your good nature, it will be of great interest to you."

I couldn't see what all this was leading up to; I said so. "And," I added, "if you're going to try to persuade me that what was said on TV last night was nonsense, you're out of luck."

She gave a wan little smile that penetrated her natural sophistication and made her seem suddenly appealing in a little-girl way. "No, I assure you—that is not my aim."

Like tumblers spinning in a fruit machine, facts were clicking together in my head about this woman. But when they had meshed, they still failed to explain a lot of paradoxes: why she was a friend of Sam Francis, for example; why Angers had specifically warned me to steer clear of her.

Something that did make sense, though, was an impression that had just come to me—an impression that for reasons I could not fathom she was trying to approach me on an unemotional level, as a man would approach another man, resolutely not capitalizing on her womanly charm.

"All right," I said with sudden decision. "One hour."

Relieved, she rose and led me out of the hotel; before a huge Pegasos sedan parked at the curb, she took keys from her handbag and indicated that I should get in. I hesitated, remembering the possibility that had struck me yesterday evening—that I might be being watched, perhaps for my own protection. I was going to raise that matter with Angers when I went down to the traffic department this morning.

Noticing my hesitation, she gave a faint smile and held out her tiny gold key chain to me.

"You may drive us if you prefer," she suggested. I shook my head and got in.

The great car moved as though on rails; we hardly seemed to have left the hotel before we were on the outskirts of Vados, in what I knew to be a Class A residential district, with small but palatial houses set in great blossom-crowded gardens. We turned aside from the main road down an avenue lined with feathery-crowned palms; Señora Posador felt for a button on the dash and pressed it. There was a hum. The wrought-iron gates leading into the driveway of one of the houses ahead swung back as though by magic, and the car slid between them. She pressed the same button again; the gates closed silently.

We did not, however, go all the way along the driveway to the house. Instead, we halted before a clump of dark green bushes, into the middle of which a narrow path led.

"We have arrived," said Señora Posador with a faint smile.

Puzzled, I got out and looked about me. "This way," she called, and disappeared down the path between the bushes. I followed circumspectly and was surprised to find, completely hidden by the bushes, a small prefabricated shed. Or perhaps more a blockhouse than a shed; the walls were at least four inches thick. A TV antenna reached up from the roof, and a thick power cable was slung over the branch of a nearby tree, leading toward the house.

Señora Posador opened a padlock that held the door fast, and I followed her inside.

At first I could see almost nothing; the only light came from one small barred window. Then she turned a switch and two fluorescents came to life. I looked around the interior. There was a chair, padded, relaxing; a twenty-eight-inch television set; and, of all things, a VERA—a full-size video recorder with two-inch tape and spools a yard wide.

"Please be seated," said Señora Posador calmly. I perched on one arm of the chair and watched her as she crossed to the recorder. In a moment the spools began to hum, and the big screen lit up.

"I will show you the program in which you appeared last night," she murmured. And at the same moment Córdoban appeared on the screen, introducing the program.

I watched in puzzlement for a while, until I was satisfied that this was indeed a recording of the same program, and then looked across at Señora Posador.

"I don't quite see what you're trying to show me," I said. "I've seen all this before, in the studio."

She switched off the recorder and spun the spool back to where she had cut it in before answering. Then she spoke without looking directly at me.

"There are few places in Vados where it is safe to watch the television, señor. This is one of them. I have here a device which I think in English is called a 'blinker.' Our name for it means 'sieve.' I have just played you that recording without the blinker."

"A blinker, so far as I'm concerned," I said, "is one of those gadgets that you can set to shut off commercials. You haven't any advertising on that program."

"No?" she said, and gave her wan little smile again. "Did you ever hear of a technique called subliminal perception?"

I frowned. "Yes, of course," I said shortly.

"You accept that that was a recording of the same program as the one you appeared in last night?"

I nodded. "It certainly seemed to be the same."

"Then watch this, Señor Hakluyt. Watch carefully."

She spun the spool forward to the first of the series of shots taken in the shantytowns and let it play over, all the time keeping her finger on a small pause switch beside the playing head. "It is sometimes difficult to find what one is looking for," she murmured. "Ah! There!"

The picture on the screen was somehow familiar, yet it was not anything I could consciously remember seeing either last night or in the playback I had seen a few moments ago. It depicted the interior of a squalid hovel. The central character was a colored man stripped from the waist down. With him were a group of children, all aged about twelve. I won't take the space to describe what they were doing. I had to turn my head away after a few seconds.

"It is no good trying to ignore this, señor," said Señora Posador coolly. "Please look at it more closely."

I got off the arm of the chair and approached the screen. There was something odd about the picture, certainly. . . .

"It's not a photograph," I said suddenly. "It's a drawing."

"Or, more precisely, a painting," she agreed. "Please watch again."

The spools hummed; she kept her finger on the pause switch, and in a moment came to another shot that was hauntingly familiar like the first. This one showed a small boy, actively encouraged by his mother, defecating on a picture. About all that one could see clearly of the picture was that there was a cross in it, and toward the top of the cross was what might have been a halo.

"Are you a practicing Christian, señor?" asked Señora Posador.

I shook my head.

"Most Vadeanos are Catholics. They would at once recognize that as a copy of the picture of the Crucifixion which hangs over the high altar in our cathedral. It is by one of our most distinguished artists."

She let the spools run forward a little more. The next picture at which she stopped showed a man with a whip as big as a threshing flail, lashing the naked back of a little girl. After that the one with the Negro was repeated, the children still in their obscene postures; and so through again in order.

"I doubt if I need show you any more of this sequence," said Señora Posador quietly. "Let us contrast these pictures with what was interspersed in your interview."

The tape spun forward some distance. Córdoban, on the screen, said, "*Aquí está el señor Hakluyt,*" I came smiling into the range of the camera, and she stopped the spool.

I saw myself—or at any rate a recognizable likeness of myself—dipping my fingers for holy water into the font at the entrance to the cathedral. Another few yards of tape: I was shaking hands with *el Presidente,* and then in a few more moments I was kneeling before the bishop I had seen coming out of the elevator at the TV studios. Finally, before the sequence began to repeat, I was shown—this was so crude it nearly made me laugh—as an angel in a long white gown, holding a flaming sword over the monorail central, from beneath which little figures ran like frightened ants.

"That is enough, I think," said Señora Posador. She shut off the recorder. "Now I think you understand, no?"

Confused, I shook my head. "I do not," I said. "Not at all!"

She pushed aside a number of empty tape-cartons and lifted herself up on the bench beside the recorder, slender legs swinging. She took out one of her black cigarettes and lit it thoughtfully.

"Then I will do my best to make it clear," she said offhandedly. "You know, you say, what subliminal perception is?"

I frowned. "Well, I know the principle—you project a message on a TV screen or a movie screen for a fraction of a second, and it's alleged to impress the subconscious mind. They tried it out in movie houses with simple words like 'ice cream,' and some people said it worked and others said it didn't. I thought it had gone out of fashion, because it proved unreliable or something."

"Not exactly. Oh, it is true that it was not reliable. But indisputably it worked at least part of the time, and of course in most civilized countries it was immediately recognized as a powerful political weapon. If it could be made consistent in its effect, it could be used to indoctrinate the population. One of the first people to emphasize this was—Alejandro Mayor."

Memories of hints contained in Mayor's first book confirmed this. I nodded.

"It so happened," said Señora Posador, looking at the glowing tip of her cigarette, "that twenty years ago Juan Sebastian Vados was campaigning for the presidency in our country. It was the first election after an unpopular dictatorship. The television service had just been brought to the country—at first it served only Cuatrovientos, Astoria Negra, and Puerto Joaquin—and its director supported Vados.

"Who first saw the possibilities? I cannot say. It was all kept very secret. In most countries use of subliminal perception is banned by law, because its effectiveness—oh, it has been made reliable by testing!—it is inhuman. But in Aguazul there was no law. The single obstacle was that most of our people were, still are, illiterate. Yet that in its way was an advantage; it was soon found that even for persons who could read, pictures worked better than words. A message in words you can argue with, but pictures have the impact of something seen *con los ojos de sí.*"

She was still staring at her cigarette, but plainly was not seeing it, because the ash was growing and trembling and she made no move to disturb it. Her voice became taut and a little harsh.

"Vados, with advice from Mayor who had become a friend of his, employed this knowledge. He broadcast very often in this technique a picture of his opponent copulating with a donkey, and—since television was rather new to us and very many people watched very much of the time—his opponent was called foul names as he went through the streets, his house was stoned daily, and—and in the end he killed himself."

There was a pause.

At length Señora Posador recollected herself, shifted a little on her perch, and threw the ash from her cigarette aside.

"And so, my friend, it has continued. Those of us who know what we know—and object—never go to the movies; we never watch the television without a blinker. With practice has come skill, and what you have seen here is typical of the technique as it is employed today.

"It is now known for certain to many of our citizens that the squatters in the shantytowns practice bestial cruelty to their children, that they offend the morals of the young, that they elaborately blaspheme against the Christian religion. It is likewise known that you are a good man, a good Catholic, and a close friend of the president, whom you may never have seen in your life."

"Once, in a car the other day," I said. "That's all."

She shrugged. "I saw you smile at the picture of yourself as an avenging angel," she went on. "Yet even that is carefully planned. Many persons watching the program may have been children who believe in such things. Others—many, many more in the small towns and villages and even in Cuatrovientos and Puerto Joaquin—are simple and uneducated, and likewise hold such things to be literally true. You are a free man, Señor Hakluyt, compared to anyone walking the streets of Vados. You come here; you can go away again; it will not matter that your thinking has been influenced in Aguazul. But it would be better to watch no more television."

"Are you trying to tell me that *all* the TV programs are loaded with this kind of crap?" I demanded.

She slipped from her perch and bent to open a sliding door set under the bench where she was sitting. "Choose any of these," she invited, indicating a row of tape spools filed on a shelf. "They are programs transmitted during the last few months. I will do the same again for you."

"Don't trouble," I said distractedly.

She looked at me with something approaching pity. "As I imagined, Señor Hakluyt, you are a good man. It shocks you to discover what methods are employed in the most governed country in the world!"

I lit a cigarette, staring at her. "I was talking to Dr. Mayor last night," I said after a pause. "He used that same phrase. What does it mean? What does it really mean?"

"To the ordinary citizen? Oh, not very much. Our government is subtle as governments go—always it is the velvet glove where possible. For most of our people, the twenty years of

Vados's rule may truly be described as happy. Never before was Aguazul so prosperous, so peaceful, so satisfied. But we who know—and there are not many of us, señor—what long invisible chains we carry, fear for the future. If Mayor were to die, for example, who can predict the consequences? For all his elaborate theories, he is still a brilliant *improvisateur;* his gift is to trim his sails to the wind of change a moment before it begins to blow. With him, Vados, who is growing old— who can tell whether he has planned well enough for another to take the controls when he has gone, and keep our country on a steady forward course? And there is a still further danger: the danger that this disguised control may have worked all too well, that if change becomes necessary, we may have been too skillfully guided for too long to respond, so that before we can again forge ahead we must fall back in chaos."

She made a helpless gesture with one superbly manicured hand and cast down the butt of her cigarette.

"I try not to speak politics to you, Señor Hakluyt. I know you are a foreigner and a good man. But it is of concern to all the world what happens here in Aguazul; we have laid claim to a government of tomorrow to match our city of tomorrow, and if we have gone wrong, then the world must take notice and avoid the same mistakes. Your hour is up, señor. I will drive you wherever you wish to go."

IX

I didn't say a word as the big Pegasos carried me back to the traffic department, where I had to call and see Angers for my daily visit. My state of mind approached consternation.

I had come to Vados to do a standard kind of job, one carrying far more kudos than anything I had yet attempted, owing to the special status of the city, but to outward appearance otherwise routine.

And now I found myself faced with a task of moral judgment instead. Or as well.

What Señora Posador had shown me had shaken me badly.

Aside from the questionable ethics of using subliminal perception for political purposes, there was the purely personal reaction against being lied about to the public. That the lies were intended to make me a popular figure merely aggravated the situation.

And yet ...

For twenty years Vados had ruled his country without revolution, civil war, slump, panic, or any other disaster. He had created peace unprecedented in the century and a half of the country's checkered history. While his neighbors were wasting time and energy in internecine disturbances, he had managed to build Ciudad de Vados, to raise living standards almost everywhere, to make inroads on the problems of disease, hunger, illiteracy, and poverty. His people respected him for that; probably in the minds of most Vadeanos this city alone excused whatever else he might have done.

What was I to do? Quit cold?

If I did that, it would permanently mar my reputation; I had worked for a long time to reach my present level in my specialized profession, and to reject this much-envied job would be construed as a confession of inadequacy, no matter how sound my reasons—because those reasons were not professional ones.

From the financial viewpoint, I couldn't afford to quit, anyway.

Well, I could get around the last objection somehow. The competition in the field of traffic analysis is seldom so strong that an expert (and I class myself as an expert) can't *make* himself employment.

But what weighed heaviest with me at the moment, when I'd reviewed the matter from beginning to end, was this: that if I threw in the job now, it was certain that Angers or someone in the traffic department with a direct emotional involvement in the situation would be ordered to solve the problem to the taste of the government—or rather, of their well-to-do supporters. And Angers for a certainty would botch it.

Ultimately, I told myself, my only responsibility was to my own conscience. Whatever the other circumstances that affect-

ed me only indirectly, my job was to do the very best I could
and ensure that no one suffered by my actions—or, if not *no
one*, then the least possible number of people.

Carrying the memory of Señora Posador's bittersweet smile,
I went into the traffic department.

Angers' greeting was curt, and after it he wasted no more
time in preamble. "Where have you been, Hakluyt?" he demanded.

I looked at him in amazement. "Visiting a friend," I said
shortly. "Why?"

"Since when has Maria Posador qualified as a friend of
yours? I thought I told you she was bad company for you."

"So you've been having me watched," I said coldly. "I
rather thought so. You think I've been spending my time in
bars, maybe? Think I'm not capable of doing my job unless
someone keeps an eye on me? If that's your opinion, you can
damn well hire someone else—and I'll personally see to it no
reputable traffic analyst will come within a mile of the job!"

The snap I put into the words took the bluster out of
Angers and made him adopt a more confidential manner. He
sat back in his chair, sighing. "Look, Hakluyt, I know you're
not well posted on the situation in Vados—because if you
were, you'd avoid Señora Posador like the plague. I have to
admit you're right about your being watched. We arranged it
for your own sake. We're afraid someone may try and—uh—
put you out of the way, because to Tezol and Francis and the
rest of the rabble-rousers who make up the National Party
you're a major menace."

"If I'd been told before I accepted this job that I was going
to be made into a football between two petty local political
parties, I swear I'd never have set a foot in Aguazul," I
declared. "I'm seriously considering taking this as a breach of
contract."

I was, too; if I'd had the copy of the contract with me, I'd
have shredded it into confetti and thrown it all over the office.
I was suddenly blazing angry.

"Please!" said Angers. "I assure you that so long as you
stick to the job you're engaged to do, you're in no danger at

all. Only, in spite of my warnings, you're doing just what I told you not to do—you're getting emotionally involved. Señora Posador is a very beautiful and clever woman, and I've no doubt she sells a fine bill of goods. But let me tell you something about her she probably hasn't told you herself.

"Her husband was the man Vados defeated at the election which brought him to power, and when he heard the news, he shot himself."

A small cold hand seemed to take me by the scruff of the neck. "Go on," I said, fishing for a cigarette.

"Well—uh—I suppose it's only to be expected, because she was rather young at the time, twenty years ago, and not long married. . . . But the fact is that her husband's death preyed on her mind, and she's supposed not to be very stable. She fled the country directly afterwards, with a few of her husband's followers, and for a long time kept up a bombardment of slander about Vados's regime from other countries. Of course, it eventually became obvious to everyone that there wasn't a grain of truth in the accusations, and in the end—about five years ago, I suppose—Vados invited her to come back to Aguazul.

"Unfortunately, instead of taking this as a favor—and it was a pretty substantial act of clemency on Vados's part, after all the things she'd spread about—she kept on trying to stir up trouble. If it weren't for the fact that her husband had been a personal friend of Diaz even when they were political opponents, she'd probably not have been allowed to go on so long as she has. There is, of course, the argument that it's better to have her here where one can keep an eye on her than let her go on with her underground subversion from across the border, but people are saying she's overreached herself now, and it certainly wouldn't be to your benefit to get involved with her if she does have to be taken down a peg."

"That I didn't know," I said slowly. Angers sensed that I was in two minds, and pressed on.

"She'll go to any lengths to discredit Vados, of course. She's a very wealthy woman, and the rumor has it that she's behind *Tiempo*, which is a rag if ever there was one, and if that's so, then it's only her private pull with Diaz that's saved the paper from innumerable libel suits. The kind of dirt that *Tiempo* throws at the president and at government officials is hard to credit unless one sees it. However—" He produced his habitual cold smile. "I don't think I need labor the point any longer. A word to the wise, and all that. Let's get on to major business.

"Believe me," he continued with sudden earnestness, "I don't want to have to ask you to divert time from your work. It looks, though, as though it may be necessary. You heard— of course you did, from Caldwell—that Sigueiras has filed for an injunction to prevent us dispossessing him from his slum. Well, as usual when it's a case of foreign-born versus native-born citizen, our secretary of justice, Gonzales, has insisted on an immediate preliminary hearing, and in fact the case is down on the calendar for today.

"We've got wind of the fact that Brown, who's Sigueiras's lawyer, intends to subpoena you as a witness."

"Does he now?" I said neutrally.

"So we're told. We thought we might take the wind out of his sails by asking you to appear as an expert witness on behalf of the city council. It would create an awfully bad impression if you were to appear for Sigueiras; people would jump to the conclusion you were on his side, no matter whether what you said was favorable to his case or not."

I frowned. "I'm not sure that I fancy appearing for either side, to be honest," I began.

Angers shrugged. "Oh, I shouldn't worry unduly. We believe Brown is only trying to pull a stunt; if we call you as well, he'll probably give up the idea and then there'll be no need for you to appear at all. Brown's an ingenious devil."

"I've met him," I said. "That's the way he struck me."

"Oh, yes. He's handled a previous case for Sigueiras. And being a New Yorker, he has a great advantage—he conducts his examinations in English himself when the need arises, as well as in Spanish. Working through an interpreter has draw-backs, naturally. One has to admit he's a most subtle lawyer, too. But Andres Lucas is leading for the city, so I don't doubt which way the case will go. Lucas is far and away the best lawyer in Aguazul."

"That's the Lucas who's secretary of Guerrero's party?"

"That's the man. He was largely responsible for drafting the charter of incorporation for the city, so when Brown comes up against him on a question of citizens' rights, he'll find he's met a Tartar."

"Speaking of Lucas, wasn't he also involved in this case of dangerous driving someone brought against Guerrero?" I suggested. "I meant to find out what happened."

Angers scowled. "Dangerous driving be damned. It's just another move in the National Party's smear campaign against Guerrero. They can't bring him down by fair means, so they resort to foul ones. The man who brought the charge—this fellow Dominguez—is another lawyer, as a matter of fact. Legal adviser of the National Party. He's forever going after either Lucas or Guerrero, and people say he really wants Lucas's prestige as leading lawyer in the country. I don't like him at all. Too smooth."

"What's likely to happen?"

"I don't know about the chauffeur, but Guerrero will get off, of course. The Nationals have two or three witnesses, but they're all well-known party members, and Lucas will make hay out of them."

He reached into a drawer of his desk and took out a thick document tied with gold thread. "This is the subpoena to appear as an expert witness for the city council in the Sigueiras case. As I say, I doubt if you'll actually be called; if you are, we'll warn you in advance. Oh, and that reminds me: unless you're absolutely tied up tomorrow afternoon, Vados has said he wants to meet you. There's a garden party at Presidential House at three P.M. in honor of our local chess champion, who came out on top in the Caribbean tournament the other day. If you can make it, I'll have an invitation sent down to you at your hotel."

"I look forward with great pleasure to meeting this president of yours," I said with emphasis.

Angers smiled. "I don't mind betting he will impress you tremendously. He really is a remarkable man."

I was in a more confused state than ever when I left

Angers' office. What he had told me about Señora Posador
being the widow of the candidate Vados had defeated for the
presidency cast a dash of cold water on my earlier reaction.
But then, of course, "going to any lengths to discredit Vados"
could hardly imply laying on a superbly elaborate hoax for
my exclusive benefit this morning.

I was walking past the Courts of Justice toward the park
where I had last left the car provided for me by the city
council, deep in cogitation, when a familiar figure caught my
eye on the steep, curved steps leading up to the entrance: fat,
sweating in his white suit, sucking alternately at a ropy cigar
and the straw stuck in a soft drink bottle. He yelled at me as
I went by.

"Hey, Hakluyt! C'mere!"

I turned aside and went up the steps, starting to smile—I
couldn't help it. Brown looked a caricature of misery. I said,
"Can I buy you that drink now?"

He scrambled to his feet and dusted off his broad behind.
"Pal, I feel I could do with something stronger than that
—horse urine. You want to know what kind of a country
you're in? Want to know what passes for law an' order in
Vados? Want to see murder?"

"I don't understand," I said.

"In there"—he jerked a pudgy thumb over his shoulder
and sprayed cigar ash down his jacket— "there's one of the
damn finest lawyers in Vados bein' ripped to shreds by a judge
who don't give a ounce of horse manure for legality, justice,
or the rules of evidence. Miguel Dominguez—heard of him?"

"Is that the dangerous driving case—Guerrero's? I
shouldn't have thought it was important enough to be tried
here."

Brown spat. "Nothin' but the best for Mr. Guerrero, no,
sir! If they'd tried to put him on in a ordinary local *justicia-
ria* where it belongs, he'd have raised hell from here to Mexico
City. It'd do you a heap of good to go inside an' see what
really goes on. C'mon!"

He took my arm and nearly dragged me into the building.
As he went, he kept up a running fire of explanations. "This
concerns you, y'know, Hakluyt. You been mentioned about

six times so far that I heard. I just got so sick I had to go find some fresh air. I was hangin' around waitin' for the Sigueiras case to be called over the other side, in the civil court, but there's a long one ahead of us an' it looks like we won't get heard till tomorrow or next day. So I thought I'd see how Mig was gettin' on, and oh, Christ, it's *murder*."

"Where in hell do *I* get into the act?" I demanded.

"Old Romero—that's the judge—he's about a hundred, an' he's forgotten anything they ever managed to hammer into his thick skull about admissible evidence—he started by makin' it quite plain he thought the case against Guerrero was nothin' but an attempt to smear him. He gave a fifteen-minute political lecture on the iniquities of the National Party, accused Mig of being a paid perjurer, said it was a damn good thing someone was goin' to clear out the bunch of peasants the National Party sponged on—that's you, natch—ach, I'm too goddam' *revolted* to repeat it!"

We came to the courtroom door; an usher rolled back a sliding panel for us, and we slipped into seats in the public block. There was a fair audience. In the front row sat Sam Francis, scowling like a fiend, and with him there were two or three other people whom I recalled seeing at meetings in the Plaza del Sur.

In the dock, in a comfortable armchair, sat Guerrero, a smug grin on his handsome face; below him in the lawyer's seat was Andres Lucas, also smiling. On the other side of Lucas's table was a man with a very white face, whose jaw was trembling visibly.

"That's him," whispered Brown. "That's Mig."

The judge was a wizened man—not perhaps a hundred, as Brown had claimed, but certainly seventy or more. His gavel seemed almost too heavy for his clawlike, shriveled hand. His voice was reedy and penetrating, and he was using it now. I got the gist of his remarks; he was saying:

"—cannot, of course, entertain the evidence offered by the prosecution when it is so plainly colored by personal animosity and political considerations of the basest kind. I have heard cases in this court and others for upward of thirty years; never before have I been faced with such a farrago of rubbish. I shall, of course, report Lawyer Dominguez's conduct to the appropriate professional body, and I look forward to the day—which cannot be far distant—when the persons responsible for this unprincipled attack on the good character of one of our leading citizens are swept away along with the repositories of filth and immorality where they were spawned. It only remains for me to pronounce the formal verdict—not guilty. Court adjourned."

The gavel banged; as if it had been a trigger, Sam Francis leaped to his feet and, forgetting his languages in the heat of the moment, shouted at Romero in English.

"Why, you unprincipled old bastard! You're just a—"

The gavel rapped again, but a storm of booing drowned it and the rest of what Sam Francis said. Beside me, Fats Brown scrambled to his feet, yelling execrations. The judge signaled to the clerk of the court, who ran to open the door behind the dais for him, and the ushers struggled to restore order.

"Let's get out of here," said Brown at length. "I couldn't face Mig in the state he must be in. He's just been legally slandered to death, so far as his career's concerned. Like this country, Hakluyt? I think it's a wonderful country. It's just got some stinkin' bastards in it."

"But how can Romero get away with it?" I demanded.

"Who's to stop him?" Brown snarled. "Romero's the senior judge in the country, bar the chairman of the supreme court, an' he's a rubber stamp for Vados. Ugh! Fresh air—and quick!"

He led me through the corridors to the entrance so fast that he was panting when we halted at the head of the steps. He hauled out a large bandanna and mopped his face with it, "Well, like I was sayin', you've seen what passes for law an' order in Vados. Like it?"

I didn't get a chance to answer, for at that moment Sam Francis came up to us and started to rail at Brown for what had happened. Brown took it calmly, realizing that Francis merely needed someone to listen to him and didn't care who it was.

After minutes, the flow of Francis's vituperation was cut

short as a group of laughing people came from the interior of the building. I did not have to look around to tell that Guerrero and Lucas were in the middle of them; there was also Guerrero's girl friend of the previous evening, and others I recognized as supporters of the Citizens of Vados party.

They halted at the top of the steps not far from us, and a man who had been half in the background—the driver of Guerrero's big black sedan—slipped past us to collect the car. I nudged Brown. "What about him?" I said. "Wasn't there a charge against the chauffeur, too?"

"Dismissed by Romero," said Brown thickly. "Said it was only a cover for the real purpose of the case, which was to slander Guerrero."

"Slander Guerrero!" echoed Sam Francis loudly, in a voice that was meant to carry. "How could you paint the bastard any blacker than he is?"

Guerrero stopped in midsentence and began to approach Francis with even steps. He stopped a pace or two distant, while his companions came up behind him. His eyes locked with Francis's, and there was a long, cold silence.

"Coming from you," said Guerrero at long last, "that is a ridiculous remark. You're the black one here!"

Francis's face contorted into a snarl, and he closed the gap separating them with a single stride. His thick fingers folded over into his palm with a clapping sound, and he drove his fist like a hammer into Guerrero's mouth.

Literally, the violence of the blow lifted Guerrero from his feet—literally, because the act of falling carried him back over the lip of the steps beneath us. He seemed to be diving backwards like a ridiculous dummy, and time stopped.

I had a half-conscious memory of a crunching sound that had mingled with the thud of Guerrero's body striking the foot of the steps. Then we were jostling and stumbling down toward where he lay.

One of Guerrero's companions—I think it was Lucas—bent down and touched his head. His fingers came away sticky with blood.

"Oh, you fool!" whispered Brown, his eyes on Sam Francis's heaving chest. "Oh, you double god-damned *fool!*"

People rushed up from every side. Guerrero's girl clutched his limp hand as she knelt beside his body. In a moment she was weeping. A policeman shouldered between us, ordered us to stand back, and felt expertly for a pulse. Then he got up and started menacingly to climb the steps toward Sam Francis, who was standing like a man in a nightmare, unable to move hand or foot.

Brown looked at me, with no vestige of humor in his expression. "Sorry, Hakluyt," he said in a low tone. "When I asked you to come an' see murder, I didn't figure it would turn out literally."

X

An ambulance; more policemen; court reporters on their way to lunch found a sensation thrown under their noses; there were pictures taken. The crowd milled and eddied, growing as the minutes passed.

Then a black-and-white police car howled across the plaza with its sirens screaming, and el Jefe O'Rourke bounced from it—bounced like a huge rubber doll. He had not made a very favorable impression on me in the office when I saw him the day after my arrival; he had struck me as dour and stolid. Now his affected untidiness seemed to fit him as though he had stripped for action. He barked rapid commands, and the policemen moved quickly and efficiently. The names of witnesses were taken; sightseers were driven back from the body, and a reporter's camera was commandeered for a record of the way the body lay after falling.

The crowd went on growing; it was perhaps three hundred strong within two minutes of the death. It growled as word of what had happened spread from the front to the back rows; insults were suddenly screamed at Sam Francis, standing—still frozen, like a statue—beside the first policemen who had arrived, high at the top of the court steps.

I saw O'Rourke stiffen and turn his head fractionally each time one of these screamed insults arrowed upward. The

temper of the bystanders was growing ugly; I wanted to ask
Fats Brown why O'Rourke wasn't doing anything about it,
but he had gone closer to the body and was hovering around
with his eyes bright and a taut expression hardening the lines
of his fat-creased face.

A silence fell as ambulance attendants lifted the body and
carried it into their vehicle. Several of the bystanders crossed
themselves. The doors slammed, and as though that had been
a signal, a roar went up and something hurtled through the
air—a soft fruit. It struck Sam Francis on the arm and
splashed colored pulp all over him.

I hadn't looked at O'Rourke for a few moments. Suddenly
he was moving, shouldering his way through the crowd like a
charging bull. There were shouts and cries of alarm. I lost
sight of him for a second; then his black-sleeved arm went up
over the heads of those around him, came down again viciously.

When he emerged again into the cleared circle where Guerrero had lain, he was dragging a man in a cheap white suit,
across whose left cheek a huge bruise was already showing.
The man kept shaking his head as though dizzy, and stumbled
as he was hurried along.

O'Rourke sent him spinning into the arms of a policeman
with a final shove, and then turned, breathing hard, to face
the onlookers. He didn't say anything. But gradually the
crowd melted; people dispersed, heads down, across the plaza.
Two policemen led Francis down the steps and pushed him
into O'Rourke's car; as he went past Andres Lucas, the
lawyer, his face contorted with rage, hissed something to the
effect that he would never get out of jail alive.

Then Lucas took the arm of Guerrero's girl and led her
away—she was still sobbing—and it was over.

With a final glance around, Fats Brown scuffed some dust
over the smear of blood where Guerrero had lain, and came
and took my arm.

"Let's go get a drink," he said in a flat voice. "You owe
me one, remember?"

We had double tequilas in a bar on the other side of the
square, where people were already talking in hushed voices

about what had happened. We didn't talk at first—just sat, waiting for the alcohol to help steady the world.

In the end I said, "Do you have a death penalty in Aguazul?"

Brown shook his head. "Not often. I mean they didn't use it lately. It's still on the books—choice of hanging or a firing squad. But only a half dozen guys been shot since Vados came to power, an' the last was five years back."

There was a pause. Brown shrugged and shifted on his seat.

"Guess you can needle a man just so far—an' Sam was mad as hell already. . . . That's about fixed the Nationals for the time being, of course. Vados'll laugh like a gargoyle when they tell him."

I pictured Francis's stunned horror when he saw what he had done. "Had he—had he done anything like that before?" I asked.

"Sam? Not that I know of. But I've seen men like him in Harlem—get what I mean? Saw one guy push a broken bottle in a white man's face for callin' him a dirty black bastard. An' Sam's always had a temper."

"Fact is," I said, looking at the chewed lemon in my left hand, "I half thought he might break my neck before he got around to Guerrero's."

Fats gave me a sharp glance. "You met Sam personally? Or you just ventilatin' an impression?"

"I met him. Maria Posador introduced us at my hotel."

"You're a friend of Maria's?" Fats spoke incredulously. "Hakluyt, you begin to bother me. I wouldn't have said you were the kind of guy Maria would look at twice."

"I may not be pretty," I snapped, nettled. "But what in hell makes her opinion so important? Someone with a grudge a mile wide the way she has a grudge—"

"Calm down!" grunted Fats. "Calm down! No offense—'s just that—ah, put it this way: Vados brought you here, Maria would like to see Vados pegged out for the crows, *ergo* it's a surprise to me she hasn't spat in your eye. I could be wrong. Guess I must be wrong." He emptied his glass, sent salt and lemon after the liquor absent-mindedly, and let the lemon fall in an ashtray on the bar.

"You lucky perishin' bastard," hē said. "Chances are, you won't even be called as a witness. But Lucas, damn his muckin' soul, would probably give his right arm to get me for aidin' and abettin'—an' I wouldn't put it past him to try an' drag Mig Dominguez in as well. An' we have other problems, Mig an' I. I better go home an' look up some law, Hakluyt. Want to try an' get Mig off this hook Romero hung him on. There's a loophole—I think. Mig's pretty close to Diaz—he was Diaz's white-haired boy at one time, an' they're still pals. I hafta get the copy of the court record in this morning's case to Diaz; if he feels inclined, he can tell Gonzales to discharge Romero on grounds of incompetence an' order a new trial. Leastways, I think that's the way the law stands. Could make Romero pretty damn uncomfortable, anyway. If Diaz'll play."

He got up and paid his check. "See if Mig wants to play it that way. He'd be a damn fool not to try it, at least. So long, Hakluyt—see you around."

I don't know whether Judge Romero had been right or wrong to see this case against Guerrero as a pure political maneuver. One fact, though, kept hammering at my mind. Francis had been as bitter about it as though it really were a plot gone wrong—and in the grip of a savage rage he had struck Guerrero down.

This was supposed to be a political leader. If the rest of the National Party resembled him at all, they were a bunch of barbarians.

It was time for lunch, but I couldn't face the idea of eating, or of working, either, until I'd got the shock out of my system. I went slowly back to the hotel.

In the Plaza del Sur, where there should normally have been two large rival meetings going on and sundry minor speakers, the field was monopolized by the Citizens of Vados. Under a banner hastily draped with black mourning streamers, an orator I didn't know was haranguing an angry crowd, lamenting Guerrero's death, and vowing terrible vengeance on the National Party. Someone must have got the news through to Tezol; there was no sign of him or any of his followers.

When I entered the hotel, I checked my mailbox and found

the invitation Angers had referred to—a handsomely printed gilt-edged card which I was asked to display to the person appointed when presenting myself at a garden party at Presidential House, et cetera et cetera. I put it in my wallet, wondering whether the death of Guerrero was going to mean that the affair would now be canceled.

The death was splashed all over the afternoon papers, of course—or rather paper, since as I had earlier learned only *Liberdad* could afford more than one edition a day. The following morning, though, *Tiempo* also went to town on the matter. It was lurid in the details it gave of the supposed provocation offered by Guerrero, and sympathetic—of course—toward Francis. But the best hope it could hold out for him was an optimistic assurance that he would get prison rather than a death sentence. There was a leading article on the subject by the novelist, Felipe Mendoza, whom I had previously noticed as a contributor, but it was mere empty thundering. Nothing could hide the fact that Francis had stupidly and viciously given way to bad temper—and had condemned himself to suffer for the result.

In an attempt to brighten up the picture, presumably, the paper also gave a lot of space to the allegedly disgraceful handling of the Guerrero dangerous driving case, illustrated with a photo of Fats Brown wearing a pugnacious expression and Miguel Dominguez looking saintly and put upon. Fats had apparently declared in an interview that Francis had been driven beyond endurance by the travesty of justice he had witnessed—but there was no explanation of why, supposing the case against Guerrero to have been a genuine one, Francis had been anywhere near the court unless his interest was political.

There were two other points that did emerge from the article, however. The first was that Dominguez was doing what Fats had suggested; he was going to try to have Romero removed from office and arrange another trial before a different judge. It puzzled me for a moment to wonder how they could get around the double jeopardy provision; then I remembered that Romero had dismissed the charge against the chauffeur without hearing evidence. That would probably explain it.

The second was something of Francis's background. As I had thought, he was neither Vadeano by naturalization nor a native-born citizen. By reading between the lines, I found that he had been kicked out successively from his homeland of Barbados, British Guiana, Honduras, and Puerto Rico for political agitation and had merely been continuing the same in Vados. As I had suspected, he seemed to be a professional demagogue.

I'd never liked that type; they were always unhappy unless they had a chip on their shoulder, and if they had no chip of their own, they would load up with someone else's, whether they were asked to or not. On the other hand, to give people like Guerrero, Lucas, and even Angers their due, they had an ideal of their own—they wanted Ciudad de Vados to continue as it had begun, a showpiece of the Western Hemisphere and the kind of place they had envisaged when it was founded. From a personal point of view, I shared that ideal; if the city society was ever to achieve its inherent potentialities, then it was essential to make the best of its finest manifestations.

The next morning it was a saint's day; there should have been heavy traffic. I went out early on the job, but after only a few hours I gave up. The situation was far too abnormal for my findings to be valid. The city had closed up like a clam. Outside the churches—even outside the great cathedral—there were far fewer people than usual coming from Mass; many of them wore mourning bands or had even put on formal mourning complete. Overnight, slogans had been scrawled up on walls, condemning Sam Francis and the National Party; when I went into the market district, where a saint's day should have produced an extra-heavy crowd, I found only half as many people as usual. The window of a store had been smashed in, and there were signs that there might have been rioting. A peasant's ramshackle vegetable barrow had been overturned; someone had unsuccessfully tried to set the wooden frame on fire. The little bar where Fats had stood me a drink was closed, and wooden slats from fruit crates had been nailed over the windows. The walls nearby were spattered with the traces of thrown fruit and eggs.

Under the brilliant sun, Ciudad de Vados was as still and as enigmatic as a package with a tick in it. Like such a package, though, it was certain that either the fuse would fizzle out—or there was going to be an explosion.

The tension contended with the heat; from both at once the people of the city sweated rivers.

XI

Despite Guerrero's death, Vados was going ahead with his garden party; Angers told me that public enthusiasm for the local champion who had won the Caribbean chess tournament was nearly as strong as the public anger at Guerrero's death, so they had agreed to give him his reception regardless.

I had a good view of the city by night as we drove to the television center. On the way to Presidential House I had a still better one by day. Very probably Vados had had his—or nominally the incumbent's, which meant his—home located where it was because of the splendid panorama it commanded over the city.

It was a vast white building, backed on the mountainside, at a ninety-degree angle from the airport on the landward side of the city. An airliner on one of the Caribbean routes was nosing down for a landing as I approached the main gates, but its noise was hardly more than a whisper.

Police in summer uniform, on guard at the gates, swung carbines from their shoulders as I came up the road. I wondered for a moment why I had been selected for that honor, since the cars ahead of me had not. Then I realized that they bore senior officers in dress uniform, conspicuous enough to guarantee themselves.

I pulled up at the gate and showed my invitation card to the nearest guard; he waved down his companion's gun and gave me a snappy salute before telling me to carry on. I drove on up the drive.

Marquees and tables had been set out on a hundred-yard-square lawn before the house. Steeply banked flower beds bordered the lawn on three sides; in the middle of the left-hand side was an ornamental cascade, and opposite it was a small pavilion in which a military band was playing a waltz. At the house end of the lawn was a wall running parallel to the central portico of the house; at either end of the wall a flight of steps descended to lawn level, flanked by pots of trailing, brilliantly flowered creepers. At the other end was a long pergola, also swarming with flowers, and behind that an avenue shaded by trees. There were perhaps four hundred people already present.

I noticed that between the avenue of trees and the limit of the Presidential estate was a double fence of high wire netting, screened from view inside by the trees, but briefly visible as one passed the gatehouse. The sun glinted on a searchlight glass aligned to illuminate the whole space between the two rows of fencing.

A policeman directed me to park my car on a hard tennis court adjacent to the house; here another policeman directed me to go down onto the lawn. At the head of each of the creeper-decked flights of steps stood still other policemen, who courteously checked invitation cards a second time and ticked names off on a list. The one who checked my card gave me a hard, searching look, as though memorizing the face of a potential assassin.

At first I could see no one I recognized. A waiter offered me a tray of drinks; I took something that looked promising, selected a canapé from another tray, and wandered around the lawn trying not to look more bored than I could help. This was probably far too formal an affair for me to enjoy.

Looking about me, I realized that there was a good cross section of the Vadeano upper crust here. The most conspicuous and colorful were not by any means the women, who mostly wore pastel frocks that vied with each other to be exquisitely simple. By contrast, the senior officers formed a group as gorgeous as butterflies—the army in pale gray decorated with red and gold, the navy in white encrusted with gold, and the air force in skyblue, silver, and bronze.

Then I spotted the first face I recognized—a man with a load on his mind, plainly, for he was the center of a group that included three astonishingly lovely women and was not even trying to be affable. Miguel Dominguez, the lawyer.

I was wondering at his presence when a voice hailed me in English, and I turned to see Donald Angers arriving together with Seixas and, presumably, their respective wives. The thin angularity of Angers made a comedian-contrast with the vast, white-clothed bulk of Seixas.

Seixas greeted me enormously, slapped me on the back, and offered me one of his black Brazilian cigars. Angers waited patiently for him to finish and then presented me to his wife— a faded, sandy-haired Scotswoman with slightly protruding teeth, who wore her expensive dress badly. I noticed that she kept darting little glances at Señora Seixas, who was nearly as big as her husband, with a great trembling bosom and thick white arms ajangle with bracelets, but who moved with the grace of a former dancer and carried her plain blue frock magnificently.

We talked, of course, about Guerrero's death. Seixas went into considerable detail about what ought to be done to Sam Francis, while his wife shook with suppressed amusement and Mrs. Angers debated whether she ought to voice her disapproval or not.

In the middle of a sentence Seixas threw up an arm dramatically toward the steps and then slapped his forehead and turned away as though about to spit.

Descending the steps were two gray-haired men, very much alike. One of them—the older of the two—seemed to be well-known, for he was bowing to both sides in acknowledgment of greeting, and as soon as he came down on the lawn was surrounded by friends.

"That *is* a bit thick!" exclaimed Angers with a frown. "I think Vados is going to overreach himself one of these days with his pose of tolerance."

"Well, he is very famous, dear," said his wife timidly.

"Famous or not doesn't matter," said Angers. "It's the principle of the thing. It doesn't seem quite right in view of the situation."

I'd never expected to hear a word from Angers against his much-respected President. "Excuse my ignorance," I said. "Whom are you talking about?"

"That fellow who just arrived. His name's Felipe Mendoza. He's a writer—supposed to be the Latin American William Faulkner, so they say. Writes sordid novels about the peasants. *I* can't read the stuff. But he trades on his reputation to publish scurrilous articles about the government, and the other day he attacked Seixas here in the most disgraceful manner."

"He *is* a very good writer," ventured his wife, with a flash of unexpected fire.

"Hah!" said Seixas, glowering in Mendoza's direction. "A libel is still a libel, well written or badly written, an' I think I'll tell Vados what I think of him inviting the— " He caught himself as his wife gave him a warning look.

"You're quite right, of course," said Angers, not apparently liking to agree with Seixas but wishing more to condemn Mendoza. "If it weren't for the fact that his brother runs that rag *Tiempo*, I'm certain he'd never get his stuff into print."

"Was that his brother with him—the man who looks like him?"

"That's right. His name's Cristoforo. He, his brother, and a man called Pedro Murieta who finances the publication of Felipe Mendoza's books are sort of literary dictators in the country, which is a damnable shame, because most of the stuff that's to their taste is on the verge, if not over the verge, of pornography—"

There was a shout from the head of the steps. I only caught the tail of it, but I presumed it was approximately, "Pray silence for his excellency the president," because everyone on the lawn stopped talking, the band played pianissimo, and there was movement under the pillared portico of the house.

Then *el Presidente* himself emerged, accompanied by his dark and beautiful young wife and by a nervous-looking man with spectacles, whose tie was out of place and whose hair was rumpled as though he habitually ran his fingers through it.

A burst of clapping went up, Angers and Seixas and their

wives joining in without great enthusiasm. It lasted till the group was at the top of the steps, and then Vados, smiling, indicated to the nervous man that he should step forward. He did so, blinking in the strong sun and smiling apologetically.

"That's Pablo Garcia," said Angers softly, leaning toward me. "The local chess champion, of course."

I nodded. Then Vados descended the steps to the lawn and he, his wife, and Garcia took three chairs which had sprung from nowhere against the wall at that end of the lawn.

"Well, here's where we have to start circulating," said Angers with a sigh. I gave him a puzzled glance, but then realized that everyone on the lawn was beginning to move in a counterclockwise procession. As each visitor passed the President, he or she bowed, and Vados either smiled back an acknowledgment or, in the case of the highly privileged, beckoned them to come and have a word with him. A man who was probably a secretary, wearing a dark suit, stood behind him and occasionally whispered in his ear.

He whispered as I, dutifully circulating with the Angerses— the Seixases had got left behind—came up. The presidential hand beckoned me. I excused myself to my companions and went forward.

"Delighted to have this chance of meeting you, Señor Hakluyt," said Vados in excellent unaccented English. "I have seen you before, of course—on the television—but not in the flesh, as they say."

"There I have the advantage," I said. "I have seen you, and Your Excellency's lady, in the Plaza del Norte the other day." I gave a slight bow toward Señora Vados; she really was very beautiful. But apparently she didn't speak English, and was paying no attention.

"Ah, but such a fleeting glimpse is not a meeting," Vados said.

"But I've met Ciudad de Vados," I countered. "And I've been extremely impressed by it."

"So you said on the television," Vados answered, and smiled. "It is always a pleasure to me when someone says that, even after ten years. I regard it almost as my child, you know. To have founded a city, though, is better than having a son, for a son is only an individual as oneself is, while a city—a city is the finest offspring a man can have." He gave a sudden sigh. "But, as with human children, sometimes it does not grow up quite as one would have wished. Well, that is of no matter at the moment—I will not spoil your afternoon by discussing professional matters. I hope you enjoy your stay in Aguazul, señor."

He inclined his head, and I said, "*Señor presidente*— Señora—Señor Garcia," and backed away. I was glad I'd added the last two words, for the nervous-looking man was having nothing to do but stare at the passing people. At my addressing him, even to say good-bye, he lit up like a lamp being switched on and echoed, "Señor!" with as much enthusiasm as a small boy accepting an offer of candy.

"You were honored, señor," said a voice I recognized as I rejoined the circular procession. Isabela Cortés was parading past the President on the arm of a distinguished man of about sixty who wore pince-nez in the old-fashioned manner. I acknowledged the remark.

This was a fortunate meeting, of course, because I had a question burning in the back of my mind—a question about the use of subliminal perception.

"León," Señora Cortés said to her companion, "this is Señor Hakluyt whom you saw on my program the other evening. My husband, señor—the professor of the department of social sciences in the university."

The professor gave me an uncomprehending but beaming smile and shook my hand warmly; then he gave his wife a reproving stare, and she laughed. "Please excuse him, señor," she explained. "He speaks English less well than I."

"Please speak Spanish," I said, since it appeared to be expected of me, and she explained to her husband who I was. Before she had finished, he seized my hand again and told me he was overjoyed to meet me. Señora Cortés looked on indulgently.

"I suppose you know rather few of the people here?" she suggested.

I nodded.

"Suppose we go over to the refreshment table and take

advantage of this carousel to point out some of the notables for you. Thank you again, by the way, for the performance you put on on my program the other night."

"It was very interesting," I said guardedly. We were both talking Spanish now, for the professor's benefit, and I was afraid I might not get the chance to ask my burning question—I probably couldn't be sufficiently tactful in Spanish.

A waiter offered us another tray of drinks as we stepped aside from the circular flow, and the professor raised his glass to me, beaming again.

"To a successful conclusion of your difficult task, señor," he toasted.

"If you don't mind," I said feelingly, "I'll drink to that myself."

We drank; then Señora Cortés moved close to me and began to name prominent personalities in a low tone.

"Over there, do you see?—it is General Molinas"—she was back to English, rather to my relief—"who is the . . . oh, I don't know the word: the man in charge of all the forces."

"Minister of War?" I suggested, and she laughed.

"War, señor? We don't fight wars any longer! No, he is —ah, I have it! Commander in chief. And there, of course, is our Minister of Information, Dr. Mayor, whom you know— and that is another minister to whom he is talking at the moment: Señor Diaz, Minister of the Interior."

This time I took considerable note. Diaz was a large, ungainly man—what they call in Spanish an *hombrazo*—with huge hands and a coarse-boned face revealing more than a trace of Indian ancestry. He wore a well-cut tropical suit which he contrived to make look like a flour sack, and he made sweeping gestures as he spoke; people stood well back even when they were being directly addressed by him. One of the group around him was Miguel Dominguez.

"And there—next to Señor Dominguez—is another minister: Secretary of Justice Gonzales, the stout one with the dark glasses. Then there is Señor Castaldo, who is deputy chief of the Ministry of the Interior, a close colleague of Diaz, naturally. . . . I think all the ministers of the cabinet will be here—yes, there is our director of health and hygiene, Dr. Ruiz."

Ruiz, a small and excitable-seeming man, was talking to Caldwell, the stammering man from the city health department whom I had met in Angers' office.

"There are many people here, and I do not recognize them all," Señora Cortés said with an air of vague apology, as though I had expressed perfect faith in her universal knowledge. "But there are many well-known business persons here, too—ah, you see, talking to Andres Lucas, that is Señor Arrio, whose name you will have seen on big stores here in the city."

Lucas was in full mourning and was trying to look as if he had only come to this garden party out of a sense of duty to his President. I didn't look very hard at Señor Arrio; the flow of names was beginning to make me dizzy.

Señora Cortés was looking around, at a momentary loss for another notable to point out. I seized the opportunity to break in. "And who is Señor Garcia?" I asked. "I mean, aside from being a chess champion."

"Oh, he is a chess champion, and that is all. Formerly, I believe, he was a teacher of mathematics at a small school in Puerto Joaquin, but now he is the director of the national chess school here in Vados."

"You really take the game seriously in this country, don't you?" I said.

Professor Cortés said something to his wife, which I failed to catch; he heard the answer and turned to me almost belligerently.

"And why not take it seriously, señor? It is a finer game than your football or your baseball, no? It trains the mind to think with clarity and never to move in haste without thought; it is always new and always stimulating."

"You play yourself?" I asked, and Señora Cortés explained, while her husband looked modest, that he had himself been in the finals of the national championship some years ago.

I made appropriately impressed sounds and took another drink off a passing tray.

Since the professor had now joined the conversation again,

I had to stick to Spanish for politeness. I lined up my first couple of sentences.

"I was very interested to visit your television center," I began, hoping I wouldn't put my foot in my mouth straight away. "Particularly to find that a minister of the government was—uh—directly in charge of the service."

"Very rightly!" said Cortés energetically. "I fully support Dr. Mayor in his view that television is one of the most useful organs of modern government. For example"—he waved down a budding protest from his wife—"for example, let us take this business in which you are involved. There are many things we could not possibly publish in print, for example, and which the public nonetheless ought to know about. With apologies to yourself, 'Belita, you know as well as I do that we'd have the bishop thundering at us if we ever attempted to put into *Liberdad* half the things you manage to get across on television."

He turned directly to me. "You know we are very concerned about these squatters who have invaded Ciudad de Vados—well, of course you do, you of all people. But some of the things that go on in their hovels you would barely credit—bestial cruelty, abominable immorality, everything that is worst in children of the soil suddenly uprooted and left without the stabilizing effect of the cultural milieu to which they are accustomed. I have the honor to be an adviser to the city council, and in pursuit of the duties of my office I have had to go to this slum under the monorail station and to those tin shacks on the outskirts, and the health inspectors and I—by entering without warning—have made the most *terrible* discoveries on occasion. Naturally, the danger of having such a well of corruption in the city is inestimable. And yet, back in their own villages, where they have certain social pressures operating on them—respect for the local priest, for instance, and force of traditional custom—these people are really sober, moral, even, one may say, honorable."

He spoke authoritatively. I framed my next remark cautiously; it seemed that I was going to get my burning question answered without even trying. I said, "But surely you can't show—well, I presume you mean obscene material—on television, any more than you could put it in a newspaper."

"Not in the ordinary way," agreed the professor. "Our revered bishop—why, there he is; I wondered what had become of him—oh, of course, today is a holy day, isn't it? He must have had other commitments. Where was I? Oh, yes. The bishop would have a good deal to say if we tried it. Yet the facts ought to be known to the public at large, and television is the only possible medium for reaching a wide audience consistently with the truth. So we use a technique known as subliminal perception to intersperse this kind of information in other matter—it involves a—"

"I've heard of it," I interrupted, not knowing whether to be pleased or appalled that he frankly admitted their employment of the technique.

He beamed at me. "Most useful!" he exclaimed. "Really, most useful!"

I suddenly felt convinced that here was a thoroughly nice man. I pictured him stepping through the doorway—probably pushing aside a curtain of sacking—of one of the shanties on the outskirts of Vados and confronting such a scene as the one involving the Negro and the children which Señora Posador had shown me. I thought Cortés would probably charge at the man, telling him that it were better that a millstone be tied around his neck and he be cast into the depths of the sea.

Señora Cortés looked at me rather uneasily, as though unsure of the effect her husband's declaration might have had on me. When she saw I was not going to reply at once, she spoke.

"Yes, señor, we do use our television service for such propaganda, but only when the subject is a truly serious one. As León has said, here is a subject we feel *is* enough to justify extreme measures—and since not everyone can go and see for himself, we have no alternative. There are many people in Vados who deny the facts of the case and will stop at nothing to prevent the President remedying the situation as he feels is best—some of those here this afternoon, indeed, oppose his plans. But our President is a very tolerant man."

"There certainly are people here I wouldn't have expected

to be invited," I admitted. "The editor of *Tiempo,* for instance. And his brother."

"You are acquainted with the Mendozas?" Señora Cortés asked in some surprise. I shook my head. "Ah, you merely know of them. They are a case in point. But Señor Cristoforo is, after all, a notable man in Vados, and Señor Felipe's reputation is today international—and in any case, all other differences fade before our admiration for the skill of Señor Garcia, our champion. But it is a matter for regret that Felipe Mendoza cannot find a more worthy use for his talent than slandering our good President."

"Well, why does Vados invite such people, anyway?" I said.

She shrugged. "To him, it seems, it means more that Felipe Mendoza has brought fame to his country by his books, and that Cristoforo, his brother, should love Ciudad de Vados enough to care about its future. Why, I have heard it said that because he has, to his sorrow, no children, he has taken to calling this city his only child. I believe that anyone who loves the city is assured of his friendship—so long as he does nothing to harm it."

"True," nodded the professor emphatically. "Quite, quite true. Believe it or not, he even invites Maria Posador to nonpolitical functions such as this—she was invited today, I know for a fact, because I have seen the list of guests. She did not come, of course." He looked at me inquiringly. "You have heard of this woman Maria Posador?"

"I've met her," I said. "The widow of the man Vados defeated for the presidency."

The professor's fine-arched gray eyebrows went up. But before he could comment, his wife had touched him on the arm. "León!" she said quietly.

I noticed that a general movement was taking place up the lawn and toward the house. Rows of chairs had been set out on the asphalt drive, overlooking the place where we were now standing. The band was putting its instruments away. A group of servants had brought a long rolled-up cylinder of stiff heavy cloth down to the side of the lawn and were laying it in front of the bandstand.

"Ah, yes, of course," said the professor, glancing at his

watch, and without further explanation my companions started to join the move toward the steps. We were among the last
to ascend, but the chairs were set in staggered tiers, and all the
places commanded a view of the lawn. I saw that Vados was
laughing and joking with Garcia in the center of the front row
as we filed into our places to await whatever was going to
happen.

Below us, the servants briskly unrolled the cylinder, and it
proved to be a gigantic chessboard, fully sixty feet square. As
soon as it was laid flat, the servants unrolling it retired, and
from opposite ends of the avenues of trees at the back of the
lawn, two files of men began to march out.

Those on the left wore white shirts and trousers; those on
the right wore black. The first eight on each side had plain
skullcaps on their heads; those who came next had tall round
cylinders topped with crenellated indentations. After them followed men with horses' heads, and then others with bishops'
miters; then the only women among the whole group, each
with a gilded coronet. Lastly, to the accompaniment of clapping, came two very tall men wearing crowns.

These people marched up the sides of the chessboard to the
beating of a single drum in the bandstand. Two at a time,
they made a deep bow before the President; then they turned
away to take up their positions on the board.

I was so astonished at this unexpected display that all the
"pieces" had fallen in before I managed to turn to Señora
Cortés and look inquiringly blank.

"Did you not know about this?" she said in surprise.
"Why, this is the highest tribute we pay to our chess masters.
Each year the national champion, or anyone who wins a
championship abroad, has his winning game played through
like this before a distinguished audience. This is the ninth time
such an honor has befallen Señor Garcia—a wonderful
achievement, no? But look, they are starting to play."

A tap from the drum; a white pawn marched solemnly two
squares forward. Another tap; a black pawn marched out to
face him. Pawn to Queen Four on both sides.

People settled themselves more comfortably in their seats, as
if preparing for a long session. But I was too fascinated to

relax at once. This was the most extraordinary game of chess I had ever seen. I had, of course, heard of the games that used to be played by despotic Middle Eastern rulers—by Shahs of Persia, or somewhere, where every time a piece, represented by a slave, was taken, the executioner decapitated the unfortunate victim on the spot. I had heard of attempts to stage similar games—shorn of their barbaric refinements—on boards the size of tennis courts, directing the pieces by megaphone. But from what I had heard, most of these stunts were failures, owing to the length of time involved and the risk of the actors fainting like soldiers kept too long on parade.

But this dramatization of chess, with the living pieces moving according to carefully rehearsed patterns, was something infinitely more impressive than any stunt.

XII

It was a long game, though—eighty or ninety moves—even shorn of the thinking time it must have needed in the actual tournament. I'm not a good enough player to appreciate the fine points of end-game play, and long before the forces on either side were reduced to two pawns and a rook I was feeling as restive as I had when watching Córdoban take on Dr. Mayor after dinner at the TV center.

I noticed that I was not completely alone in growing restive. In the opening stages the play was interesting enough as simple spectacle: pieces not being moved dropped to one knee to facilitate the audience's view, and there were pauses at intervals to emphasize a particularly skilled piece of development. Usually there was a spattering of applause when this happened, and once there was a burst of approving cries as well. The taking of a piece was pantomimed with short daggers, and the victim was then carried from the board by two pawns of the opposing side and dumped on the lawn. The whole thing took place almost in silence, aside from the tap of the drum which signaled each move, and the occasional clapping.

But once the slow routine of the end game set in, with the pawns solemnly moving their one square forward in monotonous alternation, almost everyone except Garcia and a few others (Garcia himself, I noticed, was reliving the game in an agony of nervousness) adopted polite but bored expressions and signaled more and more often to the hovering waiters for a tray of drinks.

The most noticeable exceptions to this rule, aside from Garcia, were President Vados and Diaz. Vados watched with as much attention as a fan at a Melbourne test (the likeness reminded me that sometime I ought to go home and see another Shield match—sometime); Diaz, on the other hand, seemed to be watching Vados almost as closely as the game itself.

Once, when the game had been halted for a particular move to sink in, Vados happened to glance at his Minister of the Interior. Their eyes met. A muscle in Vados's cheek tensed suddenly. Diaz's hands clenched, with deliberation, as if squeezing something that wasn't there. The tableau lasted a few seconds; then both at once looked back toward the game, with a suspicion of guilt, like children pretending they hadn't been disobedient.

There had been dislike in their expressions. Or perhaps not dislike, no. Something nearer to—nearer to hatred, and yet tempered with a mutual respect. I thought of all the stories I'd heard about their rivalry. Well, there it was, burning brightly. And unless habit had enabled them to control it, it was violent enough to break loose.

The pieces finished their complicated maneuverings; the white king dropped to his knees and bent his head. The black king stepped from the board, bowed before Garcia, and gave him the dagger from his side, before escorting him across the board to administer the *coup de grace* in pantomime. Vados led the applause, and Garcia stood between the two tall kings smiling and nervously fingering his spectacles.

Then Diaz looked at Vados again. This time he smiled: a great loose-lipped smile that exposed a broken tooth.

Beside me, Señora Cortés gathered herself together with a sigh.

"Well, that's over," she said with satisfaction. "Now we only have to join the line of people waiting to say good-bye to the president, and we can get away."

" 'Belita!" interrupted her husband, a distant look in his eyes. "You're going back to the studios, aren't you? I want to stay and have a word with Pablo about that king's knight development in the opening—I haven't seen him use it before."

"Very well," said Señora Cortés composedly. "I'll see you at home tonight."

Cortés pushed his way through the dissolving crowd; servants rerolled the chessboard and carted it away; I went to receive Vados's nod of dismissal and returned to my car.

This was a cock-eyed country, I was thinking as I drove away down the road to the city. Chess champions for public heroes; public opinion molded by subliminal perception, without any great effort made to conceal the fact; primitive squalor next door to buildings as modern as tomorrow. What a weird city this "child" of Vados's had turned out to be. . . .

And what was I to make of this subliminal perception business, anyway? Maria Posador had been right to assume—as she had—that I would react against it; yet now I had been told by Cortés that he had himself made appalling discoveries in the shantytowns, and Cortés struck me as a man not only of high intelligence but of a certain old-fashioned rectitude, a man to whom telling a lie, no matter how worthy a cause it furthered, would be repulsive. Again, in all honesty, I must reserve judgment, I told myself. And, in the same moment, I wondered how much of that impulse was true honesty, how much simple unwillingness to commit myself beyond the bounds of the field in which I was skilled.

It became clear as I reentered the city that since the frightened reaction of last night and this morning life had swung back toward normality; at any rate, there was a liveliness of the kind that was customary on saint's day evenings, with many people in the bars and restaurants, and occasional groups of musicians playing in the squares and on street corners. In a vague hope that I might likewise get back to normal, I collected my camera and notebooks and went out into the market quarter again.

But here the stamp of the panic that had followed the Guerrero killing was impressed heavily even now. The streets were quiet; a municipal street sprinkler had been through them, and the surface of the road was shiny with recent wet.

I passed a small shrine set in the wall of one of the houses—a crude clay statuette of the Virgin, with a niche around it and a shelf with some candle spikes in front. There were several candles guttering here, one of them with a notice stuck on it. I lifted the sheet of paper and read it.

"For the soul of Mario Guerrero," it said in Spanish. "He was killed by those"—then a word I couldn't understand but which I presumed to be an obscenity—"Indians who themselves are without souls."

"*Ay!*" said a harsh voice from across the street. "*No toce!*"

I swung my head. Two ruffian-type men stepped from a dark doorway opposite, each carrying a heavy cudgel. I tensed myself as they approached.

"*Qué hace Vd.?*" said one of them threateningly. The other, after scrutinizing my face closely, motioned to his companion to lower his club.

"*Es el Señor Hakluyt, no?*" he said. "I have seen your honor on the television. Apologies, señor—we set that candle there as a warning and a reminder to these peasants that the death of Mario Guerrero"—he crossed himself—"will not go unavenged. It will be well, if you desire peace, not to come this way again."

"Thanks for the advice," I said shortly, and made at a smart pace for the end of the street. If I was going to have to contend with belligerent supporters of the Citizens' Party, I might equally well get involved with Tezol's faction, and no contract was going to make me risk my life in a street brawl.

As a concession to duty, I went back to the main traffic nexus and spent a couple of hours counting the flow, before deciding to call it a day and going to bed.

I really needed at least another week's work before progressing to a digest of my results; on the other hand, with the city in its present abnormal condition I would probably be

fouling up my averages if I combined current data with what
I already had. Rather than waste time, therefore, I settled
down for the next two days at the traffic department, con-
verting vehicle counts into computer data and running them,
setting limits to my parameters, and developing the first
approximations for the terms in my main equations. Owing
to the relatively small quantity of data I had to hand, I
went through the job rather more quickly than I really liked.
But Angers was much impressed when, at noon on Friday,
he found me actually sketching a diagram of a tentative re-
vised layout for the market area.

I told him, of course, that I had no real idea whether or
not it would serve the purpose and that it usually took me at
least six tries to find a scheme that even approximately suited
the realities; he brushed aside the perfectly true statement as
praiseworthy modesty and took me to lunch in the Plaza del
Norte.

I didn't really like the smooth-spoken Englishman; he was
too—too dustproof. But he certainly knew highway engineering. He had, so he told me, left Britain in despair because
although that country's roads were notoriously the worst of
any major nation in the world, there was no coherent traffic
policy. He had worked for a time in Commonwealth countries
and had had a hand in the West African Coastway; then he
had helped to design two freeways in the States and the
Manhattan Southern Overflow, and after that, as in his view
the British *still* didn't have a proper traffic policy, he had
given up all intention of returning home and come to Vados
instead. When he talked about the Manhattan Southern Overflow, my opinion of him went up a notch—he had been
supervisory engineer on Section K, which I had often traveled
while I lived in New York.

We were having a minor technical dispute when a heavy
hand fell on my shoulder, and I found Fats Brown's ample
bulk eclipsing the sun.

" 'Lo, Hakluyt," he said in a cloud of cigar smoke. "Got
news you might like to hear."

He ignored Angers completely. Nettled, the Englishman
addressed him.

"Hello, Brown! We don't often see you here—have you actually secured a client who can pay his fee, for a change?"

"Your pal Andres Lucas is the one who worries about lining his pockets," said Brown unconcernedly. "I'm the guy who worries about seeing justice done, remember? I'm easy to recognize, 'cause I'm damn near unique in Vados. Like I was saying, Hakluyt," he continued, while Angers scowled, "it looks like I've managed to fix Judge Romero, thanks to Mig's pull with Diaz. Gonzales has ordered a new trial. So I came out here to celebrate. If you want to congratulate Mig, he's over there lunchin' with me. See you around, Hakluyt. So long."

He lumbered back to his own table. Angers glared after him. "Interfering blighter!" he said under his breath. "No business of *his*, our legal system, but he never stops trying to knock holes in it. Hah!" He ground his cigarette into an ashtray and stood up.

"Coming back to the office now?"

"In a little while," I said. "I have to pick up some books at the hotel. I'll see you later."

The books were a pretext; I was more interested to see how the lunchtime meeting in the Plaza del Sur was going. I'd missed the morning papers, and I wanted to know if the National Party had plucked up sufficient courage to put in another appearance yet.

But when I reached the plaza, there was no meeting going on at all. Instead, perhaps a hundred policemen were lounging under the trees, most of them smoking and throwing dice. A few of them were clustered around a chessboard on which two of their number were playing.

Puzzled, I entered the hotel. The commissionaire saluted me, and I wondered whether to ask him what had happened. Then I reflected that he probably wouldn't know, just as he had "not known" on the day of my arrival, and changed my mind altogether as I caught sight of Maria Posador in the lounge, idly moving pieces on one of the chessboard-topped tables, an unlit Russian cigarette between her fingers. She looked worried.

She greeted me with a faint smile as I came up, and gestured at the chair opposite her. "Would you care for that game of chess now, señor?" she invited. "I feel in need of a small distraction."

"I'm sorry to disappoint you," I said. "I have to get back to the traffic department. But perhaps you can tell me—why no meeting in the square today?"

She shrugged. "There was considerable disturbance there yesterday. Diaz has decreed that there shall be no more meetings until the furore over Guerrero's death has died down."

"Is the trouble very bad?"

"It is something that may divide the city into warring camps," she answered absently. She slid pieces into position with expert fingers as she spoke, leaving them set up as though to start a new game. "Thus!"

"I don't think I've come to Vados at a very healthy time." I tried to speak lightly; that was a failure. She raised her violet eyes to my face.

"Had it not been you, señor, it might have been anyone else. It was what the situation dictated, that is all. No, the death of Mario Guerrero is all part of a pattern—it is, you might say, one symptom of a disease that is poisoning our lives. There is a corruption, a fundamental rottenness—and each part of it renews the corruptness of the rest. You are doubtless aware that Señor Seixas in the treasury department has a strong interest in seeing new highways built, at whatever cost in money or human happiness, for it will be into his pocket that goes the—the financial oil that lubricates such deals in our country. Oh, this is widely known! Yet what happens when our good friend Felipe Mendoza tries to expose this bribery—he, a man whom success has not spoiled, who knows his duty to his fellow citizens? Seixas takes the telephone in his hand and speaks to his friend the judge, Señor Romero. And today he is armed with an injunction against Señor Mendoza, and in its shelter he can proceed with his shady negotiations, while the truth is hidden from the people. I become revolted, señor." She grimaced.

"But enough, Señor Hakluyt, enough of that. Have you

reflected on the things I showed to you the other day?"

I chose my words carefully. "I have," I said. "In fact, I spoke to Señora Cortés of the television service, and her husband, the professor, admitted at once without my asking that they use this technique. I don't like it myself, but according to what Cortés says, they seem to have some justification, at any rate—"

She seemed to wilt like a flower in an oven. "Yes, Señor Hakluyt. I have no doubt there was also some justification at any rate for Belsen. Good day to you."

And she lapsed into a silent reflection so complete that I do not think her eyes registered me as I passed through her field of vision on leaving.

XIII

All that weekend I felt as though I were walking down a tunnel on the verge of collapse. The threat of violence, which had bared its teeth for twenty-four hours after Guerrero died, still snarled across the city; one saw it in the way certain people walked circumspectly on the street, in the way others— who they were, of course, I didn't know, but there were many of them—stayed out of sight. This was a conflict that engaged the Vadeanos from the cabinet minister to the factory worker. I thought of what Señora Posador had said about splitting the city into warring camps.

And yet . . . well, perhaps it was Vados's firm hand on the controls. At least the threat of violence remained snarling rather than biting.

On Saturday *Tiempo*'s headlines concerned Dominguez's victory over Romero—they claimed it as a victory, at least. Not quite overshadowed by this was a spirited defense of Felipe Mendoza, over the signature of his brother Cristoforo, editor of the paper. Though there was no direct mention of the fact, I presumed this was a reaction to the event Señora Posador had told me about—Seixas's injunction against Mendoza. The article found space to praise Señora Posador as well, referred to Dominguez in the next breath, and topped off by calling Juan Tezol "loyal defender of the people's freedom." The whole tone of the article was sickly-patriotic and bombastic.

The more I sought to get ahead with my work, the more circumstances seemed to conspire to make speed impossible. And—what was worse—the more complex became the situation in which I was involuntarily caught up.

Oh, there were probably decent people on both sides—and that was half my personal trouble. Aside from Francis, who was now out of the calculation anyway, the Nationals were probably well-meaning enough, from Mendoza to Dominguez. In spite of her notorious grudge against Vados, Maria Posador seemed to have rational fears to back up her opposition, and certainly Judge Romero had treated Dominguez in a way no one of his eminence should have done.

But the political atmosphere here was of the hothouse kind. The least incident capable of being made to bear political fruit was being nurtured, protected from frost and fed with manure until it blossomed out of all proportion. The only hard case of grievance on either side, so far as I could see, was the death of Guerrero—and that, since Francis was in custody, was emotionally based.

At the time, I now realized, I had been oddly little affected by seeing Guerrero die. The incident was so brief, so nearly unreal. I'd seen men die before—twice in brawls between construction-gang workers, several times from accidents on the job or in the street. As the days slipped by and as the resentment engendered by Guerrero's death continued to fester in the city, I was coming to see that people who had perhaps never met Guerrero in their lives had been far more affected by his death than I who had seen it take place.

And that could have only one implication. No man could have meant so much to so many strangers unless he was a symbol. A symbol of very great importance.

They buried him on Sunday, after a service in the cathedral at which Bishop Cruz officiated in person. The city stopped, and crowds lined the sidewalks to watch the cortege, the women almost all in black, the men with black bands on their arms or black ribbons on their lapels, and black ties if they wore ties at all.

Symbol.

O'Rourke had every available police officer on duty along the route of the funeral procession, which was as well, for half a dozen attempts were made to start disturbances. I assumed at first that they were organized by the National Party; I learned later, however, that it was actually students from the university who had been responsible, and they were demonstrating against the National Party, not against Guerrero and the Citizens of Vados.

The funeral left renewed tension in its wake, as a ship crossing calm water leaves a swell that may endure for hours. Symbol, I said again to myself, and saw that perhaps I should seek a reason for my own unasked-for and unmerited notoriety here.

Maria Posador had said, "Had it not been you, señor, it might have been anyone else. It was what the situation dictated."

Exactly. As a neurosis caused by repression manifests itself in ways that may bear no resemblance at all to the root of the trouble, so the repressed tension in Ciudad de Vados was showing itself—here, there, disconnected as though poking from a wall of fog, seizing what focal event or personality came to hand and crystallizing briefly around it.

Ill chance decreed that I should be one of the focal personalities it fastened on. And once the process had begun, how to fight it? How to struggle against that amorphous combination of emotions, desires, fears, jealousies, now ruling Ciudad de Vados? I was beginning to feel hemmed in, chained, a prisoner, pushed at by impersonal forces, denied the most essential liberty, which I had all my life prized: liberty to do the work I did best in the best possible way.

Yet, somehow, two more days of illusory calm slipped by. I spent most of them in the traffic department, trying to force some sort of order on a chaotic lot of computer figures, struggling to reduce abstract flow patterns to terms of what José and Lola would see, hear, think as they passed on their way. I contrived nearly to forget a lot of things—among them, the suit that Sigueiras was bringing against the traffic department.

But on Wednesday morning Angers warned me that the legal resources of his side were drying up. Lucas had secured one adjournment and had taken advantage of the time to organize his case against Sam Francis—but then, there was no question of the outcome of that trial.

I shuffled some papers together, lit a cigarette, and sat back to look at Angers, rearranging my thinking. I said, "So you mean that subpoena you gave me may have to be used?"

"So Lucas warns me," said Angers.

"Now there's a point," I said. "I don't get one or two things about this legal setup here. This Lucas seems to have fingers in a hell of a lot of different pies. I thought it was practically universal for lawyers to stick to either the criminal law or the civil law. Yet this guy Lucas keeps cropping up in both civil and criminal cases. Why?"

"You ask some complicated questions," sighed Angers. "I suppose the short answer is that it's part of the Mayor theory of government. Mayor has influenced Vados a hell of a lot, you know. And among his other principles is one to the effect that all contraventions of justice are the business of the state. So in Vados itself—although not yet in the rest of the country, I believe—there's no real distinction between civil and criminal. A private citizen who can't afford to litigate against someone he thinks has injured him can apply for the state to prosecute on his behalf, for example. And that kind of case actually occurs every now and then.

"But in Lucas's case, it's rather different. Actually, he is a criminal lawyer. It's just that his position as legal adviser to the Citizens' Party involves him in a good many associated cases. And, of course, having helped to draft the charter of incorporation for the city, he also gets called in when a case like this one of Sigueiras's comes up."

"He sounds like a busy man."

"He is."

"Didn't you tell me to expect a subpoena from Fats Brown as well, by the way?" I recalled. "What happened? I never got it."

"Things haven't been going too well for Brown," said Angers rather smugly. "I'm told that when he heard we were going to call you, he discarded the idea. Lucas says he's been floundering a bit in court, too. Apparently he's upset by what this fellow Dominguez did the other day."

"Brown doesn't strike me as the kind of man that upsets easily," I said. "What did Dominguez do?"

"Oh, didn't you hear? Well, there was a disgraceful article by Cristoforo Mendoza in *Tiempo* last weekend, in which he gratuitously defended Dominguez against what Judge Romero had said about him—and Dominguez wrote to them and to *Liberdad* saying he didn't welcome assistance from the organ of a party whose leaders were given to committing murder in broad daylight."

"And *Tiempo* published the letter?"

"No, of course not. But *Liberdad* did."

I nodded slowly. "So he's transferred his allegiance to the party that commits its murders stealthily by night, I suppose?"

"What exactly do you mean by that, Hakluyt?" said Angers, his tone implying that I ought not to mean anything at all.

"Nothing," I said peaceably. "Nothing. I'm neutral, remember? So I suppose it's my duty to regard both political parties as equally repugnant."

"There's a difference between the Citizens of Vados and the National Party," said Angers stiffly; before he could get going on the nature of that difference, I apologized and told him to finish what he was saying about Dominguez.

"There isn't any more," he said shortly. "Except that, of course, Judge Romero is sharpening a knife for Brown. Brown is supposed to have put Dominguez up to it—did you know?"

"Up to writing to *Liberdad*?"

"Oh, come now!" said Angers in a tone of irritation. "Of course not! I don't quite see what you're playing at, Hakluyt, but you seem to be deliberately obtuse today."

"I've got a head full of data," I said. "These political machinations make a hell of a lot less sense to me than the stuff spewed out by a computer. When am I supposed to show up in court?"

"Possibly this afternoon. I'll let you know before lunch."

They told me to be on hand at two-thirty. I shouldn't have bothered to be punctual; I spent the afternoon kicking my heels in an anteroom before the usher came to tell me the court was rising for the day. I used up a few well-chosen words on the subject of the law's delays and was going out past the door of the courtroom when it slammed open and shut and Fats Brown stormed down the corridor ahead of me. When he was some distance away, he must have recognized the glimpse he had had of me in passing; he stopped in his tracks and turned to wait for me.

"Evenin', Hakluyt," he said. "Warn you, I'm gonna make mincemeat outa you when Lucas brings you on. I like expert witnesses—lunch off 'em every day. They take themselves too seriously. Let's go have a drink. Unorthodox for the plaintiff's lawyer to drink with the defendant's witnesses—probably get hell for attempted bribery if Lucas hears about it. Hell with it all. C'mon."

It made no difference to me whom I drank with, after wasting the entire afternoon. I went with him to the same small bar we had gone to after Guerrero's death. Brown ordered one of his appalling local soft drinks; I had an aguardiente. We clinked glasses.

"No good askin' you what you're gonna say in the box," Fats ruminated after his first sip. "You'd go all high-hat an' say you'll answer the questions put to you. Better at improvisin' my attacks on expert witnesses; find their weak spots an' enlarge on them. Hope I'm not worryin' you."

"Not much," I said.

"Won't talk shop anymore," he went on. "Um—hear about Mig?"

"Dissociating himself from that article in *Tiempo* the other day? Angers just told me about it."

"Ah-hah. Guess Mig an' I were the only two guys in Vados who knew about it beforehand. Clever! Wish I'd thought of it!"

"You what?"

He gave me a faintly surprised look. His eyes nearly disappeared in rolls of fat as he wheezed into an enormous laugh. "You thought it was a run-out? Oh-ho-ho-ho! Hakluyt, you're dumber'n a Vadeano when you try! That was strictly for the—hey, of course! It was strictly for the boids, and here's a Boyd who swallowed it. Heh-heh-heh-heh!"

I waited for him to finish chortling. "Since you think it was so clever," I suggested, "suppose you tell me why."

"Pipeline for the scandal of the legal world, that's me. Sure I'll tell you. Mig was in a pretty sticky position. Romero had smeared him 'bout as thorough as he could. He had to get himself out of it in the eyes of the reputable citizens of Vados, get? So up he stan's an' makes this dignified an' lawyerlike statement—all hogwash, but like I said, Vadeanos are dumb once you get out of the gutter, where they're sly as foxes. Anyway, people give him another look an' say, 'Not such a bad guy! That's pretty good!' Result—swing of public opinion. Romero's wondering if he'll stay around long enough to finish what he started on Tezol. Didya know it was Romero tried that case? No? Trust the old coot to grab himself anything where the National Party's involved. Hates their guts."

"So I gathered," I agreed. "But how do you mean—finish what he started on Tezol? Did he pay his fine?"

"Romero gave him time to find the cash. Prob'ly thought he'd make him squirm a bit. Anyway, here's Romero, he says to himself, right, this guy Dominguez is chickening out, won't have the guts to push through what he started against me. So what does Romero do? He goes on TV—one of this bastard Rioco's little programs, sat around for days while he was tryin' to make up his mind. I got advance word of it from a pal at the studios—they're finally going to shove it out. Tonight. He's goin' to lambaste Tezol an' take a swipe or two at Cris Mendoza for good measure, an' say what he's gonna do when that fine's not paid." Brown sipped his drink. "Think he'd have learned his lesson by now, wouldn't you? They make out he's a fine respectable upholder of justice an' all that crap. Well, figure for yourself what'll happen when

Mig shows him up as an ol' blowhard who don't even know what evidence means!"

"You mean when this case against Guerrero's chauffeur is tried again?" I said.

Brown finished his drink and nodded; his cheeks shook. I finished mine also and called for a repeat.

"Confusion to you in the witness box!" Brown said with a big grin, and lifted the glass.

"Down with lawyers," I replied.

The television set at the end of the bar came on; it was six o'clock. I saw the familiar face of Francisco Córdoban smiling down at me. I deliberately turned my back. Whether or not the picture they interspersed with the programs by subliminal perception were a fair representation of the state of things, I preferred to form my own judgments.

I had a sudden vision of Maria Posador, perched on the bench in the concrete shed where she had shown me those pictures, her long slim legs swinging, her lovely face drawn and serious.

"Well, see you tomorrow," Brown said after a pause, gulping the contents of his glass. The CO_2 in the drink came back in an unashamed burp. "Make a mess of you—promise. 'Night."

I stayed only a few minutes longer myself and then went back to my hotel, intending to have dinner there. First, though, I went upstairs to clean up and change my shirt—the day was hot and sticky, and even the air-conditioned court building had wilted the one I was wearing.

There was a man sitting in my room reading one of my textbooks.

I stopped with one hand still on my key, in the act of withdrawing it from the lock, and said in an incredulous voice, "Who in hell's name are you?"

Unconcernedly, he shut the book. Then he rose very leisurely to his feet. "Good evening, Señor Hakluyt," he said. "Please come in. Close the door, if you don't mind."

I took a good look at him. He was six feet two and broad-shouldered. He had big hands, which held the fat textbook as though it were a paperback. He had dark brown skin, darker than sun-tan, and his hair was inclined to be nappy. He wore a gray suit, a real silk shirt, expensive hand-lasted shoes. Diamond cuff links. Platinum watch. Wealthy.

He outweighed me by about forty pounds; he outreached me by inches in every direction. Obviously, I couldn't throw him out. Well, either he was here for some good reason—in which case I had better hear what he had to say—or he wasn't. And if he wasn't, maybe I still ought to hear what he had to say. I shut the door.

"Thank you," he said. He spoke good English with a vanishing trace of a local accent. "I should apologize for the intrusion, but it was necessary, I assure you. Kindly be seated."

With a generous gesture he offered me the chair he had been sitting in. I shook my head.

"Well, our talk may take some time, but if you prefer to stand, let us not argue." His eyes twinkled. "My name, señor, is José Dalban, and I have come to discuss with you the subject of your presence in Ciudad de Vados."

"I'm here," I said shortly. "What else is there to say?"

"Oh, very much! Very much indeed! Such as why you are here, and what you are doing. Now please"—he raised one hand; the broad palm was very bright pink—"do not try to be elusive and say you are only here because you signed a contract and you are doing only what that contract calls for. What I wish to make clear to you is what your contract implies—what misery and deprivation for how many human beings."

"Señor Dalban," I said, taking a deep breath, "I've probably heard all this before. I know quite well that if I do what I came here to do, a lot of people are going to be made temporarily homeless. I can't see, though, that anything could be much worse than the so-called homes they have at the moment. Sooner or later the government is going to have to face the problem squarely; till then, what I do isn't going to be as important as you seem to claim."

"I represent," he said, not answering me directly—he sounded as if he were launching into a prepared speech—"a group of private individuals who are afraid that if the government's plans are put into effect, there will be civil war in Aguazul, and that soon. I have come to suggest to you that you might consider changing your mind. You would not, of course, lose by doing so. You might even profit."

"Out of the question," I said. "For one thing, I'm a freelance expert. I've worked for years to build up my reputation. If I quit this job, it wouldn't just be a contract I'd broken; it would be a setback to my professional status."

"Señor Hakluyt," said Dalban, blinking rapidly, "we are businessmen, we for whom I speak. We are not poor. If it were necessary, we would guarantee your earnings for life—outside Aguazul."

"The *hell* with money!" I snapped. "I do this work because it's the work I want to do! And let me tell you this. Getting rid of me would solve nothing. Nothing at all. If I don't do the job, since the government seems determined to have it done by somebody, Angers and his crowd in the city traffic department will probably be turned loose on it. They're not competent. The result will be a botched makeshift worse than what you've got already."

Dalban looked at me steadily for a long while before speaking again. "I apologize," he said at last. "I had been of the impression that you did not know what you were doing. I realize you have given much thought to the matter. The only cause for regret is that you have come to a wrong conclusion."

"If there's going to be civil war in Aguazul, then it's not going to be my fault," I retorted. "The suggestion is ridiculous."

"You must accept, señor, that your departure would materially improve our chances of escaping that civil war." Dalban kept his voice level. "I fully realize that you did not choose the key position in which you now find yourself; however, it will be the act of an intelligent man to recognize the fact that you are of importance and that your least decision now affects many people beside yourself."

He smiled. "Therefore I must say this. Either you change your mind voluntarily—or means will be found to compel you to do so. You will find me in the telephone directory if you want me: José Dalban. Good night."

He went past me and opened and shut the door with a swift coordinated movement. The instant he was out of the room I went to the phone and rang the reception desk, demanding that Dalban be stopped before he left the hotel, demanding how he had got into my room in the first place.

The receptionist, bland-voiced, echoed the name. "Dalban, señor? Yes, I would recognize Señor Dalban. But he is not in the hotel."

Infuriated, I realized that bribes must have passed somewhere. Large ones, which would stick. I demanded the manager and got no satisfaction out of him, either. Blank-faced, he poured out streams of denials in his own defense—adding assertions about the rectitude of Señor Dalban and the unlikelihood of his doing any such thing as I accused him of.

"Who is this bastard, anyway?" I demanded.

"Why, he is a businessman of great distinction and wealth, señor! Even if he were to desire to do such a thing, he would not come himself—he would send an agent!"

"Get me an agent," I said. "Of police. And with speed!"

A blank-faced man who might have been the manager's elder brother was brought; with an air of pandering to the whim of a mad foreigner, he took down particulars in a scrawling hand and promised to report it at the police station. I had a suspicion that report would never materialize; in a last burst of annoyance I called police headquarters and demanded to speak to *el Jefe* O'Rourke in person.

O'Rourke wasn't there. A sour-voiced lieutenant took my name and promised to investigate. By the time I was through with him, apathy had dulled my anger.

It didn't really matter, anyway. The city council was supposed to have been having me followed outside the hotel, for my own protection; I only hoped the protection worked. But whoever Dalban was, and whomever else he represented, they were thinking with their muscles. If threats and bribes were their chosen technique, then I wanted nothing to do with them. I was going ahead with my job come hell or high water.

Still, there were times, and this was one of them, when I felt I was a stubborn idiot and wished I wasn't.

XIV

"Much the sort of thing I'd have expected the Nationals to try," said Angers thoughtfully. "I'm glad you told Dalban to go to hell, Hakluyt—I always thought you were a pretty square sort of fellow, in spite of our differences."

In his way, I supposed, he meant that as a compliment. I returned it by taking it as one. I said only, "Is Dalban tied up with the Nationals, then? If they can afford to buy me out, then why haven't they paid this fine Tezol owes?"

Angers shrugged. "I wouldn't put it past them to let him go hang. Peasants are two a penny, and the men behind the National Party—the ones you don't hear about, but who really matter—are said to be pretty unscrupulous."

"I hope that's not gospel truth. If it is, I'm in for a thin time. The hotel staff were almost certainly bribed to deny admitting Dalban to my room—but I had hoped to get more action from the police than I did."

Angers gave vent to a short coughing sound that might have been a cynical laugh. "I'm not surprised myself," he said. "If there's any truth in the rumors I've heard, Dalban ought long ago to have been run out of the country—would have been unless he had the police in his pocket. You're muddying some pretty deep waters, Hakluyt."

"So Dalban informed me."

His wintry smile put in a brief appearance. "Don't let it get you down. You're a valuable piece of property, if I may say so. Despite what Dalban said, he isn't really in a position to pull anything; he's precariously balanced already, and the slightest error would bring him tumbling down. He can talk, but his threats are empty ones." He frowned. "And yet I don't know that the matter can be left there, because attempted bribery of a government employee is a serious offense."

I was tempted to say something about the stories of corruption I'd heard since my arrival, but refrained. Angers looked at the wall clock and got to his feet.

141

"We'd better go down to the court," he said. "Session begins at ten. I don't expect you'll be kept waiting today."

In the corridors of the court building there was hustle and bustle—or the nearest approach to it that you get under a Latin American sun. Angers excused himself to go and have a word with Lucas, and left me standing alone, looking about me for people I knew. I caught sight of Fats Brown talking to Sigueiras in impassioned Spanish; aside from the color of their skins, the two were oddly alike—fat, untidy, given to loud talking and gesticulation.

"G-good morning, Mr. Hakluyt," a voice murmured near me. I turned to find Caldwell, the young man from the city health department, together with an aggressive little man with hard eyes behind his horn-rimmed glasses and a shock of ruffled hair. I remembered Señora Cortés had pointed this man out to me at the presidential garden party, but could not recall his name or office.

"Good morning," I said. "Are you involved in this?"

"Of c-course," he said with dignity. "My d-department's proof of nuisance is very important."

His companion spoke up suddenly. "Forgive Nicky's bad manners, Señor Hakluyt. Permit me to present myself. My name is Ruiz, Alonzo Ruiz, and it is a pleasure for me to meet you. I am a doctor," he finished with a sudden lessening of his vehemence.

I remembered and shook his hand. "You're the—uh—the director of health and hygiene, aren't you? Glad to meet you. You're giving evidence, too, I take it."

"Assuredly, señor! Why, I have statistics to demonstrate that the presence of this slum of Sigueiras's has raised the typhoid rate in Ciudad de Vados one hundred and twenty per cent in the past ten years—"

An usher walked down the corridor announcing that the court would be in session in five minutes; Angers hastened back as I was starting to look for the anteroom where I had spent yesterday afternoon and wishing that I'd brought a good book.

"It's all right, Hakluyt," Angers said breathlessly. "I arranged with Lucas to ask the judge to let witnesses sit in court today—something about special circumstances. He'll fix it."

He did. Three minutes after the judge had taken his seat, an usher escorted me into the courtroom. I was given a place near Angers and sat down under the glaring eyes of Fats Brown. Presumably he'd just had a fast one put over on him, and he wasn't enjoying it.

I looked around the court—this was a room identical to the one where Dominguez had had his ears pinned back the other day—and stiffened as I recognized two of the people in the public seats. Side by side in the front row were Felipe Mendoza—and Maria Posador.

She looked at me expressionlessly, her red lips slightly parted, and at length shook her head once, as though I had failed in some important test. Annoyed, I turned my head away.

But that was interesting, finding those two here. Another case with political implications. It looked as though half the courts in the city were becoming battlegrounds for the rival factions.

Having recovered from his annoyance, Fats Brown got up with a bored air and asked leave to address the court.

"I should like to make it plain," he said, "why in my view it makes no difference whether or not witnesses sit in court. Obviously it makes no difference. Failing perjury, nothing can hide the simple fact that the city traffic department, the city council, and that man Angers over there have conspired to deprive my client of his citizen's rights and many hundreds of people of their homes."

The bang of the judge's gavel coincided with Lucas's fierce, "Objection!"

"Sustained," said the judge. "Struck from the record. Señor Brown, when appearing before a jury, interjections of that kind serve some purpose. I assure you I'm unimpressed by them."

"Yes, your honor," said Brown, unabashed. "It was purely for the benefit of the reporters."

The judge—he was a distinguished-looking man of about

fifty—half-smiled. Plainly he made allowances for Fats; equal-ly plainly, the fact annoyed Andres Lucas. I glanced at what I presumed was the press table and saw five men and a girl exchanging amused whispers.

"So many reporters?" I said under my breath to Angers. He glanced in the direction I indicated and gave a nod.

"*Liberdad, Tiempo,* a commentator from the radio, and I should think someone from the local papers in Cuatrovientos, Puerto Joaquin, and Astoria Negra."

"This case must be attracting a lot of attention."

"Haven't you seen today's papers? It is."

The judge was frowning down at Angers; he sat back with a mutter of apology.

"Continue, Señor Brown," the judge invited.

Having got his first thrust in, Brown seemed to have calmed down. He had obviously presented most of his case the previous day; he reviewed it now, referring to witnesses who had deposed that they had no alternative accommodation, that in their view Señor Sigueiras was a public benefactor rather than a nuisance, and that they could not have stayed in their villages because their water supply had been diverted to Ciudad de Vados.

Then he quoted the city's charter of incorporation at some length and asked leave of the court to recall his witnesses if need be to rebut counter-allegations made by the defense. Then he rested his case.

Here Lucas took over, and I had to admit that the man was a master of legal expertise. With assured authority, he took Brown's interpretation of the relevant clauses of the charter and tore it to shreds—Fats looked definitely unhappy while this was going on. But obviously the mere letter of the law was not in dispute in this case; the city definitely had a right to subordinate citizens' rights to redevelopment plans. What Sigueiras was saying was that if it hadn't been for the intention to dispossess him personally, there wouldn't have been any redevelopment plans; Brown was attempting to show on his behalf that the city council, the traffic department, and Angers—named conjointly in the suit—were motivated by malice rather than by a desire to benefit the citizens.

So it ultimately came down to the question of nuisance. And Lucas, winding up his opening speech, announced that he proposed to get rid of the imputation of malice and prove the nuisance beyond doubt.

The judge, sitting with a smile of appreciation on his face, recollected that it was time for the noon recess and stepped down.

He resumed his seat for the afternoon session with an air of expectancy; so did all of us. Lucas proceeded to call Angers, and Angers stoutly denied the imputation of malice. He made a good impression, I thought, studying the judge. But when Fats Brown lumbered to his feet, he had a sleepy, dangerous twinkle in his eye.

"Angers, are you honestly stating before this court that it's bothersome to you to have this ground under the monorail central lying idle, when there ought to be a main road across it?"

"Of course not."

"Does its present employment interfere with access to the station? Or with the flow of passengers?"

Angers frowned. "It's definitely a nuisance to passengers."

"That's not the point. Is it? What's at issue is the motive of your department. Have you any specific proposal for redevelopment of this ground?"

Angers suddenly looked acutely uncomfortable, and stammered over his reply, with a glance at me. Lucas rose to intervene smoothly, saying that a later witness—me, presumably—would deal with that point. But Brown's thrust had gone home, and he exploited it.

"In fact," he wound up, his voice dripping sarcasm, "you decided that as cover for your attempt to evict Sigueiras you'd hire this outside expert and invent—yes, invent!—a new use for his ground so as to cheat him of his legal rights. Yes or no?"

"I—" began Angers, but Brown had thrown up his hands in disgust and sat down.

I began to see how Brown had acquired his reputation. All Lucas's careful smoothing-over couldn't hide the fact that a great hole had been knocked in Angers' statements. I saw Señora Posador and Mendoza looking satisfied.

Lucas had less luck still with his next witness—Caldwell. The poor guy stammered more than ever. Trading on this, Lucas made a great show of sympathy and got the court's leave to introduce affidavits covering some of the evidence about the menace to the health and well-being of the citizens at large caused by Sigueiras's slum.

Brown was not so kind. He kept Caldwell in the box for almost an hour, forcing one admission after another—that conditions in the slum were no worse than others in Puerto Joaquin; that there was no adequate alternative accommodations; that, in short, poverty was the root of the trouble and of everyone in a position to do anything to ameliorate it; only Sigueiras had taken practical steps to help the sufferers.

I leaned across to Angers, who was still sweating after his brush with Fats Brown, and whispered, "Clever, isn't he?" I wasn't looking forward with much enthusiasm to my own examination.

"Very," said Angers, forcing a ghastly smile. "I don't like to think what *Tiempo* will say about today's proceedings."

Ruiz now entered the box with an aggressive air and stood with both hands on the rail before him like a captain on the bridge of his ship, looking around the court. He showed every desire to talk, and talk Lucas let him—about health statistics, about the high incidence of disease, about the moral corruption among the slum-dwellers, about fears that people had expressed to him lest their children should associate in state schools with the children of the peasants, about the direct relation he had discovered between the growth of the slum and the typhoid fever rate in Vados. . . .

The day's time was almost up when Lucas finished his own questions, but long enough remained for Brown to start on his, and only a few words had been exchanged when it became clear that Ruiz had dug his heels in and was not going to yield an inch. Brown began to mop his forehead at intervals; Ruiz spoke more and more like an orator making a major speech.

In the public seats, Maria Posador and Felipe Mendoza

grew tense and frequently exchanged glances; correspondingly, Lucas and Angers began to relax and every now and again to smile faintly. Angers leaned toward me and whispered, "He's doing very well, isn't he?"

I nodded.

"Very sound man," Angers continued softly. "He's the President's personal physician. One of the best doctors in the country."

"I don't *care* about the situation in Puerto Joaquin!" Ruiz was exclaiming heatedly. "I'm only concerned with the situation in Ciudad de Vados, which is what this case is about! I'm saying that this slum represents a menace to mental and physical health, and the sooner something is done about it the better. It doesn't really matter what, so long as it's got rid of."

"Have you finished your examination, Señor Brown?" the judge put in.

Fats shook his head.

"Then I'm afraid you'll have to continue it tomorrow. Court adjourned."

I noticed that Brown's forehead was deeply etched with lines of thought as he left the court with Sigueiras, hands clasped behind him, plodding alongside.

Angers had to join Lucas and Ruiz for a further discussion of the case; accordingly, I was leaving the building by myself when, near the exit, I passed Señora Posador and Felipe Mendoza talking together. I said a word of greeting and would have gone past, but Señora Posador called me back and introduced her companion—"our great writer of whom you have surely heard."

I gave Mendoza a cold nod. "I read your attack on me in *Tiempo*," I said shortly.

Mendoza frowned. "Not on you, señor. On those who hired you, and on their motives."

"You might have made that a lot clearer."

"I think if you had been in possession of more of the underlying facts of the situation when you read my article, it would have been perfectly clear, Señor Hakluyt."

"All right," I said, a little wearily. "So I'm an ignorant outsider and the circumstances are highly involved. Go ahead and enlighten me. Tell me why this case is attracting such a lot of attention, for example."

"Please, Señor Hakluyt!" said Maria Posador with a distressed look. "It is for us rather than you to be bitter about it."

Mendoza regarded me with burning eyes. "You are an outsider, señor, let us not forget that. We fought hard to preserve in the city charter the birthright of those who belong here, against encroachment by outsiders. This land on which we are standing, señor—it is part of the country, not just of a city, and the country should come first. The foreign-born citizens care only—as I think you also do—for the city, but we—we feel for the earth itself, for the peasants who scratch it with ploughs, and their children who grow up in its villages. Now, regrettably, some of our own people seek to destroy the very liberties we struggled to preserve on their behalf."

"Surely," I said, "the foreign-born citizens have a stake here, too. They gave up their own lands voluntarily; they invested their efforts in Ciudad de Vados, and they don't want to see their work wasted. Ruiz was stressing that when he insisted that this case now is concerned purely with the city—and after all, if it weren't for the outsiders, the city wouldn't be here."

"Ruiz!" said Mendoza with violence, and twisted his mouth as though about to spit. "The hypocrite Ruiz! Listen, señor, and I will tell you what lies behind that smooth and aggressive face!"

"Felipe," said Maria Posador in a warning tone. Mendoza brushed the word aside and thrust a forefinger through the air toward me.

"Think on this! Our President was married before. As a good Catholic—hah!—when his first wife became an encumbrance, he could not think of divorce. She fell ill. He had Dr. Ruiz to attend her. Within a week she was dead, and yet—and yet—Vados has made Ruiz his director of health and hygiene."

"I—you're trying to tell me Ruiz killed her," I said.

"You should not speak recklessly, Felipe," Señora Posador sighed, and I turned to her.

"You're too right! I've read some of this guy's articles in *Tiempo* which ought never to have seen print. You can't go around tossing out accusations of bribery—or murder—with no evidence to support them."

"There is evidence," Señora Posador contradicted, and kept her violet eyes set on my face. "Enough evidence to ensure that if the regime falls, there will be a firing squad waiting to deal with the good doctor—if he does not flee first."

"Well, what the hell has stopped you from using the evidence if it exists?"

"The fact," she said coldly, "that he who would destroy Ruiz by using it will certainly destroy himself if Vados is still in power; he will then destroy Vados and perhaps the country. We are realists, Señor Hakluyt. What does it matter to us if one murderer goes free when to condemn him would be to tear Aguazul with civil war? There are men walking the streets here with worse crimes than murder to answer for. Come, Felipe—and *hasta la vista,* señor!"

She took Mendoza's arm, and they walked toward the exit, leaving me with a peculiar taste of ashes in my mouth.

XV

There was a saturnine policeman waiting for me when I returned to the hotel—a man called Carlos Guzman, who spoke good but heavily accented English and presented himself as a sergeant of detectives.

"It is about a threat that was made to you," he said, and left his words hanging.

I said, "Go on."

"Allegedly, by a certain José Dalban," he said. And waited again.

I took a deep breath. "Look," I said. "Why not say what you have to say and get it over with?"

He glanced around; we were in the lounge of the hotel. Not many people were present, and none of them were in earshot of a low-toned voice. He sighed. "Very well, señor. I would have thought you might prefer to discuss it in more private conditions—but as you wish. We are unable to make proceedings on your unsupported word."

"Well, that's no more than I expected," I snapped.

He looked unhappy. "It is not that we doubt you, señor. But you must realize that Señor Dalban is respected and well-known—"

I decided to take a long shot on the strength of a hint Angers had dropped to me. "Especially respected by the police, hey? Respected so much that you turn a blind eye on his affairs."

Guzman colored a little. He said stiffly, "Your honor is unjustified in his remarks. Señor Dalban conducts a business of import-export, and—"

"And traffics on the side in unofficial goods, I'm told." I more than half-suspected Dalban's main business might turn out to be in marijuana or something like that; Guzman's reply shook me rigid.

"Señor," he said with a reproachful shake of his head, "is your honor a Catholic?"

Startled, I indicated no. Guzman sighed. "I am, strictly. And yet I would not condemn Señor Dalban for what he does—I come of a large family, and we were very hungry when I was a little boy."

I began to see that I'd jumped to a stupid conclusion somewhere. "What exactly *is* this shady business of Dalban's?" I said slowly.

Guzman glanced around. "Señor, in a Catholic country it is not a respectable matter. But—"

I began to laugh. Suddenly, for all my recollection of his bulk and manner, Dalban seemed far less menacing. When I had mastered my amusement, I choked out, "Just—contraceptives? Nothing more illegal than contraceptives?"

Guzman waited woodenly till my face was straight again. Then he said, "Even they are not illegal, señor. They are—let us say unpopular in influential quarters. Yet we think, some of us, that he performs a good service for our people."

"All right," I said. "Granted. He still came to me and told

me that if I didn't get out of my own accord, he'd see to it
that I was got out forcibly."

Guzman looked unhappy. "Señor, we are prepared to offer
you a bodyguard if you wish—a man who would remain with
you day and night. We have good men, well trained. You
need only say the word and they are at your command."

I hesitated. Before learning of Dalban's real claim to notoriety, I would probably have accepted; now, thinking the question over, I was suddenly reminded of what I had seen on my
first day in Ciudad de Vados—the policeman stealing my
money from a beggar-boy's pot.

"No," I said. "No, I don't want a bodyguard from your
police. And I'll tell you why."

He heard me out with his face immobile. When I had
finished he gave a nearly imperceptible nod.

"That is known, señor. That young man was dismissed the
following day. He has gone back to Puerto Joaquin to work
in the docks. He is the only support of his family, and his
father was killed in Puerto Joaquin in the great fire. Perhaps
the beggar from whom he stole was also the only support of
his family."

He rose to his feet. "I will inform *el Jefe* of what you have
said. Good evening, Señor Hakluyt."

I didn't reply. I had a curious sensation, as though I had
stepped on what seemed to be firm ground, and instead found
myself floundering up to my neck in a river. A river that
threatened at every moment to sweep me off my feet.

The Sigueiras case made practically no progress the following day. With incredible persistence Brown hammered at Dr.
Ruiz; with corresponding doggedness Ruiz stuck to his guns.
Brown got more and more bad-tempered, though the directness and subtlety of his questioning endured; Ruiz got more
and more vehement, and it was a considerable relief when the
judge adjourned the case until Monday.

Most of all, it was a relief to me. During the course of the
week, the city had quieted down. I felt things were near
enough back to normal for me to go out and assemble the
supplementary data I needed to clarify my tentative conclu-

sions. For one thing, Lucas was deputy chairman of the Citizens' Party, and seeing how busy he was, I hoped the political front might remain quiet for a while—at least until this Sigueiras case was over.

Accordingly, I went down on Saturday to the market area.

The first time I passed the little wall shrine where I had seen the candle burning in memory of Guerrero, I looked for it, but it had gone, and there was no sign of the notice attached to it. I felt a curious sense of relief—as though somehow the influence of symbol-Guerrero was to be measured by that candle.

The relief didn't last. Sunday morning saw the whole thing flare up again.

The immediate excuse for the disturbance was an article in the Sunday edition of *Tiempo* regarding the Sigueiras case. It said a number of pointed things about Ruiz, about his close association with the president, and about how this association dated back to the death of the first Señora Vados.

I couldn't judge how the article would strike someone who had no additional information. To me, though, in view of what Mendoza had said about Ruiz, the implications were unmistakable. I could only assume that Cristoforo Mendoza was hoping to provoke a suit for libel and bring the whole thing into the open—against the advice, presumably, of Maria Posador.

Suppose the evidence existed to show Ruiz a murderer; the consequences would be appalling. If the case was ever allowed to come to trial, the attack on Ruiz would become an attack on Vados himself, for sheltering a murderer and conniving at his crime; Vados would probably liquidate his accusers, the opponents of his regime would rise in arms—and, as predicted by Maria Posador, civil war would tear Aguazul apart.

Or maybe it wouldn't even be such a roundabout route as that which led to civil war. Someone at least must have understood the message the article contained, or the message had been following it on the grapevine, for Sunday afternoon was the first time for many days I saw National Party supporters standing up boldly to followers of the Citizens of Vados. I saw, in fact, a knife fight developing—I didn't stay to see the finish—between a tall young man with a huge *sombrero* who had openly declared his belief that Ruiz was a murderer, and a couple of well-dressed teen-age youths who were slumming in the market quarter.

The fight began in a bar where I'd gone to quench a thirst founded mainly on boredom. The job was now at the stage where it threatened to become pure routine—indeed, I could have earned myself a free weekend by detailing a couple of Angers' staff to get me my information. But then again, I'd have lost the immediacy of the data. It wasn't only a question of how many vehicles of what types where and when; it was also knowing from experience what their drivers were—telling from the way a driver approached a stoplight whether he was a resident, a regular visitor, or a complete stranger in Vados; whether he was in a hurry or at leisure; whether he knew where he was going or was stuck in the wrong lane.

But I had to break for a drink and a rest occasionally. I could do it with a good conscience; the standard of driving in Vados was extremely high, bearing out a cherished theory of mine—that bad roads make bad drivers. In Vados, with its elaborately planned street system, one seldom grew impatient, rarely had to sit fuming in a traffic jam, wasted little time hunting elusive parking spaces, never had to pick one's way gingerly between twin rows of stationary cars in a narrow street. Consequently people didn't try to hurry so much, didn't try to cut corners and take risks to make up lost time, didn't lose their tempers and try to teach other drivers a lesson.

I only wished everything in Vados went as smoothly as its traffic.

It was getting late when I stopped off in another bar, hoping I wouldn't find a knife fight in this one also. Television was on, but the screen was turned away from half the room, and the sound was directionalized. I had just placed my order at the bar when a voice bellowed behind me.

"It's Hakluyt, goddam it! The li'l Boydie himself!"

I glanced in the mirror before turning around. It was Fats Brown, sitting at one of the tables between a long-faced Indian and a woman with a tired, middle-aged face who was just looking at him, infinite sadness in her eyes. There was a nearly empty bottle of rum on the table. He had spilled quite a lot from his glass. His was the only glass.

"C'mon and join us!" he invited, raising his arms. He had lost his jacket somewhere, and he had sweated his shirt into crumpled limpness. "C'mon here, Boydie, an' have a cigar!" He moved his hands as if feeling for the breast pocket of his jacket and naturally didn't find it.

I could hardly refuse; besides, he'd probably have changed his tune and insulted me if I had. I went reluctantly over to the table.

"Can't stay long," I warned him, praying he was sober enough to register the words. "I'm on the job."

"Job, hell!" he said. "Can't be working on Sunday night! *Nobody* oughta be working—oughta be celebrating with me." He burped.

I looked at his companions; the woman caught my gaze and gave a sad slow shake of her head. Brown went on loudly.

"Meet my wife—won'erful woman! Doesn't speak English. Ol' fiddle-face is my bro'er-in-law. *He* doesn't speak English. Mis'able bastard, isn' he? Won' celebrate! Won' help me celebrate!"

A bitter, writhing grievance underlay his words. I said, "What are you celebrating, Fats?"

He looked at me owlishly, clasping his hands around the glass and leaning forward on the table. "Confidentially," he said in a thicker, lower tone, "I'm gonna be a father. Whatya think of that—huh?"

I didn't connect, and he read my reaction in my face. He grimaced. "Yeah, so she tells me. Well, *she* says I'm gonna be a father. An' I never met her before in my goddam' life. Ain' that hell? Gettin' to be a father an' not gettin' any nookie outa it? Whadda *you* think, Boydie—ain' it hell?"

I said, "Who's this 'she'?"

"A li'l bitch called Estrelita. Estrelita Jaliscos." He closed his eyes. "A tart, pal, if ever I saw one. Painted, dressed like crazy—might be pretty, I guess, 'f you could see her through the crap smeared on her face. Comes to me today an' says, 'I'm gonna have a baby.' Tells me if I don' give her ten thousand dolaros, she's gonna tell Ruiz it's my kid. Hell, with ten thousand dolaros she could pay Ruiz his fee—'s a kinda job he does pretty well, I hear. Should be—he's had *plenny* practice." He opened his eyes again, reached unsteadily for the bottle, and slopped some more into his glass. He offered me a shot; I shook my head.

"Pal," he said pleadingly when he had gulped a mouthful, "I'm a happy married man, know that? Tha's my wife there— not much to look at, but the goddam', finest woman I ever met!" He almost shouted the last phrase. "What would *I* wanna lay a teen-age tart for, hey? I'm too old, so help me— y'know I'm nearly sixty? Know that? I got a boy practicin' law in Milwaukee an' a daughter married in New York. I'm a *grandfather,* pal! An' this stinkin' Estrelita bitch says—ah, hell, I tol' you a'ready."

He interrupted himself long enough to take another drink.

"Maybe it's her own idea," he resumed. "Maybe not. She don't have enough brains to figure out a son'vabitch idea like this. Maybe somebody put her up to it. Coulda been Angers, 'cept he's so righteous an' limey an' King's English he prob'ly never heard of havin' babies. I figure—know what I figure?"

I shook my head.

"I figure it's Lucas, rot his soul! Mister, what's this gonna do to me? It's gonna finish me, know that? Have people laugh at me in the streets, know that?"

He jabbed a stubby finger at me. "Y' don' believe it, hey? Y' don' think one little thing like this could wreck me for good! Well, I'm *tellin'* you. I'm on the wrong side! Me, I oughta be distinguished an' respectable an' expensive, like Lucas an' his gang. I'm a foreign-born citizen; *they* think I oughta be like Angers, rot his tin-plated hide. *They* think I'm a disgrace 'cause I spend my time an' effort tryin'a give these poor bastards who *own* the country a decent lawyer's arguments. With me? Get me? 'Cause I don' worry myself sick 'bout whether or not I collect the whole of a fee; 'cause I know law and say when it's on the other side, they'd love— just *love,* pal!—one teeny hook to drag me down. An' then they'd stamp on me."

He put his head in his hands and fell silent. I felt embarrassed, watching the compassionate gaze his wife bestowed on him, and tried to avoid looking at her. But the only other place I found where my eyes would stay still was on her brother's long lined fiddle face. There was no other description.

"Señora Brown," I said at length, and she raised her eyes to mine. "*Tengo un automóvil—desean Vds. ir a casa?*"

"*Muchas gracias, señor,*" she answered. "*Pero no sé si mi esposo desea irse.*"

"Fats," I said. I shook his shoulder gently. "Like a ride home?"

He lifted his head. "You got a car, pal? Me, I never had a car since I came here. *Ten thousand* she wants, the li'l bitch. Me, I don' earn ten thousand in two years!"

"Like a ride home?" I insisted. He nodded, unseeing, and got awkwardly to his feet, like a hippopotamus coming from a wallow.

"I'd like to smack her behind for her—dammit, she's a kid, pal, just a kid. It's not even as if I *liked* 'em young an' skinny. Ask m' wife! Ah, maybe not. Useta run aroun' a bit, true enough, but hell, that was twen'y years ago!"

We got him to my car. His wife gave me the address and sat in the back seat comforting him, while the brother-in-law sat beside me. I glanced at Fats in the mirror occasionally; he quieted down when we were on the move, and sat gazing into space. There was something almost pathetic about his attitude. He was holding his wife's hand and stroking it like a shy teenager at a movie.

It was not a long trip. The Browns lived in a block of medium-priced apartments a mile or so away; I dropped them off there and made sure that between them his wife and brother-in-law could get him indoors. Señora Brown dropped me a sort of curtsy as I turned to go, and her half-whispered, "*Muchas gracias, señor!*" stayed in my ears all the way back to my beat.

About a quarter of an hour after I returned to the main traffic nexus, the bored-looking policeman in the booth overlooking it showed the first sign of activity I had noticed in all the time I had spent here. A little light began to shine in intermittent flashes beside his telephone handset. Hastily he snatched the microphone and punched buttons. Red lights shone from lamp posts; his voice boomed from the loudspeakers. The traffic came to a halt.

There was a wail of sirens, and two motorcycle cops and a squad car raced into sight, shot past, disappeared again. A few moments later there was an ambulance. The policeman in the booth, his job done, hung up the microphone and took his thumb off the button. The traffic moved on.

It was not until the papers came out the following morning that I learned the errand of these policemen and the ambulance. Apparently a girl called Estrelita Jaliscos had fallen to her death from a window in the apartment block where I had dropped the Browns last night, and Fats himself was nowhere to be found.

XVI

Sigueiras was literally in tears when his suit reopened on Monday morning. It was hardly surprising. Fats Brown's place had been taken by a substitute lawyer with no interest in the argument, who tamely allowed things to go ahead when he could have secured a long enough adjournment to acquaint himself with Fats's groundwork. Lucas, coldly triumphant, cut his own case short without calling me; the new lawyer made a hash of his concluding speech, and the judge ruled, as was inevitable on the facts presented to him, that the redevelopment plans were not motivated by malice, Sigueiras's slum was a public nuisance, and citizens' rights did not extend to cover public nuisances.

Sigueiras had to stand up and shout at his lawyer to get him to file notice of appeal; there were shouts and complaints from people in the public seats—it was great to leave the court and breathe fresh air outside.

This morning I had noticed a stranger sitting in court; as I left in company with Angers, he came up to us—a tall, black-haired man, faultlessly dressed, whom I had a vague idea I had seen somewhere but did not know.

"Good morning, Luis!" said Angers warmly. "And congratulations on your new appointment! Hakluyt," he added, turning to me, "you must meet Señor Luis Arrio, the new chairman of the Citizens of Vados."

Arrio smiled and shook my hand. "Delighted, Señor Hakluyt!" he exclaimed. "I have been hoping to make your acquaintance since your arrival. I saw you at Presidential House the other day but did not contrive an introduction."

So that was where I'd seen him. And the name also rang a bell now. Multiple stores. I'd seen it in half a dozen places in Vados alone, over large and small branches.

"Well!" he continued. "So as it turned out there was no call for your assistance in this little matter that has been settled today. The judgment, of course, represents a further triumph for—might one not almost say civilization over barbarism? Like your own work, Señor Hakluyt, this will help to make our beautiful city yet more beautiful!"

"Thank you," I said shortly. "But—being a foreigner, not a Vadeano—as far as I'm concerned, it's just another job. One that I almost regret having taken on."

He looked sympathetic immediately. "Yes, that I very well understand. So your esteemed colleague tells me"—he gestured at Angers—"that rascal Dalban and his associates have made threats to you. Well, I can personally assure you, señor, that you have nothing to fear from them. We, the Citizens of Vados, will see to that—and you may rely on our guarantee."

He looked forthright, like the statue of *el Liberador* in the Plaza del Norte, but there was something more than just a pose in that. As far as he was aware, he was speaking the absolute literal truth. I took the statement at its face value.

"Yes, Señor Lucas and I will ensure that you meet no further incidents of that kind," he pursued. "I am convinced it is all a matter of correctly informing the people—once the citizens see what benefits these changes will bring, there will be no further hindrance. Señor, you must do me the honor of dining with me and my family one evening during your stay."

"I'd be delighted," I said. "Unfortunately, I can't accept at once—I'm spending most of my evenings out on the streets studying the traffic flow."

"Of course!" he exclaimed, as though chiding himself for stupidity. "Your work occupies you all day and night, does it not? Not the profession I would have chosen, señor. I admire your self-dedication. Then if it cannot be dinner, let it be luncheon, and let the time be now, here in the plaza." He glanced at Angers. "You will join us?"

Angers nodded; the three of us, and Lucas who joined us a few minutes later, took a table under the palms.

Much of the conversation was concerned with the affairs of the Citizens' Party. While if flowed past me, I had a chance to study my companions.

There was Lucas, of course. I had seen enough of him in action to know that he was a brilliant lawyer—he lacked Fats Brown's gift of identifying himself with the cause he was pleading, but his faculty of analyzing arguments with detachment more than compensated. He struck me as a cold man; he could be an angry man—as I had seen when Sam Francis killed Guerrero—but I doubted if he had it in him to be fanatical.

Nor had Angers. Dogmatic, certainly, and stubborn. But— well, Angers was almost *too* much of a type. The reason was probably not far to seek: perhaps it was simply the common expatriate habit of overemphasizing one's personal background in reaction against alien surroundings.

I'd have been hard put to it to find a reply if someone had asked me, "Do you like Angers?" His own manner discouraged any strong feeling of like or dislike toward him. I should probably have replied, in an unconscious imitation of Angers' own British accent, "Oh, he's all right!"

Which was probably exactly what Angers himself would desire.

As for Arrio, I characterized him as an actor. A man who had adopted a role, probably when young, and found that it served him so well he eventually came to live it. I found the role rather impressive; having decided that the man had become the part he played, I could not be less impressed simply because it was a part. Now the role and the individual were inseparable.

So here were three leading citizens, leading voices of those who spoke in Ciudad de Vados. Steady men. Probably as reliable personally as they were solid in their business. I had, I realized, still been unconsciously worrying about Dalban's threats and trying to mask the fact from myself. Now I had been assured of Arrio's support, which seemed worth having, and I felt relieved of an imaginary burden.

The meal broke up, Arrio apologizing and explaining that he had to go to the television studios and record an interview for tonight's current affairs program; they were doing a feature on his new appointment. I asked him to give my regards to Señora Cortés and Francisco Córdoban. Wryly, I wondered in passing whether they would put out a picture of Arrio in the guise of an angel; certainly he would look better in the role than I had.

When he had left us, Lucas, Angers, and I strolled back across the square. After a moment, deep in thought, Angers spoke up.

"Relieved at not having to face a cross-examination by Brown, Hakluyt?"

"In a way," I admitted.

"Oh, he is one large bluff!" said Lucas offhandedly. "Did he perhaps say to you that he ate expert witnesses for lunch?"

"As a matter of fact—"

Lucas nodded, smiling faintly. "He said the same to our good Dr. Ruiz, but he was not taken in. Strange about what has happened, no?"

"Strange?" echoed Angers. "The sort of thing one might have expected, surely."

"I suppose it is," Lucas agreed abstractedly. "I hear—did I tell you, or did Luis?—that *el obispo* is also tonight on television, by his special request."

"Really?" said Angers in a slightly bored tone; presumably the whim of a Popish bishop held little interest for him.

"And I have *heard*—just a rumor, true, but I have definitely heard—that he intends to speak his mind on the matter of morality in Vados."

Their eyes met, and it was instantly clear what Lucas was implying.

Angers smiled reluctantly. "Not by any chance a sermon on the text, 'The wages of sin is death'?"

"Anything is possible," shrugged Lucas. We had reached the sidewalk and had paused in a group with traffic rolling by. "I gather he is considering giving permission for the dead girl to be buried in consecrated ground."

I butted in. "You mean he's already made up his episcopal mind that she was murdered—didn't kill herself? Look, I saw Fats Brown and his wife and brother-in-law yesterday evening in a bar—in fact I drove them home. I heard his side of the story, and he swore blind he had never seen this—this tramp before."

They were both looking at me with quizzical expressions.

"Speaking professionally, Señor Hakluyt," said Lucas after a pause, "I assure you that what Brown may have said to you is of no interest in law. If he is innocent, why has he hidden? Oh, admittedly many things might have happened—she might have thrown herself from the window in desperation, she might have been frightened and fallen back, she might have been struck in an argument, all possible! Yet Brown's brother-in-law tells us that she was hard and self-possessed and seemed well in control of herself. Not distraught, so that she was likely to resort to suicide when she knew she could obtain—uh—sufficient provision for herself from the father of her unborn child."

"Aside from the fact that he categorically denied being the father," I insisted, "Brown told me she wanted ten thousand dolaros, and he didn't have that much."

"He could probably have got it," shrugged Angers. "No, he obviously panicked; presumably, then, he felt he was in too awkward a position to defend himself. If it were just a matter of money, I'm sure he would have been worth ten thousand to the National Party as a capable, experienced liar."

"Lawyer?" suggested Lucas.

"I know what I mean," said Angers, and barked a laugh.

Lucas glanced at his watch and started. "Well, excuse me," he said. "I have much business to attend to. *Hasta la vista,*

Donald—Señor Hakluyt." He gave a polite little dip of the head and went across the road.

"Well, I think things are going to liven up a little in Vados now," Angers commented. "With Arrio and Lucas working together, we should see progress."

"You think Arrio a better choice than Guerrero?"

"No question. Excellent fellow, Arrio—man of decision. I like men like that."

I didn't watch Arrio on television that evening, or the bishop. But when I passed the little wall shrine in the market on my way back to my hotel, dead beat at one in the morning, there were several candles burning. I glanced around for any sign of men with clubs like those who had greeted me just after Guerrero's death, saw no one, and ventured to examine a slip of paper stuck to one of the unburnt candles.

It said on it, "Estrelita Jaliscos."

Poor Fats, I thought. I remembered how pathetic he had been the night before. Then I recalled how drunk he had been, also, and how unstably poised between anger and self-pity. It had to be admitted: Lucas was right. So many things could have happened to Estrelita Jaliscos; one of them might conceivably have been murder.

By now it had become a habit for me to read *Liberdad* and *Tiempo* every morning; my original intention to improve my Spanish had become secondary, as I spoke it much of the time. Now I read the papers to keep abreast of what was happening in the city. I took up *Liberdad* first as usual the next morning and found that of course it had everything its way today.

The appointment of Arrio was the main story, together with a report of what he had said on television. Next to it was an account of Bishop Cruz's diatribe on Vadeano morals, and that was so strongly worded it made me blink. According to the bishop, Ciudad de Vados was going to be mentioned on Judgment Day in the next breath after Sodom.

He didn't mention Fats Brown by name, but there were a dozen barbed references to those who lead the young into sin, and with it there was an ingenious argument to the effect that, since this rush of depravity in what had formerly been (so the bishop stated) a highly moral and reputable city could be traced to its source in the shantytowns and more especially Sigueiras's slum, then Brown's spirited defense of Sigueiras must have been due to a desire to perpetuate these hotbeds of vice.

That was a kind of argument I thought was dead with the two Joes—Stalin and McCarthy.

Brown's disappearance was the next major story; there was a picture of the secretary of justice, Gonzales, declaring that he would be found, another of *el Jefe* O'Rourke scowling over the sheet-draped body of the girl, and a story saying that the police were working on various leads. I'd read the same thing practically word-for-word in too many different countries to go through it in detail; I glanced at the next story and found it was a report on some regional chess championship, so I picked up *Tiempo*, wondering how they were going to save any face at all in view of what had happened. They couldn't very well defend Brown except vaguely, in general terms; perhaps they would try to distract attention by attacking a scapegoat—

I was right. It was just the identity of the scapegoat I wasn't expecting.

In the middle of the front page was a crude cartoon; it depicted Ciudad de Vados as the Garden of Eden. Standing before it was an angel with a flaming sword, scowling down on ragged peasants—a man holding his hat in his hand, a woman with a baby at her side—who were saying, "Why is it a sin to be poor?"

And across the angel's robe in big black letters was scrawled my name.

XVII

I was still staring incredulously at the drawing when a discreet knock came at my door and the chambermaid brought in my morning mail. Automatically, my mind not on what I was doing, I slit the two envelopes she gave me and glanced at the contents.

The first was a letter from a friend of mine in the States to whom I'd promised to write and then—as I usually do—had put it off. The second was the front page torn from a copy of this morning's *Tiempo,* identical with the one I was reading except that the cartoon had been ringed with red and a single word added in English beside it: "Well?"

"Dalban," I said aloud. "Who else?"

Well, Dalban or whoever was responsible, this was going to stop. Now. *Tiempo* seemed to get away with a hell of a lot of libel and near libel, but Maria Posador had told me that Seixas obtained an injunction to prevent them from accusing him of taking bribes. Someone was going to have to organize the same for me. Right now.

I put the torn page back in its envelope, stuffed the envelope in my pocket, and went to the traffic department to see Angers. I told him what had happened, showed him the red-ringed cartoon, and then slammed my fist down on his desk.

"Right!" I said. "There's a law about this sort of thing. Get something done!"

Angers bit his lip. "So you think it's Dalban behind this, eh? I suppose that's logical, after the threat he made to you. Your best course, Hakluyt, would be to have a word with Lucas—suppose I call him and see if he's free to join us for lunch?"

He picked up the envelope and glanced at the postmark.

"Posted early this morning or last night, about half a mile from the Plaza del Sur—at least, I think that's the postal zone in that area. Early today, more likely, unless whoever was responsible got hold of an advance copy of the paper."

He picked up his interoffice phone and told his secretary to get Lucas for him. I waited, feeling my first hot-tempered reaction cool perceptibly.

Lucas was free; he was engaged in sewing up the case against Sam Francis, which was mainly a matter of collating the evidence of witnesses. I told him my story over lunch in the plaza that noon.

He nodded gravely when I'd finished. "Yes, Señor Hakluyt," he said. "You have what is, I think, called a hard nut to crack in both these problems. The Mendoza brothers are very skilled at *almost* libeling persons they disapprove of, without being so rude as to bring the fury of the law about their heads. Since, however, you are not a citizen but, so to say, a guest of our government, I think it well worthwhile to investigate the possibility of a suit over this attack. At the very least, we can obtain an injunction to muzzle them for the time being."

"That would help," I said. "But it's not enough. I want Dalban investigated. If he is responsible, then I want something done about him. I had no action out of the police when I was threatened by him, except the offer of a bodyguard—and I turned that down because of another experience I'd had with the police just after I got here."

Lucas made a note in a small memorandum book. "I will make inquiries for you, señor," he said. "It is, alas, no secret that a man with the right influence can—uh—discourage the enthusiasm of our Vadeano police force. Dalban certainly is one of them. But as it happens I am interested to know myself what has been going on with Dalban; I expected him to make a move before this."

"What sort of move?" demanded Angers.

"You doubtless recall the fine that was imposed on Juan Tezol? So far it has gone unpaid, aside from a couple of hundred dolaros scraped together by fanatical supporters of the party. But the twenty days' grace before the reckoning are up today, and many people have been wondering whether Tezol is indeed valuable enough to those behind the party for the money to be forthcoming."

Angers nodded. "You have a point. If the fellow doesn't get ransomed, it means his usefulness is at an end—because he and Francis were so closely linked, one assumes. Some of Francis's dirt must have rubbed off on Tezol, then."

"Of the two, Tezol is probably in fact the dirtier if not the darker," said Lucas reflectively, and gave a faint smile. "Yes, it will be interesting to see if those thousand dolaros materialize."

Angers was deep in thought for a moment. At length he said, "You seem very ready to accept that Dalban is at the bottom of this, by the way. Has he in fact any influence with *Tiempo?* I always understood that Maria Posador was behind it."

Lucas shrugged. "To my way of thinking, Maria Posador is also a—a what is it called? A decoy, precisely. I think that her acceptance of Vados's invitation to return to Aguazul greatly diminished her influence. Now it is always Dalban that I watch."

He checked the time and started to get up. "You will excuse me; I have spent too long talking. Rest assured, Señor Hakluyt—this affair of yours will quickly be regulated."

He acted remarkably promptly. On my breakfast tray at the hotel the following morning was an envelope containing two items: the first, a certified copy of an injunction issued by Judge Romero with, pinned to it, a slip of paper saying, "With compliments from Andres Lucas." And the second, the morning's issue of *Tiempo*.

Today the most conspicuous item on the front page was a yawning gap, bearing a facsimile of the official censor's stamp and a note to the effect that this section of the paper had originally contained material which contravened such-and-such a subsection of the Public Order Act.

This was more like it. As I found later, police had descended on the *Tiempo* office early this morning, acting on Judge Romero's instructions, and had removed another article about me from the actual stone on which it was set up.

Looking through the rest of the paper, I discovered that Romero had had a busy day yesterday. Tezol, his fine unpaid, had been arrested on Romero's order last night and was now in jail, without Dalban or his associates—who were supposed to be backing the National Party—lifting a finger to help him.

The Nationals seemed capable of some really bloody things on occasion. I had no doubt that so long as this illiterate peasant orator had been useful to them, they were only too happy to have him trust them; when it came to a pinch, they'd dropped him without a word.

I turned to the inside pages and there found an example of
the Mendoza brothers' cleverness, of which Lucas had spoken
yesterday. Felipe Mendoza was at it again, hammering his
well-worn theme of bribery in the treasury department and
vested interests in highway corporations. Owing, I presumed,
to the injunction Seixas had previously obtained against the
paper, he wasn't mentioned by name; nonetheless, all the "for
examples" given in the article would have fitted him like a
glove, down to the jug of sickly cocktail he kept on the desk
in his office. This gave me cause to frown. So having an
injunction against the Mendozas wasn't as watertight as I had
hoped. I'd have to go on watching for trouble in this quarter.

Well, there was hope in another direction. Lucas had spoken
of investigations into Dalban's part in the affair; if they paid
off, I might be able to get on with my job in peace. Frankly,
by this time I was wishing to God it was over and done with.

I made a mental note to call Lucas and thank him as soon
as I got the chance, and finished my breakfast in a considera-
bly better mood than I'd been in twenty-four hours before.

Sitting in the lounge with an air of extreme dejection,
studying a chess problem and idly moving a pawn back and
forth as though unable to decide what to do with it, was Maria
Posador.

What the hell *did* she do at this hotel when she had a
house a little distance away? Did she just like it? Come here
for the company? Use it as an office for whatever she did with
the National Party?

I went over to her. "Señora Posador! I'd like a word with
you."

"You are welcome, Señor Hakluyt," she murmured without
looking up. "Be seated." She gestured at another chair, an
unlit Russian cigarette between her fingers.

I sat down and leaned forward, elbows on knees. "Maybe
I'm more welcome than what I want to say," I said. "Are you
responsible for what *Tiempo* has been saying about me
lately?"

She dropped the pawn she was toying with, sat back,

crossed her legs. "I am responsible for nothing *Tiempo* says or does. Who informed you that I was?"

"That's beside the point. What is your connection with *Tiempo?*"

"I have sometimes given money to Cristoforo Mendoza— no more than that."

No evasion, so far as I could judge; a plain answer to the question. I relaxed a little. "If you're a friend of the Mendoza brothers, maybe you can tell me why they're picking on me at the moment."

She was silent for a while, regarding me. She said finally, "Perhaps, Señor Hakluyt, you are thinking of news papers." Two words; she made the distinction perfectly clear. *"Tiempo* is not a news paper. It cannot be, because *Liberdad* is not. These are tools for shaping the opinions of people. Let me put it this way. *Liberdad* is little more than a—spare wheel for the television and radio services; it carries extra weight among those highly literate and influential persons who, after all, are the operative factors in our country. Against this, the opposition has *Tiempo*—and word of mouth. It has been a great achievement of Vados, to retain public confidence in his propaganda services; often, after twenty years, government organs speaking for a regime have outworn their public acceptance. People say, 'I no longer believe! I have read—or seen—or heard—too many obvious falsehoods.' Not here, señor."

"That explains nothing."

"On the contrary. Are you an angel, señor?"

"What do you mean?"

"You would not claim to be an angel. Yet have you raised so many objections to the way the television service has presented you? Against this, *Tiempo* tried to present something less favorable, admitted, but perhaps nearer the true state of things. We are all human, fallible, not all-knowing. And of course, you deny permission to state this side of the case. I do not blame you. I wish only that we spoke for the same cause."

"For the hundredth time," I retorted, "I'm not taking sides in the internal affairs of Vados. I'm hired help, and treating me as though I were—were a hired assassin is unjustifiable."

"Whether you recognize the fact or not," she said calmly, "you are a symbol now. Better that you should leave with your work unfinished than that you should altogether lose your power of decision and perhaps be destroyed by the disaster that now impends."

"You seem very certain that there will be a disaster," I said. "And what are your friends the Mendozas doing to stop it? Nothing. They seem to be helping it along. I saw a knife fight on Sunday evening over that attack *Tiempo* published against Dr. Ruiz. Fortunately it doesn't seem to have caused anything worse so far."

"Only because the case collapsed, señor. Only because Señor Brown disappeared. I think Felipe was foolish to insist on publication of that attack; still, as I have told you, I have no influence on the policy of *Tiempo*. I merely believe it right and necessary for there to be counter-propaganda of some sort in Ciudad de Vados."

"All right, so there has to be an opposition press. I grant that. What I want to know is: must it be libelous and irresponsible?"

"Under the circumstances, it must be as extreme as the law permits. Milk and water, señor, will not tempt readers away from stronger drink. As to Dr. Ruiz—well, his time of reckoning will come. I am glad Felipe did not continue as he had intended, though—otherwise there might now be barricades in the square, and perhaps you would have been knifed."

She looked down at the chess problem on the table. "Believe me, Señor Hakluyt, I am sympathetic; our problems are not your problems, but they exist. And we in Vados cannot cease to fight our own battles merely because one stranger is involved, to whom we wish no harm. Is that reasonable? Will you agree with me?"

I threw up my hands. "I have to hand it to you, señora, you put up a most rational case. It still doesn't make me happy about this treatment I'm getting. Just one more thing, though. Are you also acquainted with a man called José Dalban?"

Her eyes widened fractionally. She gave a quick nod.

"Then tell him from me next time you see him that if he lets out another peep about me I'll have him hit from so many sides he won't know what's happening."

"Explain further."

"He'll know what I mean. He's threatened me more than once now; the third time I promise to spit in his eye." I took a deep breath. "Frankly, Señora Posador, I was told it was a tossup who out of you and Dalban, was responsible for the attacks on me. I'll accept your assurance; from Dalban I wouldn't take an oath on a crucifix."

Her voice kept carefully neutral, she said, "I will tell him. If I see him. You must understand, Señor Hakluyt, that again you have preconceptions. It is my impression that you think in terms of ordinary political parties; you mistake the similarities between our government and other governments for identities. There is a president, a congress, a cabinet which as in the *Estados Unidos* is appointed by the president—but these parties, the Citizens of Vados and the National Party, exist only in Ciudad de Vados. You knew that, possibly. But you did not go on to think that Puerto Joaquin has more than twice so many people as this city, and that our other two large cities, Cuatrovientos and Astoria Negra, combine to make as many people as live here. Beyond that, there is the whole country. It is against the isolation of this city that we fight—against the city as a privileged country-within-the-country. How long have you been here? Three weeks, is it not? This is a struggle that has continued for more than ten years, and in the course of its growth it has struck its roots in every corner of all our lives."

Her long fingers sorted the chessmen on the table before her. "Almost," she finished musingly, "it threatens to replace chess as the national obsession."

I made no reply.

"I think it would be appropriate," she said after a pause, not looking up from the board, "to play that game I suggested now. In token of our—friendly enmity?" She added the last two words on a rising, questioning note.

I hesitated before nodding. She smiled, deftly concealed a

black and a white pawn in her hands, and offered their
smooth gold backs to me. I indicated the right one; it proved
to contain white.

"Your honor," she said, and at last lit the cigarette she had
kept waiting between her fingers for so long.

Well, she was bound to wipe the floor with me, I thought.
I'd never played seriously, and probably most schoolchildren in
this chess-mad country would make hay out of any opposition
I could muster. Still—I tried pawn to queen four and lit a
cigarette for myself.

Queen's Gambit Accepted: that shook me a little, but I
ploughed on, trying to remember the orthodox attack. I soon
found that Black wasn't doing anything orthodox at all, aside
from developing major pieces brilliantly. After move eight, I
leaned back, cogitating.

"I think I've done something rather stupid," I said. "As far
as I can see, I've laid myself open to massacre somewhere."

Señora Posador nodded without smiling. "I regret that you
have. This combination of mine was played against our champion Pablo Garcia in the Caribbean tournament last month—
it so happened that I was discussing it with him yesterday,
and I thought I might try it out."

"Well, but Garcia is a grand master," I said. "I suppose this
was one of the games he lost."

"Not at all," said Señora Posador indifferently. "He won in
twenty-seven moves."

I looked at the board. I was faced with a choice between
losing my Queen or putting her back on the home square;
either way I got a move behind and lost material in a few
moves' time.

"I'm sorry," I said. "I'm no grand master."

"If you will permit, then. . . ." She leaned over and delicately tipped pieces back to restore the position at move four. "I
recommend this—you see why, of course. Then as previously;
now so, so, so. Then take the pawn, and the situation is
altogether different, no?"

"Is that what Garcia did?" I suggested, studying the new
setup.

"Oh, no. That is what he decided afterward he should have

done. It leads to a resignation by Black in fifteen moves or so. Garcia is a lazy man, he says. He only plays long games when it is unavoidable."

"Well, the one that was acted out at the president's garden party in his honor was long enough," I said. "About ninety moves, I think."

"His opponent refused the offer of a draw; he was stubborn. Which would you prefer, señor—to continue or start afresh?"

"Let me try again," I said. "I haven't played for months, and I never played well. But I ought to do better than that."

We started over; this time I managed to hang on, and the game went to about forty-five moves before I found my queen neatly trapped and resigned to avoid systematic slaughter.

"Better," said Señora Posador with clinical approval. "If you would permit me to give you some advice, Señor Hakluyt . . ."

"Of course."

"It is a matter of combination. Each move must be seen in relation to the whole. And this applies also in real life. I suggest you consider this point. Good morning, señor."

And with that final cryptic remark she rose, smiling, and was gone.

I told a waiter to take the chessmen away and bring me a copy of this morning's *Liberdad*; having seen *Tiempo*, I wanted to know how the day's news looked through government eyes.

As usual, here were substantially the same items in a completely different order of precedence. Almost half the front page was given over to an attack on Sigueiras's slum, with editorial comment to the effect that now his rearguard action to preserve his notorious public nuisance had failed, the citizens of Ciudad de Vados should take vigorous action to hasten the process of clearing it away.

There was a change of attitude detectable here: almost, I thought, I could discern a note of hysteria. Up till now *Liberdad* had soothingly been at pains to explain that the matter was in hand and the paternal government would soon put things to rights. Today there was distinct impatience and more than one hint that the government wasn't doing as well as it should. A heavy black box beside some pictures of the ragged slum-dwellers contained an accusation of the kind I thought was *Tiempo*'s prerogative here—Castaldo, deputy to Diaz in the Ministry of the Interior and one of the many officials I'd seen talking with Diaz at Presidential House, was supposed to have tried to shield Sigueiras from the long overdue clearance of his human pigsties. What he'd done, it seemed, was chiefly to nominate the substitute lawyer who took over Sigueiras's case from Brown. Having seen this substitute in action, I couldn't find that a particularly heinous offense—Sigueiras would probably have got on better with no lawyer at all. However, there it was; presumably, since *Liberdad* was the official organ, Señor Castaldo was being readied for dismissal.

Well, if *Liberdad* was going to start throwing mud like this, what kind of fireworks would *Tiempo* have to produce? Most likely they'd reopen their broadsides against Dr. Ruiz, and I wasn't looking forward to the probable consequences.

It struck me as curious that I hadn't heard anything for some time of the attempt to disqualify Judge Romero after his behavior in the Guerrero case. Maybe, because of public sympathy with Guerrero after his murder and public antipathy to Fats Brown after his disappearance, Dominguez had judged it unwise to press the matter too hard. Still, I wasn't complaining; Romero had issued me with that injunction against *Tiempo*, and so long as that remained in force, Romero, for my money, could sit on the judicial bench here or anywhere.

I folded the paper and sat thinking for a while. Or more exactly, not thinking so much as feeling. Feeling the city in terms of people. Trying to fit it into the country as a whole, as Maria Posador had suggested.

I couldn't. The trouble was this: Ciudad de Vados didn't fit into the country. It wouldn't fit, perhaps, into any country in the world. Had it been just its buildings, you could, of course, have fitted those in; the difficulty stemmed from the people, the particular people, the particular types, classes, beliefs, prejudices under which they labored. I had a moment of insight, trying to see the city through the eyes of a villager whose water supply had been taken for it: I, as it were, remembered with the peasant's memory how other people from across the sea had come with strange and wonderful things—horses, guns, metal armor—and how the world had turned topsy-turvy.

Maybe the Conquistadores were here again. Maybe I was—without wishing it—one of them.

I got up, sighing, and went down to the traffic department. I now had a considerable mass of data processed; not unnaturally, Angers was eager to know what the results would be. It cost me something of an effort to reorientate my thinking in the correct direction.

"The heart of the problem," I said when I'd succeeded, "is definitely the market area. There's nowhere else in Ciudad de Vados, except in the middle of the Plaza del Oeste, where a market could organically grow up—and there's legislation covering the plazas, so that's all right. If you can get your costing department to run a rough estimate on what I give them, we can find out by tomorrow morning how much of my four million my draft scheme will eat up. Then there'll be a matter of a few more days to iron out snags. Not long, I think.

"Then once your market is disposed of, your squatters' livelihood is largely gone; they'll have to beg or peddle their stuff. In a few months, especially if the government gives 'em a shove, the trickle back to the villages will become a torrent; pretty soon the number of squatters will drop to a handful, and inside a year the climate of opinion should permit evicting those who remain. As I get it, this is the Vados technique."

"Well, don't take my verdict," Angers answered. "It's up to Vados and Diaz to fight it out. But it sounds fair enough. A year, you say? A long year it will be. Still . . . And how about that eyesore of Sigueiras's?"

"As I've said before, that's far less important than it looks. The way things are moving already, Sigueiras can be legislated out of his slum without any opposition except from his tenants. Frankly, I'm surprised it's taking so long."

"Maybe the reason is—you've seen *Liberdad* this morning?"

"The piece about—what's he called?—Castaldo? Yes, I saw it. I was much more interested to see the hole in the front page of *Tiempo*."

Angers looked smug. "Yes, I was right to suggest you get on to Lucas, wasn't I?"

"I must call him up and thank him."

"Any further trouble from Dalban? No? I was having a word with Arrio last night; it seems he's likewise interested in Dalban's goings-on. Something to do with his business, mainly. But he's also learned a few things about the wealthy supporters of the National Party—like Dalban—which he says aren't exactly nice. This question of Tezol's fine, for example. I mean, Tezol was just an illiterate villager, but he was very useful to Dalban and his associates because of the influence he had with the uneducated classes, and it seems like a rotten thing to do to let him be jailed for want of a sum any of them could have given without noticing. There are some pretty unpleasant characters on the National side, Hakluyt."

"You've said almost exactly what I thought," I agreed.

Angers glanced at the clock. "Well, can't jaw all day," he said. "I hope your plans work out well."

I spent the rest of the day translating processed data into man-hours and cubic meters of concrete and gave the results to the costing clerks at five-thirty. My head was spinning with figures; I decided to take a break before I got a headache and went out for a drink while they started the costing.

I walked out into a changed city—a city suddenly come to life like a sleeping giant irritated by the biting of a flea, turning and twitching this way and that without being able to trace the cause of its discomfort.

Someone had thrown red paint all over Vados's statue.

Police in the Calle del Sol were bundling young men into trucks; there was blood on the ground, and one of the police held two wet-bladed knives.

During the lunch-hour meeting in the Plaza del Sur, Arrio had been hanged in effigy from a tree by enraged supporters of Juan Tezol, in protest against his being jailed. Police had

had to clear that up, too; the evening edition of *Liberdad* spoke of a hundred arrests.

My car had had the air let out of its tires.

And Sam Francis had committed suicide in jail. . . .

XVIII

That night Ciudad de Vados reacted as a sleeping lion reacts when it becomes aware of a human presence. The lion does not move, except to open its eyes. Yet its body ceases to be relaxed. Inside the tawny pelt a thousand living springs are wound up instantly to maximum tension.

The only occasions when I'd ever walked up to a sleeping lion had been on the outside of a cage of steel bars. But I was inside Ciudad de Vados. I was inside the mouth of the lion.

I did something that night that I hadn't done for years. I felt the need to get loaded with Dutch courage. When I was through at the traffic department—not that much work got done—I went to the bar of the hotel and drank steadily for three hours. The lights went out around me; at one in the morning I was still looking at my hands and seeing them shake. I wanted to leave this place. Now. Today.

Once, a long time ago, I met a newspaperman who had had to cover the great Chicago race riot of the twenties. He had found it difficult, he said, to describe to me exactly how he felt to be in a city divided against itself. If he had walked up to me now in the bar of the Hotel del Principe, I could have told him to save his reminiscences—I knew from the inside how he felt.

He was an old man, but he still closed his eyes and shivered gently when he recalled those terrible days. I wondered between drinks whether I, too, would remember with similar clarity when I was sixty-odd—and decided that I probably would.

Have you ever seen a fragment of ice dropped into super-cooled water? The mass sets solid on the instant, like a man confronted with the head of Medusa—and in just such a way had Vados frozen in face of the news first of Tezol's imprisonment, now of Francis's suicide.

Suicide? whispered gossip at every street corner. *No, of course not. A beating by the police? How should I know? But—*

Enter rumor, painted full of tongues.

A fine of a thousand dolaros? Why did so small a sum go unpaid? We are poor—but there are those who say they agree with us, and some of them are rich!

Hence: *The defenders of our rights have been robbed!* And from there it was a slip of a mental gear, a less-than-jump to a conclusion close at hand, an automatic identification by thousands of people given to thinking in identities, to the plain statement.

"We, the people, have been robbed!"

I ought never to drink on my own. A few drinks give me mental clarity; in company, I could keep my consumption down because of the amount of talking I did. I'd got two reputations that way—as a good conversationalist and as a bore. On my own, I always reached too far too fast in search of still greater clarity, and wound up fuddled.

When I threw myself into bed, I fell deeply asleep for the first part of the night. About four or five o'clock I began to toss and dream. I was wearing an awkward nightshirt that kept tangling my legs; I had gone to a Latin American carnival dressed as an angel with a flaming sword, but the sword was pasteboard. Dark, piteous faces kept rising before me. I slashed at them with the sword, knowing it would not harm them. Yet every time I slashed, the heads rolled and spurts of blood two feet high leaped into the air. Desperately I tried to control the sword, but even when I let go of it it kept slashing and slashing, and the heads rolled until they made a monstrous grinning pile around my feet and my nightshirt was soaked with blood.

In the morning my bed was damp with sweat, and that was not due to the warmth of the night. It had been warm every night since I arrived.

I washed and shaved and went down to the lounge without having eaten my breakfast. I had that curious unsatisfied hollow feeling that isn't quite a hangover but is compounded of too many cigarettes, slightly too much to drink, and not at all enough sleep. I called for the morning papers and then didn't bother to open them; my mind was too distraught. I wasted a bit of time smoking a couple of cigarettes and went down to the traffic department to see Angers.

"Morning, Hakluyt," he greeted me. "Just looking at those costings. Your scheme seems pretty sound—works out under two and a half million dolaros."

"That's bad," I contradicted grumpily. "It oughtn't to take more than half the appropriation—after all, it's only half the job. I'll take a look at it and cut the corners off; then if I can't get it below two million I'll have to start over."

"But there's no need for that," said Angers, looking at me in mild surprise. "I'm sure we can raise the additional—"

"Four million I was told; four million it can very probably be," I interrupted. "Oh, don't let it bother you. I can lose half a million out of that, I imagine. I was generous as hell with the estimates—weighted them for rise in cost of living, suppliers' greed, everything. And for bribery in the treasury department."

I don't know why I added that. Angers gave me a sharp stare.

"You oughtn't to go around saying things like that, Hakluyt," he warned. "Even if you have been reading *Tiempo*."

"Are they after Seixas again this morning? I haven't opened my papers today."

Angers shrugged. "Nothing special this morning, so far as I know. But this blighter Felipe Mendoza has been insulting Seixas right and left recently. I don't much care for Seixas personally, as you know, but I don't believe a word of what Mendoza says, and in any case it is extremely bad for the prestige of the department to repeat his accusations."

He rattled the papers before him into a neat pile. "Well, I'd like to put this scheme before Diaz, anyway. Any objections?"

"Provided you make it clear it's by no means final, I suppose you can if you like." I took out cigarettes and gave him one. "What do you think of the situation in Vados today?"

"Terrible," said Angers succinctly. "I've never seen anything like it. Somebody actually threw a stone at my car on the way to work this morning. And there wasn't a policeman in sight."

"Police learn early not to be on hand when they're really needed." I thought of the scant help I'd had from them when Dalban started to threaten me. Well, Lucas had that in hand. I hoped.

"Speaking of police, though," I said after a brief pause, "I'd appreciate having a few of the local force along with me today."

Angers nodded. "I'll tell O'Rourke," he said, making a note on a scratch pad. "So you've changed your mind about that bodyguard you were offered, have you? Can't say I blame you."

"I don't *want* a bodyguard. But if I'm going down into that hole of Sigueiras', I suppose I'd be safer with an escort."

He took a few moments to decide that he had heard me correctly. Then he drew a deep breath. "What makes you think of that all of a sudden?" he demanded.

"I've been saying—and believing—that this slum was a simple problem, not calling for elaborate answers, and that it's been dragging on and dragging on. . . . I want to see what it's like down there. I want to see the extent of the human problem involved."

He fiddled with the ball-point pen from his desk stand. "Human problems don't exactly fall in your province, do they?" he ventured. "I should have thought you could safely leave that to the city council."

"You misunderstand me. I'm sticking to my own speciality all right."

He didn't press that line further. He countered, "But you must realize that to go into that place just now would be worse than walking into a den of lions! It's Tezol's home, for instance; now that he's in jail and Francis has killed himself, it would be—would be foolhardy!"

"As it happens," I said, "my middle name is Daniel. Boyd Daniel Hakluyt. I've already thought about the consequences —I still want to see for myself."

"Couldn't Caldwell give you an idea?" Angers insisted. "Or

someone else from the health department? There are several
people on the staff who've been down there—"

"I'm tired of 'being given an idea,'" I said wearily. "I was
given a wrong idea when I first came here, and there've been
enough wrong ideas foisted on me since to make me suspicious as hell. I want to form some ideas of my own."

"Very well," said Angers stiffly. "I'll arrange it for you. It'll
have to be this afternoon, I'm afraid, because I have an
appointment with Diaz this morning that I can't put off."

My rather grudging respect for him rose a notch or two. I
said, "You mean you're coming with me?"

"Of course. Sigueiras's main quarrel is with me; I wouldn't
want you to think you were collecting something aimed at my
head if there is trouble. I'll ask O'Rourke for a suitable
escort—come to think of it, it might not be a bad idea for
them to say they're looking for Brown."

"Would that hold up? Haven't they searched the place
already? I'd have thought it was an obvious hideout for him."

Angers shrugged. "I don't know whether they've searched
the place or not, and I don't care. It would be a good
excuse."

"I wonder what's become of Fats," I murmured, more to
myself than to Angers, but he caught the words.

"Does it matter?" he countered. "The one certain thing is
that he hasn't dared to show his face in Vados again, and I'm
sure that's not a bad thing."

I didn't say anything. Whatever else anyone said, though,
Fats Brown had left an impression on me: the impression that
he was an honest man.

It was roughly what I had come to expect of the Vadeano
police that for the afternoon's sortie they laid on eight armed
officers in two cars—after previously having established that
Sigueiras himself was going to be out in the city somewhere.
They seemed to be good at shows of this kind; less good at
the practical side of police work.

It would have suited my purpose much better if I'd been
allowed to go with a single policeman as escort, but I was
made to understand that, while they couldn't stop a foolhardy

foreigner from committing suicide this way, the lives of their men were too valuable to risk so lightly. Somehow this went with the Spanish-speaking personality—in Spain itself, the *guardias civiles* are a species that hunts invariably in pairs; here in the press and hurry of the New World it seemed that nothing short of four times that number would do.

Moreover, they insisted that we each take a police automatic; Angers, possibly picturing himself as Beau Geste or someone of the kind, accepted enthusiastically, but I did my best to refuse the one given to me—after the way my reputation in Vados had been distorted, I thought carrying a gun was a final straw. When I had to give in, I made sure the holster was well out of sight inside my jacket, and hung the sling of my camera across it.

The cars skidded to a halt on the same graveled patch of ground where the traffic department's car had halted on the occasion of my first visit. A group of children playing a singing game on the lip of the depression below the station caught sight of us and scattered, crying a warning. The officers piled out of the cars and hurried toward the entry; perhaps they didn't realize what they were letting themselves in for, because one after the other they lost their footing on the slippery slope and raced in undignified manner toward the bottom.

Angers and I followed more slowly. One could sense the wave of silence spreading through the congested heart of the slum as news of the police's presence was whispered ahead. It was as though the massed human beings were melting into a single hostile organism, like a carnivorous plant on the approach of a fly.

At the entrance a courageous little dark-skinned woman was trying to bar our way. When the police repeated the ostensible reason for the visit, she shook her head determinedly. Fats Brown was not there, had never been there, and never would be there. Everyone was saying he had fled the country.

"Then you won't mind us looking through the place if you aren't hiding him," said the lieutenant in charge of the squad with heavy irony, and thrust her aside.

We threaded our way one by one into darkness and stink.

Two of the police had brought powerful flashlights; they turned them on now, and I saw how this slum had been created. Rough wooden or tin partitions, slatted floors, and rudimentary ladderlike stairs had been attached as best they could be to the original bare steel strutting and concrete buttresses of the monorail station. There was no provision for sanitation, of course, and ventilation was taken care of only by the gaps accidentally left between the ill-fitting sections of board.

Whole families somehow existed here in each of the drawer-like compartments. For furniture they had old boxes, for beds heaps of rags, for cooking stoves sheets of tin with a few glowing sticks heaped in the middle. The smoke mixed with all the other smells and was easier to bear than most.

There were garishly colored prints of the Virgin on most of the walls, along with last year's pinup calendars from soft drink companies. Occasionally a family ran to a complete home shrine with a crucifix and a couple of wax tapers.

"Don't they have a lot of trouble with fires here?" I asked Angers, and he snorted.

"Sigueiras is careful about that sort of thing. He knows perfectly well that if this place caught fire, the firemen would just make sure it didn't spread to the station overhead, and otherwise let it burn itself out. Burning would be a good way of cleaning it out, come to that."

There were no burros actually in the heart of the slum— but only because if anyone had tried to bring an animal that heavy into the place, its hoofs would have gone straight through the rickety flooring. But there were pigs, and there were chickens, and there were certainly goats somewhere out of sight—their presence was unmistakable.

The police threw back curtains—there was hardly a real door in the place—without ceremony. The word had gone ahead of us; we surprised no one in the kind of situation that Professor Cortés had assured me was commonplace down here. People turned blank faces to us or scowled or half-rose with an ingratiating smile and made meaningless gestures of invitation. Children hesitated between watching the strangers and running to hide; they seemed undernourished and all were dirty, but there were few that were visibly sickly or diseased. I saw cases of eczema, rickets, and something else I could not put a name to—six or eight in all out of perhaps a hundred-odd children.

The extent of the slum was tremendous once one was inside. After twenty minutes we were a long way from the outside air, and the surrounding, dimly sensed hatred was beginning to prey on my nerves. We were going down a particularly dark passage, the police flashlights cutting stark blades of white through the thick air, rough-cut slats creaking under our weight—when a woman in a peasant's *rebozo* went past us, head down, carrying a basket. Something about the way she walked struck me as familiar; I paused and looked after her. I never forgave myself for that flash of sudden memory.

For Angers noticed it, and turned to follow my gaze. When he saw the woman, he stiffened.

"By God!" he said softly. "That's Brown's wife! What would she be doing here—unless he was here, too?"

XIX

Angers had spoken in English; the policemen nearest us at that moment did not take in the sense of his words. He rounded on them with a sudden burst of incredible, untypical rage—I had not thought his shell of self-possession could break down so completely.

"Don't just *stand* there!" he exploded. "That's Brown's wife! Get her back here!"

It sank in. Two of the officers scrambled into the dimness. There was a cry. In a moment they were coming back, grasping Señora Brown's arms in strong hands. She struggled, panting, but she was growing old and these police were young and vigorous. Her *rebozo* fell back around her shoulders.

"So it is you," said Angers softly. He took one of the flashlights and shone it full into her face, dazzling her. She half-turned her head to escape the glare.

"*Dónde está su esposo?*" Angers said fiercely.

She gave him a murderous scowl. "*No sé,*" she said flatly. "*No está aquí.*"

I think it was in that instant that she recognized me and remembered who I was; at any rate I suddenly caught a flash of hatred from her dark eyes. I turned away, not wanting to be a party to what happened next.

Angers took out his pistol and slowly slid the safety catch off; the tiny noise it made was very loud in the confined space. "All right," he said, not taking his eyes from Señora Brown's face. "Go down the way she came and see if you can find him."

Obediently the policemen released their grip on Señora Brown's arms. She rubbed the place where their hands had dug into her flesh, but otherwise did not move. Angers leveled the pistol at her chest; her only response was a sneer.

But when the policemen moved purposefully past Angers and off down the passage, she could not control a shudder of terrified anticipation.

"Angers," I said softly, "you ought to be ashamed of doing this."

He didn't look at me as he replied, his voice cold and thin and drained of all human warmth. "Brown is wanted for murder. You know that. If he's here, we mustn't let him get away."

The woman did not understand what he said, of course—she spoke only Spanish. But her gaze followed the armed police officers as they flung back rickety tin doors and swept the squalid cubbyhole rooms with their spears of light.

They came, a short distance away, to a division of the passage. Angers gestured to Señora Brown to go after them; at first she hesitated, but a meaning jerk of Angers' pistol persuaded her. She yielded and began to walk.

Helpless, I followed.

At the division of the passage the policemen had paused and were hotly disputing which way to go. Snatching his eyes from his captive for an instant, Angers snapped a command at them. "In the left fork there is no floor!" he said. "Go down the right branch, you fools!"

Indeed, the boards laid between the struts and girders gave out a few paces along the left-hand branch, and beyond was a yawning gap that swallowed up the light of the torches. The policemen nodded and went cautiously up the other passage. I think I was the only one who saw that the woman relaxed a little as they went. I didn't say anything. Maybe if the police drew a blank, they would give up.

They were half out of sight behind a jutting partition, perhaps thirty or forty feet from us, when Angers again indicated to his captive that she should move to follow them. She went readily enough. Angers fell in behind her, and I was on the point of going after him when something moved in the left-hand fork of the passage, where there was only that open pit instead of a slatted floor.

A huge hand came out of the blackness.

It aimed for the nape of Angers' neck; if it had struck fair, Angers would have dropped like a pole-axed steer. But it didn't—maybe the reach was too far, maybe a foot slipped, maybe Angers detected its coming and managed to move aside a precious couple of inches. It struck him only behind the left shoulder.

I had time to think, dispassionately, that Brown had doubtless had the floorboards taken up along that branch of the passage in order to prevent people tracking him down; I had time to think that if he hadn't been stupid-brave to save his wife from a danger that might have passed her by, he would have lived.

In fact, he died.

Angers turned with the blow; possibly the impact spun him around more quickly than he could have managed by himself. The gun in his hand belched sudden flame, and dust shook down about our heads with the explosion. It was chance, it was reflex, it was the hand of fate, and the bullet destroyed the face of Fats Brown like a drawing being wiped from a slate.

The police started to come back; the woman screamed one long terrible cry that echoed in my head for hours—and I ran.

I found my way to the outer air before the news of what had happened. That was all that saved me from having to join Angers and the police in their bloody retreat. For as soon as what had happened was known, the people of the slum turned on the intruders. When they came out, Angers, deathly pale, was bleeding from a cut across his face; one of the policemen was dragging his right leg as if he could not feel it any longer; all of them were smeared and spattered with filth.

I didn't ask what had happened to Brown's wife. I assumed she was with her dead.

The police ignored me. One of them went straight to the two-way radio in his car and called headquarters for reinforcements. Angers, dabbing at his face with a handkerchief, said something about fixing Sigueiras for good this time—for harboring a murderer—and I said something insane about a man being innocent until proved guilty.

He turned his eyes on me. I saw they were quite hard.

"No," he said. "You're wrong. Our laws are like the *Code Napoléon*. The onus is on the accused."

Faces full of hate came to the entrance of the slum; eyes stared down at us, and children threw more filth that spattered across the clean shining cars. One of the policemen fired three shots, and the faces vanished.

Distantly we heard the howl of police sirens hurrying toward us.

I went up the slope to the station and caught a monorail to the Plaza del Sur. Nobody tried to hinder my going.

I wasn't really thinking as I went. My mind seemed to have ceased its high-level functions, as though my skull had been poured full of cold water. Afterward quick snapshots of things I had seen on the way remained in memory—faces in the monorail car, the sight of traffic in the streets below, the reflection of sun on the windows of buildings, a headline in a paper from Puerto Joaquin that someone was reading as I left the car at Plaza del Sur station. But I wasn't thinking. I had stuck, as though walking up a down escalator, in front of a billboardlike vision of Señora Posador, informing me that whether I liked it or not I had importance in the scheme of affairs.

Enough importance to kill a man.

If I had not conceived this irritable plan to enter the slum for myself, if I had not checked and turned as Señora Brown went by . . . Here you could point to decisions of mine; here you could say, "He did this, and therefore this followed."

The afternoon lay hot and bright on the Plaza del Sur. It was almost empty of people. I went straight across it and entered the hotel.

Sitting alone in the lounge, the habitual unlit Russian cigarette between her fingers, was Maria Posador. Someone had been with her; two glasses rested on the chessboard-topped table beside her, two brands of cigarette were crushed in the ashtray. She was reading through a letter, with eyebrows drawn together.

I went over to her; she raised her face and gave me a cool nod.

"I thought you'd want to know," I said harshly. My voice sounded unfamiliar in my ears, as though another man were speaking through my lips. "They found Fats Brown."

She jerked upright in the chair. "*Diablo!* Where, in the name of God?"

"In Sigueiras's slum—where else?"

"I had thought him safely out of the country! Señor, what have they done with him?"

"Angers put a bullet through his head," I said, and the frozen golden face under the dark sleek hair with the violet eyes and the rich red lips was overlaid in my vision by the sight of the other face as it ceased to be a face at all.

Maria Posador had halted at my words like a movie when the projector motor fails; after a long second she flowed into motion again, but a mist had come up in her eyes, and I do not think she saw me clearly.

"Of course," she muttered. "Of course, that was to be expected."

I waited in silence. In a while she stood up, very erect, and gave me a little stiff half-bow. Then she walked away, crumbling the cigarette in her hand so that flakes of tobacco scattered behind her elegant, expensive shoes.

I turned toward the bar.

Later, they put television on, and I was too apathetic to move away. The program opened with news: Brown's death. I saw the same graveled ground where I had stood earlier; there were military trucks deployed around it now, and people going to the monorail station crowded curiously in the background. Troops went into the slum, came out with Brown's body; the watchers saw it, recognized it under its covering of sacks. Hats were lifted. People crossed themselves. Behind, many of the slum-dwellers were chased into sunlight, beaten with fists and batons, hurried along with the butts of carbines. Like impounded stray dogs, they were driven into the army trucks, sat with bowed heads, and waited to be taken away.

There was a hunt going on for Sigueiras. He was somewhere in the city. As soon as he was found, they would charge him with concealing a wanted man.

They interviewed Angers, looking heroically injured with a bandage on his head, on the current affairs program at five past eight. I was still in the bar; I hadn't any stomach for food. I'd just been sitting there. They also put Bishop Cruz on, and he thundered episcopally about the wages of sin as he had done before, the day after Estrelita Jaliscos died.

And then they gave a sort of credit line to those who had helped in this brave hunting-down of a desperate killer— unquote. In among the rest they dragged my name.

I felt a sort of dull resentment harden within me. Hell, maybe Brown *had* laid this Jaliscos girl, in spite of all his denials; if he hadn't, maybe he *had* pushed her out of a window; if he hadn't done that, either, it was sure—I myself had seen—that he had it in mind to kill Angers. All granted, all granted. He wasn't a desperate killer; he was an honest man on the wrong side. And I wasn't going to have any part of posthumous attempts to convict him without trial.

Maybe it was a sort of habit, conditioned into me by my work; up to now, I'd been passive, reacting, absorbing, accepting, just as when I started a new job I had to spend a long time acquiring facts and feelings. Now I was past that stage. I was going to start saying what I thought and doing what I believed to be right. And I could start by raising a little hell at the TV studios.

I went out to my car and drove there as soon as the program ended.

Rioco, the producer of the program, was on the point of leaving the building. He seemed very tired; at first he failed to recognize me, and when he did, he hardly seemed to be taking in what I said.

As I was starting to repeat myself, however, he brushed his hand impatiently across his eyes. "Yes, yes," he muttered. "I did hear what you said. But what can I do? This is a policy question—you must take your complaints to Dr. Mayor."

"Why? What's it got to do with him?"

He snapped at me. "You don't think *I* decide what goes out on our programs, do you? The most important ones we broadcast? If you want your name kept out of our reports, you'll have to tell Mayor, because he handed down an order to play up your part in the affair at seven-thirty this evening. If we'd had time, we'd have come down and got you to give an interview, like Angers."

"You would not!" I said when I could draw breath again— the sheer presumption of the remark staggered me momentarily. "All right, if I have to see Mayor, I see Mayor. Where do I find him?"

"Maybe in his office—on the first floor." Rioco gave a savage grin. "I wouldn't tackle him now if I were you. He's not in the best of moods—"

"What kind of a mood do you think *I'm* in after all the lying trash you've been putting out about me?" I could feel my nerves fraying as if Rioco's voice were sawing them on the sharp corner of a block of sandstone; I stamped past him and went up the stairs two at a time to the next floor.

Mayor's office was well guarded; there was a receptionist, male, muscular, as well as a receptionist, female, pretty. I walked past both of them while they were still putting on their "good evening we recognize you of *course*" smiles and threw open the door to Mayor's sanctum.

For a moment everything was silent. I had expected Mayor to erupt, but he did nothing of the sort—he showed astonishment for a second and then mastered it. His visitor, who had been talking to him, broke off and swung around on his chair. I recognized, of all people, Dalban.

I was at a loss for a moment, and Mayor recovered his composure altogether. He sat back, settling his glasses on his nose with a fingertouch, and spoke with ponderous humor.

"Your business is obviously urgent, Señor Hakluyt. What is it?"

I ignored him and addressed Dalban. I could hear bitterness and rage struggling in my voice. "You'll be delighted to know, señor, that what your threats and bribes couldn't achieve is being successfully accomplished by this—this Mayor here. Minister of Misinformation and Accusations, so I understand."

It was at this point that I first realized I was very drunk indeed.

I stood back inside my head and allowed myself to go on talking—I couldn't do anything else. I said, "They say the bigger the lie the better the chance of people believing it. He's been telling the whole of Aguazul this evening that I was right-hand man to hero-boy Angers in the rounding up of a dangerous killer called Fats Brown. That's a hell of a big lie, and probably a hell of a lot of people believe it. Well, I don't —and after all, I was only *there*. What I saw was murder. I'm telling you that straight. I've stood practically every kind of pushing around this pretty-in-theory, stinking-in-practice government of yours can dish out, Mayor, and I'm saying now that this last lie makes me want to vomit on your nice clean desk!"

On the last three words I beat my fist on that desk, each time harder, until the last time the two phones jumped in their cradles.

Mayor had heard me out without expression. Now he moved plumply in his chair. He said in his surprisingly mellow voice, "Señor Hakluyt, you are excited. I well understand the shock you have suffered; this is not the first violent death to which you have been a witness since arriving here. But it is our duty to present facts to the public."

I said, "Facts! Facts! Lies aren't facts!"

"It's a fact that this slum under the monorail central is a

place where a suspected murderer can hide, isn't it? Or do you deny that self-evident truth?"

"Suspected! He wasn't condemned or even tried, except in the minds of the people who believe your falsehoods, and now he never can be tried. That's a fact—and you haven't given that to the public, have you? You and your 'most governed country,' Mayor—let's face it, you've degraded yourself into a mouthpiece for government propaganda, and this television service you've created is no more than a megaphone for an arrogant dictator, with hypnotic attachments! 'Know the truth and the truth shall make you free'—hide the truth and you get what you're after: a country where everyone believes what they're told and never gets an inkling of the dirty truth behind the pretty lies!"

Mayor's face was purpling; before he could speak and before I could formulate the climactic insult I needed to finish my tirade, Dalban's rich voice cut across the room.

"Señor Hakluyt, I here and now apologize to you. To bribe or threaten you was ill-judged. I believe you are an honest man. I have often desired to say exactly what you have said to this corrupt barrel-of-wind Mayor. But even with my not inconsiderable prestige I have dared do little more than remonstrate—as I came here to remonstrate tonight. Now I do not care any more. I think you are perfectly correct. I think Mayor is a dangerous megalomaniac, and Ciudad de Vados is an unhealthy town in which to live so long as he is forcing his perverted propaganda on our citizens. He and the professor of so-called social sciences Cortés who foists the same predigested pap on our intelligent young students to stop them from saving themselves would be better—off—dead."

I felt vaguely embarrassed; maybe it was the drink. Or it was the unmistakable sincerity in Dalban's tone, which made me feel that I had been looking at him up to now through some officially issued dark glasses.

"I do not any longer think we need speak of your leaving Aguazul," Dalban continued thoughtfully. "Dr. Mayor, you have heard what I said; now you have heard what Señor Hakluyt said. Are you prepared to undo the effects of your vicious lies?" –

Mayor sat very still; we looked at him. I was vaguely aware that the receptionist, male, muscular, was standing in the doorway with a helpless expression, as if waiting for a command to remove us both. I thought at first Mayor might yield, for sweat pricked out on his forehead and two bright red spots burned high on his cheekbones.

But when he at last spoke, his voice was hard and firm.

"My broadcasting service is the organ of our government," he said. "It is not to be controlled by the whim of private individuals. Señor Hakluyt, you are a distinguished visitor doing a valuable service for our city; you are likewise a stranger, and at the moment you are very drunk. We—and when I say we, I speak for the cabinet—we can overlook this breach of manners. You are fortunate in your privileged position. But I will not withdraw anything that has been said."

"I've sold your government nothing except my services," I said harshly. "Whatever you may be able to do with your own puppet-citizens, you can't do it to me."

He ignored me. "As for you, Dalban!" His gaze shifted, and I suddenly felt that I was looking at a man who wielded conscious and astonishing power. "You have been a damnable nuisance for too long. The patience of the government is great, but not inexhaustible, and this time you have overreached yourself. You are finished."

He just sat there when he was done. I felt a hand on my shoulder; the tough male receptionist had come up to me and jerked a thumb to indicate the door. Dalban, with dignity, was rising to his feet.

"On the contrary, Dr. Mayor," he said quietly, "I am just about to begin."

And he strode from the room.

I followed, wishing I had not drunk quite so much. A million things I wanted to say to Mayor boiled in my skull, but none of them would come to my tongue. What was left of my ability to think logically directed that I should obey the command to leave; if I stayed, it was inevitable that my frustration would drive me to attack Mayor physically—I should have liked to strangle him with the cord of his telephones. But that wouldn't have solved anything. And I'd have been thrown out bodily.

Outside, in the cool night air, with the illuminated façade of the building looming above us, Dalban stopped and turned back to me.

"Again I will apologize, Señor Hakluyt," he said, curiously humble.

"I'll accept that," I said. "But I don't undertake to forget that you threatened me. I thought that honor was at a premium here. And yet—"

He gave a somehow ghastly chuckle. "And yet your encounter with Mayor has perhaps disillusioned you, no?"

"I'd like to—oh, hell, I don't know what I'd like to do to him. I thought he was a sound man; maybe he was when he was just a political theorist. But—corrupted by power, maybe. *I* don't know."

"This country may owe its twenty years of peace to his methods," said Dalban, and glanced up toward the lighted windows. "But Mother of God, it has cost us dearly!"

"What will you do now?" I said.

"Who knows? We will find a way, señor. The worst things in the world cannot endure."

There didn't seem to be anything to say after that, so I went back to my car and drove, very slowly, with cool air on my face, back down the mountainside into the city.

XX

Something howled, screamed, and rattled past the hotel. I blinked wildly at the pattern of lights drifting across my ceiling—I always prefer to sleep with the curtains open—interpreting them into nonsense.

I got out of bed and stared down toward the street.

A fire engine, its siren crying like a soul in torment (I thought of Brown's wife at her husband's death), swung around a corner and tore off into darkness. A helicopter buzzed past, seeming so close that I could have jumped up beside the pilot. Two police patrol cars took the same route as the fire engine.

By this time I was beginning to understand what was going on, and I lifted my eyes toward the hills. There was a glare up there—a red, shifting glare that was patently no sort of street lighting. A plane crashed into the mountainside was my first guess; then I realized that it wasn't necessary to implicate a plane. The broadcasting center was on fire.

I glanced at my watch as I went to fetch my binoculars. Three-ten A.M. A dead time of night. From the way it showed up, the blaze had had plenty of time to take hold before it was discovered. Perhaps there was no one in the entire building.

But surely there would be sprinkler systems in a place like that, and probably also an alarm system connected directly with fire headquarters—

I stopped myself making empty guesses, because whether or not there were sprinklers and alarms, they hadn't saved the place. Through the glasses it was an impressive sight. The antennae, stilted and stiff atop the hard square outline of the building, seemed to be walking with vast deliberation into the mouth of hell. A section of wall and roof would slip; accordingly, one leg of one of the masts would dip, like a man taking a short step forward. After that, the mast would wait, as children do when playing Red Light, for an opportunity to move again.

I couldn't see the fire engines—they were hidden from view by intervening buildings and the slope of the ground—but their presence could be detected wherever the red glow dulled with the impact of their thousand-gallons-a-minute pumps. I considered going out to see the fire from close at hand; then I decided that anybody who did would certainly interfere with the serious job of fighting the flames. Though Vados's traffic flow was excellent, even a single extra vehicle on the road up to the broadcasting center might delay an essential ambulance or another fire engine.

So after ten minutes or so I went back to bed.

My mind was slightly muzzy. It wasn't until I'd lain down again that the full impact of what I'd just seen came home to me. Vados's Minister of Information and Communications wouldn't be broadcasting any retractions, or anything else, today, tomorrow, or for months to come.

And if Vados's government was really dependent on the operations of Mayor's public misinformation service to mold the pliable opinion of Vadeanos, then for that period *el Presidente* was going to be like a man with one hand tied behind his back.

I thought of what Dalban had said, standing outside that imposing building which the age-old force of fire was now reducing to a shell. And I wondered. . . .

Wondering, I dozed off. But I wasn't allowed to get much rest. It was still before daylight, only a little after five o'clock, when I heard voices at my door.

"*Este cuarto es el No. 1317*," said a hard, low voice. "*Abria la puerta.*"

It was uttered in too quiet a tone to be addressed to me, but the number of the room was certainly mine. I sat up in bed.

I hadn't given back the police automatic that had been forced on me for the visit to Sigueiras's slum. I eased it from its holster and sat waiting with one hand on the light cord.

When the door swung open and a man stepped through, I tugged the cord and jerked the muzzle of the gun through an attention-drawing arc. "*Quién está?*" I said loudly. "*Y qué hace Vd.?*"

The man swore loudly and came forward. I saw a scared-looking member of the hotel staff behind him. "*Policia*, Señor Hakluyt," he said.

I lowered the gun. It was Guzman, the sergeant of detectives I had encountered previously—the one who had offered me a twenty-four-hour bodyguard after Dalban first threatened me.

"All right, Guzman," I said aggressively. "What do you want?"

"The señor will please come with me."

"The señor will do nothing of the kind. The señor will see you and the entire police department in hell first. Go away and come back at a reasonable hour."

His saturnine face did not react. With an air of extreme patience, he answered, "There has been sabotage at the television station, Señor Hakluyt. Last night, we learn, you visited it for some purpose or other. You will certainly be able to help with our investigation."

"How? I went to tell your precious Dr. Mayor what I thought of him. Rioco saw me arrive, and José Dalban saw me leave. So, if he had any eyes, did this man who's supposed to be following me when I leave the hotel. Why don't you ask Mayor?"

"Because Dr. Mayor is nowhere to be found." Guzman spoke unblinkingly. "It is known that he remained late last night to prepare directives about today's news on the radio. They have not yet been able to reach his office because the fire is too hot."

He glanced at his watch. "The señor will come with me. *Pronto!*"

"You win," I said, sighing. "Here, suppose you take this. It belongs to your department, anyway."

I handed him the gun. He took it without expression and stood waiting while I dressed. Then he escorted me down to a waiting car, and we were hurried around to police headquarters.

They took a statement from me, laboriously, with great detail, and then abandoned me to sit on a bench in a small anteroom and smoke my cigarettes, one after the other, for almost four hours. Someone brought me a cup of strong, unsweetened coffee around seven-thirty, and I managed to have someone go out for sandwiches for me.

Eventually a clerk came and fetched me to go into *el Jefe*'s office, where O'Rourke himself and Guzman were waiting for me. O'Rourke looked defiantly weary, his eyes red and sore, his tie knotted almost at his waist, his shirt unbuttoned to show the mat of hair on his chest.

"You are in luck, Señor Hakluyt," said Guzman, tapping the statement that had been copied down from me earlier. "We had no trouble locating Señor Rioco, who could swear when you arrived, and Señor Barranquilla who—shall we say?—saw you off the premises." He gave a parody of a smile. "And it is likewise confirmed what time you returned to the hotel. Therefore, if you did not climb from your window, you remained there during the crucial times."

"Crucial times for what? And haven't you got hold of Dr. Mayor yet?"

"Oh, yes, señor. He was found at ten minutes past seven. That is to say, his bones were found. He was trapped in his office and burned to death."

I saw O'Rourke's red eyes on me. He had hunched his shoulders together and was leaning forward on his desk with hands half-closed as though preparing to seize—something— and throttle it to death.

I said slowly, "This is incredible to me. I'd have thought there would be fire alarms, sprinkler systems—"

"There were, señor. The line to fire headquarters, which connects the alarm, had been short-circuited. The sprinkler systems may have operated or may not. We cannot say. The building is empty except for one watchman between half past midnight and half past five A.M. The watchman was also killed, it seems. But him we have not yet found."

"But—damn it, that's a modern building. I was awakened up at about ten past three by the fire sirens, and when I looked at the television center, it was burning as though it were made of matchwood, not concrete! How was it done?"

Guzman hesitated. O'Rourke glanced at him and snapped a curt query in Spanish. "What does he want?"

Guzman replied quickly, "To be told how it was done."

"Tell him—what does it matter!"

Guzman nodded and switched back to English. "There were eight thousand liters of oil stored for the generators which power the transmitter if the main electricity supply runs low. It would appear that an incendiary bomb was placed in the oil store. As soon as the wreckage is cool, it will be investigated."

I thought again of Dalban saying, "On the contrary, Dr. Mayor. I am just beginning."

Not that Vados would be a worse place to live in with Mayor dead. But to have had a hot-tempered wish translated into stark fact so quickly was unsettling, and I was acutely afraid that I might turn out to be the material witness whose evidence caused Dalban's arrest on a murder charge. I didn't want to get more involved than I was—

"Señor Hakluyt," Guzman was saying. I blinked back to the present moment.

"Yes?"

"Señor Barranquilla has also testified that in Dr. Mayor's office he overheard José Dalban declare that Dr. Mayor would be better off dead. Did you also hear this?"

I hesitated, seeing O'Rourke's tired eyes on me, and in the end nodded. "I think he said something like that," I confirmed reluctantly.

"Thank you, señor. I think that is all. But we may need to contact you again."

Had it been intended as murder? Had it been chance that Mayor had remained in the building, or was the moment of the sabotage chosen because Mayor was there alone?

And *was* that what Dalban had meant when he declared he was just beginning?

There weren't any answers to those questions.

As soon as I left police headquarters I bought the day's papers and went into a restaurant to read them over coffee and rolls. My head was buzzing; I had to force myself to concentrate, but if there was anything the papers could add to my personal knowledge of what had happened yesterday, I badly needed the information.

Liberdad, naturally, was playing up Fats Brown's death as the end of a desperate villain—the same tune that the television service had been whistling yesterday. There was a long article on an inside page by Luis Arrio, now chairman of the Citizens of Vados, that contained an attack on Dalban. The fire was, of course, not mentioned—this was on an inside page and would probably have been put to bed early the previous evening. It was concerned mainly with what he had done to me; he had villainously tried to put off the day when the good Señor Hakluyt would sweep away Sigueiras's breeding ground for crime and criminals. Arrio warmly praised Andres Lucas for his handling of the Sigueiras case and went on to quote Professor Cortés extensively on the social problems of the slum.

Why the hell did they have to go on making *me* responsible for the continued existence of Sigueiras's hell-hole? I'd done my best to make it clear that any solution of that one in terms of traffic would be artificial and that what was wanted was a good healthy governmental decree about it. In any case, now that Sigueiras was wanted for harboring a murderer, the whole thing would straighten itself out.

Tiempo had really let itself go—mainly on me, as though the force of Romero's injunction had expired. Which it had not, of course. This morning I didn't much care; I was as ready to hate the guts of the people of Ciudad de Vados as they seemed to be to hate mine.

And to add to the recklessness of today's issue, Felipe Mendoza had gone back to his attacks on Seixas, and this time was imputing directly that Vados knew about Seixas taking bribes, but connived at it. They weren't going to get away with that kind of thing for long.

But I didn't spend time thinking about that. All I wanted now was *out*. I'd finish the job, if that was allowed me— and at present it seemed that it wasn't allowed. Without being asked, I'd found myself caught up in Vadeano affairs that didn't concern me, and now they were tangling me at every turn.

I wanted to get the job over. And for precisely the same reasons I wanted to quit—for a while at least—and give myself a chance to start thinking straight again.

Today, moreover, I did not want to see Angers. My first nausea was cooling, but I doubted that Angers' selfsatisfaction and smugness with what he had done would have shrunk at the same rate. If they hadn't, the sight of him was likely to make me explode. Oh, true, Brown would certainly have killed Angers, or manhandled him severely, if he hadn't missed or slipped; true, he was a presumed murderer and had fled rather than attempt to prove his innocence as the law required. . . . He nonetheless seemed to me an honest man, and honest men don't grow on trees.

All too often, though, that's where they end up. Hanging.

I went to the pay phone in the restaurant and called the traffic department to leave a message saying I wouldn't be in today. Then I went out aimlessly and within a short time found myself in the Plaza del Norte. It was thinking of Brown, perhaps, that brought me to the Courts of Justice.

I was standing staring at the statues in the middle of the square (someone had cleaned the paint off Vados's statue) when a squad of police cars howled into sight from the direction of police headquarters and went with sirens wailing down the Calle del Presidente Vados.

So many cars going out together meant something big, even making allowances for the well-known habit of the Vadeano police of going hunting in large numbers. I idled slowly along the sidewalk. After a minute or two the squad cars were followed by two large lumbering trucks.

I paused at a roadside stall and had some more coffee and tamales; before I had finished, the police cars came racing back. They halted before the Courts of Justice and their occupants got out. Three or four men in plain clothes were being forcibly led along by uniformed officers.

I almost poured my coffee down my shirt as I recognized two of the prisoners. They were Cristoforo Mendoza and his brother Felipe.

Now what?

I waited until the trucks also returned—they took fifteen minutes longer over the round trip. When they pulled up, the men in charge—police again—started to unload bundles of newspapers baled for distribution, stacks of the etched plates from which newspapers are printed, files and filing cabinets, huge boxes full of paper.

I thought to myself, well, I'm god-damned. They're closing down *Tiempo*.

And I felt something cold walk down my spine.

XXI

I thought of Maria Posador saying in that calm voice from which she seemed to try to eliminate all possible suspicion of emotionalism, "I believe it right and necessary for there to be some sort of counter-propaganda in Vados."

And I suddenly felt that the remark contained a truth as stunning as a blow.

When a dictator silences the opposition's means of influencing public opinion, then is the time to get the hell out of his domains. Up till now, presumably, *Tiempo* had not menaced Vados seriously, nor had any other source of information opposed to his régime. After all, one TV broadcast, reinforced with the "evidence of my own eyes" of the subliminal perception technique, was worth a dozen issues of any newspaper.

Was this new step due to his losing the weapon of broadcasting? Did he feel that his grip was in danger of slipping, that *Tiempo* now represented a major threat to his security? I speculated frantically for the hour it took me to establish the real facts behind it.

Today Judge Romero had a hangover.

So far as I was able to make out, that was the root of the decision. Physical discomfort has often in the past brought nations, let alone single cities like Ciudad de Vados, to the brink of disaster. It was not so long since one sick administration, composed of bodily unwell men, had nearly blown the whole world to pieces through their continued ill-temper.

In attacking me and Seixas in their issue of today, the editor and staff of *Tiempo* had, of course, infringed the injunctions against them which Romero had issued. And Romero, not taking time to consult me or Lucas, acting for me, as to whether I wished this to be regarded as an infringement of malice, had decided to haul the Mendozas in for contempt of court and to confiscate the unsold stocks of the day's issue.

And he wasn't playing. Police had closed the offices and were standing guard at the doors. There wasn't going to be another issue of *Tiempo* for a long time to come.

It took the news an hour or so to spread through the city. When it had spread, the reaction was immediate and thorough. The National Party, deprived of its only organ of propaganda, raised a howl that could probably be heard in Puerto Joaquin. Demonstrators were pouring into the Plaza del Sur long before the customary starting time for the daily speakers' session, bearing improvised banners and placards attacking Romero specifically and the administration in general. The Citizens' Party was not slow to follow suit; the pegs on which they hung their protests were, of course, the burning of the broadcasting center and the death of Mayor.

The police descended in force to try to clear the square, but it was hopeless. I stayed to watch until it wasn't safe any longer, even from inside the entrance of the Hotel del Principe. The staff closed the doors and stood by under the direction of the anxious-looking manager, ready to barricade the ground floor if they had to. And it looked for a while as though they might have to—the rival mobs first swore at each other, then began to clash: a fist-fight here, knives drawn there, until there was a full-scale riot brewing.

The police did what they could—perhaps more than I had cynically expected—but they were limited to placing under arrest an individual here and there who didn't have too many of his own side within easy reach. They were just nibbling the edges of the crowd.

"They will have to send for troops," I heard someone say nervously in the hotel lobby. "Why do they not send for the troops?"

"What could even troops do to quell this?" answered someone else.

And then nature took a hand.

All morning a damp wind off the ocean had been piling up gray thunderhead clouds against the inland mountains; now, just as the riot was starting to flare, the storm crashed down on the city. Their grievances dying in the downpour, soaked, cold, and uncomfortable, supporters of both sides dispersed to shelter while the police, sighing with relief, escorted ambulance men into the plaza to pick up the injured.

But this was merely a respite. The tensions that had so nearly exploded would be fulminating beneath the surface for at least the rest of the day, and if it turned hot again so that tempers frayed . . .

And this because an old man had dined too well last night! I cast around in my mind for someone whom I could approach for information as to whether anything was being done to put right this thoughtless and potentially disastrous act. It occurred to me that Luis Arrio ought to know; if the chairman of the Citizens of Vados didn't, who would?

I told a waiter to get Arrio on the phone for me, hardly expecting success at the moment, but he was reached for me in minutes—on the strength of my name, it appeared. Getting notorious in Vados had compensations.

"Señor Arrio," I said, "I've just been watching what might have been a full-scale riot in the Plaza del Sur. Can you tell me what's being done about this suppression of *Tiempo*?"

"Oh, that has gone ahead very satisfactorily," came back the dismaying answer. "The editor has been jailed until he purges his contempt, and the staff have been forbidden to engage in further journalism until he does so. He'll be out of the way for some time, probably, and by then the situation should be calmer—"

"You mean they're going to let Romero get away with it?"

A pause, as though wondering if he had heard me correctly. Then: "Why not, señor? It is the law!"

"The people in the square outside this hotel are paying damned little attention to the law!" I said harshly. "They think—and I agree—that this is a piece of criminal idiocy!"

"It is the law, señor," he said frigidly, and put down his phone.

I felt as nervous, frustrated, and eager to do something as though the disaster that impended hung over myself personally; whom else could I get in touch with who might understand the danger of the situation?

The only idea that came to me was Miguel Dominguez. He'd been a friend of Fats Brown's, of course, and because of that he wouldn't particularly care for me personally. Not if he believed what he saw on television. On the other hand, he had this hold over Judge Romero—he was trying to get Romero disqualified for his disgraceful handling of that case against Guerrero and his chauffeur. Maybe if he had succeeded or was near success, Romero's orders of today could be set aside.

The rain was still pelting down. I drove over to the Courts of Justice, wondering if I would find him. As it happened, he was in court today dealing with some minor case; an usher told me it would be adjourned in a few minutes, and I waited in the passage till then.

I had expected a colder reception from Dominguez than the one I actually got—not that that was any too warm. But I was spared the need to deny what had been publicized about my part in Fats Brown's death.

"I was told by José Dalban what you said to Mayor in his office," Dominguez informed me. "I am glad to hear that. We were much afraid you cared more for your contract than you did for the rights of the situation."

"I don't," I said shortly.

"I accept that. What can I do for you?"

"Well, as I understand it, Señor Dominguez," I said, "you were going to try to get an impeachment of Romero, or something of the sort. Is there any hope of hurrying it up? Because closing down *Tiempo* seems bound to cause disaffection—there was practically a riot in the Plaza del Sur today—and surely, if Romero was removed for incompetence, there'd be a chance of salvaging the situation."

He gave me a shrewd, searching stare. "Continue, Señor Hakluyt," he said in a voice that had suddenly acquired a purr. "I think you are about to speak good sense."

"This is the way I see it," I said. "If the Nationals are deprived of their paper, they're going to riot. Only the storm saved Vados from a minor civil war today. The government has lost its television station—who did that, we don't know, but what the hell, anyway? They've got twenty years' advantage! I should have thought that even if Vados himself wasn't prepared to crack down on Romero, Diaz would have done so by now, or Gonzales. Luis Arrio was trying to tell me a little while ago that 'it's the law'—but law or not, damn it, it's bad politics and bad psychology!"

He was actually smiling now—not broadly, but smiling. "Good, Señor Hakluyt. Very good. Yes, it is true that we have taken action to secure a new trial of Guerrero's chauffeur. And we have put in motion the procedure for impeaching Judge Romero for his behavior on that occasion—at which, now I come to think of it, I believe you were present, no? Unfortunately," and here he frowned,

"owing to the tension created by Guerrero's death, it was
judged advisable not to progress too rapidly in the matter,
and it will still be a few days before anything definite is done.
In the meantime, God knows what may happen. You may,
though, accept that Judge Romero, who has been too long in
his place already, is, as you say in English, 'washing up.' "

I was too relieved to correct him. "Then what?"

"Then all his subsequent judgments will be null and void
and all cases at which he has since presided will have to be
retried. Of course, this implies that his injunctions against
Tiempo will fall, and no one else on the judicial bench will be
so stupid as to ban the paper completely." He spread his
hands. "But between now and then other things may happen. . . . I agree with you, señor. We must not delay longer. We
must take steps now, at once, and I will see to it."

Only a little less worried than when I arrived, I left him on
that note.

The main story in the next morning's edition of *Liberdad*—
this was Saturday—was about Dominguez demanding an impeachment of Romero. Diaz had formally given orders for an
investigation into the matter. The paper's hackles had risen in
righteous anger; a polemical and furious article by Andres
Lucas on an inside page, bearing the signs of hurried writing,
profiled Romero and his career. Lucas declared that this was
the crowning insult to a man who despite being reviled by his
enemies had served his country faithfully during a long and
distinguished career—the sort of defense I could imagine him
putting forward in court when he was convinced his client was
guilty.

In any case, Romero was out of the reckoning after this; as
Dominguez had put it, he was "washing up." And, reading
between the lines of Lucas's article, I got the strong impression
that he was suddenly afraid of Dominguez—perhaps seeing in
him that rival who might usurp Lucas's position of supremacy
in the legal world in Aguazul. How real, I wondered, was that
threat? Not very, if Lucas had the might of the Citizens' Party
on his side.

Coincidentally, I saw Lucas that evening. He was eating in

the restaurant in the Plaza del Norte, for although the weather was still cool, it had not rained today, and the tables had been set out again under the palms.

The look on Lucas's face made me suddenly think back to the expression Juan Tezol had worn the day I saw him trudging toward his home under the monorail station, wondering where he could find a thousand dolaros to meet the fine Judge Romero had imposed on him. In the end the powerful backers who had used him as the figurehead of the party had discarded him—made him a martyr. I imagined, realizing it was imagination, Lucas picturing himself in the same situation and perhaps for the first time feeling in his bones what a dirty game politics can be.

I couldn't feel sorry for him now.

Angers turned up at my hotel on Sunday; he had called me before he came, and I had been a bit brusque with him. But he came nonetheless, a little nervously, a little less self-possessed than usual—almost, I would have said, a little ashamed.

I let him find an opening when we had sat down in the hotel lounge. I didn't say anything; I didn't even try to look anything in particular.

He had brought a portfolio with him. He covered a minute's awkward silence by searching in it for some documents, and at last, having found them, cleared his throat.

"I—uh—have bad news, I'm afraid," he said. "Diaz has studied that plan for the market area you gave me. He says he can't approve it. Ht wants a lot of changes. I tried to object, of course, but—"

I said wearily, "I warned you. It's too expensive as it stands, for one thing. And Diaz is at perfect liberty to criticize individual points. So long as he hasn't questioned the actual traffic flow, that's fine. I thought I'd made that clear when I gave you the draft in the first place."

Angers looked at me. He didn't reply for a moment, and before he did he had to drop his eyes.

"You feel pretty bad about what happened to Brown, don't you?" he said.

"Yes."

He opened his hands, palms up, and looked at them, seeming not to know how to go on. Eventually: "So do I, damn it! I—I was *scared*, Hakluyt. You must understand that. When I felt him hit me on the back and I turned around to look into his face—it was like a maniac's or a wild animal's! What else was I to do, in Heaven's name? If I'd hesitated, I'm certain he'd have tried to kill me with his bare hands."

"You weren't exactly treating his wife in the way an English gentleman is supposed to," I said.

He flushed scarlet, all the way to the roots of his hair. "She—she—oh, hell, Hakluyt! Brown was a suspected murderer, whatever else anyone says, and he'd run away to hide instead of staying to face a trial the way an innocent man would have done—"

"Stop trying to convince yourself," I said. "I saw the way you loved that gun the police gave you. Why the hell can't you stick to your own job? You're a highway manager, a traffic organizer, not a one-man crusade for the moral improvement of Ciudad de Vados! And I don't think the conceited pleasure you got out of playing Sir Galahad was worth the life of a good lawyer and an honest man."

His face was interesting over the next few moments; it began to go dignified, hesitated, flushed again, and ended up tattered, like a papier-mâché mask that has been out in the rain.

"I don't suppose there's anything I can say to convince you you're wrong," he said.

"Probably not."

He took out a cigarette, but didn't light it. With it waiting between his fingers, he gave a bitter smile. "You just don't like us or our country, do you, Hakluyt?"

"I haven't been given much reason to like it."

"No. . . . But I think you might try to understand people like me, the foreign-born citizens. We—we hitched our wagons to the star of Ciudad de Vados, as the saying goes. We put our hearts and souls into this city. We gave up all the other things our lives might have held for us—chances of possibly greater wealth, greater success, elsewhere—because we saw in Ciudad de Vados something we could shape to our own desires. There was a line of poetry"——he looked suddenly self-conscious——"that used to keep running through my head when I first made up my mind to come to Vados and settle here. It said something like 'reshape it nearer to the heart's desire.' Well, that's why. That's why, when we see people like Brown and Sigueiras making an unholy mess of our——our dreams, if you like——we find it pretty hard to take lying down. Oh, maybe they have their reasons, maybe they're doing right according to their lights, but we gave up everything for the sake of this city, and when people forget that, who never had to give up anything because they never *had* anything till we came along and gave it to them, it makes us *furious*."

I didn't comment. Angers waited a few seconds, half-hoping for a favorable answer, and at last got to his feet. "Will you be down at the department in the morning?" he asked.

"I'll be there," I said. "I'll be there."

XXII

At about half past ten that same evening José Dalban committed suicide.

The astonishment that followed the news was almost solid: thick and cloying, hampering the mind's attempts to make sense of it like heavy wet clay. *Why?* He was rich—perhaps only a few thousands short of being a millionaire. He appeared successful and influential; that success was founded, as Guzman had told me, on something not very respectable in the eyes of Vadeanos, but it was not illegal. He had a reputation as a clever speculator. And his private life seemed placid enough: he was married, had four children of whom two were at Mexico City University, and a congenial mistress in Cuatrovientos whom his wife knew about.

It was odd, I reflected, how sometimes one never managed to round out one's mental picture of a person till that person was dead, as though a subconscious reflex held one back, insisting that until a man was dead no picture of him could be accurate or complete.

Certainly, in the twenty-four hours following Dalban's death, I got to know very much more about him than I had during his lifetime.

By the end of those twenty-four hours truth was beginning to emerge. José Dalban's enterprises were ripe for the undertaker. Like all speculators, he was operating on other people's money a lot of the time; it so happened that at the moment he was extended far beyond the limits of his own resources. And in that strange, abstract, barely-more-than-half-real way that seems to turn bits of printed paper into deadly weapons, Luis Arrio had seized the chance to plot Dalban's destruction.

That destruction was now following his death.

Piece by piece, Arrio had acquired control of every loan Dalban owed, a few mortgages, several advances against security—and had notified Dalban that he intended to foreclose on everything he could. The total amount involved was about two million dolaros; more than three-quarters of a million was due or overdue for repayment.

So, having drunk two glasses of fine brandy, which steadied his nerves and unsteadied his hands, compelling him to slash four times before he achieved success, he cut his throat.

I heard most of this from Isabela Cortés and her husband when they called in for a drink at the Hotel del Principe on Monday evening before going to the opera. I had asked Señora Cortés what she thought of the destruction of the broadcasting center, and she positively exploded with rage.

"When they find the saboteurs, let them be publicly burned alive!" she snapped. "An evil deed belonging to the past that Alejo labored so many years to bury—a past of irresponsible violence and internecine hatred! I feel half ashamed that I still live to walk in the city when Alejo has suffered that dreadful end!"

"On the other hand," said her husband with unexpected mildness, "this is the first time in many years that we have been able to spend three consecutive evenings together, 'Belita."

"Do not joke about death, León!" Señora Cortés went pale. "Ciudad de Vados, I swear, has never before been like this, with José Dalban dead, and before him Mario Guerrero, and—what can have come over our people? Tell me that!"

Her husband took the question literally, not rhetorically—which in view of his position was reasonable. He rubbed his chin with the back of his hand as he considered.

"Frankly, 'Belita, you have asked an impossible question. One can assume that some—some crucial factor in the long-standing disputes to which we have become accustomed has now come to a head. But to isolate that factor—why, it would be the work of a lifetime."

It was then that we spoke of Dalban's death, and I learned something about the causes of it.

"In one way, Señor Arrio has done a public service," Cortés mused. "For too long Dalban had been making a fortune out of the base impulses of our people"—this I took to be an oblique reference to his monopoly of the contraceptive market—"and in so doing has encouraged them to continue."

"In more ways than one—so some people might maintain," said his wife. "Have you thought of the effect it will have on Señor Mendoza?"

I thought, of course, she was referring to Cristoforo Mendoza, editor of *Tiempo*. Since *Tiempo* had been closed down, I didn't see that the loss of Dalban's financial aid mattered much one way or the other—unless the order to close the paper down had been rescinded, and if it had been, I hadn't been told.

But apparently that was not the point, for Cortés gave his wife a stern look.

"Isabela, you are well aware that in my view Mendoza's books will be no loss to the world, even if he never writes another—"

"Excuse me," I put in. "I don't see the connection."

Cortés shrugged. "Dalban's vanity required him to seem to be also a patron of the arts. In keeping with the pattern of his other activities—all of which seem to have been concerned with pandering to the lower tastes of the people—he had made Felipe Mendoza a protégé of his. He had given him a

house and had occasionally paid him a salary when the sales
of his books were not high."

"I see. But surely, if Mendoza still needs a patron, he will
have no trouble finding another? After all, he has an international reputation—"

"So had the American Henry Miller," said Cortés stiffly.
"But neither he nor Mendoza wrote the sort of book I would
permit to be read in my house."

"Approval or disapproval apart," said Señora Cortés, "one
has to admit that he is creative—and original. No, Señor
Hakluyt, Felipe Mendoza may not find it so easy, certainly
not in his own country, for as you may perhaps have heard,
all his works are on the Index, and consequently he labors
under disadvantages."

"And is that not his fault?" began the professor belligerently. They would have launched on a heated argument had not
Señora Cortés abruptly noticed the time and realized they
were late for the overture.

I was very thoughtful after they had gone. The girl with the
guitar who sometimes turned up here in the evenings, especially when there was to be a big performance at the opera or
one of the theaters, was singing—more to herself than an
audience—at the other end of the bar. I took my drink and
went and sat where I could listen to her.

The way things were now, it almost appeared that my
arrival in Vados had been a trigger to set in motion a chain
of violent and sometimes bloody events. But that was ridiculous. It must simply be chance or coincidence. Most likely,
both my being brought here and the events that had followed
were symptomatic of the same web of rivalries, hatreds, and
jealousies. In other words, at the moment everyone in Vados,
from *el Presidente* himself down to that girl with the guitar,
were puppets dancing at the mercy of forces beyond the
control of individuals.

Here in Ciudad de Vados, of course, they had made a
determined attempt to control those forces—as Mayor had
claimed, this was "the most governed country in the world."
Yes, but maybe the success they had seemed to achieve was
no more than illusion. You could only disguise, not govern,

the dark impulses at the bottom of the human mind, the inheritance of prejudice with which every man, woman, and child walking the streets in every city on earth was laden down. You couldn't govern those. At most, you could dictate when they should be turned loose—and sometimes, when the pressure behind them had built up to a climax, you couldn't even do that.

"Señorita," I said to the girl with the guitar, and she turned grave dark eyes to me. She wasn't pretty; she had a large nose and a large mouth, with one crooked tooth in her upper jaw. "Señorita, what is your opinion of the books of Felipe Mendoza?"

She looked taken aback. "I do not know, señor," she said. "I am a good Catholic, and Catholics are not permitted to read his books. That is all I know."

I sighed. "What do you think about the death of Señor Dalban?"

"They say he was a very evil man. Perhaps his conscience troubled him. Certainly he must have been a great sinner to have killed himself as he did."

"Suppose, señorita, that a jealous rival of yours were to steal from you everything that means anything to you, every-thing whereby you make your living—your guitar, your songs—seduced your boy-friend if you have one, so there was no hope for you—what would you do then?"

She frowned, as if trying to decide my purpose in asking such questions. After a moment's reflection she said virtuously, "I should pray, señor."

I turned toward her. "Listen, señorita, I am not an inquisi-tor. I'm just a stranger in Vados who wants to know what people think about all these happenings of the past few days. Consider! Señor Dalban was *killed*, just as surely as if some-one had held the knife with which his throat was cut. His business was ruined, he was plunged suddenly into debts that he couldn't pay, everything he had worked for all his life was snatched away, not as a visitation from God but because a rival businessman was envious of him. Isn't envy a sin?"

"Oh, yes, señor! A vile sin!"

"Exactly. Can it be right that somebody like Dalban should have his life's work destroyed to satisfy a rival's jealousy?"

She didn't answer. Probably I was posing her questions which her confessor would regard as highly technical and best left to trained theologians.

"As for the man who was so jealous," I went on. "You have heard of Señor Arrio?"

"Oh, of course! He is a very good man. My father work in one of his stores; he is assistant manager, and maybe one day he will be manager." Realization dawned. "You mean—it was Señor Arrio who was so jealous?"

"Of course, Señor Arrio is very rich; Señor Dalban was also quite rich. Naturally they were rivals."

"That I do not believe," she said firmly. "Señor Arrio must be a good man. All the people who work for him say so, and he has set up many good stores in our country, not only in Ciudad de Vados."

"Somebody ask Job's opinion of that," I muttered to myself.

"Besides," she said, as though arriving at an important conclusion, "if Señor Dalban cared more about money than about saving his immortal soul—and he must have if he killed himself merely because he lost his money—he was certainly a wicked man. The love of money is the root of evil."

"Then who loved money the more—Señor Dalban or Señor Arrio, who took all Dalban's money away from him although he himself is already very rich?"

That floored her completely; she sat staring wide-eyed at me as if I were stirring her personal cosmos around and around with a spoon, and she had lost all her bearings. I tried another tack.

"You remember Señor Brown, who was killed the other day?"

"Yes, señor. I read about it in the newspaper."

"What do you actually know about the matter? What do you think he had done?"

She looked down and spoke hesitantly. "Well, señor, everyone knew what Estrelita Jaliscos was like, so what he had done—well . . ."

I was about to rescue her from her painful embarrassment when the significance of what she had actually said went through my stupidly thick skull. I almost spilled my drink as I shot forward in my chair.

"Did you say 'everyone *knew*' what she was like?"

"Why, yes!" She put her hand up to her throat as though my violent reaction had made her dizzy. "What is wrong?"

"You did say they *knew*?" I insisted. "Not 'everyone knows'? You knew what sort of girl Estrelita Jaliscos was before all this happened? You haven't come to that idea because of what the bishop has said on television, for example?"

"No, señor! What would we need to be told, in the district where I live? We have seen for many years how she carried on. She was going out alone with young men when she was only fourteen; she drank liquor—aguardiente, even tequila and rum. And it was said she—she even sold her honor." The girl uttered these last remarks with a faintly defiant air, as though challenging anyone to contradict them.

"In short," I said, "Estrelita Jaliscos had a reputation as an accomplished tart."

"Señor!" she said reproachfully, and blushed brightly. I turned and signaled the bartender.

"If you were really as sheltered as you try to make out," I said, "you wouldn't even have known what the word means. You've given me some very valuable information, and I'm going to buy you a drink on the strength of it. What'll it be?"

She giggled nervously. "First I must sing you a song," she said. "Manuel, there behind the bar, is a friend of my father, and all the time I am here he keeps his eyes on me. I will sing, and then when you give me the drink you will say it is because you like my singing, understand?"

I gave her a sarcastic look. "I suppose you go out with boys, too," I said.

"*Señor!*"

"All right, that wasn't an invitation. Go ahead and sing. How about *La Cucaracha*?"

"That is a bad song, señor. It is all about marijuana. Let me sing you a song of my own."

It was an ordinary sort of pop, such as one might have heard over the radio any day anywhere in Latin America. I watched her as she sang, and came to the decision that she was about one-tenth as much of a shy violet as she liked to make out. Probably Manuel let his eyes wander occasionally.

So nothing was what it seemed, I now discovered. Estrelita Jaliscos had been a real tart, going downhill since she was fourteen. And for her sake Fats Brown was being buried tomorrow. If he'd come to trial and evidence of character had been brought, surely the prosecution's case would have collapsed like cardboard!

Then why hadn't he risked trial? He'd said himself on the night I found him getting drunk to "celebrate" that he was sure Estrelita Jaliscos was a tart. He knew the legal setup in Vados; he could have built a case against her for blackmail stronger than any case against himself for murder.

There was only one reason that fitted his actions. He must have been damned sure that this demand by Estrelita hadn't simply been hatched in the brain of a teen-age gold-digger. He must have known, or have convinced himself, that he would never be permitted to clear himself.

Who could be gunning for him that hard? His rival lawyer Lucas?

No, of course not. Lucas didn't need that kind of out.

Or—didn't he?

There were a lot of things I needed to know about Lucas before I could answer that question. The best person to tell me them would be his other legal opponent, who had also been a good friend of Fats Brown's—Miguel Dominguez.

I wondered if I could get hold of him at this time of the evening. I got up from my chair, and the girl singing broke off with a hurt look.

"Oh, yes!" I said, remembering. "Manuel!"

The barman came down toward me, smiling.

"Bring the young lady her usual, and charge it up to me. I'll be back."

"Her—usual, señor?" He looked at me expressionlessly.

"Yes, whatever she has on these occasions. A double tequila *con sangrita de la viuda*, I should imagine." I grinned at the girl's outraged expression. "I'm sorry, señorita, but I think your song is terrible. Never mind—have *two* drinks on me while you're about it, and you'll get to be a big girl one day."

And why she didn't spit in my eye I'm still not sure.

XXIII

I must have got Dominguez away from his dinner table or something, because he sounded irritable when I called him. He thawed a little when I'd told him why I called, though not completely.

"Thank you for advising me, Señor Hakluyt," he said. "You must, of course, understand that since Brown was never brought to trial, the character of this Jaliscos girl is of mainly academic interest. But it would be kind to his widow to do something toward clearing his reputation, if possible."

I said, "But it mustn't be allowed to go at that, señor. Fats Brown was a good man, better than most people I've met in Vados. And from the bishop on down, people continue to smear him. Now that Judge Romero's attack on your good standing has been countered, your position in the legal world here is close to Andres Lucas's—"

"I wouldn't say that," he put in rather frigidly.

"A lot of people *are* saying it. Look, Fats was convinced that Estrelita Jaliscos was no more than an amateur tart who wouldn't have had the brains to pick on him without prompting. If there was someone behind her, then that someone ought to be hauled out of hiding—"

"Señor," he said, sounding almost regretful, "I think you are building too much on the word of one young lady. It would be erring as much on our side as those who condemn Señor Brown have erred on theirs if we were to jump to the conclusion that this was a vile scheme to defame him. We simply do not know. I can promise no more than that we who are old friends of Señor Brown will do our best for him and especially for his widow."

It wasn't what I wanted. But I had to make do with what I got.

They were supposed to be burying Fats the following day. I was unable to find out where. A curtain of silence seemed to have been drawn—presumably disturbances were feared, as there had been on the day of Guerrero's funeral. I wouldn't have thought he was so poor that he had to be buried at city expense, and he wasn't a convicted criminal, but when I called the two non-Catholic burial grounds in the neighborhood of the city, I was told that he was being buried in neither. He certainly hadn't been a practicing Catholic, but I called the bishop's secretary on the outside chance, and was told he was not a member of the Church and nothing was known of the arrangements for his funeral.

So Fats Brown was laid to rest somewhere—in obscurity— and I had to go back to work.

Things were going smoothly enough. Simple figuring had already chopped a quarter-million dolaros off my original estimates for the market district scheme, and the objections raised by Diaz turned out to be rather sensible ones. I let the costing clerks get ahead with it and went in to see Angers late in the morning.

He seemed to shrink a little when I entered his office, to draw further into his shell; bit by bit, as though he had at first been afraid I was going to strike him, he came back as we talked.

"The reason I've come in," I said, lighting a cigarette, "is the need for a decision about Sigueiras's slum."

Angers didn't say anything, just waited for me to go on.

I tried to sound impressive and didactic. "As I've said before, only it hasn't penetrated, it's essentially a matter of saying, 'Get out.' As things stand, apparently you have to add something like, 'Get out, we want this for warehouse space.' Fine; it'd make a good storage place. Trouble is, there's no genuine need for storage space there. The center of this city was much too well planned for that. It boils down to this: is the city going to throw Sigueiras out on his face, or am I still supposed to fake an official reason?"

"We still can't just throw him out," said Angers wearily. "Harboring a wanted man isn't a felony that carries automatic loss of citizens' rights. If it were, the whole thing would be perfectly simple. We still need a redevelopment plan before we can pass legislation depriving him."

I was silent for a moment, thinking back to that visit to the slum. I'd forgotten about the data I'd come to gather, the moment I recognized Señora Brown. But up till then I'd been reluctantly forced to the conclusion that there was nothing to choose between evicting the slum-dwellers and leaving them where they were. Left where they were, they had a home—of sorts. Evicted, their problem would become conspicuous enough to compel the government to act. They were plainly not equipped to inhabit modern dwellings—but hell, that question had to be faced every time you cleared tenement blocks or hovels, and they certainly wouldn't learn any better down in their mucky pit.

"I think I'm going to compose a long memorandum," I said. "A memorandum to Diaz."

"I could arrange for you to see him personally if you prefer," Angers suggested. The offer was like a kind of flag of truce.

"I don't think I do prefer, thanks. I couldn't be so persuasive in Spanish as I'd need to be, and an interpreter would waste time. I'll tell you what I'm going to say, anyway."

I looked at the wall map, which was open and hanging down, and took time to compose my thoughts.

"Roughly, it's this," I said at length. "I can fake a development plan that'll allow the city to throw Sigueiras out with no objections from anyone. Purely incidentally, unless arrangements are made to absorb the slum-dwellers when it goes into effect, it will also trigger off a civil war."

"That seems like a strong way of putting it," said Angers, staring.

"I'm not kidding. I'm simply saying that the answer isn't to—to build parking lots under the station or whatever. The best bet is to disperse the slum-dwellers on moral and health grounds, leave the monorail central as it is, and subsidize new villages for these people. Use the available funds, not to patch up the site, but to get them out of the city's hair. Build 'em new houses, buy 'em livestock, give 'em ground to cultivate and the tools to work it with. Hire a couple of U. N.-trained experts to teach them how to live in the twentieth century. That'll cure the problem—and it'll likely stay cured."

Angers was slowly shaking his head. "Diaz wouldn't accept that," he said. "I agree it's superficially the best answer, and of course it would be good for the city simply to get these peasants back into the country again. Mark you, I'm not sure they'd agree to go—a taste for sponging is hard to lose once it's acquired, and even in Sigueiras's stinking cubbyholes they've probably lived an easier and lazier life than they ever did in their villages. But that's not the objection I'm quite sure Diaz would raise.

"No, to accept such a plan would be tacitly to acknowledge these people's inferiority, and he refuses always to face that. He's of the same stock, and to him it's like denying his own family, if you follow me. I don't doubt that he feels inferior himself, compared to Vados, for instance. Vados is a well-educated, widely traveled man with a cultured background, whereas Diaz is an earthy man, a real son of the soil. With him it's practically an article of religious faith that his people are as good as we are—I mean, the foreign-born citizens and the native-born members of the higher cultural strata. Let's face it, Hakluyt: you know as well as I do that there's a great gulf fixed, as the saying goes. I agree completely that what these people most need is educating up to modern standards —but to a man like Diaz, admitting the need for education of this kind is equivalent to admitting inferiority."

"I don't agree. I've never met Diaz—I've only seen him once, at Vados's garden party—but I can't believe that a man who's got as far ahead from lowly beginnings as he has can't recognize a hard fact when it's presented to him."

Angers sighed. "Very well—go ahead. I'll make sure he doesn't actually dismiss it out of hand, but more I can't promise."

"I'll let you have the memo this afternoon. While it's fermenting, I'm going to take a day off. I'm going to go and take a look at these traffic nightmares you told me about in the rest of the country. This bloody town has about driven me insane, with its hypermodern façade and its seething primitive instincts. I want to go somewhere dirty for a change."

"You'll find things very different outside Vados," said Angers neutrally. "I'll tell the police you're going, so no one will worry. When do you expect to get back?"

"Tomorrow some time. Depends how bored I am."

"Enjoy yourself." The thin smile came and went. "They say a change is as good as a rest, you know."

Since my arrival, I hadn't been farther than to the outskirts of Vados. Now I took the coast road and went to take a look at what I'd been missing.

Puerto Joaquin: a bustling sprawl of a town, at the mouth of the Rio Rojo, with vast modern dock facilities only a few years old because of the great fire that had destroyed part of the city. And nonetheless, after the clean graciousness of Vados, seeming to belong to the dead past.

Cuatrovientos: the former capital, the city of riches, the oil town. With the lower labor costs obtaining here and the highly favorable level of taxation, it was a better proposition to work fields down here rather than open up known but so far untapped North American resources.

And Astoria Negra: farther south than Puerto Joaquin, also on the coast. That was as far as the likeness went. Astoria Negra was farther south, not so favorably located, lacked the facilities to handle such large vessels and had no pipeline from the oilfields. Its life was dominated by the harbor; the harbor was dominated by coastal trading, mostly in guano, and by fishing. There was a small naval station.

For me, it was like taking three steps out of modern times into the nineteenth century to come to Astoria Negra. It was almost impossible to accept how bad things were here. The average standard of living might have compared with that in the shantytowns around Vados; it was the kind of town where you scratch a house and find a slum. Not all of it was like that, of course—there were fine recent apartment blocks and a few magnificent old houses in time-blessed gardens—but most of it was like an Italian neo-realist film made soon after World War II: crumbling walls, irregular streets, puddles of water splashing underfoot.

The echoes of the conflict in the capital had hardly spread this far. It seemed that the main highway ran directly from Vados to the outer world, and its line was never touched by the local citizens. I talked with people—an old Indian, a young man with a chip on his shoulder, a peasant who carved traditional wooden figurines for the occasional tourists who came by sea and stopped over to exclaim at the quaintness of Astoria Negra before going on—in most cases thankfully—to the air-conditioning of Vados. Everyone I spoke to had just two subjects of conversation: lack of money and the local chess championships currently in progress. The woodcarver was a chess fanatic; he had in his store a dozen sets he had carved himself, all different, yet all strangely alike, the pieces having the squat, blocky appearance of Aztec idols.

No one seemed to be concerned about the future of the city, yet if there was a place crying out for some of those four million dolaros, this was it. The wrangling in Vados, to those people, was something that concerned the government, an amorphous body of ill-defined individuals who usually did the wrong thing and couldn't be got at to put matters right again—hence had been given up as of no concern to the man in the street of Astoria Negra.

Wherever I looked, I found new ways of spending money. I had hardly to give a glance along a street before my mind was crowded with plans for redevelopment and improvement. Suppose Vados had rebuilt this town instead of founding his new one—what then? Would it have repaid the effort? Of course not. This town was past help; ideally, it should now be left to die a natural death, stripped to its harbor facilities and to a widely spread out, clean new city a quarter the size extending much farther inland.

Only that would cost around a hundred million dolaros before you began to worry about demolition costs, and it would have to wait till next century, or the century after.

I went back to the woodcarver's store and bought one of his chess sets.

XXIV

I drove back to Vados in the evening, after about twenty-eight hours' absence. And in that time things had been happening.

Of course, the city hadn't been truly quiet for weeks, but it had at least displayed the sullen tranquillity of a dormant volcano; it did no more than burst a bubble of searing hot gas on the surface of its lava pool occasionally.

Now, though . . .

There were police beacons on the highway two miles out of the city; at the third of them the traffic was cut to single line and armed police officers stood guard. Each car in turn was halted, and some were turned back.

When it came to my turn, I demanded to know what was going on. The officer inspecting my papers didn't answer directly; he merely said in a neutral tone, "It might be dangerous for you to go about the city unescorted, Señor Hakluyt. You must go directly to your hotel and telephone to police headquarters that you have arrived safely. We will send to search for you if you are not there within"—he glanced at his watch—"a half hour."

"What's the reason for all this?" I pressed again.

"When the señor enters the city, he will see for himself," was the reply. He stepped back and waved me on.

I did see.

No word of rioting had reached Astoria Negra as far as I knew, and the outside news services might well have been censored also. But rioting there must have been. I passed one of Arrio's department stores which had had a home-made bomb thrown through a display window—firemen were still damping down the wreckage, and there was a strong smell of stale kerosene. There were several burnt-out cars along the streets; one street was closed because a monorail car had been sabotaged and had fallen to the ground there. The whole city now was ominously quiet.

The armed police on every street corner had now been reinforced by the National Guard. Militiamen looking uncomfortable but determined in ill-fitting fatigues, with carbines slung on their shoulders, were patrolling sidewalks, and I was stopped a couple more times to show my papers before I reached the Hotel del Principe and safety.

A newspaper placard had given me the key to these events as I drove past, and now people in the hotel bar confirmed what it said. No wonder Dominguez had been cagy when I spoke to him about Estrelita Jaliscos; he had already been preparing a pretty devastating attack, and while I was away he had fired his entire broadside.

Which is to say he had produced a witness—the dead girl's brother—who swore not only that she had been put up to blackmailing Fats Brown, but that it was Andres Lucas who had made her do it.

The National Party had marched through the streets demanding retribution, Lucas's house had been stormed and nearly set on fire, and Lucas himself was now in custody "for his own protection."

It took me a little while to fill in all the subsidiary details, but it made one thing plain: whether he denied it or not, Miguel Dominguez was temporarily the most influential man in Ciudad de Vados, *el Presidente* himself not excepted.

I got hold of a paper and read the text of the announcement Dominguez had released to the press; it was a measure of his sudden eminence that *Liberdad* had printed it practically in full. Not content with going for Lucas alone, Dominguez had described this shameful affair as just one aspect of the widespread corruption of the moment; another, he declared, was Seixas's barefaced insistence on new traffic developments to put business in the way of the construction companies in which he had an interest, and still another was the way in which Caldwell of the health department had exaggerated the situation in Sigueiras's slum to secure public support for its clearance.

Enraged followers of the Citizens' Party had come out on the streets to drive off the Nationals, and the National Guard had been called out to deal with the resulting riot. A curfew was now in force and would not be lifted till six o'clock in the morning.

I was very glad indeed to have missed this little set-to. Especially when Manuel, the hotel barman, pointed out to me the scar left by a rifle bullet that had careened through a window and ricocheted off his beautifully polished bar.

There was sporadic firing from the outskirts shortly before midnight, but the last news bulletin of the evening—broadcast over an army transmitter rigged as emergency substitute for the regular service—claimed that the situation was back to normal.

I wondered.

The first thing I heard in the morning was my bedside phone. The call was from Angers, asking whether I was all right and advising me, if I was, to stay put. I told him I was indeed all right and inquired whether there had been any reaction from Diaz on the memo I had sent him.

"Reaction!" snorted Angers—I could visualize his expression. "Don't be funny! He's got both hands full of this bloody rioting!"

The advice to stay put was good. I did walk around the plaza in the course of the morning, and watched a machine-gun post being set up in case someone was foolish enough to try to initiate the regular daily speakers' meeting. No one took the risk, of course; any crowd collected today would have exploded like so much nitroglycerine.

After reading the paper and the typed bulletin on the board in the lobby, which explained that in the event of serious trouble the hotel's cellars would be opened to clients, I played a couple of desultory left-hand-against-right games with my new chess set. That used up most of the morning. Eventually it got to be time for lunch, and to try to create an appetite I dropped in the bar for an apéritif.

"What's the latest scandal, Manuel?" I asked the barman not expecting any news.

His reply almost made me drop my glass. "It is said there will be a duel, señor. It is said that Señor Arrio has challenged Señor Mendoza to a duel."

"The *hell* you say!" I stared at him, half-suspecting he

might be putting me on, but his face was quite serious.
"What about?"

"It is about a story which Señor Mendoza has written—a
very funny story about a man of affairs. Señor Arrio says it is
meant to describe him. But if he goes to court and complains,
then everyone will say, 'So Señor Arrio thinks this is himself!
Ha, ha! Yes, we see that it is very like Señor Arrio, truly.'
And so many people will laugh at Señor Arrio. This he does
not like. So—" He spread his hands.

"But dueling isn't legal in Aguazul—is it?"

"It is against the law, señor. But then, many things are
against the law. Everyone knows privately, but of course no
one will learn of it officially until afterwards."

I saw the distinction. "And when is this due to happen?" I
inquired.

"Ah, that one does not know," Manuel answered sagely.
"If it were known, many people might go to watch, and then
the police would have to interfere. But most probably at dawn
tomorrow, and somewhere in the country."

"And who's likely to win?"

Manuel assumed the thoughtful look of a racing tipster.
"Since Señor Mendoza has been challenged, he has the right
to choose the weapons. It is known that Señor Arrio is one of
the finest pistol shots in all America. So it will be swords—
and so who can foretell?"

The story went afterward that Arrio lost control when he
drew first blood, and when his seconds managed to drag him
back, Mendoza's guts were hanging out of the front of his
shirt. They got him to the hospital, but he died there two
hours later from loss of blood and internal injuries. He was
no longer a young man, of course.

I'd never read any of Mendoza's work, yet the news of his
dying—which had no personal meaning to myself—affected
me curiously. I thought of the way people thousands of miles
away were going to feel regret at his death, when the news of,
say, Vados dying would not concern them at all. I felt almost
a touch of envy.

And then the unexpected happened. There was this man

Pedro Murieta, whom I had seen at Presidential House in company with the Mendozas; he has something to do with Dalban and something to do with the publishing house that issued Felipe Mendoza's books, and everyone seemed to know of him once his name was mentioned but scarcely thought of it otherwise—*that* sort of a man.

And when he was through, Arrio was in jail on a charge of murder.

I wondered what the position of the two rival parties was now. The Nationals seemed to have made up ground; they had lost both Juan Tezol and Sam Francis under discreditable circumstances, but the Citizens had now had Andres Lucas impeached for conspiracy and Arrio jailed for murder. Both sides could now throw an equal amount of mud.

By the weekend, though, the rioting dissolved in a stalemate. Every cell in the city was full of people under arrest. The police had used the machine-gun in the Plaza del Sur—once. After that things were quieter. By Sunday night, aside from the few store windows boarded up and holes in the road where halfhearted attempts had been made to barricade a street, there was no sign that mobs had passed this way.

Nonetheless, I had believed when I came to this city that Aguazul was remarkably free of violence for a Latin American country. Either I'd picked the wrong time to come, or the official propaganda machine had spread a highly convincing untruth.

I was pretty sure that the first alternative was the correct one. Reactions like Angers's couldn't have been simulated. Angers dropped in to see me at the hotel on Sunday evening and told me, gray-faced, that he had never known such events in the decade he'd lived in Vados. He had just seen his wife off at the airport; he had sent her to stay with friends in California until the situation calmed down.

And that was likely to be some time yet.

The only other significant development over the weekend, though, was a stern and dignified challenge against Dominguez by Professor Cortés. Cortés made no attempt to defend Lucas—nobody was attempting to defend Lucas at the moment—but he maintained that Dominguez's accusations against Caldwell were totally baseless. He had himself, so he claimed, seen far worse things in Sigueiras's slum and in the shantytowns than found its way into the health department reports.

I wasn't sure about Cortés any longer. Not now that I'd seen Sigueiras's place for myself. Of course, Cortés carried great authority, and he wouldn't be consciously lying in a matter like this. The best one could say, though, was that he had a fertile imagination. Or perhaps he just had a greater capacity for being shocked than most people.

Not greatly put out, Dominguez replied that it wasn't his unsupported word in question; the report on which he had based his statements was an official one prepared by a special investigator called Guyiran, on the staff of the Ministry of the Interior. In other words, Dominguez implied, if you're going for anybody, you've got to go for Diaz, and if you don't, your complaints won't cut any ice.

Apparently Cortés wasn't prepared to go to such lengths; he preserved a hurt silence.

There seemed to be a fantastic network of interlocking rivalries and fields of influence here. Some of it was due to the peculiar semi-independent constitution of Ciudad de Vados, which wasn't autonomous and yet didn't seem to be amenable to the national government as easily as the rest of the country. Doubtless this was due to Vados's personal relation with his "offspring." But each development seemed to be laying bare new tensions created by the city's privileged status, and people seemed to be far more aware of these tensions than they had been five weeks ago, when I arrived.

I wondered how much of the change was due to the loss of Alejandro Mayor and his inspired manipulation of the organs of information. I wondered whether Maria Posador had been right to fear for the future of the country when the creators of its highly individual technique of government died or grew too old.

The way things were now, it seemed she must have been right.

I had an early call again from Angers on Monday morning.

"A pleasant surprise for you, Hakluyt," he said in a voice that wasn't wholly ironical. "*El Presidente* himself is dropping in at the department this morning and wants you to be there. You have exactly thirty minutes—can you make it?"

"No," I said. I took forty. But Vados was late himself. He looked very much older than he had at our previous meeting, at Presidential House. It might just have been that he was tired and worried, but, of course, to have been in power for so long as he now had, he must in any case be over sixty and perhaps nearing seventy. I found him in Angers' office, poring over a relief map of the city. Angers wasn't with him. The only other person present was a man in plain clothes who sat inconspicuously in a corner, his eyes fixed on me, and whom Vados ignored completely.

"Please sit down, Señor Hakluyt," he said. "It is not at a good time that you have come to our beautiful city, is it?"

I nodded wry agreement.

He shifted a little on his chair and leaned back with one hand in the side pocket of his jacket. "In essence, señor, I have called you to ask a favor of you." He spoke as if he felt slightly shamefaced asking favors of anyone, and the effect was to make me feel—as he obviously intended—rather flattered.

"You're my employer," I said, shrugging.

"Good." Vados looked me straight in the eyes and smiled. Even at his present age he was a strikingly handsome and distinguished man. He had been fiddling with something in the pocket where his hand was hidden; now he brought it out, and I saw that it was a beautifully chased silver crucifix, not more than two inches long. He caressed it with the tops of his fingers as he spoke.

"Well, señor, I have seen the memorandum which you prepared regarding the slum below the monorail central. It was sent to Minister of the Interior Diaz, and he had occasion to refer to it at our emergency meeting of the cabinet yesterday. This is an admirable document, señor—high-principled and showing a great regard for the human beings who will be affected. Unhappily, it is worthless."

He spoke the last sentence without a change of tone or

expression, taking me by surprise. I said, "I'm sorry—I don't see why."

He shrugged. "Señor, I believe you can be a discreet man. I also believe that since you have never been to our country before and will quite happily be working in Nicaragua or New Zealand or Nebraska as soon as you leave, you will not pass on in haste what I shall say. Effectively then, señor, there is a flaming row going on over this question which you are aiding us so cleverly to solve."

"That's fairly obvious," I said. "*Señor Presidente,* you must know as a politician and a practical man that someone who is told simultaneously to do a job and only to half-do it realizes very quickly that the people telling him to do it don't know their own minds. Angers warned me that Señor Diaz would be sure to turn down my suggestion, but it's the only long-term solution."

He gave a weary smile. "Long-term solutions are no good to us, señor! In two years, yes, perhaps, but today we are merely trying to gain time, to prevent disaster overwhelming us. As you so rightly state, Diaz is unhappy with your plan. Our government is in a way absolute—that is true. But in all countries men have sometimes to resort to a coalition government in times of emergency, and in many countries on this continent—as you will doubtless realize—there is a perennial state of emergency. I am not a dictator, señor. I am the head of a government composed of men of sometimes conflicting views, who have one desire in common—that our country should be well and firmly ruled. Diaz and I are not only old colleagues—we are old enemies as well."

He looked at me for a comment; I murmured something about "I fully appreciate . . ."

"But I have one distinction. This city is—I have perhaps said this to you before, because I say it to everyone, and I say it to everyone because it is the truth—this city is my own child, the child of my mind. I am two official persons: I am president of Aguazul on the one hand, mayor of Ciudad de Vados on the other, and as regards the city, what *I* say shall be done is what matters."

I nodded.

"Good! Then I say this. My duty is not alone to the people who belong to this country without having had the choice, who were born here, but also to those who shared my vision and my—my dreams, who gave up everything life could have offered them elsewhere to make Ciudad de Vados a reality. It is not *just* that I should betray my promises to them.

"Señor, although Aguazul has grown more and more prosperous in the years I have ruled, ours is still not a very rich country. If I would give with one hand, I must take away with the other—and there is nothing I can take that is not already promised to others! I cannot allot funds for rehousing and subsidizing the squatters of the shantytowns and of the slum beneath the monorail station, not so long as there are slums in Astoria Negra and Puerto Joaquin, not so long as I require those funds to fulfill the promises I have made to the foreign-born citizens. Without them and their aid, there would be no city here—nothing but scrub and barrens.

"Understanding this, you will understand why I must direct you to prepare a scheme—some or any scheme—to wipe away the slums from this city. That will give us the breathing space we need to settle the disagreements in the cabinet, to prepare the long-term schemes we undoubtedly require. But— have you not reflected, Señor Hakluyt, that if we were today to make plans and place contracts for the building scheme envisaged in your memorandum it would be two years before we could clear out those slums? In two years, with such a focus of unrest as we have at present, there will have been revolution!"

"I think," I said, "that you'll get your revolution more quickly if you simply—"

He interrupted me, eyes blazing. "Señor, if I were a dictator and an autocrat, I could order troops into the shantytowns and drive their people into the country, have the shacks burned to the ground. I could have Sigueiras shot today and the squatters in a concentration camp tomorrow! But I am not that sort of man. I would rather that the citizens of my country threw flowers at my feet than bombs."

He slammed the little crucifix down on top of the table beside him; it gave a solid thud. "Please, señor, do not instruct me how to rule my country. Do I tell you how to solve your traffic problems?"

"Frankly," I said, "yes."

He stared at me and then began to chuckle. "Very true, alas, señor," he admitted. "But I wish only that you see my difficulty. Do you?"

"You must also see mine, then," I answered. "I have no choice except to do as you tell me, of course. But the result will be artificial. It'll be a pretext. It will be neither improvement nor development—merely change for the sake of change. I'll do the best I can. But you won't have achieved any more than if you had, as you said, sent troops to clear the shanty-towns. You will only have pretended to achieve more, and you'll have spent a lot of money on a sham."

He was silent for a while. Then, sighing, he got to his feet. "Do not ever enter politics, Señor Hakluyt. You are too much of an idealist. More than twenty years of ruling has taught me that all too often men are ruled better by shams than by realities. Thank you, nonetheless; I look forward to seeing the results of your work soon."

He extended his hand, realizing only at the last moment that he was still holding the crucifix. As he made to put it away, he saw my eyes on it and mutely displayed it to me on his open palm.

"You are a Catholic?" he inquired.

I shook my head.

He closed his hand around the crucifix. "In some ways I envy you. It is often hard to be both a good Christian and a good statesman."

"I'd have said it was impossible," I countered. "A state is concerned with people's condition here and now; almost all religions are concerned with their state hereafter. And the two pretty often contradict each other."

"Still, there is the ideal toward which we work." He sighed heavily. "A Christian government for a Christian community —and almost all my people are believers. . . . Señor, you must come and dine with me at Presidential House some-time soon. It has become rare for me to meet foreigners who have no personal interest in the way I run my country. I meet bankers negotiating loans, oilmen seeking favorable tariffs, importers and exporters desirous of exploiting our markets—and who else? Sometimes I even envy the man who might, had things been different, have ruled in my place. . . . But I waste your time in empty talk, señor. *Hasta la vista!*"

He pocketed the crucifix, shook my hand, and returned to his study of the relief map of the city as I left the room.

XXV

I had a dim recollection that when I came to Vados five weeks ago I'd felt excited and proud of having been selected to do this job.

Well, the excitement and the pride were finished. Now I was reduced to doing a scrappy job, collecting my pay, and getting the hell out. The only part of that I wouldn't regret would be getting the hell out.

It took me about four and a half hours to work out a scheme for the monorail central that was exactly what Vados wanted: two new passenger access ways, extra storage room, and a parking lot that might be half full on saints' days and holidays. It looked all right superficially, of course; I've worked the basic rhythms so far into my system that I don't think I could any longer design a bad-looking layout. But there wasn't any *need* for any of this. There was no organic unity about it. It was like—well, creating a demand artificially by clever advertising and then complimenting oneself on having filled a long-felt want. Compared with the scheme I'd worked out for the market district—which was real development, worthy, I liked to think, of the painstaking original planning of the whole city—this was patchwork.

I turned it in for computing at the end of the afternoon. It would cost more than it was worth—but then, anything of this kind was essentially worth nothing. The hell with it. I went back to the hotel and had dinner.

Vados's directive had amounted to an ultimatum. What else was I to do except get this thing over quickly?

Not long after I entered the dining room at the hotel, Maria Posador also came in. I hadn't seen her for some days, and at the back of my mind I'd been wondering where she might have got to. Now she showed up with someone I failed to recognize at first, because I'd never before seen him in plain clothes. It was *el Jefe* O'Rourke, looking incredibly wrong as a foil to Señora Posador's effortless elegance.

For someone who supposedly enjoyed a merely tolerated status in Ciudad de Vados, a bitter enemy of the president, who was alleged to be permitted to remain in the country only so that an eye could be kept on her subversive activities, Maria Posador had a respectably long list of influential friends. This particular mismatch just about capped all the others. I watched covertly while I was eating and saw that O'Rourke ate with gusto and was talking little, while Maria Posador ate rather little and seemed to be saying a lot. Occasionally O'Rourke rumbled into laughter, while his companion looked on with a tolerant smile. Their whole manner was that of old and close friends.

I was really getting curious when I finished my meal.

They came into the lounge for coffee and a game of chess after dinner, and, much to my relief, Maria Posador invited me to join them. O'Rourke commented on the fact by glancing at her, at me, and then at her again, but said nothing. In fact, his contribution to the conversation at first consisted of grunts before making his own moves and after Maria Posador had made hers.

I would never have pictured O'Rourke as a chess-player in any other country in the world, except perhaps the Soviet Union. In the States or back home I'd have said he probably played poker for relaxation. Nonetheless he played competently, with a style that fitted his personality: direct, aggressive, concentrating on the officers and not worrying much about pawn development except to ensure that his pawns got in his opponent's way rather than his own. This two-fisted technique had faults; he would probably have made mincemeat out of me, but Maria Posador was on playing terms with grand master Pablo Garcia, and pretty soon the game was going all her way.

Trying to stir up conversation, I said, "This game is so popular here I'm surprised I haven't seen any fights over it."

O'Rourke raised his head and gave me a blunt look. "In our country, señor, we know this is the game which is always honest. We save our bad temper for other things which are not so."

Señora Posador cut in quickly, "But that is not always true. You will hear sometimes of fights, if not about the game itself, then about the bets that have been made on the result of a match."

O'Rourke moved a pawn and sat back with a satisfied noise. "Betting is for fools. We have more fools than we need, anyway."

Maria Posador took the pawn, and O'Rourke scratched his chin thoughtfully. Before making his own countermove, he glanced at me. "The señor himself plays chess?"

"If you can call it playing. Ask Señora Posador—she beat me easily."

"Señor Hakluyt has some understanding of the game," said Señora Posador, her eyes on the board, "but lacks practice in the principles of combination."

"He should then use his eyes and look about him," O'Rourke retorted, and decided to castle queen side, about four moves later than he should have done. "Except that in actuality few people obey rules, there is much to be learned from what can be seen in the world."

I had a fleeting impression that Maria Posador would have preferred the conversation to turn into other channels. I snapped quickly, "In what way, Señor O'Rourke?"

"Check," said Señora Posador, taking another of O'Rourke's pawns. "I think what Tomas means, Señor Hakluyt, is the same as I was saying to you the other day. One must not think from move to move, in real life as in chess; one must remember the overall picture."

She gave me a sweet and dazzling smile, and—I thought, but couldn't be sure—trod hard on O'Rourke's toe under the table. O'Rourke caught on; I didn't get anything further out of him, and eventually I gave up trying and went to the bar.

It was almost empty this evening. The now useless television set was gone from its regular place, and where it had stood was a shabby old radio, obviously dug out of storage. It was giving out with a pep talk when I arrived; I recognized the voice of Professor Cortés, who had assumed temporary direction of the emergency broadcasting service. I listened for a little while, but there was no real meat in the words. Aside from another broadside at Miguel Dominguez—Cortés was still not convinced, apparently, of the charges he had made about Caldwell and the health department—it was a woolly reiteration of trust in God and the President to see the citizens through their time of tribulation.

Mayor had certainly been a loss to the regime—perhaps far more of a loss than the television center itself. As a publicity man, Cortés was a good dishwasher.

Shutting my ears, I said to Manuel, who was polishing glasses behind the bar, "Señora Posador spends a lot of time in this place, doesn't she?"

Manuel's dark eyes flitted across my face. "She lived in this hotel when she first returned to Aguazul after her time of exile, señor," he said. "She had grown fond of it, I am told."

"Ah-hah. For someone who's supposed to be in official disgrace, she seems to have a lot of important friends, doesn't she?"

"Many of them were friends of her husband, señor."

"Of course. Does that include *el Jefe*?"

"I believe so, señor. *El Jefe* is her guest to dinner here this evening—you have perhaps seen?"

"Yes, I saw. You're a fountain of information, Manuel—maybe you can tell me whether they've made any progress toward finding out who burned down the television center. I was just wondering when I saw this old radio you've put up on that shelf."

His eyes switched briefly to the radio and back to the glass he was rubbing. "It is said not, señor, and—and some people begin to be disquieted. For many reasons. Whoever took away our television has made himself many enemies. Because, you understand, the chess championships have now commenced, and it has been customary for them to be shown on the television for many years. Now there is no television, and it is much more difficult to understand what is being done from a spoken description on a radio."

I sipped my drink. "So presumably there are a lot of people who want to know why the police haven't already presented the culprit's head on a plate."

"Exactly, señor." Manuel sighed. "I am myself one of the people who desire that, señor. This year my son is playing in the junior division, and I wished much to see him on the television. But—" and he shrugged expressively before putting the glass, sparkling, on its shelf and taking another.

I thought over what I had just heard. So O'Rourke was in Dutch with the public, was he? I wondered why he hadn't produced some kind of scapegoat to distract public attention. Maybe he would. Maybe he and Señora Posador were hatching something this evening. I went back to the lounge to see if they were still there, but they had gone.

Obviously, they had been hatching something. Next morning's *Liberdad* stated that the police had descended on the city health department, acting on instructions from someone unspecified, but assumed to be Diaz—assumed by the paper, that is—and had questioned Caldwell extensively about the situation in the shantytowns. O'Rourke was quoted as saying that Caldwell had no right to make wild statements about the incidence of crime among the squatters; the police hadn't found the lawlessness Caldwell described, and it was an unjustified reflection on their devotion to duty to talk of it.

In other words, "Mind your own business!"

That seemed like good advice to me, too. Such as my business was at the moment. Vados accepted the plan I'd given him for the monorail central—I'd been pretty certain he would—and gave orders for it to be published at once. I got the impression that he had been pretty desperate for some favorable publicity, because naturally, since he and his city were so tied together in the public's mind, the recent disturbances had been extremely bad for his status.

I could have done without the effusive comments on my

skill and ingenuity which accompanied the publication of the plan; if that got to the eyes of any of my potential future employers, it would likely do considerable harm to *my* status, too.

What the hell!

I went over to see Seixas in the treasury department about the estimates for the project, and he greeted me with a smile that threatened to cut his head in two.

"Señor Hakluyt!" he exclaimed. "Come in! Siddown! Have a drink! Have a cigar!"

It was a tan suit, with palm-trees on the tie, today, and the cigar I got was bigger than usual. Seixas was plainly in a tremendously good mood.

"Yeah!" he said, sitting back. "An' why not? You done me a lot of good, Hakluyt! You know people been throwing mud at me 'cause I hold stock in some construction firms—you saw about that in *Tiempo* prob'ly."

I indicated that I had.

"Well, I thought I was shut of that crap when Felipe Mendoza got carved up and his brother got jailed for contempt. Not a bit—here comes this lawyer Dominguez an' starts all over. Well, this plan you turned out, *no* one can say my company gets a cut, 'cause they don't do this kinda work. They do big stuff—divided highways, overpasses, that kinda thing. So I call up Dominguez, an' I say how about it, unless he can prove I get a cut of this one he'd better shut his trap permanently. And I get this back. How's that for eating dirt?"

He flipped open the drawer of his desk and hauled out a folded letter for me to read. It was on a neatly printed letterhead bearing the title of Dominguez's law office, and said:

Señor Dominguez wishes to inform Señor Seixas that he has taken note of the message received by telephone last evening, and concedes without question the justice of the point made therein. He further assures Señor Seixas that he has not associated himself and will not associate himself with any allegations to the contrary.

"How's that, hey?" said Seixas, and poured himself another shot of his habitual nauseating cocktail.

It didn't mean much to me; it struck me that it was a most lawyerlike sidestepping of the point, seeming to say a lot, actually saying almost nothing. Still, Seixas was delighted with it, and I made complimentary noises.

"That'll show the bastard I mean business!" said Seixas, and shoved the letter back in his drawer.

With a bit of difficulty I got him down to business and managed to get provisional approval for the estimates I had; I didn't really much care what happened to such a makeshift plan, and Seixas didn't, either—maybe because his construction firm genuinely wasn't getting a slice of this one. So the matter was disposed of quickly, and that was that.

I ran into Dominguez lunching in a restaurant near the law courts the following day. He was by himself, and I saw that he was frowning over the front-page spread in *Liberdad* that had been given to my plan for the monorail central.

All the other tables were at least partly occupied; I had the headwaiter show me to Dominguez's. He looked up and nodded coldly to me, but didn't speak before going back to his perusal of the newspaper.

I said after a frigid interval, "You're perfectly right, Señor Dominguez. It's a mess, isn't it?"

He thrust the paper aside and scowled at me. "Then what have you permitted it for, Señor Hakluyt?" he countered.

"I'm *hired*," I said. "Vados gave me an ultimatum: do it his way, and disregard my personal opinions. So I've done it. I did my best to prevent it—I told Vados, I told Diaz, I told Angers, I told everyone I could reach, that if you just throw the squatters out, you're creating a fund of ill-will that may possibly end in revolution. I sent a memorandum to Diaz about it, and I'm told the cabinet discussed it, and in the end Vados vetoed it. What the hell am I to do?"

He recognized the genuine bitterness in my tone and appeared to thaw a little. "That is interesting, señor. I had not heard. Have you perhaps heard that you have a powerful ally in your opinion?"

"The most powerful ally I seem to have is Sigueiras," I said acidly. "Wherever he may be—he's still in hiding, I suppose."

"Ah—yes, in a sense. He could probably be found today, if it was necessary." Dominguez spoke indifferently. "But perhaps you have wondered why no steps have been taken to evict the squatters under the monorail central. After all, it seems they all conspired to conceal Señor Brown, a wanted man."

"I suppose something ought to have been done by now," I agreed.

"Yet it has not. And why not? Because it would be necessary to use troops for the eviction, and our commander in chief General Molinas has declared that he could not trust his men to do the work. Many of them, after all, are peasants like the squatters, who had no better chance in life than to enter our little toy army. Their officers are, most of them, upper-class dilettanti, who would sooner associate with criminals than with common soldiers. Moreover, there is an element of racial prejudice involved; as you are perhaps aware there exists in some parts of Latin America a kind of social hierarchy based on percentage of European blood, and in our army this is quite marked. It is an exceptional man who despite Negro or Indian ancestry achieves advancement."

"This is most interesting," I said thoughtfully. "Thank you for telling me."

"Do not thank me for anything, Señor Hakluyt. I wish only one thing: that we had met under happier circumstances. For as the situation is, I and those in Ciudad de Vados who think as I do are compelled to regard you as a menace, because you reinforce the capacity of our opponents to implement their highly dangerous plans. This is an honest statement, señor; I hope you will take advice, not offense, from it."

"I'll try," I said.

He folded his newspaper so that the article about my plan was concealed, and let it fall to the floor. "So!" he said. "Let us talk of other things."

"I'd rather ask you a further question on the same subject, if you don't mind," I said. "I was talking with Seixas yesterday."

Dominguez frowned. "I have no doubt what you are going to say. Seixas is a cunning man, but little else than cunning."

"I was wondering why you—uh—backed down in your attack on him. I can't make out if he really is an open scandal or simply a target for random criticism."

"Oh, he is notorious. But we have more important matters to deal with. Flagrant offenders will sooner or later hang themselves. We must expose the subtler forms of corruption."

After that we did talk of other things, desultorily, until it was time for me to leave. I had been asked to call on Caldwell in the health department, reason unspecified.

I found him in a pretty bad way. He looked extremely tired, and his stutter was the worst I had heard it since his gruelling by Fats Brown during the Sigueiras case. Distractedly, he waved me to a chair and offered me a cigarette. He was going to take another himself when I pointed out that he already had one burning in an ashtray on the desk.

He gave a nervous laugh. "I'm s-sorry," he said with an effort. "I haven't f-felt so good s-since that b-bastard O'Rourke went for me—d-did you read about that?"

I nodded.

"S-scandalous!" said Caldwell with vigor. "I'm c-certain O'Rourke has some k-kind of interest in hiding the t-truth. If it weren't for the sh-shantytowns, m-maybe he'd be out of a job."

"This sounds like the old one about doctors having a vested interest in disease," I said when I'd recovered from my surprise.

"Oh, you d-don't understand!" said Caldwell irritably. "I mean s-someone must be p-paying him what-you-call-it. P-p—"

"Protection money?" I said incredulously. "But what for?"

"Th-that's right! What f-for? *What for*? T-to k-keep quiet about what g-goes on in th-these p-places, naturally." Caldwell thrust his hands through his already untidy hair and gave me a defiant look through his glasses.

"Look," I said, "you've obviously been overstraining yourself. I've been to the shantytowns, I've been through this place under the station, and I haven't seen anything half as bad as the things they were putting over on television, for instance."

"Ah, but you went there in the daytime, didn't you?" exclaimed Caldwell, pouring the words out in a rush without a hesitation. "I t-told the newspaperman about th-that when I s-spoke to him this morning. I t-told him what the t-truth must be."

"You mean you've told the papers—I mean *Liberdad*—that O'Rourke is hiding something?"

"I t-told the t-truth," said Caldwell with dignity. "And now I'm going to p-prove it. You're an outsider, Hakluyt, s-so you're an independent witness. I want you to c-come along t-tonight and s-see for yourself."

I almost said, "You must be out of your mind!" And then I didn't. Because it occurred to me, watching Caldwell's wild expression, that that was very probably true.

I changed the remark to, "Well, what do you think *does* go on there?"

"All k-kinds of *vice*, Hakluyt! I've s-seen it. And if you c-come with me tonight, I'll sh-show you."

I frowned and didn't reply for a moment. It was logical, of course, that there would be at least a few prostitutes operating out of the shantytowns—poverty dictated it. But to accuse *el Jefe* himself of graft, and to accuse—most likely with justice—a few local police officers of turning a blind eye, were two totally different things.

"You'll come with me?" he insisted hotly. I yielded with a sigh, and he rose and shook my hand warmly.

"You'll s-see!" he said.

I went back, frowning, to the traffic department after arranging to see Caldwell at one of the shantytowns at eight P.M., and called in on Angers to consult him about Caldwell's condition.

He greeted me with comparative warmth, for him. "We're going all-out on this plan of yours," he said. "Well done!"

I scowled; this enthusiasm for what I could only regard as rubbish was getting me down. "How does Diaz feel about it?" I asked.

"Well, of course, he hasn't got a leg to stand on. One

almost has to feel sorry for him. I don't mind saying it's put me in a pretty sticky position, because of course while Diaz is nominally my chief, Vados is mayor of the city, and in this case it's what he says that counts. However, I must say the argument has been a very interesting one—it's a pity you're not a citizen, because there's an important principle at stake."

"It strikes me a still more important principle would have been to make the whole damned city self-governing, instead of crossing it up with the national government."

Angers gave his barking laugh. "They have a genius for complex things like this in Latin America, Hakluyt. You ought to try Brazil for real confusion."

"I've had enough confusion to last me a lifetime. Angers, what do you make of Caldwell's behavior lately?"

"How do you mean?"

"Well, he asked me to go and see him, and I've just been over there. He's got some crazy notion in his head that O'Rourke is being paid to conceal some kind of vice-racket— at least, as far as I can make sense of what he says. I'm supposed to be going on a sort of voyeur's tour with him this evening. Is there any foundation for this, do you suppose? Or is he just suffering from overstrain?"

"Good Lord!" said Angers, blinking. "Well! O'Rourke isn't exactly a paragon of efficiency—that's well-known. But I always thought he was a fairly honest man—if he weren't, I don't suppose Vados would tolerate him. Who's supposed to be paying him—anyone in particular, or just individuals?"

"Search me. Frankly, I think the guy's about to blow his top. Who's his chief—Ruiz? Someone ought to keep an eye on him. I mean, there's enough mud being thrown at O'Rourke already, and some of it probably ought to stick, but this is irresponsible nonsense so far as I can see."

"Well, I don't know. Caldwell's young and hard-working; he's always been the nervous type, but then one can understand that, with that stutter he suffers from. I'd be inclined to think there was something to what he says. But on the other hand it has all been denied by O'Rourke, hasn't it?"

He made a note on his scratch pad. "I'll say something to Ruiz, if you like. Maybe he needs a rest."

And yet, when I met him that evening at the appointed time and place, he seemed much calmer and more in control of himself. He wasn't alone; there were two policemen and a photographer with him. I wondered whether O'Rourke knew about the policemen—I didn't think he would approve of them helping Caldwell to gather evidence against him.

It was cloudy tonight, but warm, and the shantytown was like a set for an experimental film as we moved into it, Caldwell authoritatively taking the lead. An air of sullen hostility met us, brooding heavy over the beaten, unweatherproofed matchboard hovels, decorated if at all with torn oil-company posters and pinup calendars from the year before last. If we had not been a formidable group, we would probably have had things thrown at us. Rotten eggs, perhaps. Or knives.

Caldwell was carrying a flashlight; as we passed a patch of ground scratched with a hoe into some kind of cultivable condition, he stabbed the beam down at the plants growing there. He said, "Look!"

I looked; I saw only a plant growing.

"Th-that's hemp," said Caldwell. "You g-get marijuana from th-that." His voice was tense and triumphant. "S-see, Hakluyt?"

I wasn't surprised. In fact, I wasn't surprised at anything Caldwell showed me during our tour. We walked in on families sleeping five to a hut, and Caldwell invited me to express disgust, which I duly did. But this was no surprise; it was inevitable, given the conditions.

Before another hut we halted, and Caldwell turned to me, indicating silence. "A s-streetwalker lives here," he hissed in confidential tones. "Th-there are d-dozens of them!"

"There are always dozens of them!" I said irritably. So far the biggest surprise he'd sprung on me was his comparatively reasonable manner this evening, his air of confidence.

He walked up and flung back the door of the hut. The beam of his flashlight speared around the empty interior. "Off after more customers," he said in a low tone. "See here, Hakluyt—in this box."

His voice shook a little. I shrugged and went to see what he had found. It proved to be a crude wooden chest containing a leather whip and some boxes of contraceptives.

His eyes searched my face for a reaction. Slowly his confidence began to evaporate.

"Look, Caldwell," I said as kindly as I could, "you'll *always* get this sort of thing where there's poverty in a big city. You can't legislate it out of existence. It's been tried, over and over again. I'm afraid you haven't proved anything that wasn't self-evident."

He drew himself up and kicked the wooden box aside. "It was a mistake for so many people to come," he snapped, his stutter vanishing for the moment as it seemed to when he shot out a single phrase he had been turning over in his mind beforehand. "S-sorry, Hakluyt," he added after a moment. "I ought really t-to sh-show you what g-goes on down in S-Sigueiras's p-place, but it's d-dangerous to g-go th-there."

We went back in silence to the place where our cars were parked. Caldwell was muttering something under his breath when we stopped, and I asked for a repeat.

"I said Mendoza knew," he declared. "He wrote about it in one of his b-books. He d-described exactly the s-sort of th-thing I s-saw. *Someone* is c-covering it up now. Who? Why? We've g-got to find out, Hakluyt!"

"For the last time," I said, taking a deep breath, "how much of this alleged vice have you seen for yourself, and how much did you just get out of some dirty story by Felipe Mendoza?"

With dignity, he drew himself up. "I t-tell you I've s-seen for myself!" he forced out between his teeth.

"All right," I said, losing patience. "I haven't. And if nothing worse goes on than what you've demonstrated this evening, then all I can say is that this is one of the most moral places I've ever set eyes on. Good night!"

I walked away to my car, fuming, feeling his hurt stare following me.

Baseless or not, Caldwell found a willing audience for his accusations in other people than me.

Bishop Cruz was one of the first to join the fray. Addressing a class of graduates from the theological faculty at the university, he denounced Sigueiras as close kin to a child of Satan, and his slum as a short cut to hell.

He probably wasn't looking for the response he got.

Somewhat puzzled—so I gathered—but prepared to accept the evidence of a bishop as superior to that of their own senses, the simple-minded inhabitants of the slum grew terribly worried about the state of sin they must be living in. Accordingly, a fair proportion of them bundled up their belongings and walked out, together with their livestock, to set up a brand new shantytown on the Puerto Joaquin road.

It took forty-eight hours for the police and the National Guard to get them back where they came from, and by that time there were a lot of stories going around about police brutality. Some people accused O'Rourke directly of being involved, but he ignored the accusations and went on hammering at Caldwell. It was said, also, that General Molinas had flatly refused to send in regular army troops against the new squatters, and that the cabinet was fighting regular pitched battles at its meetings.

The second influential voice to take up Caldwell's accusations was that of Dr. Ruiz, his chief in the health department. Ruiz had been silent for a long time on this matter—cowed, perhaps, by the risk of exposing himself to further charges about the death of the first Señora Vados, or possibly feeling that Sigueiras was now done for in any case.

He wasn't, by any means, as it turned out. After Dominguez's revelations regarding Lucas and Estrelita Jaliscos, no further talk had been heard from official quarters about his harboring a wanted murderer, and bit by bit the feeling excited by the Jaliscos girl's death had died down. Apparently this wasn't to Ruiz's taste; now he jumped back in the argument with both feet, reiterating the kind of statement he had made on the witness stand when facing examination by Fats Brown.

This time he piled it on so thick it was a wonder everyone living in Sigueiras's slum hadn't long ago suffocated in the foul air alleged to be there. With the three of them—Caldwell,

Ruiz, and the bishop—on the job, clearing out that slum was going to have massive support.

One person whose support was less than lukewarm was I.

I made this perfectly clear to a correspondent from *Roads and Streets,* who'd flown down specially from New York to do a story on the redevelopment project. I took him aside into a bar and stood him a succession of whiskeys while I explained the whole sad situation.

When I was through, he looked at me sympathetically and said in a voice brimming over with emotion and straight rye, "Boy, you're in a spot, ain't you?"

After which he flew back to New York, intending to cancel the proposed story.

I was half-expecting Sigueiras to retaliate when Ruiz began to go for him; after all, he must know the stories that were current about Ruiz's "successful treatment" of Vados's first wife. Someone presumably advised him against it—which was sensible, because with Dominguez on his side and General Molinas refusing his troops for the eviction he was assured of a respite at least. All he did, in fact, was to invite half a dozen local doctors to go down into his slum and see whether there was in fact a reservoir of disease there.

"If there are sick people," he said spiritedly, "why don't people outside catch their diseases from them?"

The doctors found exactly what I'd seen—rickets, vitamin deficiency diseases, and a lot of skin complaints caused by the squalid conditions. But it wasn't their findings that took the heat off Sigueiras in the end; it was a stern directive from Vados himself. Apparently one of the current items of publicity about Ciudad de Vados was that it had the lowest death rate of any city of its size in Latin America, and they were worried in case Ruiz's assertions might affect the tourist trade.

Not that the recent rioting had helped any, of course.

Another directive came down about the same time. The university year had ended, and accordingly Professor Cortés was confirmed as acting Minister of Information and Communications. Having sampled his work while he was filling in, I wondered how Vados liked making do with Cortés instead of Alejandro Mayor; however, presumably he was the best available, and since there was no sign of *Tiempo* returning to life, after all, the government's propaganda now had no competition.

Well, no effective competition. There were a series of inflammatory news sheets that had sprung up, which were constantly trespassing over the edge of the libel laws and being closed down in consequence—only to start up again the next day or the day after under another name. Most people were resigned to *Tiempo*'s fate and regarded the news sheets as the best stopgap they could expect.

But there were some others who were getting restive. They pointed out that even though Romero had been suspended from the judicial bench and looked likely to be declared incompetent, no action had been taken to reverse his committal of Cristoforo Mendoza for contempt or to release the impounded equipment belonging to his paper.

And that was not the only matter in which there had been a peculiar delay. As Manuel, the barman, had told me, at this crucial time of the chess championships television was sorely missed, and people were demanding that the arsonists be found forthwith.

It went without saying, of course, that the National Party view was expressed by every one of the succession of news sheets, and these two were the matters at which they hammered again and again: the banning of *Tiempo*, for obvious reasons, and the failure of O'Rourke to catch the arsonists, to stave off accusations that National Party supporters had been responsible.

It was something of a surprise to me to find out how these news sheets caught on. Surreptitiously printed and distributed, one day's issue sometimes remained in circulation for nearly a week, being passed from hand to hand, and not only among people who had formerly read *Tiempo*, but also among people who merely wanted the television service back.

I had my own ideas as to who was responsible for keeping these news sheets going, of course. I'd seen no more of Maria Posador since the evening she dined with O'Rourke at the hotel, and nothing before that for some days. And she was the one who believed that an opposition press in Ciudad de Vados had to be maintained at all costs.

Maybe Vados had been premature to assume that Maria Posador was safer in Aguazul than out of it.

Manuel kept a supply of these miscellaneous news sheets under the bar for interested customers. I was going through one that I'd missed—I think it was calling itself *Verdad* in its current incarnation—when I found an interesting item which Cortés hadn't seen fit to divulge on the radio or in *Liberdad*. I had no reason to doubt it, though. It was stated that *el Jefe* O'Rourke agreed with General Molinas on the question of clearing away the slums of Vados. It would be asking for worse trouble than they had already. And the much-vaunted plan of mine for redeveloping the ground below the monorail central was nothing more than a governmental pretext to kick out Sigueiras.

Well, that was perfectly true, of course. What shook me rigid was that O'Rourke had supposedly gone on, "And if they try to put this into effect, then we'll throw Hakluyt out of the country and his plans after him."

XXVI

There is a moment in the demolition of a tower, an old-fashioned factory chimney, or a high wall, when the falling structure—weighing perhaps a hundred tons—seems to float, leaning against the air.

It lasts perhaps a small fraction of a second, but feels much longer. And in that narrow space of time the whole visible world seems to hesitate, waiting for the inevitable crash.

I was waiting for a crash now. What was worse, I appeared to be directly in the path of what was falling.

I folded the news sheet so that O'Rourke's alleged statement was uppermost, and signaled along the bar to Manuel. He was serving another customer; when he was through, he came down to stand opposite me, his eyes a little wary.

"Have you seen this, Manuel?" I asked him.

He sighed. "Yes, señor. I thought you would have seen it also before now."

"No, I hadn't. . . . What do you make of it, Manuel? What do you think yourself about my job here?"

At first, I could see, he was not going to reply. I said, hearing my voice harsh and dry, "Say what you think, Manuel. Go ahead, for God's sake."

"I have no views of my own, Señor Hakluyt," he said reluctantly. "I have a good job. I have profited much by the making of this city. Before, I was in a little hotel in Puerto Joaquin; now here I am, as you see me. Yet it seems to me that there are also people who have suffered because of the coming of the city, and it is easy to understand why they feel differently."

"Why should *el Jefe* be one of those who feel differently?"

"It is this way, señor." Manuel leaned forward with both elbows on the bar and spoke in confidential tones. "There are some of us—like myself—who are used to the great world. I have served some very rich and famous people at my bars, both here and in Puerto Joaquin when I was called to help at great receptions. I have seen how today a man can be in Aguazul, tomorrow in San Francisco or in Tokyo. To me that is good. I am the friend of all people who come to my bar.

"Then there are others, who say, 'This is ours, let it remain always ours.' It is like the difference between *el Presidente,* whom I have also served at a bar, and Señor Diaz. And I think *el Jefe*—whom I have *also* served with his liquor!—is one of the same color as Diaz. That is what I think, señor. But I am only a man behind a bar."

"And in this city—how many think like *el Jefe?*"

"As we have seen in the streets and in the plazas—many, señor. Too many."

I nodded and picked up the news sheet. "Do you mind if I take this?" I asked him.

"Please do, señor." He glanced under the bar. "Yes, I think I have two examples of that."

"Thanks. I don't know whether I can do anything about this—but I'm sure as hell going to try."

As it turned out, I didn't get much of a chance even to try.

As usual, when I went down to the traffic department in the morning, I went first of all to see Angers. Caldwell was there a few minutes ahead of me, looking even more tired than he had been recently, his face very white, set and strained, his eyes circled with darkness.

I assumed he'd come to check progress on the clearance of the slum at the monorail central; the health department was, of course, very eager to get it moving. In a way, he had.

I caught a fleeting expression of worry on Angers' face as I sat down, but Caldwell had begun to address me, and I was unable to ask what he was disturbed about.

"How about you, Hakluyt?" Caldwell said. "What do you th-think is the real reason b-behind the d-delay in clearing S-Sigueiras out?"

I shrugged. "From what I've heard, it's due to General Molinas refusing to send in troops—and to O'Rourke predicting riots if they go ahead and evict. What's more, I entirely agree, and I've been saying so all along."

"Well, you're wrong." Caldwell spoke with a triumphant air. "It's p-political. It's the National P-Party again."

Frowning, I shook my head. "I don't see that," I said. I didn't. Things had been rather quiet on the political front for the past three or four days; the Citizens' Party was like a snake without a head, having lost Guerrero, Lucas, and Arrio, all three—Guerrero dead, Lucas under arrest while the allegations of conspiracy against him were investigated, and Arrio awaiting trial for murder as a result of his duel with Mendoza. Likewise, the Nationals lacked any notable figure around whom they could rally, for Dominguez, though a supporter, was not an official of the party, and Murieta's action against Arrio had apparently been dictated by his literary friendship with Felipe Mendoza, not by politics at all.

But this wasn't Caldwell's view. Smiling, he took some papers out of his pocket.

"I've b-been at the s-state c-custodian's office this morning," he said. "I've b-been looking th-through the account b-books th-they recovered from B-Brown's office. And who do you th-

think p-paid the fee for S-Sigueiras's case against the city c-council?"

I shook my head.

"It appears to have been Pedro Murieta," said Angers in a dry voice, and Caldwell shot him an annoyed glance, as though he had been deprived of springing a great surprise on me.

Nonetheless, it was a surprise. I said, "I thought Murieta's only interest in the matter was because he financed the publication of Mendoza's novels—wasn't that right?"

"Th-that's what we were *meant* to th-think," said Caldwell significantly. "There's more to th-this than meets the eye."

He got to his feet. "Well, I'm g-going to tell P-Professor Cortés about th-this," he said. "P-people ought to know what's really g-going on."

When he had left us, I stared at Angers. "Do you think this is as important as he wants to make out?" I asked.

Angers shrugged. "I honestly don't know," he said in a faintly puzzled voice. "Before you came in, he was dropping dark hints about the extent of Murieta's complicity in some shady traffic that's supposed to go on in the shantytowns, and especially in the station slum."

"Oh, not again!" I said wearily. "You know how he took me on this guided tour of the vice spots of Vados, don't you? All he could show me was one plot of ground where someone was supposed to be growing hemp for marijuana, and one hut occupied by a prostitute who wasn't at home. Frankly, I take anything Caldwell says to me now with a sack of salt—I think he's suffering from some kind of strain, and his imagination is playing tricks on him."

"If it weren't for Dr. Ruiz bearing out what he says," Angers admitted after a pause, "I'd be inclined to agree with you."

"Well, Ruiz isn't in any too comfortable a position himself," I pointed out. "There were some pretty nasty allegations being made against him when he was giving evidence in Sigueiras's case, weren't there?"

"If there'd been any substance to them," said Angers with asperity, "you may be sure the National Party would have kept on with them. But that's a standard part of their propaganda technique—planting nasty rumors and letting them grow unchecked till someone who's actually been accused of some very small offense indeed is being described as a murderer or worse."

Whether it was part of the National Party's technique or not, that method worked extremely well for Caldwell over the weekend.

It happened this way. *Liberdad*—Cortés apparently having been impressed by Caldwell's story—published the information about Murieta financing Sigueiras's case, but took the precaution of checking with Murieta first. As it happened, Murieta was in New York for the weekend on a business trip, but his personal secretary suavely confirmed the tale. His employer, the secretary said, had been asked by Felipe Mendoza to aid Sigueiras, and owing to his well-known concern for the rights of the private citizen, had consented.

And Caldwell snapped back that apparently Murieta's view of the rights of the private citizen included the right to take drugs and indulge in sexual perversions, because this was what Sigueiras specialized in providing.

There was a charge—uttered with the theoretical approval of the city health department—that really called for an answer. But Caldwell didn't stop there. I never found out how anyone allowed him to get away with it, but he topped off his list of charges with a flat statement that Murieta was little better than a professional pimp.

In the twenty-four hours that preceded Murieta's return from New York, rumors followed this story like weeds sprouting on burned ground. I heard them, even. I was told confidentially how, in the dim recesses of Sigueiras's slum, children, virgin girls, and raddled old hags were made available at a stiff price to wealthy and debauched patrons; I was told how the air was never free of the stink of marijuana; I was even informed that the livestock in the shantytowns was kept for other purposes than feeding people.

Myself, I wondered how the putative "patrons" of Murieta's supposed vice ring would have enjoyed indulging their tastes in the uncomfortable and insanitary condition below the monorail central. But only a very few Vadeanos who repeated the rumors had any idea of the real state of things down there, and doubtless assumed that the clients would appreciate a sordid setting for their sordid activities.

By Monday the whole matter had gone past a joke, and tempers were running high. Inoffensive peasants from the shantytowns had been stoned on the streets; police had twice had to be called to the monorail central to drive away indignant bands of demonstrators and enthusiastic would-be customers; and, much to the annoyance of business people and the city tourist bureau, a large party of statesiders had noisily canceled their visit to Vados because they got wind of what was being said about the city's morals.

Caldwell turned up again in Angers' office on Monday morning, looking bloody but unbowed—not, this time, specifically to talk about Murieta, but on formal health department business. Nonetheless, Angers and I both went for him, and from his reaction I gathered that we weren't the first by a long way.

"I t-tell you I've s-seen all th-this for myself!" Caldwell kept insisting, his voice shaking with rage. The fourth or fifth repetition was too much for me.

"If you have," I snapped back, "you're probably Murieta's only customer yourself!"

I thought for a long instant that he was going to throw himself at me like a wild animal, and I automatically tensed to beat him off. But at that very instant the door was thrust open and one of Angers' assistants, looking harassed, put his head into the office.

"Señor Angers," he began, *"por favor—"*

He got no further before he was pushed to one side bodily by a huge bull of a man in an open shirt and canvas trousers which stretched so tight across his seat they threatened to split at every step he took. He was very large and very dark, and it seemed for a moment that he filled the entire doorway, shutting out the light beyond.

"Caldwell *aquí?*" he demanded; then his eyes fell on Caldwell who had dropped back into his chair as the door opened, and he gave a grunt of satisfaction. Turning, he signaled to someone behind him.

This was a rather small man, immaculately dressed in a snow-white summer suit and cream Panama hat, smoking a king-size cigarette and holding a silver-knobbed walking cane. He had a thin moustache and brilliantly white teeth.

Caldwell remained frozen to his chair.

The newcomer raised his cane and pointed it as though it had been a gun at Caldwell's chest. "You will pardon this intrusion, señores," he said without taking his eyes off Caldwell's chalk-white face. "But I have business with this cur."

Angers got to his feet with dignity. "What do you mean by walking uninvited into my office?" he snapped.

"I," said the intruder calmly, "am Pedro Murieta. I am informed that Señor Caldwell has told lies about me. He has said that I, a citizen of Ciudad de Vados against whom no man has ever breathed a foul word, am a pander. A pimp. A trafficker in immorality of the vilest kind. It is not true, before God it is not true!"

The cane whined across Caldwell's face, raising a tiny red weal where the very tip touched the skin of his cheek.

"*Say* it is not true, misbegotten son of a mangy mongrel bitch!"

And Caldwell burst into a flood of tears.

Bewildered, Angers glanced from him to Murieta to me, his eyes demanding explanation. While Murieta dropped the end of his cane to the floor and leaned on it, watching Caldwell with considerable satisfaction, I said, "Señor Murieta, do you know why he has been saying—saying this about you?"

"He is sick in the mind," said Murieta after a long pause. He straightened up and turned away, sighing. "I am not a vindictive man, señor, but this I had to do when I learned what he had published to the world about me. Yes, no doubt he is sick in the mind. We have been to his apartment this morning in search of him—with the police, for he has committed a crime in our law—and we have found certain books and pictures which suggest that he is not normal."

His sharp black eyes flashed to my face. "Did you not know? Could you or another not have stopped him? Although we shall show what he said was mere lunatic raving, it will nonetheless do me very great harm."

I said wearily, "Señor, I cannot care any longer what happens in Ciudad de Vados. I live only for the day when I can leave it."

"Leave it, then!" snapped Murieta, and turned his back on me.

The enormous man who had come in with him had lumbered out again; now he returned, with a policeman and two white-jacketed male nurses. Seeing them, Caldwell began to scream.

The complete disintegration of a human being is not pleasant. When it was over, and Caldwell was in the ambulance, I suggested we go out for a drink, and Angers, shaking like a leaf, agreed instantly.

Over a whiskey in a nearby bar, he said dully, "Who'd have expected it? He's always been such a steady fellow—hardworking, reliable—and then all of a sudden, this!"

I said after a moment's thought, "I'll make a wild guess. I'll bet you that when they go into the matter they'll find that Caldwell probably laid some tart or other in one of the shantytowns some while back, and he's collected a load of guilt in consequence. I imagine that he's always suffered because of that speech impediment; he's acquired a string of complexes a mile long."

"All this is just words," said Angers impatiently. "What I want to know is—what's it going to do to the project? We relied on what the health department was saying, and so did the public. When it turns out that it was all the raving of an idiot, what will happen then?"

"They'll probably laugh like demons," I said. And I was right.

Having a pretty primitive attitude toward mental illness, most of the Vadeanos did laugh—loudly, long, and often. Not only at Caldwell, but also at everyone else who had swallowed his story, if only for a day.

The worst sufferer, naturally, was Professor Cortés, who had allowed the story currency in Liberdad. It was extremely galling for him to have to order the printing of a full-scale retraction. He tried to cover himself and distract attention from the matter by going for Miguel Dominguez again. But the lawyer's personal position was now virtually unassailable, because of the way he had successfully demolished Andres Lucas and showed up his complicity in the fate of Fats Brown. He laughed the whole thing off.

I had half forgotten my own worries in the atmosphere of tension that followed Caldwell's breakdown, but I still kept one eye open for any further rash statements by O'Rourke. I preferred not to provoke trouble with him so long as he didn't repeat what he had apparently said about throwing me out of the country. And at the present moment he seemed to have something else on his mind—more exactly, someone else. Dr. Ruiz, in fact.

I had this from Manuel, as usual—the barman was getting to be quite a pipeline of information for me. He seemed to be dismayed because it was through him I learned about O'Rourke's attack on me, even though I'd asked for it— literally—and he tried to make up for it by slipping me reassuring snippets of gossip.

According to him, O'Rourke had told Ruiz that if he went on with his accusations, the police would prosecute him for aiding and abetting Caldwell in publishing a libel, and still more than that would start investigating the allegations that he had murdered the first Señora Vados.

There was an air of desperation about this, as though Vados were gradually wearing down O'Rourke's resistance to the eviction of the squatters. Of course, it was unthinkable that Dr. Ruiz should be officially accused of this crime—the mud that would splash on Vados would topple his regime, and *el Jefe* would find himself in one of his own cells before he was allowed to say a word in public. Nonetheless, Manuel assured me he had the story on excellent authority, so I took it for what it was worth.

"Any more news sheets, Manuel?" I asked. "Or have they been closed down again?"

"I do not know whether they have been closed down or

not, señor," Manuel said regretfully. "But I cannot obtain any more of them. Have you not seen today's *Liberdad?*"

He opened a copy of the official paper on the bar before me and jabbed his finger down on a large-headlined story. I read: Bishop Cruz had forbidden all practicing Catholics to buy or read the unofficial news sheets.

"I am a good Catholic," said Manuel, with regret in his voice. "But I had hoped to collect all of these for the information about the chess championships; the name of my son is in many of them, for he has done very well in the tournament so far."

"So you won't have any more unofficial news for me, Manuel?" I suggested.

Manuel smiled. "Señor, behind a bar one has the news anyway."

It was not a rash boast. A day later he was able to inform me of something else to which Cortés had refused space in *Liberdad* and time on the radio, which was scarcely known to most Vadeanos. General Molinas had pledged his entire support and that of the army for O'Rourke and the police; he had said that if rioting started because the squatters were evicted, he would be unable to keep his forces at the disposal of the Vados government. I found this far more interesting than what Ruiz had been saying, and what was reported at length by the official organs, which was approximately, "No smoke without fire," in the question of immorality in Sigueiras's slum. It looked as if Professor Cortés were making a desperate effort to save face over the Caldwell affair.

And that was the situation when Sigueiras exploded his bomb.

I hadn't given another thought to the threat he had made to Angers on the first occasion when he took me to see the slum; I'd dismissed it as fine words and hot air. I'd realized that the Negro was a determined man, but now, when things were practically all going the Citizens' way, he capped every desperate move the National Party had ever made with a gesture of spectacular defiance that made people all over the city—myself included—regard him with astonished admiration.

The one person who didn't, of course, was Angers.

XXVII

A couple of times since he had sent his wife off to California to avoid the disturbances in Vados, Angers had invited me to drop around to his apartment after work and have a drink with him. The first time I'd dodged out of it; the second time I couldn't—and in any case I was beginning to feel sorry for the guy. Somewhere under that shell he had cultivated there was a human being; I'd even managed bit by bit to recover from his playing cops and robbers at the cost of Fats Brown's life.

So I finally gave in.

We set off, after sewing up the day's computer figures, in Angers' car, and he'd just told me we were only half a block from his home when he slowed down abruptly and pointed ahead.

"Why do you suppose all those people are standing on the pavement?" he said.

I followed his arm. Around the doorway of an apartment building ahead, not less than fifty people were milling. Most of them were shabbily dressed. They seemed to be staring in through the ground-floor windows, gesticulating.

"Whatever it is, they're enjoying it," I said. "They seem to be laughing their heads off."

As we pulled up, we saw that many of them were literally helpless with amusement. More people were dashing up moment by moment, and the janitor of the apartment house was trying frantically to drive them away with vehement curses.

"That's my place they're looking into!" Angers snapped, starting to open the car door. "What the hell can be going on? Do you suppose there's a fire, or something?"

Then one of the windows shivered into sudden fragments, and a bored-looking burro poked its head out, nostrils wide, as though sniffing for fodder.

"God in heaven!" said Angers, and left the car faster than I had ever seen him move before. He crossed the service road at a run; the janitor caught sight of him and called to him pleadingly, but he took no notice. His goal was a new arrival with a large camera, who was down on one knee focusing for a picture of the burro. Now, having found there was nothing to eat outside, the animal was sampling the gauze curtains and not finding them much to its taste.

Angers was the last person I'd have cast as a football player. Nonetheless, the kick he launched at the camera was superbly professional. The camera was snatched from the man's hands; it soared through the air for twenty feet and exploded into fragments against the wall of the building. The would-be photographer shot to his feet with a yell of dismay, but Angers had already spun around and was thrusting his way into the crowd, a look of savage fury on his face.

I followed more slowly. There was a sound of police sirens coming this way. Once they realized the owner of the apartment was on the scene, the sightseers began to melt rapidly, and I had a clear path to the entrance. I tried to get some sense out of the janitor, but he was distraught with terror—presumably because it was his fault that the burro was in the apartment—so I followed Angers inside.

He was shaking with rage; he could hardly get his key into the lock, and when he succeeded, the door proved to have been barricaded from the inside. He glanced around wildly, spotted a heavy fire extinguisher hanging on a wall bracket across the foyer, seized it, and used it as a battering ram. The door broke from its hinges on the first blow, and we charged into the apartment.

There were people here, too—not just a burro by itself. In the foyer there were four naked children playing delightedly with a doll they had found. The doll was an Inca statuette four centuries old, but that didn't worry them. The excitement had been too much for them, and they had relieved themselves indiscriminately in odd places on the carpet. A woman so old she seemed not to have energy left to breathe or move her eyes sat wrapped in a *rebozo* on a couch, stroking a fine silk cushion with one hand and telling a rosary with the other.

At the sound of our crashing entrance, a man with a

scarred, simple-looking face looked out from one of the bed-
rooms. He had one hand full of *frijoles,* and their sticky
traces were all over his face from chin to nostrils. Behind him,
a high-pitched woman's voice demanded in a peasant accent
to know what had happened and what had the children
broken this time.

Angers looked slowly around the room. A few slivers of
glass left in the frame of a wall mirror, and a heap of colored
bits of china in one corner, explained why the woman had not
been more startled at the sound of our breaking down the
door. A stack of shabby bundles on the floor indicated that
this family had moved in with the intention of staying put;
indeed, they had already set up the family shrine on a new
lightwood sideboard, and several crude candles were trickling
streams of grease across the polished surface.

Then there was a furious rattling and crashing from the
door of the other bedroom, and it was flung open by a young
woman in her early twenties, cursing with a sonorous obscenity I have seldom heard in any language. In Spanish, the result
was magnificent. In spite of all her efforts to prevent it, a fat
pig broke away between her legs, ripping off her skirt in
passing and carrying it triumphantly wrapped round his nose
like a banner as he careened across the lounge. The simple-
faced man dropped his handful of *frijoles* on the carpet, seized
the nearest portable object—it happened to be a lamp—and
used it as a combined lance and bludgeon to drive the
squealing and grunting pig back through the bedroom door.
The door slammed. The burro commented on the fact at the
top of its voice.

The young woman grabbed her skirt as the pig fled past
her, and knotted it haphazardly back around her waist as
though she were used to this kind of thing.

I came close to admiring Angers in the next second, for he
had been standing there quite immobile while the boarpig was
chased back to its new sty, and now all he said, in a frozen
voice, was, "*Qué hacen Vds. en mi casa?* What are you
doing in my home?"

Then a squad of policemen crowded through the door. The
woman who had called from the bedroom came to see what

was happening; she, too, had her hands full of *frijoles*. The four children began to scream almost in unison, their voices pitched just far enough apart for the result to be a nerve-fraying quadruple discord. The very old woman began to weep quietly. But the young woman, cursing the police as roundly as she had cursed the pig, picked up a dozen wine-glasses from the sideboard and began to hurl them with accuracy, and it wasn't until she had been dragged into the kitchen by two burly policemen and locked in a broom closet that we got any sense out of anybody.

Looking hurt and puzzled, the simple-faced man explained. They had come from a village in the mountains. Today they had arrived. Their village was short of water this summer, and the people were very hungry. Other people—their cousins, their friends—had come to the city and found good homes, though not so good or so large as this one. So they had arrived and asked someone where they should go, and they had been brought here. It was very good here; there was a separate place for the animals, instead of them having to share the living-room, and there was much water, and the floors were soft. But there was no firewood, and nowhere to make a proper fire, so tomorrow he would have to make an oven. Today they were tired; they had just cooked up some *frijoles* over a little fire, and wished to sleep soon.

Simple.

The "little fire" had been made in the bedroom washbasin; two or three books had contributed to it, and it had left a smear of smoke-grease all the way from the basin to the window through which the smoke had escaped. And they had not, apparently, been able to believe in an unfailing supply of water. They had found out how to work the taps, and had then filled every container they could find and stowed them in cupboards, in drawers, in closets, under the beds—everywhere.

I would never have believed that so much chaos could be created in such a short time by so few people.

"This," said Angers coldly when he had surveyed the damage, "is Sigueiras's doing. You remember how he threatened to do just this—don't you, Hakluyt?"

And then I did recall what I had scarcely thought of since the first visit I had made to Sigueiras's slum.

"Ask them!" Angers ordered, whirling to the nearest policeman, throwing his arm out in a gesture that swept across the peasant family. "Ask them whether it was Sigueiras!"

No, they had never met anyone by that name. They had come to the city and asked where they must go, that was all.

"Well, how the devil did they get *in*?" demanded Angers. "Livestock and all! Get that idiot of a hall-porter here!"

Struggling to control his weeping, the terrified janitor hurried to throw the blame on his young assistant—a youth of twenty, notorious for his National Party sympathies. The janitor himself, it seemed, had not been on duty this afternoon—he had been inspecting complaints of unsatisfactory garbage removal.

And this young assistant was nowhere to be found.

"Go and look for him in Sigueiras's slum!" Angers ordered. "Quick! And get Sigueiras if he's there!"

They went; they found Sigueiras, though not the missing youth, and they arrested him.

Frankly, I didn't see what else Sigueiras could have expected. This was a magnificent, publicity-gaining gesture in its conception, but in practice it was bound to backfire. It did. As Angers immediately realized, it cut both ways.

Defiantly, perhaps characteristically, Sigueiras's only comment on the affair was that he had given Angers fair warning.

When things had calmed down a little, and the peasant family had been removed from the apartment, Angers looked about him grimly at the wreckage. "*Now*," he announced, "I want a photographer."

The pictures were all over Vados the following day: in *Liberdad*, in leaflets hastily run off on private printing presses, in posters slapped on walls. The message they conveyed was obvious almost without explanation; it ran: "This is what will happen if they rehouse the slum-dwellers! This is the way such people *like* to live!"

And they worked.

At three o'clock that afternoon the police had to use tear-gas and fire hoses to turn back a crowd of self-appointed sanitary inspectors from the monorail central—about two hundred aggressive young men and women who had armed themselves with firebrands and set out to smoke the slum-dwellers from their homes. If the jail had not been very modern and very strongly built, a similar mob would have hauled Sigueiras from his cell and tarred-and-feathered him or stoned him through the streets.

Three or four shacks were actually burned down in the shantytown on the Cuatrovientos road, and in retaliation a group of peasants rolled oil-drums filled with dirt into the fast lane of the highway. Since most of the traffic in that lane was still doing fifty or sixty miles an hour before slowing to take the city cut-off, they managed to wreck several cars; no one died, but several people were badly hurt.

Bit by bit, the temper of the city was reapproaching the point at which they had had to put the machine-gun post in the Plaza del Sur. Accordingly, I locked myself away in the hotel over the entire weekend and went for the one last remaining part of the problem: the shantytowns on the out-skirts.

After that makeshift job on Sigueiras's slum, this was a breath of sweet clean air—straightforward improvement of traffic flow patterns to eliminate the kind of backwater effect that had allowed the first small nucleus of squatters to congregate, and then had directed that the nucleus should grow. It wasn't bad when I was through; it wasn't bad at all. I only had to have it computed for costing, file off the rough bits, and then, in a few days if all went well, I could get to hell out of Ciudad de Vados and never—never—come back.

Feeling and probably looking worn out, I walked into Angers' office on Monday morning and planted a heap of papers on his desk: sketch-plans, preliminary figures worked out on my portable analogue computer, estimates, the lot. "Done," I said. "That's it."

Angers looked up at me with a sour expression and shook his head.

"I'm sorry, Hakluyt," he said. "Not done. Not by any means. Take a look at this."

He thrust a sheet of paper across the desk at me. I took it; it proved to be an interdepartmental memorandum form of a kind I had occasionally seen since arriving in Vados—used by cabinet ministers to issue instructions to junior personnel. This one was headed MINISTRY OF THE INTERIOR and bore Diaz's personal signature. It ran:

> In the matter of the dispossession of Fernando Sigueir-as. Señor Angers is forbidden to take any action to further this plan without specific directions from this Ministry.

"What on earth is this all about?" I demanded. "Surely he can't do that!"

"But he can," contradicted Angers wearily, sitting back and crossing his legs. "The situation in this lunatic city of ours makes the federal-state relationship in the U.S.A. look like sheer heaven. Don't you realize, Hakluyt, that in my capacity as traffic manager of Ciudad de Vados I'm solely responsible to Vados as Mayor, while at the same time in my capacity as highway supervisor I'm responsible to Diaz in the Ministry of the Interior? This blasted project is being claimed by both of them! There seems to be nothing left for me to do but comply in one capacity, refuse in the other, and resign in both!"

"Does this kind of thing happen often?"

"Oh, about twice a week," said Angers with bitterness. "But this time it's different. Look what came with that memo!"

He passed me a typed list of what looked like references to legal cases. There were about twenty of them. "That's Do-minguez's doing, I'll swear it is," Angers declared. "Those are cases in which the verdict went against the city council be-cause it was proved that some municipal employee involved in the case had a personal grudge against the defendant—and believe me, I have a personal grudge against Sigueiras now!"

"Well, what's that supposed to prove?"

"If you ask my candid opinion, Hakluyt, it isn't supposed to prove anything. It's just hamstringing us. It may take months to prove that these cases are totally irrelevant. Oh, this looks like Dominguez's doing all right. And devilish clever it is, as a delaying tactic."

I folded the list together with the memo and dropped them back on Angers' desk. "Well, it's no skin off my nose," I said, shrugging. "As far as I'm concerned, the job's just about over. You've got your scheme; it's not my job to put it into effect—it's yours. I'm through—and by God, Angers, I can never remember a contract I was so glad to finish."

XXVIII

More in my job than perhaps in any other, there's a complete change of viewpoint which sets in on termination of an assignment. I thought about the sometimes paradoxical consequences of this as I sat over a drink in the hotel lounge, watching passersby through the glass front wall.

Yesterday this city had been a problem to me: I was seeing its people as figures, units of pedestrian traffic. Today and from now on until I left, I was on holiday.

Oh, tomorrow, of course, I'd find out whether they'd decided to go ahead with the Pietermaritzburg expressway, and if they had, I'd offer my services. They'd probably hire me. I didn't have to be vain, but I didn't have to be modest, either—there weren't at any one time more than half a dozen specialists available with my peculiar blend of skills.

Today, though . . .

I sipped my drink and tried to imagine that I was a well-heeled tourist who had come to Ciudad de Vados in order to see, hear, feel, taste, and smell this city with more air-conditioning units per head of population than any other in the world, this monumental creation of twentieth-century man, this town without traffic jams—

And, currently, without television or an opposition newspaper. I found myself frowning into my drink, drove my inside knowledge of the situation to the back of my mind, and tried to reassume my status as a tourist.

It wouldn't work. I sighed and gave up trying. In the same

moment I realized that someone had sat down in a chair next to me and was waiting for me to acknowledge the fact. It was Maria Posador, so I did so quickly.

"I haven't seen you in here very often lately, señora," I said. "A pity."

She gave a smile tinged with weariness. "Much has been going on," she answered obliquely. "I am told that your stay in Vados is over, also."

"Pretty well."

"Does that mean you are now leaving?"

"Not quite *now*, unfortunately. I'll have to hang around for a few days—perhaps as long as a week—while they finish the costings and so forth and make up their minds to pay my fee. But I've done my share of the work."

"You sound bitter," she said after a pause. "Have you not enjoyed your time here?"

"You don't have to ask that. Most of the time I'd have given anything to be a thousand miles away."

She took out her gold cigarette case thoughtfully, selected one of the thin black cigarettes, lit it herself. "I am told," she said through aromatic smoke, "you are not pleased with what you have done."

"I haven't tried to make a secret of that, either. In fact I've done the opposite, I hope. Hell, I was told when I first got here that my job was going to be that of a sort of white corpuscle killing off disease germs in the bloodstream of the city. I rather liked the idea at first. Then I found it was a filthy job. A white cell isn't much different from the bacteria it has to dispose of—do you imagine the germs plead with it to spare their lives?"

"No," said Señora Posador rather frigidly.

"All right," I shrugged.

She was regarding me with her deep violet gaze as though trying to phrase difficult thoughts into words. She said in the end, "Señor Hakluyt, I am not greatly impressed by your disclaimers of responsibility. I think you are a shallow person; you judge too much by appearances and have little gift for understanding what lies deeper."

Nettled, I answered, "Part of my job is to understand what lies deeper!"

"Then you cannot be so good at your work as you think you are." She put it flatly, not admitting contradiction. "What is your opinion of *el Presidente*, for example?"

"As a man or as a president? They're two different things."

"The man and the president are one," she retorted. "I wish you to answer directly."

"All I can say, then, is that he's a pretty good ruler, as his kind go. He's ambitious, but he'll certainly leave behind some solid achievements when he kicks off—"

"And they will still be cursing his name in the back streets of Astoria Negra," said Señora Posador unemotionally. "Also there are places in Puerto Joaquin where they nightly roast his image at the fireside before falling asleep. Oh, perhaps I am unjust to say you are shallow—but you appear shallow because you are a rootless man; you live where you work, and you work everywhere. Do not let this brief stay in Aguazul delude you into thinking you understand the situation."

And more quietly she added almost to herself, "For it will go on after you have left the city."

"I know that," I said soberly. "I think I do understand, pretty well, what forces are at work. But I haven't had time to explore them, trace them to their source. I've just seen them impersonally affecting the lives of people I know. You say I'm shallow, but it isn't true. It's simply that detachment is necessary to my job. I'm pretty good at remaining detached now, and yet there are some times when I can't. A few moments ago, when you arrived, I was thinking how different it is to be able to regard Vadeanos as people instead of units of traffic— but you can't separate the two completely. A person *is* a unit of traffic if he lives in a social group; he's a lot more besides, but that doesn't prevent it. And in a way you can parallel the behavior of people as traffic and people as just people. I'm certain that someone like—oh, Alejandro Mayor, for example, if he'd lived—could develop the kind of math I employ to describe far more general activities than simple point-to-point progress."

"Please go on, señor." Sudden interest showed in Señora

Posador's face; she leaned forward as though not to miss a word.

A familiar-looking trio came in through the main entrance; people I had seen before, on my first day in the city. The mousy man with the notebook and the sheaf of pens was still shadowed by the same two gigantic escorts. He marched importantly up to one of the waiters, asked him a solemn question, which the waiter answered respectfully, and then went out again.

"What's the question this time?" I asked Señora Posador, reflecting in passing that I hadn't yet seen the result of one of these opinion polls published.

"Something to do with dispossessing Sigueiras," came the impatient answer. "But please continue!"

I was only too ready. "Yes, in fact, I had an impression from some of Mayor's early work that he might be aiming for something of the kind. Look, I can generalize about people as though they were identical molecules of gas; in fact, most of the formulae I employ are adapted from hydrodynamics and fluid mechanics. When people crowd into a subway on the way to work, they're driven by a force which may be more abstract but is certainly no less efficient than a high-powered fan. That force doesn't care if Auntie Mae has had a bad night, or the baby cried till four A.M., or Pedro overslept and hasn't had his cup of coffee to quiet his grumbling belly. There's a definite force at work, moving people, compelling them to form a visible flow.

"Now take advertising. Advertising isn't actually a force—the motive power is compounded of some basic impulses, like hunger, thirst, the need for clothing and shelter, and some superficial impulses. The urge to keep up with the neighbors, for instance. Nonetheless, advertising men can and do channel this impalpable flux. They can launch a campaign of which the end-product is once again physical action, visible movement. In other words, people will go to a store and buy. That's infinitely more subtle, but it's still capable of direction, it can still be defined in predictable terms. You can say, 'So many people will probably buy this product in such a period,' quite as confidently as I can say, 'So many people under such and such circumstances will be fouling up the subway system ten minutes after the offices close.'

"So as far as I can see only the sheer impossibility of gathering a totality of data about all the individuals involved prevents us from developing a system of forecasting and influencing all the actions of a person in his entire daily life."

"Señor," said Maria Posador a little faintly, "it is well-known that Alejandro Mayor sought to achieve total control of our people—I myself showed you one method he employed. But are you saying that people *can* be controlled in this way?"

"People *are* controlled," I said in surprise. "Look, the man in the subway going to work of a morning has no more real control over his own activities than—well, than a piece on a chessboard! Because he has to earn a wage, he has to go to work. He can choose his kind of work, within strict limits. Maybe he likes—oh, meeting people and talking to them. So he wants to be a salesman. Unfortunately, that product doesn't sell very well. His family gets hungry, so he takes a job he loathes, processing company data for computers. It pays more, perhaps, but it pays in practice slightly less than what it would cost to install a machine to read ledger-postings with a scanner system.

"What other choices has he? He could quit work altogether, but if he has a family to support, he won't. He could cut his throat; sometimes people do. But he's a Catholic, and suicide is a mortal sin. So there he is, on that subway train at the same time as everyone else."

"You're a cynic, señor," said Señora Posador. Her face was pale under its golden tan; her breath came so quickly that even in those few words I could hear a quaver.

"No, I was lucky," I said. "I think—I hope—I actually saw this sort of thing coming when I was in college. I read Mayor's first book, *The Administration of the Twentieth-Century State,* and as I said, there were pointers in it. . . . So I picked a job where there were openings for only a few specialists, so few their work wouldn't be worth automation. Result: I have comparative freedom to choose my jobs, I enjoy the work I do because I'm good at it—and am, as you tell me, rootless."

"So you are master of your fate, and we in Ciudad de Vados are not?" suggested Señora Posador, her violet eyes troubled.

I shook my head. "I said *comparative* freedom. Ultimately, I'm at the mercy of the same impersonal forces. I have to eat and drink and sleep and wear clothes and all the rest of it, and I have a fair burden of nonessential desires created by advertising and habit—I smoke, I drink alcohol, I like to enjoy myself when I'm off the job. I'm still a chessman. A pawn being shifted hither and yon across the face of the earth by the same processes that have shaped history since man first discovered how to walk on his hind feet."

"You puzzle me, Señor Hakluyt," said Señora Posador after a pause. "You must be aware that your work here has laid the foundations for a long and bloody struggle—"

I interrupted her by slamming my fist into my open palm. "Laid the foundations *hell!*" I snapped. "Don't accuse me of not understanding the situation, much less being fooled by remarks like that. The current situation was implicit in Vados's first decision to found his city, and that in its turn may have depended on the fact that his wife was too damned vain to spoil her figure by having children—or maybe he's impotent or sterile, but whichever way it happened, he needed a surrogate. Whatever the reason, the same forces are driving him that drive the rest of us. I've done my best to make things better, not worse. Oh, I've been under orders, so all I could do was cushion the blow where I could, but if Vados manages to avoid open revolt within the next few weeks, then he'll get two years of comparative peace—that's my guess—and two years from now the situation will be no better, no worse, than it is today. The problems will be different, but they'll still exist. Maybe then they'll tackle the root causes—poverty, lack of education, those things. Then, again, maybe they won't. People don't do logical things like that."

"A few moments ago you were saying people were predictable. Does that not imply that they are logical, too?"

"No-o-o. . . . You run out of logic about the time you start taking imponderables like religion into account, or genetic predisposition. In theory, I imagine, there are logical reasons to be got at; one can imagine in some far future society people will say, 'This man has propinkidinkidol of utterbimollic acid in his genes, so he'll have cold feet, so he'll be a good customer for electric blankets'—only even then it'd probably turn out he got shocked as a kid and he's so scared of electricity he won't use anything but a plain hot-water bottle."

Señora Posador was staring into space. "I remember the first time—oh, when I was at school, señor, learning English in a junior class. That was when I first heard the word 'cussed.' The teacher said it was slang, and we should not use it. But I like the word. It expresses something so—so human—"

She spread her graceful hands in a helpless gesture, at a loss for a precise definition. "But if what you say is to be believed, if one could—given the time and the necessary information—treat individuals as readily as you forecast the behavior of crowds, hurrying for a train, why, there is nothing left for anyone. Except to be one of the persons who gathers and uses this information, rather than a—a victim."

I shook my head. "No, no. There is so simple a way of interfering with the process that it could never become reality."

"How so? You have said just the opposite—"

"Well, you yourself provided me with one example. After you showed me how television was used to force ideas on Vadeanos, I simply stopped watching it. Do you suppose that a chessman possessed of conscious thought would calmly sit on its square and wait to be taken if it knew the rules and the state of the game? Not likely. It would sidle quietly to another square where it was safer, or scuttle across the board when the players weren't looking, to crown itself a queen.

"No, the sort of absolute system I've been talking about couldn't work unless everyone was ignorant of what was happening. Outwardly there would have to be no change at all in everyday life. You and I and that waiter over there would have to be able to eat and drink and sleep and fall in love and get indigestion as always—so what would be the difference, anyway? Maybe such a system is already in operation—how would we know? We're like pawns on a chessboard who do know the rules and the state of the game, but we prefer to ignore that knowledge because we have no legs, and we can't leave our squares unless we're moved."

Señora Posador sat without moving, looking at nothing, for a long moment. She said at length, "You paint a bleak picture of the world, Señor Hakluyt."

"Not very. We're bound to accept that we're restricted by forces beyond our control. So long as they remain beyond anyone's control, we're all in the same boat, and we don't care. But to be ruled, and to know one was ruled, by people who were controlling those impersonal forces—that would be different."

"Yet we are ruled by people; often there have been absolute regimes, and even you, with your freedom of action—are you not ruled by men controlling economic forces, by those who pay you, in the most immediate case?"

"That's nothing to disturb me, is it? But what I am afraid of is—let's say the situation where in a restaurant at noon the cooks prepare exactly *so* many of each different dish, because they know that, faced with the day's menu with such-and-such items on it, just that number of their patrons will select just those dishes, and nothing at all will be left over. You see, there is a subtle horror in that. No one, except the cooks, and perhaps not even the cooks, would realize that anything had changed."

Visibly, literally, Señora Posador shivered.

"I'm sorry if I've upset you," I said. She came back to herself with a start, and glanced at her watch.

"Not at all, señor. Not more than usually, to be frank. I find you a disturbing person in some ways—but I cannot say how."

She rose to her feet, still with a faraway expression. "You will forgive me, but I have an appointment in a little while. I hope that"—she smiled slightly—"the impersonal forces will direct that we meet again before you leave. *Hasta la vista,* señor. And—good moves in your game."

I stood up quickly. "Thank you. I hope the same. Will you

not have dinner with me before I have to leave—perhaps help me make the best of my few days' holiday?"

She shook her head, not smiling. "No," she said calmly. "I cannot see you any longer as a person, you understand. I can see you only as an agent of the forces against which I am struggling. I would prefer it otherwise—but . . ."

She shrugged and turned away.

XXIX

I was restless that evening. I had intended to relax in the hotel bar, but I couldn't relax at all, and in the end I decided to go for a stroll; the evening was fine and clear, and there was a light breeze.

I was thinking as I started out about the man who had been my seat-companion in the plane coming down from Florida, the one who had boasted about his European accent and his country of adoption in equal proportions. I had found his card again in my wallet as I was paying for dinner this evening. The name was Flores. I recalled telling myself that I knew more about his city than he probably did, although I had never visited it.

What *had* I known? Anything at all? I couldn't have said then, as I could now, that that man driving a European sports car rather too fast through the main highway nexus was probably a supporter of the Citizens of Vados, and that consequently the long-faced Amerind lighting a candle and crossing himself before the wall shrine in the market was prepared to hate him on principle. I couldn't have said that the old woman carrying a sleepy-eyed baby through the glittering evening streets probably worried more about the health of the family livestock than of the child—for a crippled and sickly child might still be able to beg, while a crippled and sickly animal was good for nothing at all.

Lord, there was power waiting for anyone who had the determination and patience to employ knowledge of human beings!

Of course, demagogues and dictators all through history had used such techniques. Only they had been amateurs, empiricists, and their lack of knowledge led to eventual ruin. You couldn't rule people totally—they were, as Maria Posador put it, too cussed—unless you were responsible not only for externals like their living conditions, their right to walk the streets in freedom, their binding laws and regulations, but also for far more subtle things: for their prejudices, their fears, beliefs, and hatreds.

I'd been talking wildly about developing mathematical tools on the analogy of the ones I used every day, to cope with general as well as particularized behavior. Now it occurred to me that perhaps I already had some of those tools.

Suppose, for example, I went from here to work on the Pietermaritzburg project. It would certainly be the biggest planned traffic system in Africa if it came off. There I'd have to make allowances for the local system; I'd have to complicate simple suggestions to make provision for *blankes* and *nie-blankes*. Even here that held good. Making allowances for the local system . . .

Why had I been brought into this, anyway? Not because a genuine traffic problem existed; rather, because legal and political factors combined to dictate that a traffic problem be solved in order to smooth over an unpopular decision. I wanted desperately to believe that I had done the best I could. But the fact remained: I hadn't done my job. I mean, I hadn't done *my* job. I'd done the dirty work for people without the necessary special knowledge to do it themselves.

It was as well that I was an outsider. I could leave Ciudad de Vados behind me, and with it the dispute between the Nationals and the Citizens, between foreign-born and natives, between Vados and Diaz; and when the results were all in, I might be found to have set a precedent.

Oh, there were similar cases on the books—there was Baron Haussmann's work in Paris, and there was the clearing of the St. Giles rookery in London, when street-planning and slum clearance had been used to get rid of nests of crime and vice. But there the primary object had been to improve the city. To coerce social change by altering the balance of factors that had led to undesirable conditions—that was subtler, and very different. Inherently different.

Good God, I had been right, at that!

I had been walking, lost in thought, for several hundred yards without knowing where I was going. Now I stopped in my tracks, and a young man and a girl coming arm-in-arm behind me bumped into me. I apologized, let them pass, and resumed my aimless stroll, repeating under my breath, "I *was* right!"

Sometimes you can have knowledge right in the palm of your hand and never use it, because you don't recognize it for what it's worth, or because you aren't the kind of person it's worth anything to. I hoped the second alternative applied to myself.

For I had just realized I had power I never knew about.

I explained it to myself step by step, saying *look at it this way*. Here in Vados, capital city of the "most governed country in the world," they conceive the idea of applying my indirect leverage to enforce a desired social change. They don't have the knowledge to work the trick themselves; they know the next best thing, though—where to lay hands on the knowledge, as I would look up figures in a table of logs.

Now it had been done, it would be copied. Recipe: specialized knowledge.

I remembered hearing about a time-and-motion man—forerunner in some ways of my own discipline—who achieved one of the earliest major successes in the field when they gave him the problem of improving the ground-to-upper-floor communications of a skyscraper, whose lobby was swamped with people entering and leaving and whose elevators were crammed to capacity.

He studied the situation—and recommended putting an information booth in the lobby. Result: people entering slowed down, perhaps went to the desk, at least hesitated while they decided not to. And the flow of people thereafter moved at a pace which the elevators could handle.

I could do that. In South Africa the hatreds engendered by *apartheid* smoldered always below the surface. Suppose I designed a main station so that two segregated streams bumped each other or crossed each other, so that neither had the easiest access to its own part of the train, or to waiting rooms and conveniences. Plan skillfully; estimate the irritation caused and allow for it to become unbearable on a blazing hot day at the time when, tempers frayed, people are going home from work tired out. It needs just one man in a crowd to push another, to be struck down—and explosion!

If the critical points were too obvious, people might see them in the plans and demand changes. But who would think such factors had been built-in deliberately?

Almost, they could have done this when they were planning Ciudad de Vados. They didn't have access to enough information, of course. They couldn't have foreseen that Fernando Sigueiras would be a stubborn man with a streak of mulelike tenacity, or that Felipe Mendoza would become famous outside his own country and language group, or that Judge Romero would become incompetent and crotchety in his old age.

But they could have deduced that peasants deprived of water would move to the city. They could have guessed that the native-born citizens would be jealous of the foreign-born. They could have guessed a good many more things—no, not guessed. Reasoned out. Only they didn't know what they knew.

And I did have the knowledge, and I had been used. Made to go through motions like a—a pawn on a chessboard.

I found myself on the fringe of a large crowd and looked to see where I had got to. I had somehow found my way to the Plaza del Oeste, and I was now facing the public tournament hall. Posters announced that tonight the finals of the Ciudad de Vados regional competition in the series for the national chess championship were being played off. Pablo Garcia was advertised to play.

When I paid attention to what the crowd around me was saying, I discovered that they had all come in the hope of seeing the grand master because there was no television any more.

On an impulse, I thrust my way through the crowd to the box office. There were many people in the lobby, hurrying to their seats. The girl clerk in the box office shook her head with a smile.

"The señor is plainly a stranger in Vados," she said smugly. "Otherwise he would know that all tickets were sold—as usual—the day before yesterday."

She turned to exchange someone else's reservation form for his tickets; I went back to the entrance, wondering why I had taken the trouble to go and ask anyway, since there were few things I fancied less this evening than sitting and watching a chess match.

Obviously, though, a lot of people didn't share my tastes. I could hardly get down the steps now for a huge swarm of schoolchildren eagerly waving their tickets and chattering with excitement.

Suddenly a siren sounded outside. As though by magic half a dozen policemen appeared, thrusting the bystanders off the sidewalk and clearing the approach to the hall. One of the officers recognized me just as he was about to shove me back with the rest of the crowd, and courteously asked me to stand back from the entrance. I did so, just as el Presidente's car pulled up.

A dapper little man in full evening dress—probably the manager of the hall—and a stout woman whose gown was ornamented with an official-looking rosette incorporating a checkered motif greeted Vados and his wife as they emerged from the car. Smiling and bowing in response to the claps of the onlookers, they came toward the entrance.

And as he passed, Vados caught sight of me.

"Señor Hakluyt!" he exclaimed, halting in his tracks. "You have been unlucky in obtaining a ticket?"

I admitted that I had. "But it's of no importance," I said. "I was just walking past, and I came in on the spur of the moment—"

"But it is of the greatest importance!" said Vados with enthusiasm. "I am told your work is finished and you will be leaving us soon. It is unthinkable that you should go without seeing a great national institution like a chess match!" He turned peremptorily to the dapper man following him. "Place another chair in the presidential box!" he commanded. "Señor Hakluyt is my guest."

I cursed the man's generosity, but I could hardly get out of it now, so I murmured dutiful thanks and fell in behind.

The box was large, with an excellent view of the four tables which were in play together. Even so I was a bit of a nuisance, for in addition to Vados and his wife and the stout woman with the rosette—who turned out to be the organizing secretary of the city chess federation—there was also Diaz, who was already in his place when we entered.

He rose to shake hands with Vados, and a flash from the body of the hall immortalized the moment on film. A gust of applause swept the packed audience, and the national anthem was played—recorded, presumably, for there certainly wasn't room in the hall for a seventy-piece symphony orchestra. A one-man band would have had trouble finding space.

The various grand masters who had come through to the finals took their places; Garcia, bobbing his head and smiling, received a tremendous ovation. Then the chief referee called for silence, and play began.

Everyone in the hall could follow the play easily enough; there were opera glasses to study the tables in direct view, and additionally the various moves were repeated on large hanging illuminated signs, grouped in fours, all around the hall. I remembered having seen similar signs, not yet illuminated, outside the entrance, without realizing their purpose.

For a while I made a great show of appreciating the opportunity of seeing the match. Then the heavy thinking set in, and I began to get bored.

I stole a covert glance at Señora Vados; she sat with her face in an expression of absolute blank tranquillity, and I judged she had mastered the art, so useful to a public figure, of turning off her mind.

I also looked at Diaz, wondering what was going on inside that dark skull. Having directly countermanded Vados's instructions to Angers, he must be feeling pretty tense in his president's company; indeed, I saw the muscles on the backs of his large hands knot and unknot, and sometimes he swiveled his eyes to scan Vados's face.

As for Vados, he seemed utterly absorbed in the play.

A scatter of applause which the stewards failed to kill ran through the audience, closely pursued by indignant hushing sounds. I saw that Garcia was sitting back with a smug expression, while his opponent literally scratched his head in cogitation.

A clever move, presumably. But I was getting more interested in the audience than in the play. Who were these chess fans? They seemed to be a complete cross-section of Vadeanos; there a shabby man like a factory hand was playing through Garcia's game on a much-worn pocket set balanced across his knee—he was on the wrong side of the hall to see Garcia's board clearly and had to take the moves off a sign. Two places from him a woman was knitting and chewing gum while staring at the players; then there was a block packed solid with children under eighteen and over twelve.

Across the hall, in the more expensive places that commanded a perfect view of the most popular table—Garcia's, of course—were men in tails and women in low-cut dresses who looked as though they had set out for boxes at the opera rather than seats at a chess match. Yes, both the *blankes* and the *nie-blankes* were—

What was that? I caught the idea by its disappearing tail and hauled it back into the front of my mind. Surely I must have been dreaming about the pieces on the boards: black opposed to white. For this was the wrong country.

I looked again, straining my eyes past the brilliant hanging lights, and felt a shiver down my spine. Coincidence, perhaps—but it was true. Diaz, for instance, sat on Vados's right, and for the most part the audience on that side of the hall were long-faced Amerinds or recognizably mulatto. Oh, there were plenty of Caucasian faces, too, but on this side dark skins lined up in groups of half a dozen together. The situation across the hall was reversed: the dark skins were spaced singly among the rows of lighter faces.

I'd seen this phenomenon the day after my arrival in Vados, and I hadn't understood its significance. I remembered very vividly how I'd felt isolated among the dark-skinned crowd listening to the native musicians raise funds for Tezol's fine, under the trees in the Plaza del Sur. Maybe I'd seen it since without noticing it because it was accepted automatically.

Nonetheless, it was certain that the two sides, playing out a game more deadly than chess on the squares of the city, were divided like chessmen into black and white.

XXX

"Ah!" said Vados suddenly. "That is good. That is perfect!"

A pawn move by the grand master Garcia had just gone up on the signs; for a few moments no one except the players and the referees were paying any attention at all to the other games. I joined my gaze to everyone else's. But I hadn't been following the development of Garcia's game very closely, and I didn't see that it was a spectacular move.

Everyone else did, including Garcia's opponent, who spent five minutes in close study of it and then thrust back his chair, shaking his head. The audience dissolved into applause.

Garcia smiled a little vacantly in acknowledgment and shook hands with his opponent before patting down the noise for the benefit of the other players. A general move for departure washed through the audience, as those who had obviously come only to see the champion triumph slipped away.

In answer to a signal from Vados, Garcia came up to the presidential box to receive congratulations, a waiter appeared with coffee, brandy, and biscuits, and Vados spoke in low tones with Garcia and Diaz. I paid little attention; I was too interested in my own new discovery.

Why should these politicians love chess so much if they were not hankering after just such orderliness and obedience to rule in the real-life government of their people? Chess, so the legend goes, was invented to amuse a prince. To console him for the unpredictability of his subjects? I wondered.

I came back from my reverie to find that Vados was gazing

irritably at me. I apologized for not hearing what was said, and he repeated it.

"I was saying, Señor Hakluyt, that I had invited you to dine at Presidential House before your departure, and there is now little time. Would you care to join us and grand master Garcia tomorrow evening?"

"I'd be delighted," I said. "I'm sorry to appear rude—I was thinking about chess and the art of government, as a matter of fact."

I spoke in Spanish because I had been addressed in Spanish; the result was that Diaz and Vados together snapped their stares on my face. Taken aback, I glanced from one to the other.

"Really?" said Vados after a pause. "In what connection, may I ask?"

"Well," I said lamely, "I'm not much of a chess-player, and I'm certainly no politician. I was—uh—thinking that the resemblance is pretty slight, because pieces on a chessboard have to go where they're put. People are—uh—more difficult to control."

Diaz relaxed and addressed me directly for the first time. "It comes perhaps as a relief to us to watch a chess match and dream that things might be so well ordered in the sphere of government."

"Just what I was thinking," I agreed heartily, and Diaz and Vados exchanged looks. The tension between them sparked almost visibly, like lightning crackling between a cloud and a tree. I guessed that each of them was thinking, "If only we could settle our problems as simply as a match like this. . . ."

"Let us be going, then," Vados said briskly to his wife, who gave a smile and a nod of ready consent. "Señor Diaz will accompany us, yes?" The dark, ungainly man nodded.

They took effusive leave of the stout woman who was secretary of the chess federation, of Garcia, and lastly of me, with a handshake, an automatic smile, and a quick, "*Hasta mañana,* Señor Hakluyt!"

I stayed, smoking a last cigarette, until another of the four boards broke up, and then left the hall. It was about eleven

P.M. The chess federation secretary informed me that the tournament would continue all day and evenings if necessary for the rest of the week, and that the regional finals winners would meet for the national championship the week after next.

"And I suppose the winner is bound to be Pablo Garcia, as usual?" I suggested, when she mentioned the timetable to me.

"I am afraid so," she sighed. "People begin to lose interest now, because he is so far ahead of all our other players."

But it didn't seem to me that people were losing interest. I went back to the hotel and found that everyone except the tourists in residence was in the bar, where the radio was giving a—well, it was hardly a running commentary, but at any rate a report on the match in progress, interrupting a program of recorded music every time a move was made. Manuel had set up four peg-boards behind the bar, and transferred each move to the appropriate board when it was announced.

I'd had enough chess for one evening; I went into the lounge and found that here at least the chess fever was less prevalent. There was one game in progress—Maria Posador was playing against a man I didn't know—but at least no one was talking about the championships that I could hear.

I kibitzed on Señora Posador's game until it wound up, and her opponent disappeared for a few minutes. As soon as he had gone, she turned to me with a smile.

"You have had a pleasant evening, Señor Hakluyt?" she inquired.

"I've been at the chess match as Vados's guest," I said.

She nodded noncommittally. "And you enjoyed the play?"

"Not much. I was much more taken with the audience." And for no other reason than that I felt my discovery was important enough to share with someone, I mentioned the curious division between swarthy and pale which I had noticed in the hall.

"Oh, in some ways you are quite right," she answered reflectively. "In part the conflict in Ciudad de Vados is a conflict of color. But that is incidental, not central. By the way, I should congratulate you. I have only just realized that you speak very good Spanish—when we first met, I invariably addressed you in English, but now I speak my own language with you and you answer well."

"I've moved around a lot," I said, shrugging. "I've got into the habit of acquiring languages. Arabic, Hindi, a bit of Swahili. . . . But please go on. What do you mean, incidental?"

She spread her graceful hands. "There is no real color problem in Latin America in general, you see. That we have a dark native population and a high proportion of foreign-born citizens with lighter skins is a product of the special circumstances under which Vados founded the city. It aggravates the situation, perhaps. But it did not cause it."

"I see. Well, maybe I have a hangover from my own background. You probably know there's not much of a color problem in my country, either—Australia—but it's nonetheless color-prejudiced as hell, with its keep-Australia-white immigration policy and the rest of it. I don't care any longer; I've worked around the world, and I don't find brown people harder to get on with than white people. But maybe some of that prejudice has stuck with me. Maybe I see problems where they don't exist."

I offered her a cigarette. As usual, she shook her head.

"I am afraid I do not care for that pale tobacco, señor. Please, though, make trial of one of mine. I think these of mine are of more character than ordinary cigarettes—they have a certain superior aroma."

She flicked open the little gold case and slid a cigarette out for me with her thumb. I took it.

"I think," she said, waiting for me to offer her a light, "it is better to see problems than to overlook them. Had we been more aware of such prejudice in some—not all, but certainly some—of our foreign-born citizens, we might be less troubled today. Naturally the newcomers brought their opinions with them. Possibly some of those opinions were infectious."

She bent to take a light from me, and then glanced at her watch.

"Another day ended," she said with a sigh. "Indeed, it is very late now. I must be leaving, señor. Should the gentleman with whom I was playing chess return, please make my apologies."

"With pleasure, señora. *Buenas noches.*"
"*Buenas noches,* señor."

I sent for a nightcap and lit the black cigarette—finding it aromatic, but too bland for my taste. There was no sign of the man she had been playing chess with.

I waited only a few minutes, in the end. I grew very sleeply all of a sudden, tossed off my drink and went up in the elevator to my room. I must have sunk into a deep stupor as soon as I had undressed and got into bed.

I awoke with cramp and discomfort in every limb. The surface on which I was lying was hard and cold, and I knew that if I breathed deeply, I would cough. I had to breathe deeply. I did cough—rackingly, with a violence that made my throat sore.

Then sudden shock brought me to my feet. I was in total darkness. I had been lying on a cold concrete floor—merely putting out my hands to stand up had told me that. But—what in hell was I doing on a concrete floor? I had nothing on but pajamas, and my feet and hands were frigidly cold from the still, slightly dank air in this place.

Where in God's name. . . ?

I hadn't a lighter or a match; I had nothing at all except my sense of touch. Alert, tensing myself against anyone who might be in the room—if it was a room—and straining not to cough again, I felt in front of me like a blind man, taking a half-pace at a time. In a moment I struck something hard: a bench, about waist-high, littered with small objects I could not identify.

Fumbling over the bench, I touched a wall, and started to grope along it. My head felt as though it were stuffed with horsehair; my throat was rasped from my violent coughing. I wondered wildly whether I was engulfed in a nightmare or whether this was real.

My shaking fingers touched a switch. I threw it, not caring what the consequences might be. Nothing happened, and I started to creep farther forward.

Suddenly a startling pattern of lights leaped into being just in front of my face, and I staggered back, almost losing my balance. Things dropped into perspective with astonishing precision.

It was a cathode ray tube I had turned on. And by its fitful, irregular glare I could see that this was the concrete shed—the blockhouse—where Maria Posador had brought me to show me her recording of my appearance on television.

I looked around wonderingly. What the hell was I doing here?

Before I had had time to digest my situation, there was a clinking sound. I spun to face its direction; it came from the heavy padlocked door. Someone was putting a key in. I could hear tense breathing.

I snatched a length of metal bar from the nearest bench and snapped off the switch controlling the cathode ray tube. In the renewed darkness I saw irregular glimmers from a hand-held flashlight, seeping through the crack at the edge of the door. Cautiously, I moved toward the glimmers. Whoever had put me in here was going to get as good as he gave.

The door swung back—thrown back violently. I leaped forward, seeing in the dim light of dawn that the newcomer held not only a flashlight, but a gun.

Then my bare foot landed, with my entire weight behind it, on a thick electric cable crossing the floor.

The pain was shocking. I lost my footing, lost my grip on the metal bar—and the gun cracked.

Something hit the fleshy upper part of my left arm; it felt as though a pair of gigantic red-hot pincers had closed on the skin. The impact spun me around and sent me sprawling across the floor. Rough concrete burned skin from my cheek and the palm of the hand with which I tried to break my fall. My head rang with dizzying pain.

Light bloomed from the ceiling; I tried to turn my head, but all I could see was a pair of soft moccasin slippers and the lower part of a pair of biscuit-colored linen slacks. A voice said softly, "*Madre de Dios!* Why should *he* be here?"

Maria Posador herself.

I heard a clinking sound as she hurriedly pushed the gun and the flashlight onto a bench; then she was kneeling beside me, probing my blood-smeared arm with precise, gentle fingers. I dug my voice harshly out of my raw throat.

"I'm not unconscious, you know," I said stupidly. "I—"

Another fit of coughing seized me. Maria Posador rocked back on her heels, staring down at me in astonishment. "But you!" she said, shaking her head. "But—you! I—I—oh, we must get you to the house. And quickly!"

I wasn't thinking clearly for the next few minutes. I got to my feet somehow and stumbled out into the dawn with my left arm hanging limp, my right around her shoulders. The grass was cool and soft under my bare feet; the fresh, clean air steadied me and blew the clouds from my brain.

When we came in sight of the house itself, Maria Posador cried out for aid; a man who might have been Filipino threw open a window and stared out, his face blank with sleep. In a moment, though, he had comprehended the situation and was hurrying down to us.

I simply took the line of least resistance; I allowed myself to be guided into a room and laid on a divan. I set my teeth while she cut away the arm of my pajama jacket and wiped the wound with a cloth wrung out in hot water brought by the Filipino houseman. A fat, motherly woman who reminded me by her cast of face of Fats Brown's wife came with brandy, and when my arm was bandaged I was made to sip a glass of it.

In a little while I was able to sit up. The bullet had gone clear through, making a shallow groove in the flesh rather than a hole, and the substance of the muscle was hardly touched. I could even move the arm—stiffly, but without great pain—when it was dressed.

Maria Posador watched me with her face quite expressionless.

"I will not ask your forgiveness," she said at length. "Once before—soon after I came back to Aguazul five years ago—there was an ambush laid for me. I was beaten about the head and left to die."

She reached up and drew back her sleek black hair from her left temple. With a quick twitch she removed one of the tresses—a postiche. Where it had been, a patch of red, granular scar tissue showed on her scalp.

She left it visible just long enough for me to take in its meaning. Then, deftly, she restored her hair to its original immaculate state.

"So," she said levelly. "It was because of that, you understand. I have not been out very often to that place since the television center was burned down. But last night I heard a strange noise, and it occurred to me to—well, to see if there had been trouble. It was perhaps foolhardy to go out alone, but what could I do?

"And then I came to the shed, and I saw fresh scratches on the lock, as though someone had tried to open it with a wrong key. So I returned to get my gun, and—there you were."

I nodded. There was a little more brandy in the glass at my side. I sipped it carefully. "I must have frightened you, coming for you with that iron bar," I said. "But—who did it? Who kidnapped me and brought me here?"

"We will find out," she said in a voice like ice breaking. "We will find out."

There was a silence. The motherly woman came back into the room carrying a tray loaded with breakfast—hot coffee, glasses of fruit juice, half a dozen native cold dishes in little glass bowls.

"Drink coffee," said Maria Posador stonily. "It will aid the refreshing stimulus of the brandy you have taken."

I shivered a little, although the room was very warm. I said, "You know, if it hadn't been for that cable I trod on—which knocked me off my balance—I'd be dead now. I'm sure of it."

She gave a grave nod. "I have no doubt that was what was intended."

Something clicked in my mind, and I gave a grunt of astonishment. "That cigarette you gave me last night—was it —*was that cigarette doped?*"

I half-rose to my feet, my mind flooding with suspicion. She looked at me calmly.

"Not so far as I am aware. Who could have obtained my

own case? Who could have ensured that I gave you that cigarette and no other?"

"You could," I said. There was silence for a while.

"I could," she said at last. "But in that case—would I have missed my aim?"

"Possibly. You might be—oh, hell, you wouldn't have had to go to all that trouble." I subsided, feeling that I had said several stupid things.

"Of course not," was the calm comment. "You are a weapon in a struggle which trembles on the verge of open civil war. Enough people hate you for it to be possible to find an assassin to destroy you. No, señor! Your destruction was to have been linked to mine, plainly! Well, that has failed. But it may be tried again. I would suggest to you that you leave the country at once, today, but some formality would certainly be found to hinder your going . . . . I am sorry that you should be involved as you are. But, as you yourself have said to me, we are at the mercy of impersonal forces."

"I don't think these forces are so impersonal," I said grimly. "I think I'm being pushed around by individuals' whims—as though I were one of those men who march around that life-size chessboard at Presidential House! What kind of impersonal force carried me up here from my hotel room and put me where it was an even chance you would think I was lying in ambush for you? It looks to me as if someone—whoever, Vados or Diaz or someone—were pushing me *and you* about exactly like bits of carved wood being shoved from square to square on a board!"

"Señor," said Maria Posador heavily, "you must understand that for twenty years *el Presidente*—with the guidance of the late but not lamented Alejandro Mayor—has ruled his country by means direct and indirect. He has moved not individuals but whole masses of people at his whim. Once, a long time ago, I was capable of feeling as you do about the fact—but I was very young when my husband . . . "

Her voice broke suddenly. "Sixteen? Seventeen?" I suggested gently.

She nodded, not looking at me. "Seventeen. I was married very young. Oh, things have changed for me—once I swore I would follow where he had gone, once I swore I would wear black until I died, again I thought I would enter a convent. . . . Then here I am, as you see me." She gestured up and down, indicating her tailored shirt, her biscuit-colored slacks, with all their air of some expensive resort.

I cupped my hands around the thick pottery mug of coffee I had been given; there was still much heat in it, and it stung my palm where the skin had been grazed.

I said, "Up till last night I was proposing to get out of Ciudad de Vados as fast as I could, and be glad to see the last of the place. Now I'm not any longer just waiting to collect my pay. I'm not interested in that sort of thing anymore. It's a different kind of pay I want, and who's going to settle the account I don't know. But someone is. Someone most definitely is going to pay."

XXXI

The motherly woman scuttled into the room, her face wide-eyed and anxious. "Señora!" she exclaimed. "There are police cars at the gate! Pancho will try to delay them, but it cannot be for long."

Maria Posador reacted with instant decision. "That will probably be because someone has warned them to come here and seek a corpse. Quickly—you must go into the cellar. I have a concealed retreat arranged down there, against emergencies."

We were already moving as she finished explaining; it was like a priest's hole in an old English house, comfortable, well ventilated, and completely hidden. It was a relic of her early days after her return, when she was still half afraid that Vados regarded her as a menace to be eliminated at the most convenient moment.

"Myself, I have never had to use it," she added. "But— others have. More than once political opponents of Vados have found safety here; I wished to offer refuge to Fats Brown, but he chose otherwise, and . . ."

And I was scrambling inside.

It was awkard with my injured arm, but I made it, and I waited there tensely for more than an hour, wishing I'd asked for cigarettes to ease the strain.

Eventually the houseman let me out and helped me back upstairs, where I found Maria Posador sitting in a chair and tapping thoughtfully on the arm with perfectly kept nails.

"Would you care to guess," was her first remark, "who it was who grew worried about you and sent the police here to make inquiries?"

I shook my head.

"It was Señor Angers."

"Good God! But—oh, I suppose it was on some flimsy excuse like you having been the last person I was seen talking to last night."

"You have a good understanding of the minds of our police. Of course, they work on uncomplicated principles. I managed to drive them away temporarily, but I must arrange to conceal the effects of the bullet I fired at you—it will have left traces on the wall, of course, and may have broken something, though I do not know. And someone, it is said, heard the shot. I think it would certainly be best for both of us if you were to remain in concealment here for a little."

"I'll cheerfully keep out of the way of the police till this evening," I said. "But I have a date tonight that I wouldn't miss for the world. I'm invited to dinner at Presidential House, and I want to tell Vados what I think of his beloved city now."

She smiled. "I learned very early in life that one's involvements go always deeper than one intends. One is linked with a particular world. Often one would prefer it otherwise. But there are certain ties and obligations that cannot be dissolved. Were I to have abandoned my country, moved somewhere where I was unknown, I should still have been fastened securely to my old self by knowledge of duty unfulfilled. . . ."

Wistful sadness filled the mellow voice, the violet eyes.

"Very well, then," she finished in a brisker tone. "You will remain here until evening. You will require various things— clothing, and so on, which I will obtain for you. And when you wish to go to Presidential House a hired car will call for you. The driver will be a discreet man; whatever has been said in the city regarding your disappearance, he will ask no questions."

Twice in the course of the day the police returned—the first time armed with a search warrant, which implied that somebody at any rate was pretty sure where I was; the second time in the person of *el Jefe* O'Rourke, who apologized to Señora Posador for bothering her and gave the interesting news that Vados had turned the heat on him. As far as he himself was concerned, he was satisfied that I wasn't here.

To outward appearance, of course, I wasn't. I was in the hiding-place in the cellar again.

Clothing arrived as promised—evening dress rented from a company in the city, which fitted me excellently. I put it on when O'Rourke had been there and it was fairly certain that I could emerge from hiding safely. My arm was stiff, sore and cramped, but I could move it without dislodging the dressing, and there was no bleeding.

I had not been told any particular time to arrive at Presidential House; and it seemed to me that eight o'clock would be about right, and Maria Posador confirmed my guess.

She offered to lend me her gun, but I refused; I wasn't as ambitious as Angers to play cops and robbers, and in any case I couldn't hide it if I took it. Someone might ask me awkward questions if I tried to go into Vados's home with a gun, and if anybody was going to ask awkward questions this evening, I intended it to be myself.

The hired car turned up sharp on time. Taut-faced, worried, Maria Posador took leave of me as I went out to it.

"Almost I envy you," she said wistfully. "Maybe there are advantages in rootlessness, after all. What happens here in my country hurts me—all the more because I know that if I myself do more than a very little to alter the situation, I shall cause more harm than good. Will you come back here, or return to your hotel?"

"I'll go back to the hotel," I said. "After what I'm going to say to Vados, I think people will stop worrying me. I hope."

"Good luck then, and be assured that we will find out if it is at all possible who sought to destroy you by bringing you here this morning. *Hasta la vista, y—*"

She didn't finish the sentence, but turned and went back indoors, shaking her head thoughtfully.

I thought, as I was getting into the car, that there was a *hell* of a woman. One of the first things I could recall noticing about her was the way she sought respect not for her femininity but for herself, and now she'd certainly got that respect from me. I could have imagined things developing a thousand different ways—only I couldn't imagine them, after all. Suppose I'd come to Aguazul at leisure, rather than on business and restricted by my own self-imposed rules. I'd more than likely have done the usual things—the round of dinners and shows and so on; I'd have wanted a companion as charming and sophisticated as Maria Posador, and I wouldn't have got her.

The hell with that sort of thing, though. I had a vague feeling that we might come out of this actual friends, and somehow that seemed like a very fair—even generous—reward.

The ride to Presidential House was a short one, for we were already half the distance from the center of the city to the hillside on which the great building was set. Almost before I knew it we were checked through the gates and up the driveway; evidently I was still expected. At any rate, the guards seemed to know I was coming.

A servant came to open the door of the car for me, and directed my driver where to park. Before going indoors, I looked down over the lawn and saw that the huge chessboard was once again unrolled on the grass. By the light of a floodlamp a few men were being rehearsed in the moves of another game.

From the outside, Presidential House was pillared and traditional; the interior, on the other hand, was superbly free of fuss. I waited under cool white discharge lamps on the buff-colored plastic floor of the entrance hall, looking at a magnificent piece of Inca sculpture set off by flowers so arranged as

to resemble votive offerings to the god. The servant who had
escorted me inside went to announce my presence.

The result I wasn't prepared for.

The door through which the man had gone reopened in a
matter of seconds, to pass him and someone else—presumably,
from his stately bearing and evening dress, the chief butler.
His expression, however, was far from matching his bearing;
he seemed to be thrown into consternation by the sight of me.

"Señor Hakluyt!" he exclaimed. "You—you were delayed,
yes?"

"I was delayed," I said. "But that was this morning. Here I
am as you see me. What's wrong?"

"Señor, dinner is—has just been—I will inform his excellency the president—"

What had got into the man? I said harshly, "Don't trouble
yourself. Vados didn't give me a time to come. If there are
apologies to be made, I'll make them myself. Is he in there?"

I walked toward the door through which he had just come;
he made a half-hearted move to block my way, and I side-
stepped, feeling tension gather inside me. Before he could get
in the way again, I was in the room.

"*Buenas tardes,*" I said. And took in the scene.

This was an anteroom; beyond it, wide double doors were
thrown back to reveal a table laid for dinner. The guests were
taking an apéritif before going in. They looked at me.

There was Vados himself, gaping like a stranded fish, his
face pale, his hands shaking. There was his wife, looking magnificent in a gown that had probably cost a thousand. Diaz
was there, his long-boned face frozen in an expression that
might have been comical. There was Garcia, looking more
than ever like a schoolmaster, blinking behind his glasses
and smiling a greeting to me. There was a woman who might
be his wife or Diaz's. And there were some servants.

A clock on the wall stated that it was five minutes to eight.

I looked past the petrified gathering to the dinner table, and
I counted. A place for Vados, one for his wife, one for
Garcia, one for Diaz, one for the unidentified woman. I felt
cold certainty clasp my mind.

Into the long moment before anyone recovered sufficiently

to speak to me, I dropped the weightiest sentence I had ever uttered. I said, "I'm sorry to disappoint you, but I'm not dead."

Diaz crossed himself with spasmic violence; Garcia, Señora Vados, and the unidentified woman gave a little unison gasp of astonishment. Only Vados remained outwardly calm. A hint of sweat made his forehead shine, but his voice was steady as he said, "Dead, Señor Hakluyt? Has an attempt been made on your life?"

A moment of dominance was upon me now, bringing with it a strange dreamlike calm, as though my mind were running a few moments ahead of the present and watching the inevitable consequences of what I said and did, ensuring that I could only say or do precisely those things which would be most effective.

I said, "Dead. *Señor Presidente*, did you invite me to dine with you tonight?"

"Of course."

"Did you inform your servants that I was expected?"

"Naturally! I fail to see—"

"You didn't set a time for my arrival, did you? It seems that eight o'clock is the time you dine. It is now"—I shot a glance at the clock—"four minutes to eight. You had given up expecting me. *You* had. The guards at the gatehouse hadn't, but you had."

"Señor Hakluyt, you are obviously overstrained—"

"Or do you tell your servants to lay another place at the dinner table each time another of your guests arrives?"

Garcia, as though realizing for the first time what all the fuss was about, turned and began to count the places at the table, jabbing his forefinger through the air. I looked not at him, though, but at Diaz, whose large, long stone-carving face bore an expression of resigned dismay.

Vados touched his moustache with a shaking finger. He said, "As to my not advising you of the time, señor, that is indeed a fault, and I apologize. But for the rest, you are making a great deal out of nothing at all. We have been told by the police that you were not to be found today, that you were missing from your hotel. There had been—uh—there had been an anonymous telephone call to say you were missing. And we had not been advised of your reappearance."

"Listen, begetter of concrete and glass," I said harshly, "and I will tell you of this city you have fathered. You have tried to govern it as one governs a game of chess; you have reduced your citizens to the status of pawns and attempted to direct their actions and even their thinking as though they were pieces of carved wood. You have tried to do this to me also, and here you have made your greatest and last mistake. I have not come here to sit at your table and eat your fine cuisine. I have come to say that a man is not a pawn, and if you try to make a man into a pawn, you must expect him sooner or later to turn on you and spit in your eye."

And Diaz—that great-bodied horse of a man, huge enough, it seemed, to draw a plough or tear a tree from its roots—Diaz put his wide spatulate hands to his heart, closed his dark eyes, folded at the knees, and sprawled across the immaculate floor in a total faint.

I had intended until that instant to end my tirade there, to spin on my heel and walk out of the room, out of the house, out of Ciudad de Vados. If I had done that, I would never have discovered what my words—my random-chosen, metaphorical words—had done to Vados.

Two servants moved to help Diaz to his feet, to stagger under his weight to a couch. Absolute silence except for their shuffling and grunting. In that silence, my resolve to leave the room forestalled by Diaz's collapse, I saw Vados's face go gray and appear to crumble at the edges, like the face of a statue much exposed to weathering.

And yet in the same moment he looked relieved, as though a very heavy burden had been lifted from him.

"So it is over," he said. "And I am not sorry."

Half-recovering, Diaz raised his head where he sat on the couch and gazed mutely at the President.

"We were told," said Vados, looking at him, "that if the knowledge escaped to one of—of *them*, it would all be over. Alejo said that, did he not, Estebán?"

"Many times," said Diaz in a groaning voice. "Many times."

"And now it has escaped." Vados looked back at me, and a ghastly smile sketched itself on his pallid face. "But in a way you do us an injustice, señor. You are no mere pawn—you are a knight."

XXXII

The words seemed to exist in a vacuum. They bore no relation that I could understand to anything that had gone before. Yet certainly an answer was expected of me. After a long, incredulous pause while I struggled to find a context for what Vados had said, I uttered stupidly, "Am I?"

"Madre de Dios!" said Diaz in a choking voice, and struggled to his feet. He swung menacingly to face Vados and would, I thought, have struck at him but that another spasm seized him and made him clutch dizzily at a chair back for support. "I did not think he knew, and now—but he did *not* know, Juan, stupid one, he did *not* know!"

He bent his head and shook it slowly from side to side. I thought the rhythmic movement would never cease.

It was as though the other people in the room did not exist except as shadowy background figures. A fierce spotlight seemed to have selected Vados, Diaz, and myself and left Garcia, the women, and the servants in a twilight from which they could not emerge. In that brilliant glare I could see the very pores of Vados's face as more sweat gathered and oozed from them, as it was squeezed forth by the terrible tension of the muscles underneath.

"So tomorrow there will perhaps be fighting in the streets," said Vados glacially. "I can no longer care, Esteban. You say he did not know; I say he did know—sufficient to destroy our work. These past few days the burden has been more than I could bear. I said at first I thought it was the better way, better than to have my beautiful city torn apart in civil war. So I did think at first. And yet those who have died because of us have died in ignorance, without choice; at least those who die in war have a chance to know that there is a war, and why men are dying."

He was mastering himself bit by bit and now became aware again of the other people in the room. He turned to his wife with a smile that came and went as though it had cost him a tremendous effort to conjure it up.

"Consuela, this is nothing with which to trouble you or Pablo Garcia—or you, madame," he added with a shadow-bow toward the unidentified woman. "I wish you to begin to dine as planned. Jaime!" he snapped at one of the servants. "Take Señor Diaz to another room and let him rest; bring him restoratives and brandy, and telephone to Dr. Ruiz if there is another attack. And you, Señor Hakluyt—I wish you very much to come with me."

I thought Diaz would protest; he glanced up, but thought better of it. I saw that he had fumbled open the front of his dress shirt and was touching a small gold cross that hung on a chain against his chest.

Vados did not wait to see if his instructions were followed; he started from the room by the door that had admitted me, and I followed, not yet having understood everything that had been said but beginning to suspect. The suspicion had the quality of nightmare.

Across the hall, into a room identical in shape to the one we had just left; across that room to the double doors at the other end, which were locked. Vados thrust a key into the lock, turned it, threw back the doors, and snapped on the lights.

This was furnished as a lounge, with low chairs, small tables, but there were also many glass-fronted cases of books, and one tall cabinet that almost but not quite disguised its construction of steel plates with a veneer of wood. Breathing heavily, Vados spun the dial of a combination lock that held its doors together.

Not knowing what to expect, I waited tensely, prepared to dodge through the door again if Vados produced a weapon from the cabinet.

Then the front swung aside, to reveal shelved rows of file covers, stacks of paper, documents of a dozen kinds—and a chessboard standing with pieces in play upon it.

For a long moment Vados gazed at the board, leaning on the door of the cabinet. Then in a sudden savage outburst of—not anger, perhaps self-disgust—he picked it up, pieces and all, and flung it against the wall. Pawns and officers bounced with little dull taps all over the room.

"I feel as though I were at confession," he said half-inaudibly, and wiped his shaking hand over his forehead.

I stood waiting by the door. At length he turned to me, and this time he was smiling as though he meant it.

"Come here, Señor Hakluyt, and I will show you. You are the cause and agent of my salvation. I have been carrying a great guilt. I have been pretending to the powers of God. Here! Look! You will understand completely."

I went forward uncertainly, only able to think he was insane.

"Look at the documents in this cabinet. There are many of them, too many to read, but you need only look at them to understand."

Still I was hesitant, and impatiently he snatched down one of the files at random and thrust it into my hands. It was bulky with papers. I looked at the superscription. Typed on a pasted label was a name—Felipe Mendoza—and below had been added by hand two different comments.

The first said: "Black king's bishop."

The second said: "Taken."

"Oh, no!" I said. Then with a sudden burst of energy, "Let me at those files!"

Vados stood back, mechanically rubbing one hand against the other while I shuffled feverishly through the files. I came to one bearing my own name, and likewise two comments.

"White king's knight."

"Taken."

I dropped Mendoza's file on a table and flung open the one bearing my name. Its contents were divided into two parts. One was a thick wad of handwritten foolscap, which I found too difficult to read with attention—there were many abbreviations, and the writing was crabbed and irregular. The other was a dossier about myself. It included photostats of the letter I had sent when applying for the Ciudad de Vados assignment, of the questionnaire I had completed about myself at the time, of the letter of acceptance and the contract engaging me. I knew about the existence of these documents; they were no surprise to me.

But there were surprising things that followed.

Someone, apparently, had shadowed me for three days in Miami before my arrival. Someone had taken the trouble to go to New York and see my last employer. Someone had interviewed half a dozen of my business colleagues in the States. And a name that I recognized was appended to the last of these reports.

Flores.

The man who had shared my seat in the plane coming here.

It was Flores's signature, too, that was appended to the most remarkable item of all. That was a typed sheet that ran:

"As directed, I have conducted an exhaustive inquiry into the antecedents of the traffic expert Boyd Daniel HAKLUYT. Owing to the extreme distances involved, I have not been able to investigate his career outside the Americas. It appears that he is indisputably of great skill in his speciality. I have heard him spoken of most highly.

"As to his personal relationships and attitudes, it seems that he deliberately avoids forming close personal relationships while engaged on a particular project. This is in accord with the pattern of his life—viz., that he works for about seven or eight months of the year and takes extended vacations for the rest of the time. The nature of his work would appear to have made him essentially a mercenary, and I have no doubt that his loyalty will be to his employer exclusively.

"As to the information I was particularly asked to obtain, while his Australian origin suggests an inherent intolerance, the fact that he has worked in such countries as the UAR and India may have offset his original reactions. I am unable to state definitely one way or the other on the basis of available data. It is, however, a platitude that childhood conditioning remains throughout life. At least one may expect a disrespectful attitude toward 'the natives.' This seems to be in conformity with the desired attributes."

Vados was watching me as I read the report, and when I

looked up, I found his dark eyes on my face. "Yes, Señor Hakluyt," he said levelly. "It would seem that our mistake lay there."

"That little bastard Flores!" I said between my teeth. "If I'd known, I'd have kicked him off the plane."

"Do not bear a grudge against him. He was acting exactly as he was ordered. And I ordered him."

He dropped into a chair and reached toward a bell. "A drink, señor?" he suggested. "I am ready to answer all your questions."

"No drink," I said. "Explanations are all I want."

"You think perhaps that I would poison you." He smiled faintly. "The time for that is past. But as you wish. Be seated."

I drew down another half-dozen of the folders at random and put them on a table as I sat down. I glanced at the names they bore, but they hardly meant anything to me. Too much of my mind was taken up in insisting to myself that I was not dreaming.

"You will perhaps not understand much of this that I am about to tell you, Señor Hakluyt," said Vados with a sigh. "You are, after all—forgive me, but it is true—a man without deep roots, without a real homeland. You have left your home behind and chosen to work all over the world as a mercenary. We misjudged how deeply that had affected you, how it had cut you off from the influences that must have shaped your personality as a young man. However, it is well that we made such a mistake."

"Look," I said, "I don't want to be told platitudes about myself. I want to know what this means." I tapped the pile of papers on the table. "As far as I can see, it says here you've been playing chess with human beings."

I could hear the still strong disbelief in my voice as if it were coming from a neighboring chair.

Vados inclined his head. "This is exact," he muttered.

"Are you insane?"

"Perhaps. But not as you mean it. Señor, I have said to you more than once that Ciudad de Vados is to me like a son. If you had a son, would you wish to see him scarred, injured, perhaps crippled for life? That much I can make clear I love my country! I have been its ruler for many years, and—oh, I have failed in many ways, but in others I have been fortunate enough to achieve great things where someone else would have patched and scraped and ended up with inferior botched work. . . .

"And there was this disagreement, this mutual hate, growing out of something I had not foreseen and wished to set right—out of the peasant squatters who poison my beautiful city like germs in its bloodstream. Yes, they, too, are men of my country, but they are my soldiers, too, and I am fighting a war. A war against backwardness, señor!

"They tell me sometimes, 'You were wrong to build Ciudad de Vados when there are slums in Astoria Negra, lairs of criminals in Puerto Joaquin.' How was I wrong? Before there was a Ciudad de Vados, what did the world know of Aguazul? It was a blot on maps, no more! There was no trade to speak of, no foreign investment, nothing but peasants and their cattle plodding through mud and dust. Oh, there was the oil, but that was not ours—it was leased for a pittance to people who could afford the equipment to work it. Perhaps you did not know that, señor. That was the way twenty years ago. Today we own a quarter of the oil-drilling equipment in Aguazul; tomorrow we shall own all of it.

"I saw this coming! I trod down other men because I had a vision, and I had seen part of the vision come true. All of it might come true, I think—and then there is this problem dragging disaster in its wake. You will have been told that civil war—ah, but I am not here to make excuses, only to tell you the facts so you may judge.

"Diaz is a good man. He, too, loves his country—our country. But he hears all the little cries of the little people and wishes to run to every one of them and give them comfort. Good, good! But I know that some must suffer for the future happiness of all. Suppose I did not allot four millions of dolaros for the task we set you—what do I do with it? Say I give ten dolaros each to four hundred thousand hungry people in Astoria Negra and Puerto Joaquin. They spend it; it has gone. And perhaps a company that was considering setting its Latin American headquarters here, which would have brought us four millions not of our dolaros but of the better, stronger North American dollar in a very few years, decides to go instead to Brasilia because Ciudad de Vados has lowered its standard. Oh, no, señor! (Yet if Diaz were in here, he and I would be shouting argument at one another. . . .)

"And in the end what happens? Diaz says that if I will not do as he asks, he will compel me to do it. Or he will oust me and do it himself.

"Am I to see my city bombed? See men and women bleeding in the gutters, at the corners of streets? I have seen that, in Cuatrovientos, before I was president. I have seen men thrown through windows; I have seen children shot down while they cried for mercy. Am I to do as others do, across the border—murder Diaz to be free of his opposition? He is a good man! We have worked long and well together, and only now do we begin to hate each other.

"So at the meetings of the cabinet we rage at one another until one day Alejo—Alejandro Mayor whom you knew, may his soul rest in peace—he comes to me and to Estebán Diaz and suggests to us—"

I saw Vados's hands tighten, one over the other; the veins stood out knotted on their backs. He was not looking at me. He was reliving the moment he was describing.

"—that since we could not resolve our disagreement except by conflict, that conflict must be bound by rules. He said we both knew rules that were acceptable. He said that he could not—oh, remember, señor, this was perhaps the greatest master of government and political science who has ever lived!—he could not determine from day to day all the actions of all the members of our population, but it would be possible to control very subtly individuals about whom one had gathered sufficient knowledge."

I could imagine Mayor as he made his proposition: his eyes bright behind his spectacles, his face perhaps shiny with excitement, his voice shaking for fear he might not get this chance to carry out the ultimate experiment in government.

"So perhaps it was a kind of madness," said Vados, his

voice dropping. "But we thought it was a better madness than some. I would not see my city torn apart by civil war; Diaz would not see his people die in a bath of blood. So we agreed, and we took our solemn oath upon it: we would fight out our battle on the squares of the city, serving us for a chessboard, with no man knowing such a game was being played."

I said a little foolishly, still uncertain whether this was a vast hoax or sober truth, "At the chess match last night—I saw that one side of the audience was dark-skinned and the other was light. . . ."

"One side of this whole country is dark-skinned and the other light. As Alejo explained it to us, one cannot predict when a man will feel hungry or thirsty unless one knows when and what he last ate or drank, and many other things. But one can say certainly that if he does not die, he will feel hungry and thirsty sooner or later. And there are certain things that do not change—a man who hates the religious will always be anticlerical, whether he be sick or well, drunk or sober. Oh, how small and unworthy it makes a man seem!

"To listen to him, señor—and we listened, for he had been at my right hand for twenty years nearly—you would have said he was a foolish mystic, a clairvoyant claiming to foretell the future. But we had seen what he could do already, and we agreed. If we had not agreed, we should have split Aguazul apart, and like the dog in the fable of Aesop that dropped its bone in the river through greed, we should have lost all that we were fighting to save.

"But no one else knew, Señor Hakluyt. Until you, no one else in the world knew what was being done."

"I don't see how it could be *possible*!" I said helplessly. "People—people are—"

"You find it humiliating that you, too, have been employed as a piece on the board." Vados looked at me unblinkingly. "I understand. But you may take comfort, for you are also the first and only to see what was being done. It is truly quite simple—so simple it can be done without the person knowing there has been a change in his life. Or so I believed, so *we* believed.

"We needed first a people which is well and firmly ruled. We had that; there is order and law in force in Ciudad de Vados.

"A division into sides was also simple. As you shrewdly say, a partial division exists into black and white, or more nearly darker and lighter. But we selected our pieces where their sympathies lay—some, like Brown, the lawyer, though white-skinned and foreigners, were with the black pieces and with Diaz; some others, although native-born, sided by prejudice with the Citizens of Vados Party and thus with the white cause.

"Then we had to agree that certain pieces should be allotted roles equivalent to the power of the pieces on the actual board. Thus Alejandro Mayor himself— I am sure he did not see what would befall him—was my Queen, the most powerful piece on the board, and wielded equivalent power affecting everyone in the country, through the television, the radio, and the newspaper *Liberdad*. And we also agreed that should a piece be taken, it must be rendered incapable of further influencing the real world. That meant—"

"That meant death," I said. I was looking at some of the names on the files before me. Fats Brown was dead; Felipe Mendoza was dead; Mario Guerrero was dead. . . .

"For some, it meant death," agreed Vados grayly. "Not for all. After the first few I felt this was worse than—but no matter, it is finished now. Yes, I was saying, it was then amazingly easy to predict and to coerce one's pieces. Let us take a very clever thing which Diaz did against me. He wished to—to take Mario Guerrero. He knew Guerrero despised and hated Francis, that if they were brought together, Guerrero would insult him, and that if he insulted Francis's skin, Francis would strike him in uncontrolled rage. Had Francis not killed Guerrero with his fist, moreover, he would in all probability have sought him out afterwards and killed him then, for every previous time he had been so insulted he had grown insanely violent. He had left two countries because of this . . . I had hardly believed that people were so uncomplicated!"

"What about me, then?"

"Oh, you obeyed orders, you furnished me with plans which we demanded, in some ways you reacted as foreseen—but you were sometimes so difficult! We thought you would dislike Brown, who was so unlike you and who so much hated distinctions of race. Instead, you became friendly with him. And Maria Posador, widow of the defeated rival, widow of him who had *not* built this city of which you thought so highly—we expected you to be as ice one to the other, perhaps that you would approach her as a beautiful woman and be repelled and insulted by her. But there again, no! So I was faced with an irremediable weakness in one of my pieces, which Diaz might too readily have exploited. In consequence, I moved you only a few times. But in the end the weakness turned against Diaz, and in seeking to take you from the board and also to abide by the agreement that each piece should take what it took, he was forced to an unwieldy contrivance—and it failed."

"You—you were aware of who the other's pieces were?"

"All but the pawns we knew of beforehand. We agreed at the beginning that the power and value of pawns vary with the progress of the game, and that therefore we should name our pawns, one to the other, as they came into play. But the officers we named first of all, and agreed on their powers; that took long, even with Alejo as arbitrator."

"You mean Diaz allowed one of his opponent's pieces to act as—as referee?"

Vados shrugged. "I think we understood," he said in low tones, "that what Alejo cared about was not that one or the other of us should emerge the victor, but that the game should be played. It was to him an ultimate goal; whatever the result, nothing in life would ever mean so much to him again."

"Then he deserved what he got."

"Perhaps he did."

I reverted to my questioning. "But I don't see how you could *move* a piece!" I said despairingly. "How was—how was I *moved* from square to square?"

"Oh, you were very difficult, señor! The others—they almost moved themselves. I knew, for instance, that Judge Romero would condemn the suit against Guerrero as political trickery, because he had dined with me the night before and I had heard it from him. If he had not produced the idea himself, I would have guided him in that direction. And then I knew always what Alejo would broadcast, for although he did not know how the game was progressing—that was a secret between Estebán Diaz and myself—he knew of its existence and acted as I advised him. So likewise did Diaz with Cristoforo Mendoza and *Tiempo*. I knew that Angers hated Brown, regarding him as a traitor, for he was white and English-speaking and had married an Indian woman and gave his services to Sigueiras. Many times it was not necessary to order one piece or another to move—not directly to order it. It sufficed to give a single piece of information or advice and allow it to work in their minds as leaven works in dough. So, to bring about the downfall of José Dalban, I had to do no more than advise Luis Arrio that he—or perhaps an agent of his—had burned down the television center. This was true! Then, said Arrio, if the police will do nothing against him, I will act myself by destroying his business—and he did. But before God, I did not foresee that he would kill himself!"

"And you mean you solemnly stuck to the rules of the game when you knew perfectly well that Dalban had done that—and killed Mayor in doing it?" My voice cracked on the last word. "You mean you let it go so far that you actually stopped the police from going after Dalban so that Arrio could get at him instead?"

"Yes, I do assure you, we would study the board as it was; we would select the next move to make, *make* it—disregarding what the person concerned did of his own accord, because we had to justify every single move one to the other and show how it was effected. Then we would change the position of the pieces here and wait for the next move to be made. The game in fact was played out there in the city—that board in the locked cabinet served merely as a reference."

He looked now worn out, as though he had undergone a terrific physical strain. His voice had been getting steadily lower, so that now I had to lean forward in my chair to catch his final words.

"We kept faith with each other," he muttered. "We moved always according to the rules."

I felt altogether helpless. For no reason except chance, without my demanding it, I suddenly found myself in a position of power over this man who had power I could scarcely believe—and had used it.

Could this story be true? Or was it all some vast shared delusion, shared by Vados and Diaz, shadow-played out to hide from themselves the fact that they were allowing their mutual disagreement to destroy what they wished to preserve?

The more I studied the terrifying contents of the files I had taken from the cabinet the less I was able to persuade myself that this had not in fact been done.

I thought of my cynical—well, speech—to Maria Posador about the impersonal forces that move human beings. I thought of the sensation I had sometimes had since coming to Vados—the sensation that I was being unwillingly involved in the clash of opposed interests. Maybe I *had* had a clue to what was happening.

I opened one of the folders—a very slim one, with only a few summary notes inside. The name on the cover was that of General Molinas, the commander in chief.

On top of the packet of papers inside was a handwritten slip, presumably by Vados himself. It said:

"Wondered at first why D. selected him for his side; felt him to be more sympathetic to white. As it turns out ... N.B.: investigate reliability of."

And that snatched me back at one jerk from fantasy to the world of hard facts.

I said, "At least this could not happen anywhere else."

Vados raised his head sharply. "It could have been done anywhere! Anyone could have done it—with Alejo's skill to guide them and his audacity to persuade them to try it."

"No!" I said violently. "And God be thanked that that's not true! You said your first need was a well and firmly governed population. What you mean is a population too damned apathetic to care that it's being pushed around on a chessboard. You have to begin with a dictatorship; you have to begin with 'the most thoroughly governed country in the world.'

"For the sake of your vision, you've bled the spirit out of half your people; for fear that your pretty new town would suffer, you've insulted the personal dignity of everyone in it. With your camouflage—like these mock public-opinion polls—you've given the average man in the street a comforting sense that his views count; at the same time you've used every underhand trick to ensure that his views are molded into the same passive conformity as everyone else's. The only reason you were able to employ the prejudices and fears of your victims to drive them around this chessboard of yours was because you created them! You didn't create my prejudices, and so you failed to control me.

"I don't have to claim some special credit for mucking up this bloody scheme of yours. You dug the trap and fell into it yourself, in just the same way as when you called in foreigners to build your city for you because you didn't have any faith in your own people. Lord, even if your plans had worked out and Maria Posador's bullet had gone through my head instead of through my arm"—Vados winced and made as though to clasp his head in his hands—"this attempt to reduce the realities of life to a game of chess would still have failed.

"Here you're swearing that you stuck by the rules, and yet this file here shows that you're planning to get rid of General Molinas because he doesn't think the same way as the rest of his officers, doesn't share your contempt for the ordinary people of Aguazul! He's one of these chessmen, but do you honestly imagine the army as a whole would have observed the rules of chess if you'd beaten Diaz and got the chance to impose your wishes? Do you suppose that if Diaz had played so skillfully that he threatened to eliminate Bishop Cruz, who's also supposed to be one of your pieces, the clergy would have sat quiet and watched him knocked down? The idea's nonsensical!

"And Diaz himself! And you, for that matter! Staring defeat in the face, would you or he have still stuck to the rules? If Diaz cares so much about his own people that he accepted this crazy scheme in preference to starting a civil war, he must care for them enough to welsh on his agreement and try another method if he's beaten. Maybe we're all nothing but bits of complex machinery responding to stimuli on a totally determinate basis; it often seems to me in my job that we are. But that applies to *all* of us, and none of us can claim what you called the powers of God to dictate the thoughts and emotions of others.

"Well, you've brought yourself and your country and all your ambitions to the edge of disaster. What the hell are you going to do about it?"

XXXIII

I suppose that, although I had intellectually accepted the truth of what had been said, I didn't yet *feel* that it was true. It was so patently unreal, so "Alice Through the Looking Glass." Otherwise, I could never have remained as calm as I did. I had forgotten, or was not reacting to, the fact that this man—Diaz, rather, since I was one of Vados's own "pieces"—had come within inches of arranging my death this morning.

Of course, it is in any case very hard to accept the possibility of one's own death; one is so accustomed to thinking of oneself as being indefinitely alive that in mental self-defense one tends to drive the idea out of one's mind as soon as one can. Maybe that was why I scarcely felt angry anymore. I felt angry later—blindly angry—but in these last few minutes while I was speaking with Vados, I had kept a clear and detached viewpoint, like that of a man whose mind is still lucid although his body rages with fever.

Vados did not reply to my final question. I repeated it.

"What the hell are you going to do?"

"God knows," he said wearily. "Whichever way I turn I see nothing but disaster. What *can* I do?"

"You're asking me?" I said bitterly. "I'm only one of your chessmen, remember? You've turned loose forces that have got beyond your control. You must have been crazy to think that the death of someone like Guerrero and Mendoza could be called a move in a chess game. Had you just forgotten about everyone else in the city? Didn't the feelings of Fats Brown's wife matter to you, or Mendoza's brother, or whoever else cared for the people you've killed?"

All the anger that had been repressed inside me suddenly undamned, and I roared at him. "Who the hell told you you had to *fight* over this bloody mess? You call that governing a country—getting yourself into such a damn stupid position you haven't got any way out except killing people? You may have built Ciudad de Vados and brought prosperity and all the rest of it, but obviously you've done it to pander to your own selfish ego, because you must despise everyone else if you can treat them like bits of wood."

He tried to break in, but my feelings were rising and I ignored him. "You were prepared to stamp down thousands of people just so long as your pretty new buildings didn't get dirty, weren't you? Why the hell didn't you give up a few square yards of Presidential House and make room for some of those poor bastards living in Sigueiras's slum? *He* didn't want 'em there, living like animals—or maybe you think he did. God, but I'm glad I'm not in your shoes. Compared to you, a slave trader has clean hands."

Vados sat limply, like a badly stuffed rag doll. "I cannot deny it," he said. "It is all true."

I made a disgusted noise and went over to the cabinet, to drag down the rest of the files from their shelf. I went through them methodically. Some of the names on them hardly meant anything to me personally: Guyiran—that was one of Diaz's people from the Ministry of the Interior, and I hadn't met him; Gonzales—that was the Secretary of Justice, and I hadn't met him either. But some of them meant a lot to me: Angers, Brown, Posador . . .

I counted them. Thirty. Two short. "Who were the kings in this lunatic game?" I said harshly to Vados.

"Why, we ourselves," he said with a shrug.

I sneered. "A very natural role to adopt, of course. The one piece that can never be taken! Like a general directing the massacre of an army from a bombproof shelter."

He winced a little. I went on shuffling through the files.

"Señor Hakluyt," he said after a pause, "what will you do? I have delivered myself into your hands as I would not to anyone except my confessor—and he is bound to keep secrets."

"Don't try to soothe your conscience like that!" I snapped. "You could ring for servants and have me thrown out. You could deport me tonight. You could silence Garcia and Diaz and even your wife—they say you're no stranger to that kind of thing. You needn't even bother deporting me. You could shoot me out of hand. Nobody knows where I am except a hired-car chauffeur and Maria Posador.

"What the hell do you think I am? A kingmaker? Am I maybe supposed to run out into the streets and shout the news so that the people can throw you out on your ear? Nuts! Who'd believe me? Even if I showed them these files, they wouldn't. Oh, you've been clever, and the only person who might believe me would be that poor sick bastard Caldwell." I happened to have a file labeled "Caldwell" in my hand at the moment; I pushed it through the air toward Vados, slapping it with my open palm.

"*I* didn't know what you were actually doing to me. Who else would know? The people you've 'moved' all over the board would deny that anyone had been controlling them. But you've done for yourself, nonetheless. You've had twenty years of your own way, more than most people ever dream of. Now you'd better start facing the facts of life again instead of the rules of chess, because if you don't, a firing squad is liable to be facing *you*."

He sat dumb. Perhaps there was a picture show going on behind his forehead, with men and women bleeding into the gutters of his beloved city. I thought that was more likely than that he should be worrying about a firing squad for himself. He looked so completely abject that for a few moments I was on the verge of pitying him.

I said, "Damnation! Government's your business, not mine! Get busy with placating the people—pension Fats Brown's widow, because he wasn't guilty, and you know it—oh, what am I telling you this for?"

I had absent-mindedly opened Caldwell's file as I was talking. Now I glanced down and saw a slip of paper inside, with a few words in Vados's writing:

"30. Pablo says best is P-B5."

And in that moment I stopped pitying him altogether.

"So even in this you cheated," I said softly. "Even when you swore you were abiding by the rules, you cheated. And you asked Pablo Garcia—grand master Garcia!—what your next move ought to be."

I flung the file across the room; it opened and shed its contents on the floor like white leaves falling. Vados half-rose, bracing himself as though he feared I would hit him. I shook my head.

"I can't think of anything I want to do to you that you haven't got coming anyway," I said. "All I want is *out*."

I felt actual nausea rise inside me, and that lent force to the final word. Vados got distractedly to his feet.

"I—I'll send for your driver," he began, but I cut him short.

"Not just out of the house. Out of the country. Anywhere will do. But tonight!"

A telephone shrilled quietly in another room. It stopped almost at once. Vados half-turned and then sighed. "Very well, Señor Hakluyt. I shall not be sorry when you have gone. Maybe then I can begin to build up myself as I would wish to be again. At this minute I feel I am only a shadow of the man I thought myself to be."

"*Señor Presidente!*" came a sharp cry. The door of the room was flung open; it was the chief butler, almost babbling. "Señores, forgive me, but they have telephoned to say there is fighting in the city. General Molinas has ordered mobilization of the reserves, and a mob has attacked the monorail station, which is now on fire!"

I looked at Vados. I didn't have to say anything.

Stony-faced, he began to pull himself together. One could almost see the resolve stiffen inside him as his back stiffened, as his shoulders squared.

"Very well," he said at last. "Call Señor Hakluyt's driver to the door. Tell Jaime to go to the safe and obtain twenty

thousand dolaros and give them to Señor Hakluyt; if there is
not enough cash, he must make up the difference with a sight
draft. Then he must go to the Hotel del Principe and obtain
Señor Hakluyt's belongings and go with them to the airport.
Arrange yourself that an army plane is available to take Señor
Hakluyt wherever he wishes to go."

"But the——" began the butler in astonishment.

Vados blazed at him, "Do what I tell you, fool, and be
quick!"

Dazed, the butler shrugged and left the room. In a great
silence Vados looked at me without seeing me.

"All I have secured is a postponement of what I most
desired to avoid," he said musingly. "And at what a cost to
my conscience—perhaps to my soul. . . . But that is between
me and my people. To you I will only say—*adios*. Forgive
me."

He must have read in my face that I would not have
shaken his hand, for he turned on his heel and left the room.

In a few moments the butler returned, bearing the money—
I didn't trouble to count it. My car was at the door. I went to
it with a sense of overpowering relief, as if I had been released
from shackles I had worn since birth and never known I had
on.

"The airport," I said to the driver as I climbed in; he
nodded and let the car roll forward.

I felt partly as though I were running away, partly as
though I were escaping from unjust bondage. And that was
parallel to the true situation. I was running away, because
unknowingly I had helped to create this terrible situation; I
was also escaping, because I had not understood.

Beyond the gatehouse, we could see out over the city. The
flaring of the monorail central was like a red hole in the
jeweled face of the city. There was a black hole, too—all
the streetlights had been extinguished for an area of ten blocks
near the Plaza del Norte. The driver stared incredulously for a
moment—of course, I realized, he might not yet have heard—
and accelerated slightly.

Then, about a quarter-mile down the road, a light leaped

up and faded behind us. I swung around in my seat. Another
flash followed, and this time I caught the trail before the
explosion. It was a rocket.

Now the façade of Presidential House had two notches torn
from it, like gaps in a row of teeth. The emplacement must be
across the other side of the city, I reasoned, and the aiming
was fantastically good.

"Hurry!" I snapped at the driver. He nodded and increased
speed a second time. I was afraid of reaching the airport only
to find that Vados's authority no longer held good and the
promised plane had been diverted to another purpose.

I was lucky. The plane was waiting, with its pilot, who was
cursing the fact that he had to leave Ciudad de Vados at this
of all times, but who respected an order direct from his
president sufficiently to obey it regardless. Since Vados was
quite possibly dead by this time, I judged it better to leave
without waiting for my belongings. I gave a hundred dolaros
to an overzealous customs officer to get him out of my hair,
and within ten minutes of reaching the airport I was aloft.

The plane was a little side-by-side jet trainer, with the one
cockpit for pilot and student pilot. I glanced at my companion's round dark face.

"If you wish to circle the city. . . ?" I suggested. He gave me
a puzzled look and then nodded, banking the little plane into
a sharp turn.

"We may be shot at," he pointed out. But he waited to say
that until we were already swinging around the city.

The fire at the monorail station was dying bit by bit, and
greasy smoke masked some of its glow. But it was no longer
alone—we could see a dozen such fires now, some of them
large and brilliant. A second rocket battery had opened up
and was lobbing its missiles at random into the town; one of
them by chance fell near the cathedral in the Plaza del Oeste
and knocked the three-hundred-foot cross to a canting angle.
A mob carrying huge flaming crosses (whose idea was *that*, I
wondered) had descended on the shantytown on the Puerto
Joaquin road to wreck and burn, and it was clear even from
our height there were thousands of people in the crowd.

"*Madre de Dios*," said my pilot simply and flatly. "Ah, *madre de Dios!*"

And then, as he disgustedly drove the aircraft into a fast, steep climb, another crowd began to detach itself from the lights of the city, like a snake winding slowly from an egg. This one was flowing up the hill to Presidential House.

So there was an end to the rules of the game. Now there would simply be slaughter.

The city grew smaller behind us. The height ticked up on the altimeter—five hundred, eight hundred, a thousand meters. I thought of everything I was carrying away with me—all the burden of knowledge that weighted me down. Knowledge without which any man, anywhere, any time, might be turned into a chesspiece and moved across some vast imaginary board, behaving and reacting with all the predictability of a lump of carved wood.

So maybe no one would believe me. So probably the files which detailed the incredible game played on the squares of Ciudad de Vados were buried under rubble in Presidential House. So maybe I'd have to carry that burden of knowledge by myself. Was that a good reason why I should also carry the burden of guilt? And I was guilty without realizing it. Anyone is guilty who has so far renounced his right to think and act rationally that someone else can press his buttons and make him dance.

I reached across and tapped the pilot on the shoulder. I said, "If you wish, you may turn back."

There were phones in the lobby of the airport reception building; fortunately the system was still in full operation. I dialed with fingers that felt more like thumbs, and with a surge of relief I heard Maria Posador's own voice, tense and urgent at my ear.

"Listen," I said. "You've got to listen. You're not going to want to believe me, but you've got to listen, because what I'm going to say is very, very important."

"Boyd!" she said, recognizing the voice. "Yes, go ahead. Please go ahead. I'm listening."

Author's Note

The persons, places, and events described in *The Squares of the City* are, of course, entirely imaginary.

The techniques whereby the human "chessmen" are described as having been moved are—regrettably—*not* entirely imaginary. Certainly they do not exist today as they are pictured here. Nonetheless, they are foreshadowed in the methods of present-day advertising, which are being more and more often applied to politics, and history is full of what one might call nonprofessional application of tricks like the Big Lie and guilt by association which in the hands of accomplished and determined men have served to direct and control the thoughts and actions of large populations.

The game of chess itself is not imaginary at all. It is Steinitz-Tchigorin (Havana) 1892, precisely as recorded in the Penguin handbook *The Game of Chess* by H. Golombek. Every move of the game has a counterpart in the action of the story, with the partial exception that castling is implied and not overt. The individuals who correspond to the "pieces" have powers roughly commensurate with those of the pawns and officers they represent.

Naturally, since none of the "pieces" are aware that they are being "moved," including the narrator Boyd Hakluyt, many events not directly equivalent to the moves of the game are recorded in the story. But the moves are all there, in their correct order and—so far as possible—in precise correspondence with their effect on the original game. That is to say, support of one piece by another on its own side, threatening of one or more pieces by a piece on the other side, indirect threats and the actual taking of pieces, are all as closely represented as possible in the development of the action.

The game is three moves short as played in the story, owing to the failure of Maria Posador to kill Boyd Hakluyt and Hakluyt's discovery of the truth. As originally continued, Black resigned on move 38.

For the benefit of the curious reader, I append a table of the "pieces" involved in the game, with a note—where applicable—of their ultimate fate.

Pieces

White

QR	Bishop Cruz	QRP	Estrelita Jaliscos
QKt	Luis Arrio	QKtP	Dr. Alonzo Ruiz
QB	Judge Romero	QBP	Nicky Caldwell
Q	Alejandro Mayor	QP	Andres Lucas
K	Juan Sebastian Vados	KP	Mario Guerrero
KB	Donald Angers	KBP	Seixas
KKt	Boyd Hakluyt	KKtP	Isabela Cortés
KR	Professor Cortés	KRP	Enrique Rioco

Black

QR	General Molinas	QRP	Fernando Sigueiras
QKt	Maria Posador	QKtP	Fats Brown
QB	José Dalban	QBP	Pedro Murieta
Q	Cristoforo Mendoza	QP	Sam Francis
K	Estebán Diaz	KP	Juan Tezol
KB	Felipe Mendoza	KBP	Guyiran
KKt	Miguel Dominguez	KKtP	Castaldo
KR	Tomas O'Rourke	KRP	Gonzales
	(*el Jefe*)		

Taken in the course of play—White

QKt (Luis Arrio) denounced to police by Pedro Murieta for killing Felipe Mendoza in a duel.

QB (Judge Romero) removed from office for incompetence at instigation of Miguel Dominguez.

Q (Alejandro Mayor) burned to death in television station following threats by José Dalban.

THE SQUARES OF THE CITY 319

QRP (Estrelita Jaliscos) killed in fall from window in apartment belonging to Fats Brown.

QBP (Nicky Caldwell) suffered mental breakdown following exposure of his false charges against Pedro Murieta.

QP (Andres Lucas) imprisoned on charges of complicity in blackmailing of Fats Brown brought by Miguel Dominguez.

KP (Mario Guerrero) killed by Sam Francis for insulting the color of his skin.

Taken in the course of play—Black

QB (José Dalban) bankrupted and driven to suicide by Luis Arrio.

Q (Cristoforo Mendoza) jailed for contempt by Judge Romero following the closing of his newspaper *Tiempo*.

KB (Felipe Mendoza) killed in duel with Luis Arrio.

QRP (Fernando Sigueiras) jailed after moving peasant family into Angers' apartment.

QKtP (Fats Brown) shot by Angers when under suspicion of murdering Estrelita Jaliscos.

QP (Sam Francis) said to have committed suicide in jail while awaiting trial for murder of Mario Guerrero.

KP (Juan Tezol) jailed by Judge Romero for nonpayment of fine.